For Colleen
Cal lun tau seryan ede to maynd…

*Not the power to remember,
but its very opposite, the power to forget,
is a necessary condition of our existence.*

— Sholem Asch

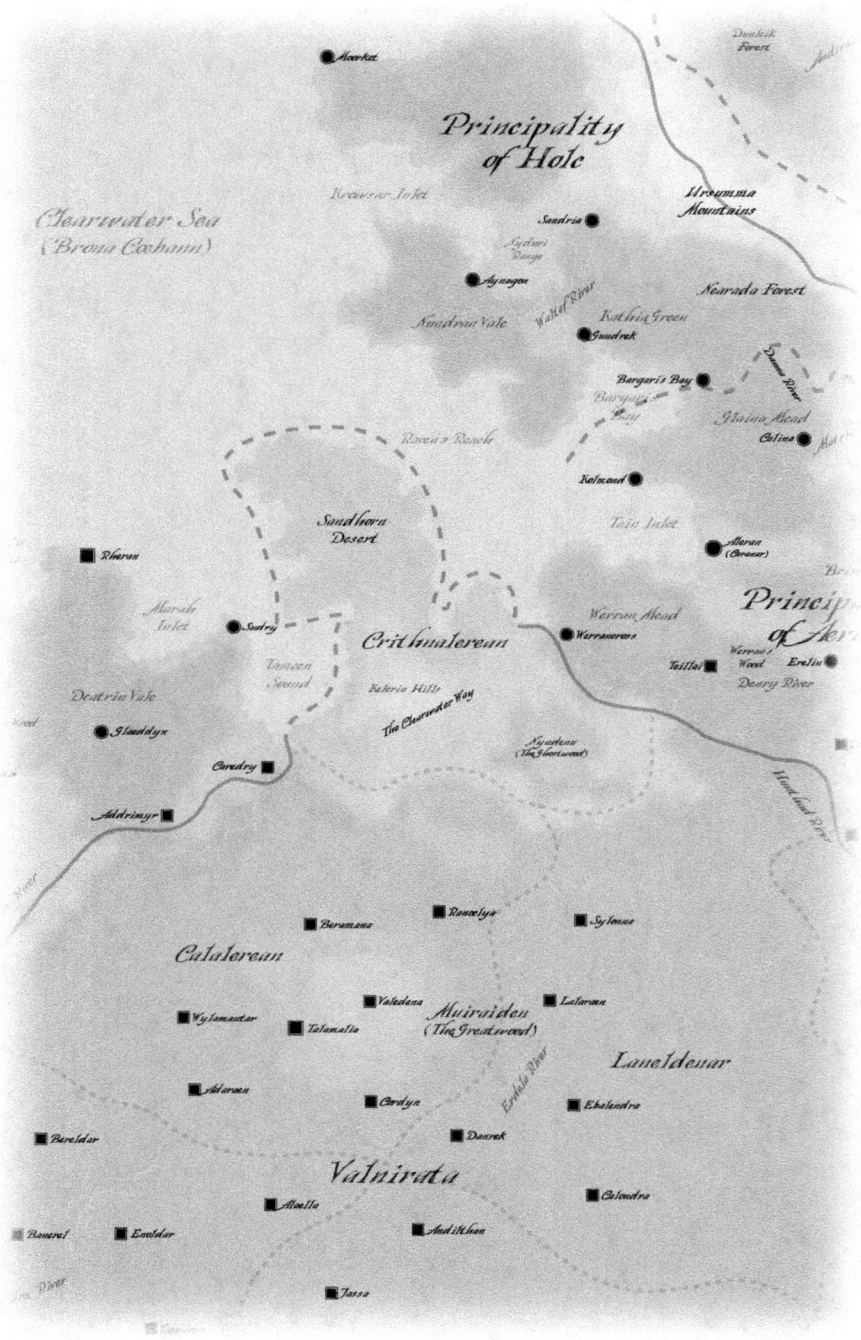

— CHAPTER 1 —

RANGERS DOWN

"GREEN SCOUT MARKED!"

Like the crack of a whip, the distant shout of one of the first-squad rangers split the shadowed stillness of the forest, a following of echo-sound hanging for a moment before it was swallowed by the stifling air. The faint hiss of arrows sang out an instant behind, and Chriani marked the shift and shimmer of the sound to count three distinct shots, far off and unseen.

His hearing was better than the other rangers of second squad, who reacted only to the voice sounding out a measured distance ahead of them. All of them listened now for the faint thud of hoofbeats to mark the movement of the rangers of first squad, and of the trouble pursuing them.

A flash of hand signals passed between Sergeant Thelaur and second squad, Chriani and his five fellow rangers drawing to a quick halt in response. The sergeant was a dour veteran half a head shorter than any of the soldiers under her command. But in the five months that command had included Chriani, he had come to recognize that her instincts were sharp and her hearing even sharper. Nearly as sharp as his own, in fact, to judge by her quick sign of three fingers to mark the count of the Ilvani archers. They were somewhere ahead in the green shadow of the Greatwood, spreading to all sides as a deep and impenetrable gloom.

"Green scout marked!" the voice came again, farther off now.

"East!" Thelaur hissed to Chriani and the rest. "Three and three. Stay low." At a touch from the sergeant's boots, her horse slipped forward, Chriani in the first rank of three rangers close behind her.

When a ranger called a warning, *green* was code for moving east — named for the green of the Greatwood that rose like a wall along Brandishear's eastern frontier. *Blue* meant a scout was moving north, for the vast expanse of the Clearwater Sea that spread beyond the headlands of Rheran, the great capital and Chriani's former home, five months behind him now. *Gold* and *grey*, west and south, for the grasslands that marked much of Brandishear's border with the Greatwood, and for the bare slopes of the Analatia Mountains that Chriani had never seen.

In the complex series of call signs he had learned over his five months on the frontier, there were codes for rangers under attack, codes for rangers wounded, codes for tracks found and followed. There were codes for signs of a war camp, or for predators of the four-legged variety prowling the twisting switchback trails that the Ilvani and their sure-footed horses marked out between the great trees.

There were codes for rangers down, and for rangers captured — special call signs meant to warn allies that you were caught and com-promised, meant to sound like calls for help in the event that an Ilvani warrior of the Valnirata held a long-knife to your throat. In five months of scouting and skirmishes along the edge of the Greatwood and pushing within it, the rangers of Chriani's company hadn't had to use either of those. Not yet.

Their horses moved at a jog to hold their strength, silk ties wrap-ping off bit joints and stirrups, muffling any clink of metal as they moved. Chriani and the other rangers hunched low, cloaked in green and brown. The forest around them was a perpetual haze of emerald twilight that seemed to mask all movement — shadow and mist slashed through by the twisting strokes of great tree trunks rising up to shroud the sun. Their branches were set with unnaturally broad and scaled ev-ergreen leaves, glimmering gold to jade green depending on their age. These were the great limni of the Greatwood, home to the Ilvani who called that forest *Muiraìden.*

Chriani flicked his horse to the right to skirt a gnarled trunk, and a fall of blood ivy dropping from a twisted branch the thickness of his leg. The shower of serrated leaves was pale and wan in the faint light, but it wasn't the plant's toxic touch that made him wary. As they made their way along the twisting trails behind the sergeant, the rangers of the squad had stopped and doubled back five times already. It was a common happenstance when following the Ilvani, whose trails were crossed and crossed again with dead ends and false starts. The scattered formation in which the rangers rode while within the forest served double duty, lowering the risk of an entire group falling to ambush even as those in the middle and back ranks could seek out clear paths while the lead rider repositioned.

The silence in the forest hung over all their patrols like an ever-present shroud, dampening the sound of their horses' hooves even as it seemed to make the breathing of mounts and riders louder. Today, though, that silence was tinged with a feeling that set Chriani's nerves on edge — and all the more so because he had no idea as to its source.

Chriani and the rest of the rangers had been scouting in pursuit of an Ilvani raiding band since first light. They all had bows drawn and arrows nocked, scanning the shadows intently. However, Chriani was the only one who knew they were alone for the moment, the gloom shifting and shimmering like ever-fading fog against the sharp sight of his eyes.

He had his father's black hair, the same steel-grey eyes. He never spoke of the sight that was the gift of those eyes and his father, who had once called the Greatwood home. The sight had saved his life on more than one occasion, even as hiding the fact of that sight had saved his life more often. He wore his hair tied back and low, always covering his ears, concealing the faint peak at their tip.

Of the rangers ranked around Chriani now — his squad mates, sworn to service with him — he judged three that he suspected would never speak to him again if they were to see his ears. One for certain who would try to kill him on the spot if the secret of Chriani's sight or the parentage that had bestowed it on him were ever known.

The five who rode beside and behind him under Thelaur's command were new-made rangers as he was, all of them freshly commissioned in the prince's guard and on their first field assignments. They were younger than him, as were most members of the troop as a rule. Two years or more for most of them, and with at least a quarter of the troop's guards barely broken out to breast or beard. Those years were the length of time it had taken Chriani to make rank. The cost of a lack of ambition, and an anger he carried with him still.

The circumstances under which he'd make rank had become a tale told quietly and with no small amount of animosity throughout the prince's guard, preceding even his arrival to ranger duty. He had made rank as squire, then been granted his commission to guard in the space of two weeks — a promotion whose quickness made it unusual enough. But then came the rumors that gave his sudden advancement a sense of dark secrecy and bright notoriety all at once. Notoriety for the story of how Chriani had helped deliver the Princess Lauresa to Aerach as the only survivor of a ranger squad ambushed by the Valnirata. Secret for the real truth behind those rumors, which none of the folk of Brandishear or the soldiers of the Bastion knew.

Chriani's first night in the ranger camp, bunking with his assigned squad, they had replaced his bedroll with silk sheets. Fate only knows where they'd come from. *For the Prince's Whore,* the note tacked to them read. If Chriani had held out any hope that the anger always holding him back was a thing he'd left behind when he left Rheran, the feeling as he crumpled the note erased it.

When he left Rheran, when he had taken the assignment with the rangers that he'd been wanting for far longer than he could ever admit, Chriani hoped that things would change. Hoped that things had changed. But like the secret of his sight, like the reason for his promotion, his relationship with the Prince High Chanist of Brandishear was a thing Chriani kept secret. And as long as that was the case, he suspected that nothing would ever change enough.

As the troop rode its patrol, its three squads were scattered by design, with first squad riding ahead of Sergeant Thelaur and her rangers, third squad behind. Standard formation and assembly for forest patrols, where the noise of a full troop would call down an Ilvani ambush in short order.

The ambitions of the rangers' forays into the Greatwood were modest. They stayed clear of the deep wood, rarely ranging more than half a league within the perimeter of the forest. That frontier of the Valnirata was an empty expanse of trees that mirrored the Ilmari's own frontier — the empty belt of wild grassland kept cleared of settlement for fear of Ilvani raiding, and of incursions by the beasts that dwelled in the Greatwood and were found nowhere else in the principalities of the Ilmar. Fell wolves and drakes, trolls and wyverns. The Ilvani drove them from the forest and against the farmsteads that dotted the frontier, it was said. They trained them to the taste of Ilmari flesh by feeding them on captured scouts and errant woodcutters, and on children plucked from their beds in the dead of night.

They were good tales, as tales went.

The Ilvani patrols that shadowed the movements of the Ilmari along the frontier were the *carontir* — the elite ranger scouts of the Greatwood. Only rarely, however, would those scouts slip out to harass the Ilmari farmsteads nearest to the Greatwood's twisting wall of trees. More common by far were rogue Valnirata riders slipping past their own patrols to do the same. It was likely those rogue Ilvani that the troop was pursuing now — raiders that had crossed the boundary of the forest for two weeks past, harassing the close-standing farmsteads by dark of night. No casualties had been reported, but barns had been burned, flocks sniped and scattered by bowshot.

Three days before, the troop of Guard Sergeant Thelaur had been ordered to end it.

Chriani's sight, his hearing, even his sense of scent were things he had learned to trust long ago. Even so, no threat came to eye or ear now, the air close and thick with the forest's familiar musk of rot and loam. He was already slowing, though, wary, when another hand signal from Thelaur ahead of him made all the rangers rein up sharply. She stood at a fork in the path, both branches twisting out into shadow that made it impossible to read their direction for more than a dozen paces.

As Thelaur considered their course, Chriani tapped two fingers to his thumb. The faint pulse of sound was a signal among the rangers, used whenever calling out by voice might bring a Valnirata arrow from the shadows. He got Thelaur's attention, but then raised her ire when he spurred forward to get within whispering distance.

"Something's wrong," he hissed.

"An attempt at specificity would be welcome, master Chriani. Or should I strike a guess?" The sergeant's whisper carried a sharpness like steel scratching glass. Chriani had heard her offer honest commendations that left people shaking. Other people, at any rate. Even after five months in her squad, Chriani's performance had given Thelaur precious little to commend so far.

"Just a feeling. There's something..." Chriani began, but Thelaur stopped him with a chopping motion of hand over hand. She made no attempt to hide her anger as she signaled him to fall back, motioning Ettroch in the third rank to take his place behind her. Chriani's horse slipped back and was turning even before he spurred it, as if it recognized the command more clearly than he did.

He had trouble following orders. That's what his first report from Sergeant Thelaur had said. Also, his second and third. It was an echo of every inspection, every presentation, every assignment he had ever taken at the Bastion — the castle of the Prince High Chanist in Rheran. The Bastion had been Chriani's home for more than ten years, since the day Barien had taken him in. Barien who was a sergeant of the prince's guard, and who had been friend and confidante to Prince Chanist. Barien who was dead now, and whose death had been the point at which Chriani's life changed.

For ten years in the Bastion, Chriani had learned and grown at Barien's side. The initial quickness and determination he had shown was shaped by the veteran warrior to a skill with the bow that few other tyros of the guard could match. However, in all that time of shaping,

Chriani had never learned to care about the official strata of rank and title on which life in the Bastion was based. More importantly — and more frustratingly for Barien — he had seemingly taken great delight in actively fighting against the even more important strata of seniority and experience.

If it were ever possible to aggravate a person in a position of authority over him, Chriani would do so. As an unranked tyro, he had enraged other tyros, ranked squires, and guards alike. Sergeants and other officers. Barien had watched it happen. Had laughed about it as often as not. But he'd been steadfast in reminding Chriani that when the anger was done, those squires and sergeants and captains would remain his peers and superiors. And he would find himself stuck where he was unless things changed.

"Find yourself a new path," Barien had told him more than once. "Or you end up walking behind the same people your whole life, whether you see them or not."

Over five months of riding the frontier, Chriani had tried not to think of the path that brought him there. The path he had finally chosen, setting out on a cold morning from Rheran, seemingly a lifetime ago. He turned his mind away from that short spread of days that had transformed his life, like a season of storms had scoured his world and left it remade. Transformed.

Only one other person knew the truth of what had happened to Chriani. The truth of the path that had changed him, and that truth would stay safe with her.

No.

The thought came sharply to his mind as it always did. Not a thing he'd forgotten, but one he had tried to forget. A reminder that in fact, two other people knew the truth. And in that thought were all his reasons for wanting to forget.

He set his horse to the left of a rotting nurse stump sprouting a half-dozen new trees, Chriani not liking the snarled look of the underbrush to the other side of it. As he did, a familiar itch rose at the forefinger of his right hand where it gripped the reins. Another memory that wasn't memory, the sensation came and went. A reminder in touch and feeling that Chriani had lost that finger once. Had watched as it was hacked off cleanly by an Ilvani exile, left to rot on the forest floor.

The animys of restoration had grown it back for him at the end of his path of change, courtesy of the Prince High Chanist's own healers. He had refused them at first when they came to him, intent on owning the injury for life as a reminder of what he'd been through. They explained it wasn't an offer, but an order from the prince high himself. Payment for services to the crown.

All of it seemed so long ago now. An itch in mind, like the itch of his once-missing finger. A memory someone else had passed to him, not something from his own life. A secret he would keep as he kept the secret of his sight, his hearing. His father.

Another thing he might be killed for if the truth were ever known.

In the back rank, he was less important as point watcher, his keen eyes no use where the trails ahead were obscured by a screen of trunks and low-hanging branches and the constant fall of evergreen leaves. Ambush from behind was always a risk, but he trusted his hearing to warn him of any approach or bowshot, even as he focused his sight on the ground at his horse's feet.

Something about the trail tugged at his mind, harrying at his senses without revealing itself. Something wrong, like he'd tried to tell Thelaur, but he still had no idea what it was. He hung low across his horse's neck to scan the dirt and moss of the track, half-thinking about dropping down to his feet for an even closer look, but not wanting to risk the sergeant's wrath.

All at once, he made a fast halt, hauling straight back on the reins to bring his horse to a stop. As he stepped it backward three paces, Chriani chopped his hand to his palm three times, loud. The two other back-rank riders skidded to a stop and wheeled back toward him, even as they echoed the signal for the riders ahead. To a casual listener, the steady staccato beat would sound like the fast thump of wings. A grouse sailing clear of some obstacle before touching down again. It was the signal for *fall back, imminent danger*. Every bow was ready and nocked, every eye to the trees, horses guided by knees and instinct as they circled in close.

Thelaur split the line, a smallsword in each hand as she stopped beside Chriani. He was already on the ground, close up and peering at the sign that had stopped him.

"Explain," she hissed.

"There," Chriani said, though in truth, it was a moment before even he saw it. From the mad jumble of markings and impressions that movement and nature laid down on the trail, his senses had caught it even before his mind could make sense of it. The edge of a single hoof print, a horse unshod. Regular notches in the leading edge of the toe callus. An impression created, like three circles cut into a half-moon. "We need to move. Fall back to…"

"Explain," Thelaur said again, louder this time. Her voice was ice.

"Ilvani horse track," Chriani whispered. He marked off one print beneath circled fingers, shifted back to mark off another. A long pace apart, the horse moving quickly. The Ilvani rode their horses unshod, trusting to the strength of callus built up on the soft forest trails, and to varnishes with which they painted their steeds' hooves. It was hard as iron and long lasting, but no Ilmari alchemist had yet been able to re-create it.

"I've seen this horse before," he said. "More than once." It had been three times, in fact, the memory coming back to him. "The farm-stead patrols. Twice, a week past. Then the first time a week before that, the half-blood shepherd with his root cellar burned and his flock and best dogs shot. Each time we followed the raiders' trail, I've seen this mark, lord."

Chriani used the honorific of rank rarely heard in the presence of anyone below captain outside the Bastion. He knew in advance how little it would do to improve Thelaur's mood.

The iron-hard hooves of the Ilvani horses left marks as distinct as any boot print, but Chriani was certain he was one of the few in the troop who ever bothered to read them. The softer dirt of the open fields where the raiders ventured forth from the forest by night held the tracks best. Here within the forest, across its tangled floor of leaf mold and loam, dark earth torn through and pounded down by the horses' passage, only the barest hint of the prints could be read. Not enough to note the faint but distinct details worn into the tread of each Ilvani steed. Not except this one.

"So as we pursue those raiders," Thelaur hissed, "you're somehow surprised to find them ahead of us?"

"Not ahead of us, lord. Beside." Chriani pointed in the two direc-tions along the axis of both tracks, then marked out the edge of the nearest beneath his hand again, hoping against hope that Thelaur would actually see it. Shadow on shadow, a faint impression in the dark. But it was there, he was sure of it. "This one, cutting across our path northward, even as we move east. They've slipped off the trail to wait for us while we follow first squad."

If Sergeant Thelaur's look could kill, Chriani understood that he would have been dead, burned, and spread as ash months before. He ignored that look this time as he had all the rest.

"They're setting an ambush, sergeant. We need to fall back."

Thelaur spit in response. Chriani felt and saw a surge of impatience shift through the other riders as they edged away.

"Your shadow chasing and your thoughts of yourself as a tracker try my tolerance," the sergeant murmured. "You've cost us time and light." She called out to the others, voice louder than was safe. An edge of anger in her that Chriani knew was all for him. "East, three and three, before third squad rides over us."

She spurred her horse forward as Chriani angrily swung himself up to the saddle. As the sergeant pressed on ahead of him, an ash-grey Ilvani arrow took her through the chest.

It happened slowly, as it always did.

The hiss of the arrow and the scattering of leaves were loud in Chriani's mind. The warning he shouted sounded out through the shimmering green shadow of the wood — "Black scout marked! Black scout!" An immobile ambush. Rangers down. A call for anyone within earshot to fall in, come to the rescue. But his voice was lost to his own ears as he tracked the flight of arrows erupting from the shadows to all sides.

He saw and heard eight archers, then stopped counting. He felt the panic rising from all sides as horses and riders scrambled to get clear, saw the confusion as the other rangers circled. All new-made guards like him, younger by two years or more. Panicking now as their sergeant clutched feebly at the gout of blood that fountained out around the dark shaft, the serrated hunting head still clinging to fragments of flesh and leather where it had punched out her back.

Thelaur's horse took the brunt of a second volley as it screamed and reared. Chriani had to fight to twist his own horse around, grabbing Thelaur as she slipped from the saddle. The muscles of his shoulder and back screamed in protest as he twisted to pull her across him, felt his horse balk as he turned it hard.

The light of life was already gone from the sergeant's eyes, the blood soaking her cloak and armor spilling warm across Chriani's arm. He hung onto her all the same as he let his senses loose, felt as much as heard the hiss of horses moving within the leaves. Almost surrounded, but he saw the one opening still left to them, marked the sliver of path it held.

"Ride!" he shouted. "On me!" Then with a kick, his horse was off, the others following close behind.

The sun was well past high, the great roof of limni overhead eating the daylight hungrily and showering the forest floor with faint stains of green and gold. Dusk was on its way, the gathering gloom of the forest's early night already pursuing them from the east as they rode.

"Gold scout marked!" someone behind him was shouting, setting their westward trajectory back toward the forest wall. The voice was punctuated by intermittent arrows flashing past them, Chriani marking their trajectory as he shifted the squad's course, trusting his horse to hold the trail. A single glance back showed him the Ilvani, riding bareback at speed. Their armor was green leather when they wore it, but many of the Valnirata rode only in light cloaks of mottled green and grey, their clan war-marks set across them in twisting lines of black. Their fleet horses were painted patchwork with mud, letting mount and riders all but fade away unseen within the shadows.

He needed to make sure the rest of the squad stayed close, even as he had no idea what he would do if one of them fell. He was desperate to retrace the route they had followed into the forest, knowing the disaster that would come of hitting one of the Ilvani's dead ends at speed. He was even more desperate to reach for the horse bow at his hip, but it was taking both hands and all his strength to hold Thelaur fast across the saddle. She hung head down and limp, the blood that dripped from her caught on the clutching wall of leaves and branches as it whipped past.

"Red scout stands!" came a familiar voice from the trees ahead. Rangers holding, countersigning Chriani and the other riders' approach. Too close.

Something twisted in his stomach as he shouted, "Break right!" Not one of the rangers' codes, but just a desperate warning. He hauled his horse hard to the side, felt it scramble off the path just in time.

Thelaur had been right. Third squad had almost ridden them down in the time it had taken Chriani to fail in explaining the tracks he'd seen. They were scattered across three sections of trailhead, ranked around a broad grove of new limni growing within a hollow marked out by the crumbling stumps of three once-great trees. Six riders led by Umeni, ranking guard of the troop under Thelaur.

One of those six riders was Kathlan, sitting her horse at Umeni's right hand. It was her voice Chriani had heard. He was afraid suddenly, felt a chill trace up his spine. He was aware of his breathing, the pounding of his heart as Kathlan expertly slipped the chestnut mare she rode back and away, giving him and the others room as they slewed their foam-flecked horses to both sides.

"Ilvani!" he shouted, to Kathlan and Umeni and all the rest. "Through the grove! Shoot from cover!"

The rangers at his back continued on their course with a sureness that surprised him, Kathlan following suit as she turned her horse and spurred ahead. But the attention of Umeni and his other riders was focused entirely on Thelaur slumped across Chriani's horse. Her sergeant's insignia was barely visible in the gloom.

"Report..." Umeni said as he tried to get his horse in front of Chriani's. He was Thelaur's second, had control of the troop by right in her absence.

"Move!" Chriani struck Thelaur's horse on the flank, driving it forward as he rode past.

They had bows drawn and arrows nocked, horses twisting between the tight screen of the trees as the Ilvani shifted behind and around them. The hiss of arrows was a moment's warning, the haze of dark shafts arcing toward them from three directions. Even to Ilvani eyes, though, the screen of trees was a wall that those shafts were shattered and split off against as fast as they were fired. As they always did, the Valnirata warriors fought in an unsettling silence. No battle cries, no orders called out. No sound from the dying.

A warning shout against spell-fire came from somewhere to Chriani's right. Spellcasting was second nature to the Ilvani, but the warmages of the prince's guard were few and far between. He saw knives of white light flash within the trees, heard the cries of rangers and horses as they were struck but ran on.

Kathlan was racing hard and close beside him. She was the best rider in the troop, and showed it by the way she twisted her horse through brush and undergrowth. She might be the best rider of all Chanist's rangers one day. But even so, Chriani had to fight the urge to vault toward her, hold himself in front of her as if that would make any difference to the peril riding hard on their heels.

"Folk get strangely stupid," Barien had told him once. "Protecting what they love."

Even held to his own saddle, Chriani was conscious of trying to cover Kathlan as he swiveled toward the targets he still couldn't shoot at. Those were unfortunately plentiful, his eyes pulling detail from the shadow, counting fifteen Ilvani in a wide formation. He had seen four of them hit so far, the rangers catching them through breaks in the trees, when something changed.

"...break through!" Umeni was calling, but Chriani missed the rest of the guard's frantic cry. Something was wrong. He felt it. Sensed the chill tracing his spine that told him his eyes had caught something his mind couldn't yet see.

Around them, the Ilvani were pressing, holding tight to the rangers as they raced through the grove. The steady pulse of arrows hadn't slowed. But the timing was wrong. Erratic. The thought came stray to Chriani's mind, burning in him with an instinct he couldn't name as he lurched his horse forward with a quick kick. He pulled himself next to Kathlan, feeling both their horses shy at the uncomfortable closeness as they ran.

"What are you...?" was all she got to say as he hefted Thelaur's body from his horse to hers. Both horses stumbled, but the sergeant was light even in armor. As Kathlan clutched at the body, Chriani pulled his bow from the hitch at his saddle.

"Ride hard," he shouted to Kathlan as he pulled away. Then he called out "Lomyr! Collyn, Taedry!" With the exception of himself and Thelaur, those three were the best archers in the troop. A half-dozen paces ahead and beside him, all of them glanced back. "On me! Now!" Then Chriani dug in hard to wheel his horse, spurring around, then running hard back the way they'd come.

Far to the front, Umeni shouted after him with a strangled cry. "Hold formation!"

Chriani ignored him, not looking back.

He had seen an Ilvani fusillade once. Only once. On that path he'd taken to a changed life, he had watched a cloud of shafts spill out of the darkness into a running battle with unerring precision, only a moment ahead of a mounted assault. He hadn't known the Ilvani tactics then. Had spent his life blissfully distant from the Greatwood and all the myriad ways one might die there.

He had learned much of the Valnirata Ilvani's combat in the first months of taking his place of rank in the Bastion, and newly commissioned to the prince's guard by the Prince High Chanist himself. He had learned more in the five months of his assignment to the rangers, and of patrolling the boundaries of the forest. And all of what he knew now, and of what he remembered of that dark night from a year and a half before, was that the Ilvani war-clan fighters used their arrows always as a prelude to running their foes down. But these had stayed out of sight, circling. Waiting for something. Giving him and the three who had followed him a chance.

A twisting track through bracken and low branches took them out of the grove and onto the trails again. He had Lomyr and Taedry beside him, the sound of Collyn's horse coming up from farther behind. He let his eyes pull all detail from the shadows, following the trails torn up by the Ilvani horses. The hiss of arrows came from ahead, but still trained on the main body of both squads, the trees screening Chriani and the others as they closed. The forest to both sides was green and black, leaf-shrouded sunlight and shadow flashing past. The trails were uneven, broken through by the great limni's twisting roots. Chriani's horse stumbled once, his knees locking tight to the saddle.

He was the first to break through the screen of trees to bring the Valnirata troop into sight. It was a carontir patrol, not the border bandits they had been pursuing. They wore no livery, but Chriani recognized the sureness of their riding, the speed with which they shot.

Three paces in front of him, an Ilvani set two grey shafts flying from her bow, sending both into the wall of the grove where the fleeing Ilmari could be seen as flashes of grey and green. The Ilvani had time to register the sound of horses behind her as she wheeled. Chriani's shot took her under the arm as she tried and failed to flatten against her horse's neck in time. The momentum sent her tumbling from her mare's bare back, hitting the forest floor in a tangle of limbs and dead leaves.

In a heartbeat, the air around Chriani and the others was a haze of arrows. Ilvani and Ilmari alike unleashed a storm of bowshot. Both sides were shooting for each other rather than their horses, knowing that the mounts were an easier target, but knowing also that a horse could take multiple arrows and run on. Especially at this range, one well-placed shot could take a rider out of the fight with ease. Chriani ducked down more than once as a wide-bladed shaft twisted past his head. But as he had hoped, the unexpected attack from the flank was sending the Ilvani scattering, creating a gap to one side.

"Umeni, break left!" he shouted over the thunder of hoofbeats, not bothering with codes anymore. A call came in answer, the Valnirata breaking even farther as bowshot from the troop crossed over in front of them. The Ilvani riders were slowing, shifting to both sides now, the careful order of their assault broken.

Tearing through the trees a half-dozen paces to the left, a wild-eyed Ilvani warrior turned her horse hard as she saw Chriani appear beside her. Their bows came up at the same time, both shots crossing over. The sharp bite of steel hit high on Chriani's right arm, a flare of pain rising even as his return shot struck home.

The Ilvani was naked to the waist, golden hair flowing behind her, arms and shoulders and breast knotted with the dark tattoos that were the war-mark of the Valnirata. Tight lines twisted along her skin in black and green, laying down glyphs and sigils that spoke of clan and family, the battles she'd fought, the enemies fallen before her. Chriani's arrow took her along the edge of that mark but didn't drop her. Her teeth were set with a feral rage as she forced her horse alongside his, a long-knife flashing in her hands.

A touch to his quiver told Chriani he was out of arrows. He swung the bow instead, hearing it and the Ilvani's cheekbone break at once. The knife flashed past him as the rider went down.

Ahead, he saw light. A sudden shift from green shadow to blue and hammered gold, the open sky turning molten along the horizon with the setting of the sun. They were within sight of the forest wall and the open grasslands beyond, a hundred paces away.

Under normal circumstances, Chriani would have called them safe as they hit open ground. The horses and horse bows of the war-clans were both made for speed and maneuverability in tight quarters, not for straight range. As well, over five months of playing cat-and-mouse along the forest's edge, the Ilvani carontir had shown little reluctance to pass beyond their woods. But this attack was already unusual in too many other ways.

"Ride hard!" he shouted, though the steady thunder of hoofbeats behind him made the order unnecessary. He hadn't looked back to see if he'd lost any of the three who'd followed him, but he could see Umeni on his far right flank now, three riders still with him.

Kathlan was one of those riders. Chriani felt something bright surge within him as she outpaced the others, even with Thelaur's body draped across her legs. As they all ran, she pulled closer to Chriani where the trails began to split and widen to open ground.

From behind him came a low hiss. A sharp exhalation, a sound of fury and frustration that carried even over the thud of hoofbeats and the horses' rasping breath.

"Laóith irnash!"

The hissing turned to words that rang out behind him. One of the Ilvani, his voice twisted by rage as he screamed an oath. *We hunt the vile, we hunt the hateful. We hunt the Ilmari.* The Valnirata's hatred of the Ilmari and their homelands ran deep, and gave their epithet *laóith* a dozen subtle meanings. Chriani didn't understand the warrior as he shouted again, though.

"Lóech arnala irch niir! Lóech niir!"

He risked a look behind him. The Ilvani warriors always fought in silence. No battle cries, no orders ever heard.

He saw the rider three lengths back, snaking through the thinning screen of trees. His hair was long streaks of grey and gold, tied tight and flowing fast behind him, his eyes flashing molten gold in the half-light. His leather was cut away at the shoulder for ease of shooting, his bow up and a black arrow at the string, set dead on Chriani. On the wrist of the Ilvani's bow arm, a blood-red light was flaring.

"Chriani irnash! Lóech arnala irch niir!"

It happened slowly, as it always did.

Chriani heard his name hang across the gulf of shadow and the screen of leaves that wrapped them both. His name, shouted by an Ilvani warrior he'd never seen before. He felt his reflexes slow, felt a chill twist through him as the black arrow snapped from the bow.

"Chriani!"

His name again, but from the right side this time. The endless moment surrounded him, giving him time to see Kathlan from the corner of his eye. She twisted her horse in to drive his a half step to the side as they both broke through the sentinel trees at the forest's edge. Then she muffled a cry as the arrow that would have taken Chriani in the back punched into her shoulder instead with the crunch of breaking bone.

A surge of pain and nausea twisted through Chriani, spreading from his gut and threatening to knock him from the saddle. One hand clutched at his stomach, then swung around to his back to see if he'd been hit, but there was nothing there. The other hand grabbed at Kathlan, but she shrugged him off where she lashed her reins tight around one hand.

A wave of brightness washed over Chriani, and a pulse of clean air. They were out and free, racing across open ground and through a field of autumn-gold oat grass, blown to gentle waves by a rising wind. He twisted to look back, saw Umeni and the others following close. He waited for the volley of arrows across the clear and open space behind them, but it never came. There was just the dark wall of the forest rising, the sloped canopy of leaves rippled by the wind and glowing green-gold in the day's last light.

Of the Ilvani, there was no sign.

— CHAPTER 2 —
THE DEEP WOOD

AT A HUNDRED PACES from the trees, Umeni's voice rang out over the breathing of exhausted horses, the drumming of hooves. "Rangers hold!"

They were all looking behind them, waiting for the Ilvani that Chriani knew instinctively were long gone back to the green shadow. His heart was racing, pain twisting through him as he let his horse slow, easing it into a walk. His mind was working even faster, a spill of furious thought cascading through him too fast to focus on.

The Ilvani had called his name.

"Blood, mother, and fuck me..."

The edge of pain in Kathlan's voice brought Chriani back to something like a focused state of mind. She was on her knees on the grass, her horse wandering off to where Umeni and two others approached it. Sergeant Thelaur's body was still draped across its back.

Kathlan had a wad of cloth held to the arrow where its head was buried in her shoulder, its black shaft gleaming in the light of the setting sun. Her face was pale, but the slow ooze of red-black across her armor told Chriani the arrow had missed the fast blood.

"You'll be all right," he said as he slipped from his horse. He stumbled as he stepped toward her, righted himself.

"Spoken like someone who doesn't have an arrow in the arm."

"Just hold it for now. Take healing when it's drawn. Staunch the bleeding, flush the blood-fever."

But as Chriani knelt close to her, reaching in to help her keep pressure on the wound, he lurched as the nausea hit him in a second wave. Something hot and sharp was burrowing inside him, like a broken dagger nesting in his gut. Kathlan had to reach out to steady him, her hand as he brushed it awkwardly away showing the blood welling on his own arm.

Her tone softened just a little. "You're hurt."

"No," Chriani said, and it should have been true. The arrow had cut him, but he couldn't feel it through the rising wave of pain that occluded all else. Poison, maybe? But there was no burning in the wound itself. He'd felt the chill of blood-shock before, knew this was something else. Only the hammering at his heart was familiar to him.

He was afraid, he realized.

He'd seen Kathlan shot in front of him, an arm's length away. And it had terrified him. He recognized that fear. Felt it surge out from the space he'd been carrying it since the day they rode out from Rheran for duty on the frontier, even as he tried to hide it. He knew how she'd react if she saw it in him.

"Don't do this," she said quietly. Too late, then.

"I'm not doing anything..."

"You're paying mind to me where it isn't needed, and I'm not the only one noticing."

"You need healing. Thelaur should have had a draught with her..."

"Thelaur's dead, and Teobryn and Geran," Kathlan hissed, low enough that only Chriani would hear. "And there's at least three others who need healing more than I do right now. I'm shot and both squads are in shambles, but I'm not where I need you nursemaiding me just yet. And I need the rest of troop seeing you treat me like I can't handle myself even less."

Chriani stood shakily in response, felt a wave of dizziness pass through him.

"See to your horse," Kathlan said. "Then see to yourself. Or thinking on it, see to my horse, then to yourself. It's worth two of you any day."

Chriani walked back to where his horse and Kathlan's were pacing, trembling. Kathlan's chestnut mare had been brought from the Bastion stables, a horse she'd reared and trained herself. He knew she was right about its worth. As he pulled both horses to a slow walk, he caught the glances from the other rangers, the quick flick of eyes from him to Kathlan and back again. It told him she was right as well about them noticing.

Chriani had to struggle to walk and cool both horses at once, but they settled in time. The rangers kept their mounts saddled against the risk of unexpected attack, but as they walked them, they pulled their saddlebags loose and were cooling the horses with the last of their water, wiping them down with felt as they moved.

The sound of hoofbeats to the north along the forest wall caught Chriani's ear before any of the others could hear it. As they did so a moment later, a surge of panic pushed through the rangers, bows drawn. But he had already recognized the sound as their own horses, their cadence different from that of the lighter Ilvani steeds. It was the riders of first squad that Thelaur's rangers had been in pursuit of when everything had gone so wrong. They were seven strong and all accounted for, Chriani saw, their horses barely winded.

Umeni strode out to meet them from where he'd been kneeling at Sergeant Thelaur's body, wrapped now with his own cloak and hers. She was lying in the tall grass, her weapons beside her. The arrow that killed her was set atop her body, pulled from her chest but not broken. Standard procedure for any Ilvani weapons and ammunition claimed on patrol, the war-mages wanting to read them for magic. The arrow that had struck Kathlan had that look about it. Another reason not to draw it until she was safely back at the camp.

Chriani irnash!

They'd been hunting him. The Ilvani had called his name.

By the time the horses had fully calmed, the nausea and the churning fear had passed. Chriani's thoughts were focused, playing back the frantic last moments of their escape in mind and memory. He tried to tell himself he had only imagined it. The voice coming steel-sharp on the air, masked by the pounding of hoofbeats and his own heart.

Chriani irnash! Lóech arnala irch nür!

We hunt Chriani. A call for his blood, and the other words that he didn't understand but whose fury he felt all the same. He had frozen at the sound of that voice. Had felt it reaching for him, like the calling of his name was a sight line on which the arrow had been hung. But how would the Ilvani know him? Commissioned for only a year and a half. Most of that time spent in the Bastion guard, then five months with the rangers along a frontier whose most significant battle had been fought only today.

Chriani felt a rising anger, recognized it as the frustration of having something looming before him that he somehow couldn't see. A screen of thought and churning questions were hanging like moss and shadow from the trees, shutting down the path he knew lay somewhere beyond it.

It was his mother who had first taught him to focus his thoughts, focus his mind. Seeing even at a young age how easily angered her son could be, how quick to leap to distraction — or perhaps seeing something in him of the mind of his father who he'd never really known. Quick to judgement, quick to anger.

Chriani remembered a night by the fire. A winter he recalled before the summer when his mother had died, thrown by her horse and too far from a healer's touch.

She had told him of how the fire warms the hearth, and he remembered sitting with her before its bright blazing light. But fire was safe only when it was slowed, she said. One spark, one crack of flame would dazzle the eye and sear the skin, the touch of that fast fire burning. He remembered holding out his child's hand toward the flame, just long enough to feel it grow uncomfortable before his mother lowered it toward the hearth, and the softer warmth there. Heat drawn in by air and stone, to be soaked up slowly. Warming without burning.

The Ilvani had been pursuing second squad, sweeping past them on both sides. An ambush set, the track Chriani had seen that Thelaur hadn't believed. The Ilvani pursuit had hemmed them in but not pressed the clear advantage. The riders waiting for something.

First squad had ridden out of the Greatwood without a mark on them, the Valnirata seemingly ignoring them.

The Ilvani had called his name.

Instinct and anger were like the fire, Chriani's mother had often told him. Reminding him, trying to teach him to not react to the quick thought, the quick fear. Let it build slow to show the truer thought, and the real fear beneath it.

"Chriani." Umeni's voice from behind him chased questions and memory alike from his mind.

"We need to follow them," Chriani said even as he turned. The thought and the words coming in one stroke, unbidden.

Umeni stood two steps ahead of Makaysa, ranking guard and leader of first squad. She was of an age with Chriani, and someone he had known at the Bastion. She'd made tyro a year after him, but had stayed at the citadel less than four years before making squire, being sent to the rangers, and never coming back. She wore a look of quiet contemplation now to contrast Umeni's dour countenance. Still, both showed the same surprise in response to Chriani's words.

"We'll send a rested squad back from camp to retrieve the fallen," Umeni said coldly. "Not that such a decision needs any suggestion from you."

"I'm not talking for the bodies. We need to find the Ilvani…"

"And while I'm sure that might be relevant to some other discussion, this discussion concerns your breaking rank and formation without order or authorization."

It was Chriani's turn to show surprise. "You're welcome," he said.

"Excuse me, soldier?"

"My apologies. You're welcome, lord. We need to follow the Ilvani. Now."

As a tangible surge of antagonism rose in Umeni, Chriani saw Makaysa smirk behind him. Among the guards, there were only minimal distinctions of rank but plenty of battles for seniority, he knew. He and all the others who wore the falcon of Brandis stitched in silver at their shoulders earned the right to lord themselves over squires and tyros at their whim. But guards likewise fought subtle battles to ascend the tiers of commissioned rank and responsibility, which determined how the guard sergeants and other officers would lord it over them in turn.

"Your actions," Umeni said, "put two squads at potential risk. You called archers to you with no order or corroboration..."

"Thelaur was dead. Who should I have...?"

"Me, fool. As ranking guard of third squad..."

Chriani turned his attention to Makaysa, a calculated taunt to Umeni's rapidly rising sense of indignation.

"Before Sergeant Thelaur was killed, she had been advised that second squad were being pursued. We saw signs..."

"Enough!" Umeni said, loud enough that Chriani knew he meant for his voice to carry.

"First squad called out *green scout marked,*" Chriani said to Makaysa. "You came under fire, yes? But there was no pursuit, because the Ilvani were using you to draw second squad in."

"For what reason, soldier?" Makaysa's tone suggested that even if she had no interest in Chriani's story, she would embrace it for the rage it was inciting in Umeni.

"That's what we need to find out..."

"Rangers, mount up!" Umeni shouted over him. "Field formation for the return to camp. Eyes on the forest as we go."

Umeni's squad reacted quickly to his order, the other rangers less so. Chriani looked past the seething guard to see Kathlan on her feet, her arm slung and tied tight to her chest to keep the shoulder and the arrow from moving. She was loading her saddlebags one-handed, getting ready to ride.

Other eyes were on him, but Kathlan's expression was the only one he felt the need to read. He saw the warning in that expression. A sense not of disapproval, but of impatience. Of an irritation that flared up with each increasingly erratic thing Chriani did — and with the quiet worry that came with wondering what he might do.

He knew that look. Had seen it countless times since he and Kathlan had been assigned to the rangers. "Eight years a tyro," she had told him during one particularly long and rain-filled day along the road from Rheran, "and doing everything in your power to keep that streak going as long as you could. But you've made rank and commission and got a future to think of. You're done with the games now."

It hadn't been a question, so Chriani hadn't answered it at the time. He'd seen the look in her eyes, though. The same as he saw now.

Umeni stepped in front of him, blocking his view. More quietly, the ranking guard spoke. "I'll ask the same questions about your games in the forest when we return to camp, soldier. Only there'll be captains present this time, and I don't think they'll find your insubordination as amusing as you…"

Chriani's foot lashed out to hook between Umeni's legs, sending the guard face-first to the dirt with a quick twist. "Thank you for the horse," he said to Makaysa, seeing her smile waver. Then he was running.

He had seen the horses of first squad loosely staked near Thelaur's body, had marked off the distance in his mind even as he drove Umeni to the ground. Bootsteps came a moment behind him, as he expected. Knowing that Umeni would try to charge Chriani in his rage before calling to anyone in his squad — or worse, Thelaur's or Makaysa's squads — to stop him.

Chriani snatched up the reins of the first horse he reached and kept running. The animal showed no surprise as it lurched to speed alongside him. Then he swung himself up to the saddle at a run, digging his heels in to feel the horse spring forward from trot to gallop. Umeni was screaming something behind him, but he didn't bother to hear it. The forest loomed as a wall of shifting green before him. He didn't look back.

Chriani felt the anger flag even as the shadow fell once more, the forest looming around him as he drove the horse through along the same trail that had led them out of the Greatwood. Behind him a moment before, there'd been the faint gold of grass and fields shimmering through the trees. Now his eyes were adjusting to the gloom as he left the brightness of the sky behind, saw the fainter brightness spread around him where the canopy of leaves let its drizzle of faint sun through.

He had no idea what he was doing, no idea what he was searching for. But in that complete lack of planning was an uneasy familiarity, Chriani knowing it should have bothered him more than it did.

He played the fight back in his mind as he rode, tried to assess and count off how many of the Ilvani had fallen. How many might be left. Eight was the number he kept coming back to, so he held it hopefully in mind. He thought about the risk of ambush, then discarded it. They had let first squad go, that thought circling in his mind still, tugging at him.

He had no idea where the Ilvani had come from, how long they'd been following Thelaur's second squad. But Makaysa and her rangers had appeared from the trees less than half a league from where Chriani and the others spilled out from the forest wall. If the Ilvani had wanted ambush, if they wanted blood for revenge or to pay for the escape of their chosen targets, first squad would have presented them a perfect opportunity. Instead, the survivors had vanished.

All he had to do was find them. Simple.

Chriani shook his head, heard all the voices of his youth calling him a fool in his mind. Barien, Kathlan. Makaysa once, back when both were tyros. He'd almost forgotten it. A shared watch in the armories one night, and Chriani trying to impress her by showing off his skill with a thrown dagger against one of the main chamber's battered ceiling posts. Except he'd missed and sent a stack of shields to a noisy tumble. The sergeant-at-arms heard him. It hadn't ended well.

In the few times their paths had crossed in the camp, Makaysa had made no sign that she recognized or remembered him. Probably for the best.

Chriani let his horse slow as the trail took them back toward the last point of the battle. There, through the gloom, he saw bodies. Two Ilmari soldiers and their horses, scattered at a distance along the forest's skein of twisted paths. One Ilvani horse lay dead a short way off, but there was no sign of any of the Valnirata warriors that had fallen. Those bodies would have been dragged away from the battle site, Chriani knew, to be given whatever rites were practiced in the Greatwood. The Valnirata didn't return their dead to their homes or families. Just hid them away in the darkness of the forest close to where they fell, leaving them to nature but out of sight of enemies who might desecrate them. Even if he'd had time to look for those Ilvani dead, Chriani knew he'd never find them.

He dismounted to check the Ilmari fallen, though, saw their weapons gone and bodies looted. Arrows had dropped them both.

Teobryn and Geran, Kathlan had said their names were. Chriani wouldn't have known it otherwise.

The horses had their saddlebags emptied, the Valnirata clearly taking their time as they fell back. He found the signs of that retreat easily enough, tracks marking where the light Ilvani steeds had circled before veering off along a trail that opened up to the north, breaking northeast before it vanished into shadow.

Within the field of hoofprints as they funneled off to a single chaotic line, Chriani saw the familiar track. Three circles cut into the half-moon. He was still staring at it when he heard the sound of horses rising from behind him.

As before, he knew it wasn't the Ilvani even before he caught first sight of movement through the trees. He felt a shard of anger spike, having counted on Umeni being too obstinate to follow him. The horse he'd stolen had a standard-issue shortbow clipped to the saddle, light for his taste but serviceable, and good enough that he could have sent warning shots behind him. Chriani left it there as he swung on and spurred ahead, though. No point in giving Umeni any more reason to shoot him in response.

Even as he slipped the horse at speed into the dark screen of the trees, though, it was Makaysa's voice he heard calling to him.

"Blue scout shown green. Blue to green." North to east. Announcing that she had seen him, was following his course. Then a louder call. "Clearmoon's full light. Chriani!"

Chriani reined to a stop. He lingered for a moment, heard the others approaching at a trot. Not giving chase.

Clearmoon's full light was the call that all was well. Clear and safe to approach. Its counter, designed specifically to be used by rangers captured or cornered by the Valnirata, was *Clearmoon, dark night*. Not many of the Valnirata Ilvani spoke the Ilmari language in one of its regional dialects, so that the rhyme of the two calls made it difficult for the Ilvani ear to tell which was which. This allowed the hope that a captured ranger could attempt to sound a warning if tortured into calling allies into ambush.

Chriani swung the horse around, stiffly cantered forward from deep shadow to the paler light of the open paths.

Makaysa was leading five of her rangers, nodding to Chriani as she drew abreast of him. He wondered for a moment where the last rider of first squad was, then realized stupidly that he was astride that rider's horse. He didn't know the others by name, but if the dark looks they gave him were any indication, they knew who he was.

"You shouldn't ride off ahead like that," Makaysa said. The familiar smile played across her lips, her eyes bright in the shadows. "Someone might think I hadn't ordered you to join me on this sortie."

Chriani felt a look of profound surprise twist across his face, fought to quell it as he nodded. Makaysa was covering for him, but what her reasons might be, he had no idea. Perhaps annoying Umeni was reward enough in the complex game of ambition and power the ranger guards all played.

"Sorry," was all he could think to say.

"Sorry what, soldier?" Makaysa had angled herself so that only Chriani could see her smile widen.

"Sorry, lord."

"Much better. Now enlighten me as to why I've called this patrol."

The mockery in her tone shouldn't have bothered him, but Chriani felt the faint burn of anger rising in his chest as he turned away. He gestured to the dark side trail ahead. "The Ilvani looted the bodies, interred their own, then rode north and east. Not time for a full rest, though. Riding as hard as they were, they're moving slowly to cool their horses. With fresh mounts, we've got a chance to catch them. Lord."

He added the honorific in reaction to Makaysa's look. He saw wariness in that look, but also the knowledge that her decision to follow Chriani through to whatever he was seeking had been made even before she rode into the forest behind him.

"If they're retreating, they're moving for the deep wood." Makaysa glanced up from the bottom of the well of green shadow. "We're losing the light as it is." For the benefit of the other rangers, she added, "Loose formation, ready to fall back. We follow Chriani."

They rode fast to make the most of the fading sun, Chriani already knowing that even he would need light by the time they made their way back. The twilight of day in the Greatwood faded to an absolute darkness by night, the great trees converging overhead to swallow the pale light of moons and stars alike.

He'd seen that darkness only once so far, on the night patrol that had responded to the burning of the shepherd's root cellar. That was the first time he'd seen the half-moon hoofprint, clear beneath the torchlight as they'd followed the trail into the wood, just far enough to ensure the Ilvani were gone. Away from that torchlight, the night-time forest had vanished even before Chriani's eyes. A vast emptiness outside the bright spread of firelight, the wind shifting branches to wrap each rider in shadow.

With Chriani on point now, they followed the trail easily, the Ilvani not bothering to hide their passage. Still, he spent as much time focused on the side trails and open spaces as he did on the twisting main track, watching for any sign of horses splitting off. He'd seen nothing so far, though, the Ilvani seemingly unconcerned with being followed.

They rode in silence for the most part, the occasional slap of hand to palm sounding out a warning that turned out to be mostly shadows. They saw wolves twice, but only at a distance. These weren't the great fell wolves but their smaller cousins, cautious enough that even as a pack, they would think twice about taking on horses and warriors in concert.

They were passing the second of those packs, Chriani watching their bright eyes as the squad slipped by in silence, when the light changed. He slowed his horse, held up a hand in warning.

It was an unfelt moment. A subtle shift like the start of a change in the wind. They had ridden a little over a league, he judged. Behind them was green shadow, the twilight of the Greatwood's dusk still hanging. Before them was a deeper gloom that only Chriani's eyes could pierce. He saw no threats, the trail continuing clear and unbroken ahead. Just the darkness.

Tales from the wars the Ilmari called the Ilvani Incursions talked of the network of trails the Valnirata carved through the deep wood as shifting day by day, twisting like something alive. A troop's worth of tracks would end suddenly in a wall of trees, no way to get beyond it. Open trails would lead to ambush, or twist around to split a squad up and separate its riders, leaving them lost and alone.

The rangers of Brandishear patrolled the frontier. They rode the forest's edge, watching the Ilvani shadow them with patrols of their own. On rare occasions, they would slip within the edges of the forest for a day, or a week. But not since the days of the Incursions a generation before had Brandishear rangers driven in numbers into the deep wood — the heart of the forest beyond the relatively open trees of the frontier.

A year and a half before, that had almost changed. An attempt on the prince high's life, talk of a Valnirata plot. It had all just been tales in the end. Chriani had been there.

"We go in there, how do we come out?" It was the rider behind Makaysa, whispering for her ear alone, but the silence of the forest seemed to lift and raise his voice to a sharp hiss. Makaysa silenced him with a wave of her hand, but her eyes held the same question for Chriani.

He made the signal for light, two of the others drawing torches from side compartments on their saddlebags. These were special issue for the rangers — alchemically treated by the Bastion's mages to burn safe and almost smokeless, and to light themselves when a sharp blow cracked them. Chriani heard the snap, saw the pulse of firelight spread and shimmer within the trees.

The other three rangers had bows drawn, the two holding the torches drawing their swords. All looked wary. Chriani had a bow in hand, but he shook his head at Makaysa as she pulled a torch of her own. He nudged his horse closer to her.

"If they're waiting," he whispered, "the light will draw them in. So we work that to our advantage. Send the others wide, the archers behind, just out of the light. You and I on point. Stay behind me."

"And how are you and I supposed to see?"

"I've got good eyes for the dark," Chriani said carefully. It was less than the truth but more than he liked to say. He looked away to avoid Makaysa's gaze. "You just need to stay close."

Makaysa made the finger signals that gave the orders. No hesitation, no argument, but still no trust for him that Chriani could feel. Just an instinct for sticking with a course once committed to it. Not willing to show her uncertainty to the others under her command.

They rode forward as three groups, Chriani leading. The distant last light of day was a dark grey stain across the trail ahead, but it was enough for him. The other rangers split off along side trails, pressed through screens of brush to stay on Chriani's course when the trails veered.

The trees around them were growing almost trunk-to-trunk in places, their great boles arcing down to twisted roots that his horse stepped over carefully. He glanced behind him to Makaysa each time it happened, warning her with a wave but not sure whether she could see him. Her horse kept the trail, though, her expression alert. She had a longsword in one hand and her unlit torch in the other, ready for whatever might lie ahead as she crept forward with Chriani through the shadows.

He remembered that same sense of readiness in Makaysa from her time at the Bastion. A kind of expectation in her that whatever was to be faced, she would face it and persevere. An attitude from the start that leadership was just another challenge to be faced, and a thing she would claim when it was time.

He saw that in Kathlan sometimes, though never from the innate sense of superiority that Makaysa had too often shown as a tyro. And in the time since he and Kathlan came to the frontier, Chriani had wondered more than once what it was going to feel like serving under her some day. Kathlan knowing what she was capable of, rising to that capability through the same determination that let her face off against every other part of her life. Chriani falling behind her, under the weight of insubordination and the anger he would never shake.

He had no idea, he realized, what the penalty even was for stealing a horse. The thought struck him with a sense of absurdity that almost made him smile. At some point previously, he should have looked into that.

Through the screen of trees ahead, a shimmer of movement blurred at the edge of his vision. He leaned forward as he nocked his bow, saw a half-dozen Ilvani on foot breaking to both sides. As he hoped, they'd seen the light and honed in on it, not seeing him and Makaysa as they pushed up the middle.

He let his fingers slip the bowstring as he shouted, the shaft arcing high through a screen of trees. "Throw torches, thirty paces dead ahead! Shoot!" No time or place for coded signals anymore.

The figure Chriani had targeted was caught off guard. The arrow took the Ilvani high in the shoulder, sending it off its mount with arms flailing as two pools of firelight arced through the trees. That light landed across the paths of the other Ilvani where they were slinking into ambush position. Then it burst to a brilliant sheen, each of the torches flaring to daylight brightness in a space twenty paces across. It was more of the Bastion's alchemy, the torches designed to flare when thrown and almost impossible to quench when they did. It wasn't magic — or not the real magic of dweomercraft, at any rate — but Chriani had to fight the urge to make the moonsign anyway.

Catching the Ilvani off guard had been their only real hope of facing them successfully. But even Chriani was surprised by the speed of the fight. He and the other rangers were in darkness but targeting freely, the Ilvani fully lit up against the shadowed forest beyond. For their part, the Ilvani were all but blinded by the light, the keenness of their own vision not helping them where Chriani and the others spurred their horses and circled around through the trees. The long grey shafts of the Ilvani horse bows arced past them harmlessly as their own return fire struck true.

Chriani took two more Ilvani cleanly himself, striking one horse when he misjudged the arc of a long shot through a screen of hanging vines. He shot twice more to take the wounded horse out, heard it scream as it fell. The Valnirata fought and died in their deathly silence.

The rangers pushed into the light, swords drawn and steel striking. The Ilvani bowshot faded, and the forest was quiet once more.

The three-beat signal to regroup sounded out, but Chriani circled far outside the light before he fell in. His eyes pulled the stillness of the forest from the shadows as he went, making sure they were alone.

When he did return, more torchlight had been spread around the point where the rangers took shelter within a twisting stand of five broad trees. The brightness of the light set up a surreal tone within the wood, the great trunks of the limni shimmering like verdigris and bronze, green moss scrawled like veins across bark-brown skin. The brightness made the darkness beyond seem even more absolute, the rangers and their prisoners held within a bubble of green walled in black shadow.

Makaysa and the others were circling around four Ilvani on their knees, hands to their heads and blades at their backs. Three bodies had been dragged to where the horse had fallen, but the other Ilvani steeds were gone. The Valnirata trained them that way, sent them to flee if their masters fell.

As Chriani slipped off his horse, Makaysa nodded in what almost looked like thanks. "Nicely done."

"You plan well, lord," he said.

The squad leader smiled. "When you and Umeni had your... debriefing, you talked of this being a coordinated attack. The Ilvani using first squad to draw second squad into ambush?"

"As I saw it, yes. When you called green, moving east, they were already closing in around us. Waiting for us to follow you."

"But why target second squad with first squad already in view?"

Makaysa's tone carried a thoughtfulness that Chriani heard far too rarely in would-be leaders. Not in Thelaur, for all her skill in the field. Certainly not in Umeni. But the question was one he had no answer for. Not yet.

Chriani irnash! Lóech arnala irch niir!

The Ilvani had called his name.

The sound of cracking ribs pushed Chriani's thoughts from his mind. He looked up to see an Ilvani prisoner slump forward, mouth set in a grim line where one of Makaysa's rangers had sent a boot into his side. Grus was a hulking veteran guard whose name Chriani had learned only because it showed up so often in the troop's disciplinary reports. All muscle and no wit, like too many members of the guard who seemed content to stay at first rank all their lives. A picture of himself in years to come, Chriani thought.

Trembling, the Ilvani slowly straightened. He made no sound.

"Tell us what we want to know and it will go easier on you." Makaysa spoke the words in awkward and badly accented Ilvalantar, the language of the Ilmar Ilvani. An offshoot of the older tongues of the Valnirata war-clans, but close enough in nature that the prisoners would understand her. "Your actions were unprovoked attack, in violation of treaty. You targeted a sergeant of Brandishear who now lies dead. Answer for your aggression."

The stoic silence in which the Ilvani fought had seemingly carried with them. None of them looked up. None of them spoke. Grus waited for a nod from Makaysa before a second kick sent the first prisoner to the ground. When he made no sign of rising this time, the veteran lined up a third kick, his heavy boot swinging back and a thin smile on his lips.

Chriani grabbed the boot as he stepped up behind Grus in two quick strides. As he pulled and twisted, he drove his own foot into the ranger's back, sending him hopelessly off balance and crashing face-first to the ground.

A flash of blades. The other rangers were close, swords still on the Ilvani but dirks in their hands now, all leveled at Chriani. The tip of his own longsword was set to the back of Grus's bare neck.

"No," Chriani said simply.

At his feet, the veteran made no effort to hide the rage in his trembling breath, but his hands stayed at his side. No one moved.

"Pardon me, soldier?"

He saw Makaysa from the corner of his eye. She stepped closer, but her rapier was still in its sheath. "Forgive my lack of protocol," he said. "No, lord."

"Step back, Chriani." It was an order, and in a tone that said there would be no follow-up.

"On your word that the prisoners are to be left unharmed. Interrogation only. Take them back to the camp if they won't talk. The war-mages' truth magic can deal with their confession." He repeated his words in the Ilvalantar, a mix of threat and diplomacy. Not sure which was appropriate, what his role was. The Ilvani made no response either way.

"The war-mages can steal the thoughts of one as easily as four," Makaysa said.

"No."

"Fuck you with your own sword…" At Chriani's feet, Grus snarled like a cornered dog. The veteran's hands were locked to fists, waiting for any chance to strike. "Horse-bastard Ilvani kill your sergeant and this is the stones you show."

Chriani felt the tip of his sword twitch. The veteran's voice cut to seething silence.

It hadn't been intentional. A tremor had threaded his hand as Grus's blind rage washed through him. The hatred that had driven a raw wedge between Ilmari and Ilvani for generations.

Chriani understood anger. He had lived with it, had felt it shadow him his whole life. In that moment in the forest, seeing Kathlan lurch in the saddle as the Ilvani arrow took her through the shoulder, he understood only too well how easily he would have killed the one who shot her if he'd had the chance. And that understanding warned him now of all the wrong reasons he might find to do what he did. All the reasons he might have stood back once and done nothing while the Ilvani were beaten senseless for their silence.

He had pledged to turn the anger aside, to not let it rule him. He had made that promise to Kathlan. He had made other promises in his life, to be sure. But the promise to Kathlan was the one he would keep.

Riding with the rangers, his anger had been given a new outlet in combat. But as he felt Grus's seething tension, saw from the corner of his eye as the wounded Ilvani pushed himself back up to a sitting position, Chriani didn't know what he had gained from that. Ilmari and Ilvani, always too ready to kill each other. And him caught in the middle of it.

After what seemed a long while, Makaysa nodded to the others, whose daggers slid away. They took a step back but kept their blades high, close enough that the Ilvani would have no room to run. Carefully, Chriani stepped away from Grus, who shot to his feet in a fury.

"No." It was Makaysa this time. An order given and heard. Eyes blazing, the veteran turned his back on Chriani, strode quickly away toward the horses.

Chriani paced around the Ilvani. He felt the eyes of all the rangers on him, even as he felt the inherent futility of the task at hand.

"Where do you ride from?" He spoke in Ilvalantar again, but slowly. Trying his best to mask his skill with the tongue, which was far from perfect but better than Makaysa's by far. It was a thing he had learned from his mother, but which he had relatively few chances to practice. Another thing he didn't want known. Not here and now at any rate.

Silence was the only response.

"You set an ambush. You're carontir, but you acted as raiders on the Brandishear side of the frontier to lure our patrols into the forest. Then you waited for us. Why?"

"You done wasting time?" Grus asked in a low growl as the silence continued.

Where they stared sullenly forward, all the Ilvani had eyes of gold, bright and burning in the torchlight. It wasn't an unusual color among their kind, but in tone and brightness, it was strangely consistent. Chriani would have taken them for siblings at first glance because of it. Members of a family clan, perhaps, though their hair and coloring showed no other similarity he could see.

"You killed the sergeant, then held back. What were you waiting for?" He said it quickly, letting the Ilvani accent carry the words. Not sure if he wanted Makaysa to be able to follow this particular thread too closely.

One of the Ilvani made a sound then. Not words, not speech, but a sharp hiss as if her breathing had brought her sudden pain. Chriani saw a flash of gold as her gaze found his, a bright hatred burning in the narrowed eyes.

A memory slipped into place in his mind. Hidden beneath his thoughts before, then revealing itself to anchor those thoughts. Assemble them into clear focus. As he so often did, Chriani welcomed the memory with a spike of anger, cursing himself for not thinking it sooner, for all the endless distractions of his mind.

Instinct and anger. His mother's patience was something he had tried to learn, a virtue he told himself was the last part of her in him. But too often when the instinct came, it seemed to come too late.

"Lóech arnala irch niir…" Chriani said it clearly, quietly.

As one, all the Ilvani turned to face him.

The rage that twisted through their features sent a chill up his spine. The rangers' blades slipped closer, Chriani glad of it. All four of the Valnirata began to whisper, their voices faint but hanging steel-sharp on the bright silence of the torchlight.

"Lóech arnala irch niir…"

He had no idea what it meant, no idea what was passing between them. Snatches of other words came and went, but the single phrase was a refrain that each sibilant voice came back to.

"Where is he?" Chriani whispered back.

Three bodies by the dead horse. Four Ilvani kneeling before him.

He was sure there'd been eight survivors when he counted the fallen in his mind. He'd held the number hopefully, at least until the first distraction had driven it from him with no effort.

Hair of grey and gold, black armor cut away at the shoulder. The one who had shot Kathlan, the one who had shouted the words. "Where is he?" Chriani said again, but he was already moving, not waiting for a response.

"Who?" Makaysa called to him as he reached the horses, grabbing his borrowed mount and swinging on.

"One escaped," he called back. "Rode off with the horses." He spurred forward to the nearest torch, snatched it up as he passed it, held it high above his head so its light would reveal the ground, not occlude it. The tracks were easy enough to find, the Ilvani horses scattering, circling, then regrouping.

"We don't need him," Makaysa said from two steps behind. "The war-mages and their magic will get the truth of these ones." Beyond her, the Ilvani were face down and in the process of being bound by the rangers.

"Wait here." Where the horses' path twisted off into the woods, Chriani could just see a last glimmer of twilight sky above the trees. He handed Makaysa the torch.

"You're riding out alone and without light, soldier?"

"I've got good eyes for the dark," he said. "I'll ride quieter alone."

"I could order you to stay."

"Wait here," Chriani said again. Then with a flick of the reins, he passed beyond the light and was gone.

He was riding through water. That was the feel of it, the dark gloom of the forest spreading and flowing around him. Like the currents of an unlit sea, that dark surrounded him, playing tricks on his eyes in ways he didn't like. The horse's pace stayed steady, though, its own eyes equally sharp in the darkness as he rode slowly, bow drawn and arrow nocked, letting all his senses slip out around him. All was shadow and silence, and the scent of leaf rot and unmoving air.

The trail was easy to follow, but that only made Chriani warier. The stillness of the deep wood seemed wholly unnatural to him. No wind to set the lower branches of the limni moving, or to ripple the vines that twisted into nets along the edges of the path. He heard distant bird sound, the buzz of insects, but it all seemed to fall back and away from his approach.

He spotted blood ivy twice, saw where the Ilvani horses had skirted it. He saw black pools of water set around an ancient stump, had to lead the horse around them to test the firmness of the ground, not willing to trust the confluence of tracks there. He counted multiple trails, all of them old, all of them running roughly east, deeper into the forest. Across them all, the newest set of tracks traced their slow way into shadow.

Three times, he stopped when he sensed the heaviness of the air punctuated by a faint but familiar tang. He knelt to scan the shadows, scenting close to the ground to discover blood soaking into black soil. Signs that the Ilvani or one of the fleeing horses had been badly wounded, the patches appearing at irregular intervals. Places they'd been forced to stop and rest, needing to push to go on.

What with Chriani's show of defiance and the time he'd wasted remembering the things he should have remembered, the Ilvani had a solid head start. Chriani had been moving steadily, though, while his quarry had tarried. It meant he was close.

A sudden wash of light from the forest ahead coincided with the clack of stone, startlingly loud beneath his horse's shoes. Chriani pulled the horse to a stop, froze and flattened himself along its neck. Only when he had taken a careful measure of the silence around him did he swing off carefully, crouch low to the ground.

The light was the sun, filtering somehow through shadow above him. Low stone walls marked the edge of the path ahead, loose rubble strewn along it. The trees were smaller here. Stunted. The ground was bare earth and thin patches of glistening mold, none of the leaves there that normally covered the floor of the Greatwood. The reason for that became clear as Chriani's eyes adjusted to the sharp contrast of brightness and shadow, seeing the signs of gnarled branches draped in darkness. Leaves hanging not dead, but covered in some kind of mold. Silent trunks rising around and ahead of him in a bleak grove of black.

In silence, he pulled the horse from the trail, pushing into an open space behind a tumbled wall. He tied it to a thin stump, then ducked down behind the wall, shifting a dozen strides away before he stopped. He waited there a long moment, scanning the shadows to all sides for movement. Then from within a double-seamed pocket set within the inside of his belt, he slipped on a ring of black iron and vanished from sight.

Outside the haze of light that marked the sun descending below the forest wall, the ever-present gloom of the Greatwood was fading to the real dark of approaching night. But the ring draped all the world with its own haze of shadow when it was worn, so that even as Chriani disappeared within the unseen aura of its magic, he was as good as blinded where his eyes scanned the deeper shadow around him. He had expected it, though, a torch already in his hand, broken and thrown in a single motion.

A star rose bright from the gloom of the ground to arc and blaze across the open space before him. He stayed low for another long moment, needing to make sure the ring still concealed him. He knew its magic had a fickleness to it, but as long as the ring was another of the secrets Chriani was bound to keep, he'd had no real chance to fully test it. On the finger of the assassin he'd taken it from, he had seen its power fade beneath the speed and fury of a weapon attack, or of too-sudden movement. He didn't know whether hurling the torch would likewise disrupt the magic's flow around him, but he was willing to wait to be sure.

When he finally rose to look into the light, he saw the shrine.

The pulsating glow of the torch held back a gloom that was absolute, the air seeming to blaze white against a rising globe of darkness and the far-spread, twisting branches of a score of black trees. These were limni by their look, but stunted, and more gnarled than even the most ancient of those great trees. Their mold-black branches clawed at empty air like splintered fingers, their trunks marking out a broad circle around a shattered stone courtyard edged with crumbling pillars. A five-sided dais — an altar, perhaps — rose at the center of trees and courtyard alike as smooth walls of stone.

The beating of wings caught his ear. Movement in the shadows, dark shapes on the air. From out of the deeper darkness, a half-dozen crows were circling within the trees, sweeping down to settle on stiff branches. Their movement reminded Chriani of insects drawn to the light, but the space of that light was unnaturally empty. No haze of movement, no swarms of fly or moth that Chriani would have expected to see. The black grove showing no signs of life.

The crows were silent. Just shifting along their branches, taking flight again to drift over to the next trees. All of them circling around the clearing and the shrine at its heart. That shrine was Ilvani work. No mistaking it. Centuries old to judge by its weathering, but the intricate lines and inscriptions that twisted up every pillar, marked off each side of the altar, were razor sharp. A magic of the Ilvani artificers who had scribed them, going beyond spellcraft and into an understanding of form and material that no Ilmari could match. Where the markings unspooled to glyphs, Chriani recognized the lettering but not the words. The old Ilvani of the Valnirata, which he'd heard spoken but had no tongue for himself.

The torch had fallen a half-dozen strides from the near side of the altar, which cast a long shadow behind it like the gnomon of a sundial. Sprawled half-in, half-out of that shadow, Chriani saw what had drawn the crows on through the darkness.

He moved cautiously to the place where the dead Ilvani had fallen. He was watching the black birds above him, though they showed no sense that they noticed his movement with the ring's power shrouding him. The warrior was staring up open-eyed at the darkness, arms outstretched. Chriani read the signs of the dark ground, seeing where the Ilvani had dragged himself toward the stone. Then the frantic signs of him convulsing as he fell, twisting around to his back before he died. Chriani watched the body for a long while, made sure no trace of breath disturbed its stillness before he approached.

The broken stub of an arrow jutted out from the Ilvani's armor, just below the ribcage. The blood that soaked green leather and the cloth beneath was already drying. A gut shot, deep and sharp, tearing as it went. A slow death, and painful.

The arrow hadn't been his, but even if it had, Chriani would have felt no sense of victory in the scene before him. Just a faint wondering of what would have driven the Ilvani this far, this deep into the forest. What was here in this place of black trees and grey stone that would have made a difference in the end?

He circled the shrine twice, still watching the birds. Still watching the shadow beyond the haze of the torch's alchemical light. There was no sign of the missing horses, but Chriani picked up the trail on the far side of the shrine, their tracks leading off at speed into the darkness. He checked those tracks, found the mark of the half-moon with its three circles. Not important anymore.

As he approached the body at last, a faint pulse of color flared at its wrist. A stone talisman there, shining out its blood-red light against the shadow. Chriani remembered that light from when the Ilvani had attacked him. He made the moonsign this time, his hand marking out the crescent at his heart that was the sign of the night. Warding against the darkness of this unknown sorcery by appeasing it, but out of habit more than anything else. He was still invisible, the magic of his ring more dweomer than most folk of the Ilmar saw in a lifetime. The Ilvani were different, though. Arcana was in their blood, part of their nature, it was said.

Chriani slipped the talisman from the figure's wrist, saw the light flare within its dark chunk of bloodstone. It spread out like liquid across the gold claw that held it, tied tight with a black leather cord. The stone was oily to the touch, Chriani stuffing it quickly to an inside pocket of his armor. Something for the war-mages to look at later. He had no urge to bring the body back.

What he could see of the Ilvani's tattooed war-mark showed him as Calala. A warrior of Calalerean, the northwest of the four provinces of Valnirata, whose southern reaches Chriani had been patrolling for five months. He recognized some of the mark's lines on the carved stone altar, but the runes there shaped words he didn't know. He didn't feel like cutting the armor to read the rest of the mark, though he knew it might have told him more. The Ilvani's clan, at the least. But something about the shrine, the stillness of the black grove, set a sense of unease in him. A feeling that if this was the place the Ilvani had come to die, it would be best to leave him to it.

He did a last check of the body for weapons and magic, though. Secret pockets, other markings on the flesh that he might read. As he did, he saw the gleam of gold within the figure's tight-clenched hand.

Chriani squeezed the fingers open, watched as a coin spilled to the ground. He lifted the stiffening figure's other hand, saw a second coin fall.

The coins were clearly Ilvani by the intricate knotwork that etched their faces, by the angular sweep of their lettering. They were scribed, not stamped. An artisan's touch to each of them, though Chriani didn't recognize them. Couldn't read the writing even though he recognized the script, as with the glyphs that adorned the altar stone.

The Valnirata didn't trade with the Ilmari, but their Ilvani gold bought its worth in Ilmari coin easily enough when taken from prisoners or the dead. Most rangers with enough field experience set aside a comfortable pot for retirement using the small coins, which were milled with a hole at their center for stringing. The Ilvani carried their wealth that way, sheaves of coins knotted tight and looped around the neck or upper arm like jewelry.

The gold of the Valnirata coins was tinted with a reddish tone compared to Ilmari crowns. *Blood gold* they were called, for that and other reasons. The coins that had fallen from the Ilvani's hands were a pure molten hue, though. Brightly polished, unscratched.

They were warm, too, when Chriani picked them up. Magic in them. He made the moonsign as he realized he should probably have thought of that before touching them. Acting without thinking, like always.

He was about to slip the coins into another of his many hidden pockets when he caught a gleam of gold within the body's mouth.

He stared at it for a long while. Had to steel himself to pry the corpse's jaw open, watching as a third coin slipped off the blackened tongue and fell to the ground. He made the moonsign again as he picked it up, all three coins in his hand now and getting even warmer, it seemed. A weave of shadow seemed to pass across his eyes, and in that shadow, he saw that the coins gleamed not just in reflection of the torch but with their own light. A bright pulsing of gold, the same angry molten hue that filled the Ilvani's eyes.

Chriani glanced down. The Ilvani's eyes that had been gold were a deep emerald green now, their gleam all but faded where their moisture had dried and congealed to tears that tracked across dead skin.

With a shriek above and around him, the crows took to the air. Chriani's arm whipped out and away from him as he shot to his feet, stumbling back from the body. He had hurled the coins out and into the darkness almost before the thought to do so had gelled in his mind, a stark reflex of muscle and fear. He felt a spasm of pain as he did so, the wound in his arm, ignored up to now, flaring with his sudden and frantic movement.

The birds were gone back to the darkness as he ran to the horse, leaving the torch behind him but pulling another from the saddlebags. He spooked the animal as he did so, had to remember to fumble the black ring from his finger before he snatched up the reins, pulled himself to the saddle and spurred away. He didn't look back to the shrine behind him.

His injured arm was agony as he rode, a useful combination of focus and fear masking it before, but now long gone. He held himself low along the horse's neck as he raced back along the trail that had brought him there, the torch above and behind him to keep it from the horse's eyes. It lit up a narrow well around them, the motion of the ride setting it flaring, the light pulsing back from the trees where they pushed in from all sides. For long stretches, Chriani felt as though he and the horse were held suspended and motionless, trapped in a shimmering sphere of light as the forest flashed past them at speed.

When he rounded the bend that marked the haze of light where the rangers were waiting, Chriani wasn't surprised to see two of them with bows drawn, tracking his approach until they confirmed it was him. He was surprised, though, to find them already mounted, faces ashen and eyes bright with fear.

He slewed to a stop where Makaysa sat astride her horse. She was six paces back from where the bodies of the four Ilvani prisoners were sprawled across each other on the ground. Their hands and feet were still tied, their limbs twisted as if they'd been broken. The three Valnirata who had died in the initial assault had been inexplicably moved by the look of them. Within the shadow of the fallen horse, their bodies were tossed across the empty ground, backs arched and limbs splayed in some grim contortion.

Where he could see the mouths and hands of the fallen Ilvani, Chriani saw the flash of gold shine bright in the torchlight.

"We were almost done waiting for you." Makaysa's voice carried the same tone of indifference but the smile was gone. She made the moonsign as she nodded to Chriani, as if warding herself against the chance that his sudden reappearance was more than it seemed.

"What happened?" Chriani asked, though his guess at the answer was already rooting in the shadow that filled his mind. He spurred his horse past Makaysa toward the bodies, but the animal balked at the command. Three paces but no closer, as if it could sense the magic pulsing as points of golden light in the shadows.

"Something killed them," Makaysa said evenly. "They screamed as one, then shook. Some force pushing through them, twisting them like rag dolls. Then the ones already dead moved the same way, leaving them all as you see them."

The prisoners had been searched as a matter of course. No way for the coins to have been hidden on them, let alone be left within reach of their hands, bound tight with cord and twisted behind their backs. No way for the Ilvani to have placed the third coins in their slack and open mouths. In the light of Chriani's torch, their dead eyes gleamed violet and blue, brown and green.

"Ride," he said, but the other rangers were already moving. He let Makaysa spur away ahead of him, pulling up the rear as they raced away. The light of their torches pulsed bright in the darkness of the forest as they galloped west, leaving the bodies and the darkness behind.

— CHAPTER 3 —

THE HUNTER'S HEART

THEY RODE HARD TO ESCAPE the trees, Chriani sensing the others as shimmering light swerving through the darkness around him. No formation to their movement, no sense paid to whether they might be followed. Just a focus on the trail ahead, swerving to avoid branches and vines as they slipped within the light, flashed past, were gone again.

A surge of speed took Chriani's horse as it sensed the open air a moment before his eyes caught the change in the light. Then all of them broke out across the threshold of the grasslands with torches held high, Chriani seeing Grus standing in the saddle, gasping the open air as if he might have been drowning in the closeness of the trees.

Night was falling in the world outside the forest. The real night of stars and wind, not the darkness of the shrouding canopy of leaves. The warmth of the waning summer had been lingering through two weeks of clear weather, though it was beginning to grow cold by dark. The sky was clear this night, the shimmer of starlight and the last glow of the sunset bright enough to ride by, but the seven of them kept their torches burning as they turned for the camp.

Makaysa led a two-rank formation, picking an easy pace to cool the horses. Chriani checked that pace even further to let himself slip back from the two rangers he rode alongside. Not wanting to see the looks on their shadowed faces, their fear too bright to his eyes. He looked back at intervals, feeling the ache at his injured arm grow more acute as the trail disappeared into darkness behind them. There was no sign of any pursuit.

As they rode, no one spoke.

When the first lights of the camp perimeter were seen, Makaysa ordered the horn call that was standard procedure for riders returning from patrol or calling to regroup. Two short blasts repeated at intervals until an answer was heard. It wasn't a code of the same type as the forest call signs, but simply a heads-up for the close camp patrols and the perimeter guards. Less chance of being shot on sight that way.

Along the empty trail they followed, they heard griffon riders above them once but never saw them. The elite *gavaleria* aerial patrols of the Valnirata flew across the camp each night on some schedule only they knew. The shriek of their griffon mounts sent a ripple of unease through the horses, but their fast movement was all but impossible to track across the shimmer of starlight. The Clearmoon was at its last crescent but not yet risen. The Darkmoon had been waning thin for a week or more, barely visible at dusk as it pursued the sun on its descent.

The gavaleria hadn't engaged with the Ilmari on either side of the Greatwood in long years now, but their presence by night was an unnerving reminder of the mysteries the forest held. No one knew how far into the deep wood the griffons and their riders were based, or how far they ranged out from the trees. No one knew whether their missions were solely designed for disruption or whether they were looking for something. Watching and waiting as they shadowed the Ilmari camp lines and the patrols that prowled the frontier.

The camp ran no outriders after dark, but Chriani saw the perimeter guards marked out by starlight as Makaysa led them onto the main trail bisecting the rise of low hills on which the camp was spread. Bows were drawn and arrows nocked against them, archers watching darkly as they approached. Only when visual contact was made did they drop their aim.

The camps of the rangers never held to a single location long enough to become anything like a permanent presence along the frontier. Among the nearby settlements, this site was simply *the ranger camp*. Among the rangers, though, the frontier stations were named for warriors dead or retired, gone to legend or the anecdotes and grumbling of those who had followed them.

Konaugo Post was the designation for this camp. Established six months past, east of Alaniver and across the Locanwater River. The name carried a darkness for Chriani that not even Kathlan understood. The late Captain Konaugo had been a legend in the Bastion, and on the frontier where he had ridden in his youth. He had come back to that frontier with his prince a year and a half before, and had been ordered by that prince to escort the Princess Lauresa safely to Aerach along the Clearwater Way.

Chriani had hated Konaugo, as he knew the captain hated him. He'd been convinced that Konaugo was complicit in Barien's death, had doubted and distrusted him right to the end. But that end had seen Konaugo fall while executing the same duty Chriani had taken up, the same pledge he had made. To protect the princess even if it cost him his own life.

The name was for the rangers alone, seen nowhere among the banners that flew from six points around the perimeter, then again above the central clustered tents of the captains and the war-mages. The falcon that was the symbol of Brandishear stood highest among the standards, with the interlocking spears beneath it that stood for the strength and bond of all four of the Ilmar principalities. Brandishear and Elalantar to the west of the Greatwood, Aerach and Holc to the east. The horse-and-axe insignia of the Prince High Chanist's house hung below those, twisting in the breeze that picked up as the sun disappeared.

It was that same standard under which Chriani and Kathlan fought — the regiment of Rheran and the Bastion. But four more standards flew alongside it, marked with shield and blade, axe and wolf and mountain lion. The signs of the five regiments of Brandishear's eastern frontier, which made up the bulk of the camp's four-thousand-strong force.

As they passed through the first checkpoint, Makaysa gave the signal to stop as she summoned two sentries close. Chriani didn't hear the words that passed between them, but he was fairly certain he saw one sentry glance his way before turning and taking off at a run. Makaysa spurred ahead, the squad following.

Chriani brought up the rear, as before. He slowed to hail the sentry Makaysa had talked to, saw the squire's insignia in bronze at his shoulder. "Umeni's squad, and the rest of Sergeant Thelaur's," he said quietly, one eye on Makaysa and the others moving ahead of him. "When did they make it back?"

"Who's asking?"

Chriani knew the sentry to see him but had never bothered learning his name. The attitude of bored indifference was such a common feature among the camp guard that he'd yet to see the point in differentiating between them.

"Chriani, temporarily reassigned to Sergeant Thelaur's first squad under Guard Second Rank Makaysa," he said with a maximum amount of ire. "Acting head of second squad after Sergeant Thelaur's death." Though none of that was exactly true, all the time since he'd taken commission, both in the Bastion and on the frontier, had taught Chriani that there was a mutable line between actually having authority and simply sounding as if you did.

The sentry shot to something resembling attention. "They arrived just at dusk, three missing and Sergeant Thelaur dead."

"One of the injured was Kathlan of third squad. You'd have seen the arrow she was holding in her shoulder."

"She was with them, and headed for the healers, I heard."

Chriani spurred forward with a nod. Ahead of him, he saw Grus turned back and watching darkly.

Makaysa led them to the southwest stables, one of four set deep within the camp as protection from direct attack. They made their way along mud paths packed down with straw, passing between tents set onto wide platforms. Those platforms were arranged in tight arcing rows, spreading in semicircles cut through with radial paths for ease of movement within and across the camp.

The stations of the Brandishear rangers were mobile defensive, scouting, and attack platforms, setting up for a season or a year, then shifting to keep pace with weather and threats. They had long been a staple of the southern frontier, keeping watch on the old mountain passes and the Orcish war-bands that still made use of them, or hunting the fell wolves that appeared on the southern plains with dread predictability in the last days of winter.

The Greatwood had been of less concern since the end of the Ilvani Incursions of a generation ago, and it had been almost that long since the camps had been seen along Brandishear's forest frontier. The patrols that kept a watchful eye on the Ilvani had long been content to range out from the fortified towns flanking that frontier, anchored between the eastern cities — Cadaurwen and Alaniver, Welbirk and Addrimyr, and Caredry to the far north, whose gates and walls marked the entrance to the Clearwater Way.

A year and a half ago, the long sense of uneasy peace and isolated skirmishes along the forest had changed.

East and south of Alaniver, Konaugo Post was a day's easy ride from that city, and less than a league from the wall of the forest. The impermanence of the ranger camps was designed to balance their close proximity to the Greatwood, allowing them to stay close to towns and cities along the frontier for defense and resupply, but to not give the Valnirata a reason to increase their own standing forces like a permanent presence would.

Building permanent forts so close to the forest created an invitation for Ilvani raids, though it had been long years since the Valnirata had ventured out in numbers to assault settlements in Brandishear. Many said that was changing, though. The Prince's Guard of Brandishear had been actively recruiting as it hadn't for a generation. Another sign of the events of a year and a half before.

As they dismounted and led their horses toward the grooms, Makaysa brushed dust from her leathers, the other rangers pulling personal gear from their saddlebags. Chriani grabbed a waterskin from off his own borrowed horse before it went, stifling a wince where he felt his injured arm stiffening. He caught the groom's look of unfamiliar appraisal, clearly recognizing the horse but not its rider. As he drank, then splashed water to his face, Chriani thought on how that suited him fine this night. He didn't know how long he would have before Umeni found him, but the fewer people who saw him until then, the better.

"First squad on duty," Makaysa called. The others stood to attention, Chriani managing to lift himself out of the slouch of too long a day in the saddle. "But all of us are to the war-mages, now." She met the eyes of each of her rangers in turn as she spoke, but Chriani didn't nod as the others did. "Debrief on what was seen. No discussion among yourselves first. When the mages are done, the five of you are off duty." The sweep of her hand made a specific point of excluding Chriani from the second half of her orders. To him, she added, "When you're done, report to Captain Rhuddry. She knows you're coming."

Chriani understood what message the sentry had run on Makaysa's command. He nodded this time.

Guard Captain Rhuddry led the Crimson Shields, the guard regiment of Alaniver. A veteran ranger, decorated in her home city and Rheran, though from what Chriani knew of her record, she hadn't spent more than six months behind city walls in over two decades of military service. He knew her as less dedicated to discipline for its own sake than to the fighting form that discipline was meant to shape, which put her ahead of most captains in his view. But for those whom discipline couldn't shape — including Chriani — Rhuddry had very little patience. He didn't expect that would change tonight.

He fell into step with the others, striding behind and to the left of Makaysa. He tried at first to slip back to last rank, but Grus's boot at his heel told him the veteran was watching for that particular move. So Chriani waited until they passed through the main-path intersection between the mess tents, the smell of roast meat and wood smoke hanging heavy, a twisting mass of foot traffic converging from three different directions.

He waited for his moment, sidestepping easily to avoid a supplies cart slowing in front of them, bogged down on one side in a muddy rut. Then he kept on sidestepping, away from Makaysa and the others and onto a track running off behind the stores tents.

Chriani felt Grus moving before he saw him, knew that the veteran had been watching for his escape. Even still, he was barely fast enough as he twisted away. He slipped beneath the warrior's first punch, then came up into his jaw with the elbow of his good arm, stopping the shout he was about to make.

As Grus stumbled back, Chriani dropped to a defensive crouch, slipped back two paces. It was dark between the tents, the spill of fire-light from the mess fading to shadow around them. It would work to his advantage. "The mages hate to be kept waiting," he said in a cold whisper. "You're sure you want to do this now?"

Grus's answer came as a flying tackle from a standing start, coming at him so fast that Chriani managed only to get his injured arm behind him before he was hit. He wrapped his left arm around Grus's neck, holding on as the heavier warrior pushed him back, and knowing that one solid shot to his injured arm might drop him.

Grus apparently knew it too, hammering three times across the wound with a fist that struck like iron. As bad as the pain had been on the ride from the forest, it exploded like a hot brand now, shooting down Chriani's arm and back as a spasm that allowed Grus to drive him to the ground. He was on his back in the mud, couldn't move. The leering veteran loomed over him, ready to kick.

"Master Grus!" Makaysa's voice sounded out from the shadow scouring Chriani's sight. Through Grus's legs, he saw her standing at the entrance to the side track, her rangers and a handful of others close behind, watching with amusement. "You fight on your time, you follow orders on mine. Now."

With a growl, Grus once again showed his devotion to following orders by stepping quickly away. Chriani staggered to his feet, holding his arm as the pain ebbed. By the time he made it stumbling to the main track, the blood at his leather was seeping through his fingers.

Makaysa sighed as she saw the extent of the wound. "You didn't think to mention that?"

"I'm fine," Chriani said through clenched teeth.

Grus snorted, but Makaysa silenced him with a look. "Grus, lead to the war-mages. I'll get Chriani to the healers first, then meet up with you. Go."

The veteran nodded, but his smirking gaze held Chriani's for a long moment as he and the others turned away.

"Can you walk?" Makaysa asked. Her tone had softened, but Chriani shrugged off her assistance as he made his way around the intersection and took the main west track. "The healers are to the east, Chriani. Is it your arm or your head that needs attending to?"

"My arm's fine," he said evenly. "I'm returning to barracks to check on Kathlan. Then I'll see the healers. Then I'll see the war-mages, then the captain. With your permission and indulgence, lord."

"Just make sure you do it in that order." Makaysa fell in beside him. "If you bleed out on Rhuddry's carpets while you're still technically under my command, I'll be the one cleaning them."

Chriani glanced over, tried to assess the shift in Makaysa's mood. She wasn't looking at him, though. Just walking. "That was good riding today," she said at last. "Though a bit more excitement than I like on patrol. I'll look forward to not seeing you in my squad again anytime soon."

"You should take the whole troop with Thelaur gone," Chriani said. He was almost surprised to realize he meant it.

Makaysa laughed. "You'll put in a good word for me, then?"

He shrugged, felt pain lancing down his back and wished he hadn't. "You know how to lead is all. Not all of them do. Umeni should learn from you."

"Umeni is a soldier with more ambition than ability, and it'll kill him one day." Makaysa said it evenly, no sense of judgement. Chriani got the sense it was something she'd thought about. "The opposite of your problem, in fact. All ability and no ambition. Though I don't doubt you and he will both come to the same end."

Chriani stopped. Makaysa came around to face him. She was smiling as she had been earlier that day, though Chriani hadn't noticed when she'd started again.

"You find that funny?" he said. "My end?"

"Based on what I saw today, I suspect your end will be spectacularly amusing. I'm just hoping I'm not there to see it."

"I guess you can find anything funny if you try hard enough."

"I've found it's the best way to survive out here. But you in particular always amused me, Chriani. Recalling that day in the armory still makes me smile."

She had remembered. Chriani didn't understand why that felt like a good thing.

Makaysa was watching him closely, her expression suggesting she had something else to tell him. But in the end, she only said, "Good luck, Chriani," before she turned back east.

He watched her go for a moment, so that he was still facing her when she turned back.

"I was sorry to hear about Barien," she said. "He knew how to lead."

Chriani could only nod as he turned away.

He wasn't sure what kind of punishment might be in store for him, though he'd had enough practice that he might have tried to guess. Umeni wouldn't be the first superior to have him before the captains for disobeying orders since his arrival among the rangers. However, he would be the first to do so despite Chriani having probably saved his life. He didn't know whether that made him care more or less about the outcome.

Because from the moment he'd ridden out of the forest at speed for the second time — from the moment before that when the dead Ilvani's eyes went gold to green and Chriani had felt the fear — there was only one thing he cared about. One person he needed to find.

He looked for Kathlan first in her tent, but she wasn't there. *Back at sunset,* the sentry had said, and Chriani felt a faint unease. He knew she wouldn't have spent any more time at the healers than necessary, but he knew also that a wound as straightforward as hers had looked shouldn't have taken this long to deal with.

He spent a few moments to check her footlocker, her gear. Two tunics spread across her cot, untouched from when Chriani had seen her that morning. She hadn't been back.

He went next to his own tent in the hope she might be waiting there, but he saw no sign of her. A faint fear traced his spine as he thought of the black arrow. Wondering what manner of Ilvani magic might be in it. He needed to go to the healers, check to see if she was still there. Ask what had happened.

Except Chriani couldn't go to the healers. Chriani hadn't gone to the healers in all the time that he and Kathlan had ridden with the rangers, and she was the only other person in the camp who knew why.

Over five months on the frontier, he had tended his own wounds, had sought healing life-magic in his own way when he needed it. In five months, he'd never made use of the camp's baths. Instead, he and

Kathlan spent off-duty time alone at a quiet stream a short ride away, its water frigid but its pools secluded.

He spent a few moments outside his tent to brush the dirt of the forest, the dust of the grassland tracks, and a newer coat of mud courtesy of Grus from his leather. As he did, he let the scene before and around him play out, carefully marking off light in the closest tents, the movement of soldiers along the nearby paths. Then he slipped inside. The barracks tents were roomy but low, Chriani dropping to his knees so he didn't have to stoop. He sealed the door flap tight, listening carefully. He prepped water and brandy, bandages, needle, and silk thread from his field kit. He listened as he did so, all his senses on alert. Waiting to feel the ebb and flow of movement in the world around him.

He found the quiet he was seeking. Then, teeth set against the pain, slowly and carefully, he peeled off his scarred leather and the blood-soaked jacket and tunic beneath. Beneath the drying crust of red-black, a darker mark stood out on his left-front shoulder, crossing around to his arm. A knotted mass of twisting red and black lines, delicate as lace, bright as blood, dark as night. The war-mark of the Valnirata.

The mark had been tattooed upon him when he was a child. An inheritance from his father, an Ilvani exile of the Greatwood who had fought against his Valnirata kin in the Incursions. Its lines and crafting were the hand of his mother — an Ilmari who had fallen in love with her Valnirata exile against a thousand years of bitter racial hatred, and who was one of the few Ilmari who had ever learned the war-mark's art. She had scribed the tattoo on Chriani in the name of his father who had died in the Incursions. Just a memory now.

Halobrelia forest-heart. His father's house within the rigid clan structure of the Valnirata Ilvani. But against and around the mark of Halobrelia, Chriani had since scribed four names of his own, setting them down in the delicate script of the Ilvani. A year and a half before, on that path where his life had changed.

Lauresa. Princess of Brandishear, who he had loved once, and who had given up the future she had been born to in order that the Ilmar would have peace. *Barien.* Warden to Lauresa since her childhood and mentor to Chriani, taking the place of the father Chriani had spent his life remembering only as shadows. *Irdaign.* Lauresa's mother, spell-singer of the Leisanmira, who had tried to show Chriani how to set aside his fear of things he didn't understand.

The fourth name was the one that meant the most to him now.

The only one of the four who remained a part of his life, and who would for all time if he had anything to say about it. *Kathlan,* who knew the mark and all of Chriani's secrets, and who had promised to hold those secrets as she held his heart.

No. Not all.

The thought came to him as a stray shadow, twisting through his mind as he washed the cut the arrow had made. Telling him he was lying. He tried to push it away as he always did, but it churned within him like a shard of cold steel, like an arrowhead snapped off and burrowing slowly beneath his skin.

Kathlan didn't know all his secrets. Not yet.

He tensed as he flushed the wound with brandy, felt the pain rising to a burning, blood-red crescendo in his mind before it began to fade. Then he stitched it quickly, knowing he would need to seek healing magic but needing to seal off the wound, ease the pain first.

The four names that had become extensions of the mark were the only people who knew Chriani wore that mark. But Barien was gone now. Lauresa and Irdaign had left his life. Kathlan alone was the keeper of his secret.

No.

Twisting through him again. Another lie, told because the truth was something he didn't want to think on, didn't want to have to see.

One other person presently knew that Chriani wore the mark of the Ilmar's deadliest enemies, knew that his father had been Ilvani. The Prince High Chanist, who had been sworn to secrecy in his own way by the threat of what Chriani knew of the madness the prince bore. What he knew of the actions that madness had driven.

Chanist had tried to sacrifice his own daughter in the name of restarting the war he had ended with the Ilvani a generation before. He had killed Barien to protect his secret. Had sent Chriani into the center of his plots in the hope of killing him for what he knew. When that failed, he had spoken of killing Chriani in the Bastion throne room — the great meeting hall where the last words between him and the prince high had been exchanged.

Chriani remembered those words. He knew how easily Chanist could have seen them made real.

"A man might die many ways, squire."

Chriani had reflected on that threat uncounted times in the first few months of his new life. His rank and commission, and all that came with it. A clear understanding that it was Chriani alone the threat was meant for. Knowing that whatever happened, Lauresa was beyond her father's reach now. That was something, at least.

A prince sworn to his secrecy was a power that Chriani never imagined, could never have dreamed of. But still, he knew that if any person who served that prince stepped into his tent right now, his remaining life might well be measured in moments.

Five months away from the healers, away from the baths of the camp. And for eleven years in the Bastion before that, Chriani had bathed alone, had slept in bedclothes always outside Kathlan's loft, had never stripped his tunic off even in the hottest summer.

He remembered the Ilvani warrior he'd dropped when he cracked his bow across her face. Remembered the tattoo that turned her skin to a seething field of twisted lines, razor sharp. For the five months since he'd been sent to ride the frontier, Chriani had wondered in all his darker moments what would happen the day he was injured and knocked unconscious, left for dying. Kathlan not there to keep one of the other rangers from tending to him. Others seeing the secret set in black ink at his shoulder. A thing they would kill him for.

The Valnirata arrow had torn the flesh of his arm but missed the bone, thankfully. The wickedly serrated hunting heads the Ilvani favored for their shafts were notorious for leaving scars even for those who took magical healing, and more than a few rangers wore those scars with pride. The edge of Chriani's wound had severed one of the long, twisting tails of the war-mark, but he knew from a boyhood's worth of nicks, scrapes, and cuts that the tattooing of the Valnirata would somehow seal itself when the flesh was joined. The war-mark of the Valnirata never faded, never aged. Some manner of alchemy in that ancient art, of which the names Chriani had tattooed himself were only an imperfect reflection.

When he was done, he dressed quickly, then found rags to wash up the spill of blood and brandy across the tent's platform floor. He drank what was left of the brandy as he worked, felt its bright burning in his gut to remind him he hadn't eaten anything since the morning.

"Chriani..."

Kathlan's voice came from outside the tent as he was finishing. The rush of the brandy was joined by a calm that wrapped around him, held him tight. He fumbled with the door flap, had only two of its pegs untied when she slipped in on hands and knees, rising to embrace him.

She kissed him hard, pressed tight against him as if the two might be wearing each other. It was a feeling Chriani had long grown used to, but which still carried with it an intensity, a passion like it might be the first time they'd touched. Eighteen months since Chriani had pledged himself to Kathlan, and more than a year before that of her bed when it suited him. And all the time since, he had thanked fate through every waking moment that she had waited for him.

When the embrace was done, Kathlan hit him, and significantly harder than she'd kissed him. Chriani shifted to evade the backhand blow, but he was only rarely fast enough when Kathlan had hurting him on her mind.

"Have you had healing yet?" she asked when he turned back to her, his cheek stinging.

"No. So maybe don't…"

She struck him again, this time across his freshly stitched arm. He had to stifle a cry as the pain shot through him, renewed.

"What in fate's name were you thinking?" she hissed.

"I was thinking you wouldn't be hitting me quite so much, or I'd have left you outside."

She sent her other hand toward his cheek but Chriani was ready, catching her wrist in his fingers. That freed her up to slam him in the arm again, which he realized had been her plan all along as another molten wave of pain sent a haze of shadow across his eyes.

Though already on his knees, he collapsed back toward his cot, worried that if he didn't, he would simply keel over. But he twisted Kathlan's wrist at the same time, brought her around backward and wrapped his arms around her. They hit the cot together and sent it crashing to the platform, Chriani landing hard under her, but managing to hold her in a tight embrace.

A ribald call of approval rose from outside as footsteps passed the tent. Then laughter, fading.

"Are you enjoying yourself?" he whispered.

"Tremendously. Now answer the question."

"You already know the answer, Kath. I wasn't thinking. I leave that to you."

She said nothing to that. Just lay in his arms for a while.

"Were you worried?" Chriani asked at last.

"A little less when Makaysa set out after you."

"You try to ride with her?"

"Maybe."

"Umeni have to hold you back?"

"Maybe."

He kissed the back of her neck. She swung around, setting her weight against him. She avoided the wounded arm this time.

"I was looking for you," Chriani said.

"I was at the healers, then with the horses."

The stables were a place Chriani should have known to go back to. Not thinking again.

Kathlan was the daughter of soldiers both dead, and had been assistant to the Bastion's stable master when she was named a tyro of the guard at the High Spring before last, a year and a half gone. Chriani had requested that she serve under him, adjutant to a guard superior. She was old for the post, seventeen summers behind her and most tyros taking the writ by thirteen years. Chriani had made rank himself only three weeks before that, was given his guard's commission that allowed him to take an adjutant at the same ceremony.

Most members of the guard made squire and served at that station two years or more before receiving commission, making Chriani and Kathlan's unlikely advancement the subject of much whispering. Chriani was above it, mostly because he didn't care. But partly also because the suddenness of his commission came with tales swirling around it of what had happened on the Clearwater Way. Kathlan, though, became the butt of quietly whispered jokes heard among every rank of service and duty from the pages on up. A tyro at seventeen. A stable hand in uniform.

The laughter had faded quickly the first time they saw her ride.

Kathlan had always been one of the best riders in the keep, but only a select few had ever known it. Chriani. Eugen, the stable master. Barien, maybe. Chriani had never had a chance to ask him. Kathlan had lived among horses her whole life, but a bad break in her leg and a hip that had worn down over years because of it made it painful for her to ride. She would exercise horses shaking off bruises or colic, guiding them across the training grounds of the keep with as much skill as any ranger or cavalry rider of the prince's guard. A kind of joy was in her when she rode, but never for more than a short spell. When she was done, the limp that plagued her would be more pronounced for days afterward.

The Prince High Chanist's own healers had restored her leg. Powerful magic, reserved normally for the crown and its captains. Chriani had seen it done, made it another thing the prince high had promised on his behalf. He had needed to talk Kathlan into it, though. Had needed to be there with her while it was done, the healers protesting all the way. She had squeezed his hand to cracking throughout the spell-casting, made the moonsign more times than Chriani could count.

Word of that had gotten out. More jokes whispered behind her back, by tyros who had never seen life-magic, by guards angry at a new-made squire getting attention from the healers that none of them would ever warrant.

The jokes ended the first time they saw her ride.

In those first months, Kathlan had put veteran rangers to shame on patrols around Rheran. A month into mounted combat training, she was assigned to assist Hestria, the cavalry sergeant-at-arms. Three months after that came an offer to become his adjutant that she turned down. She showed a focus, a discipline, that Chriani marveled at, even as he knew how bad it made him look by comparison.

In those months, he realized he had never loved anyone more.

Only one in a hundred tyros were ever recommended for active duty, and even fewer of those for duty with the rangers. Chriani had never come close. Kathlan had been riding as his adjutant for just over a year when the orders came. The pride she showed that day, the perfect light in her green eyes was a thing he still remembered.

Because she was his adjutant, those orders came through Chriani, but he understood with absolute clarity that as far as the ranger captains were concerned, he would be accompanying Kathlan to the frontier, not the other way around.

In his tent now, the two of them lay there for a time, not speaking. A kind of peace hanging between them that Kathlan liked to call *the between times.* The moment of rest and silence between duties, the moment of waking between sleep and daylight. *Nothing else to think on, nothing else to be done except hold each other.*

Chriani remembered the first time she'd said it, one night not long after the night that had first brought them together. He'd felt as if he was humoring her then as he nodded his agreement, sensed her body tight against his in the dark. He felt differently now.

"I need to go," he said at last to break the perfect silence.

"Fine. I'll get you a horse." Kathlan lifted herself off him slowly, as if it involved some great effort. "You'll need a distraction to pass the sentries. Then stick to the river. Harder for Umeni to pick up your trail."

She laughed as Chriani swatted at her. But as he stooped to a standing position beneath the tent's low ceiling, he found himself smiling. It was a thing that happened a lot around Kathlan. A thing he was still getting used to, even after all the time that had passed.

"I need to see Rhuddry. And the war-mages."

The second piece of information caught Kathlan's attention. "What do you want with the mages?"

"What they want with me. Debriefing on Makaysa's orders. Something in the forest. Not important." He winced then as he carefully moved his shoulder through full motion. Not because of how much it hurt, but because only as he spoke of it did Chriani truly understand how much he didn't want to talk about what he had seen. What he'd felt that day.

As he hoped, his apparent pain refocused Kathlan's attention. "You need me to restitch that later, let me know," she said, running her fingers along his tunic sleeve. "You're like a drunk sailmaker with your left hand."

Chriani found most of a clean uniform in his footlocker, dressed quickly as Kathlan put his cot back together. "You'll be here when I get back?" he asked before he left.

"Count on it," she said. She held him tight again for a long while before she let him go.

There were rules about these sorts of things. *The official conduct of fraternization between members of the prince's guard,* as the regulations called it. Soldiers in the field sought each other out for comfort, especially in times of strife. It was known and accepted. Practically a tradition in its own right. Kathlan was a product of that tradition, in fact, telling Chriani when they first came together how her parents had met while on patrol in the south.

The finer details of the regulations of official conduct didn't prohibit fraternization, but were dedicated to ensuring that fraternization didn't interfere with discipline, or take advantage of rank, or come at the cost of recrimination or lovers' spats in the field. Kathlan called it liberating. Chriani found it daunting, only because the commitment he'd given to Kathlan in the deep winter of the year before was still a relatively new thing to his mind. The idea of having the captains implicitly sign off on it — the idea that what passed between the two of them in the night might end up the subject of report if it affected their conduct by day — put him on edge.

From the first, even before they'd ridden out from Rheran together in the forty-strong force from the Bastion guard reassigned to ranger duty, Kathlan had set out her own terms for keeping boundaries between them. "Call it paying sop to regulation," she'd said the night before they left, their last night in her loft above the stables. *Their loft,* Chriani had come to think of it, spending more time there than in his own assigned bunk in the Bastion barracks. "Call it keeping your head down. It's all the same to me."

"It's a waste of time and a lot of irritation," Chriani had said in reply. But he made good on the promise she extracted from him that night, and the two had done their best to keep sight and sign of their bond to themselves. Not that it had always been their doing alone. Sergeant Thelaur knew they were together, because it was no secret, and it hadn't taken her long to use that to get back at Chriani for what had become a lengthening list of failings. When he and Kathlan weren't on patrol together, Thelaur seemed always to have them assigned to the rangers' intermittent perimeter watch at opposite ends of the night, the two of them passing each other in his tent or hers for a few fleeting moments in the deep darkness.

It was dark now as Chriani made his way past the camp's central pavilions. These were a stand of five-pillar tents surrounded by a well-patrolled track, and set with a sentry platform atop a great white pine, staked and tied to hold it secure against the wind. He stuck to the shadows, watching for any movement from the captains' pavilion as he passed beneath it.

His plan was to avoid Rhuddry for as long as he could, and he knew that making his way first to the mages' pavilion was as good a way as any to do so. The captain's distrust of the camp's war-mages was notorious — even when compared to the general distrust that spellcasters held among many soldiers. For now at least, it was as good a place as any to hide from the debriefing Chriani knew was coming.

The war-mages' pavilion stood apart from the tents and meeting places of the officers, set adjacent to the armories by custom, and keeping that important corner of the camp clear of traffic and casual looting. Its standard was the symbol of the mageguard — a gout of flame set within intersecting crescent moons. That mark was a brand taken by those arcanists who served the crowns of the four Ilmar nations — and who were eventually tasked with hunting down any arcanists who attempted to avoid such service.

Chriani rapped at the outside pole of the mages' pavilion, the tent already sealed up for the night. When a voice barked out from inside, he entered.

The leader of the camp's war-mages was the boisterous and dismissive Magus Milyan, whose black robes were rumored to have reached that shade simply by virtue of never having been washed. His steely eyes behind their spectacle lenses caught Chriani's gaze as he stepped into the tent, pulling the door flap closed behind him.

"Seven stories promised me tonight, but only six rangers came to sing them. I don't like waiting." Milyan's voice carried the reedy tone of a schoolteacher, but the thickly muscled set of his arms and the long-sword at his belt showed that he took his military service seriously. He wore his collar cut low, so as to reveal the full extent of the mageguard brand he wore at his neck. Its twisting lines were set in red against the shadowed skin that marked him as hailing from Elalantar's northern isles. "Chriani, they call you?"

"Yes, lord." Chriani nodded to Milyan, then to Derrach behind him. She was one of the war-mages' many adepts — tyros in service to the mageguard but not yet branded. Chriani had dealt with her more than once, but she ignored his nod now with narrowed eyes, speaking to the nature of those previous dealings. She sorted through papers spread across a broad oak table, candles set across it and burning with an unnaturally bright light.

The tent was more books than walls, set with freestanding shelves linked together by stanchions on which hung dried herbs, glass flasks, and the skeletons of creatures Chriani didn't recognize. He was more than certain they were the bones of different animals simply reassembled into alarming forms to frighten those who visited the tent — a squirrel with a bird's long beak, a sinuous fish with hands and a snakelike tail, something like an oversized frog with bat's wings erupting from its shoulders. However, he had never seen fit to ask after the truth.

"Sit," Milyan muttered. Chriani did, taking a stool across from the room's single chair, whose height seemed specifically designed to allow Milyan to look down upon anyone he was speaking to. "Makaysa and the others have come and gone with their reports. Spare me the tedious details they have shared and expand my knowledge for a change."

From his pocket, Chriani drew the bloodstone talisman. He tossed it to Milyan without a word. He was certain he saw the mage's eyes actually light up as he snatched it in a long-fingered hand.

"And what is this?" Milyan asked before he whispered a word of incantation. Chriani fought the urge to make the moonsign as the talisman shimmered with its faint pulse of blood-red light — not because he feared this particular magic, but because he understood it. Milyan's casting was a spell of detection, reading the dweomer in the talisman. What Chriani feared was what might happen if that power passed over him to read the dweomer of his two rings.

The black iron band was hidden in his belt again, in its secret space lined with velvet over gold foil. That was a trick he had paid to learn from one of the war-mage acolytes he trained with at the Bastion after taking commission. Though the lowest ranked among the spellcasters who served the prince high, even the acolytes knew how lead and gold would block the dweomer of detection. Chriani had thus spent a considerable amount of his newly commissioned salary sewing gold foil into certain of the secret pockets of his belt, his jackets, his armor.

He had designed those pockets himself, and he was confident of their security against anything but the strictest search. One held a set of lockpicks that he hadn't had any opportunity to use in the five months since he came to the frontier. One of those picks had been his mother's, who had taught him to master it as a child. Likewise, he kept the black ring at his belt at all times except when he wore it. A sense of wariness about its power, and a subtle fear of that power somehow activating when he didn't intend it.

He had a second ring tucked in beside the black band now. One he normally wore, but which he had hidden away while he walked to the pavilion. It was cast of plain steel — a token Lauresa had given him before the end. He tried to not think of either of the rings now, or of what would happen if Milyan's power sensed them.

"Divination and revelation," Milyan said thoughtfully as he raised the talisman to his eye. "Ilvani magic. Tracking by blood. Where did you find it?"

"On a dead Ilvani whose eyes turned from gold to green. Three coins on him. One in the mouth, one in each hand."

"A tale already heard. The others…"

"Didn't see this Ilvani. I followed him into the deep wood. Found him at some kind of shrine."

Milyan twisted the talisman between his fingers, his expression looking unnervingly to Chriani like he might be tasting it. "Tell me," the magus said.

Chriani told him. The flight through the woods, the dead grove and its black trees. The crumbling courtyard and the stone altar before which the Ilvani had died. When he was done, Milyan sat in silence for a long while. From the corner of his eye, Chriani saw that Derrach had stopped her sorting, was listening intently.

He told most of the story. Not all.

Chriani irnash! Lóech arnala irch niir!

The Ilvani had called his name.

Something caught at Chriani suddenly. He felt it, sensed it tripping across his skin like a spider's touch. A twisting in his gut, his pulse rising. He was alert, glancing around the tent and behind him, but seeing nothing there. His hand strayed to his dagger, his fingers trembling.

"If I can take my leave, lord," he said, "I am ordered to the healers."

Milyan glanced up as if he had only just become aware of Chriani's presence. "I don't suppose you had any more sense than your halfwit companions to claim the coins you found?" Chriani shook his head. "But you touched them? Saw them?" the arcanist pressed. "Describe them."

"Ilvani. Old by their look, but clean like they were new. Lord…"

"More! When I stop listening, you stop speaking."

Chriani felt the anger surge, but it was muted. Caught and dragged down by the sudden unease. "Warm to the touch," he said, trying to focus. "Bright, not like the blood-gold. The same color as the Ilvani's eyes before they turned." He pulled that image from his memory, even as he felt its edges frayed by the fear that still carried over from that darkness.

No, he realized as he spoke. Not that fear from the deep wood. This was something else.

When he'd sat with Kathlan, seen her wounded, something had torn through his gut like hot iron. That sensation of pain and nausea was coming back now, no warning to it. No sense of where it had come from. "I need to take my leave, lord. The healers…"

"Can wait. This shrine. You can find it again." Not a question.

"Lord, I fear that I am not well. If we could continue this conversation…"

"This is not a conversation, soldier."

"No, lord. I mean, I don't know if I could find it. Perhaps in time."

Milyan was on his feet, digging through one of the stacks of papers Derrach had just finished sorting. "The captains and I have things to discuss. An expedition to the deep wood. Derrach, see our visitor out."

With that, the mage swept past him, Chriani feeling a pulse of chill air through the door flap that set a shiver through him. He stood up from the stool, stumbled forward to the table.

"What in fate's name?" Derrach stared at Chriani's erratic movements in horror. "You come here drunk…?"

Chriani held a finger to his lips for silence. He looked around him, watched the door. Tried to listen, but a roaring was rising in his ears. "Healing draught," he managed to whisper. "Quickly."

Since Chriani had come to the camp, Derrach had become his contact for life-magic, with her access to the stores of draughts and unguents shipped out from the healers in Alaniver. They were troop-issue only, meant to be held by sergeants and squad commanders and doled out in response to dire need. Chriani had the coin to pay for them, though — and the need. The shoulder that no healer could ever see.

"Stuff your draught," Derrach hissed as she glanced to the door in turn. "It's not a week past the last time…"

"I need it," Chriani whispered. "Something's wrong. Something happened today. Ilvani magic, or poison, I don't know…" From the purse at his belt, Chriani fished out a handful of coins, Ilvani blood gold and silver siolans marked with the crest of Brandishear. "I can pay…"

"It's not about the pay, you mindless ass. It's about me getting caught. Two draughts gone missing so quickly, Milyan will know something's going on."

In all their brief and clandestine dealings, Chriani had never seen the acolyte show anything but fear at the mention of the magus's name. She was skilled enough, to judge by her having been recruited for fieldwork under Milyan's direction. But Derrach never made any secret of how passionately she hated that fieldwork, and all the myriad ways a person could die on the frontier.

"Ten in gold."

"Get out," Derrach hissed.

"Fifteen," Chriani said. Then something hit him like a body blow, and he went down to the floor.

The offer was three times what the draught was worth, but he suspected it was his collapse that swayed Derrach's mood more than the money. The acolyte dropped to her knees beside him, frantic. Fumbling through uncounted pockets on her grey robes, she pulled out a black glass jar, quickly tore through the heavily waxed paper that sealed it. She scooped a finger's worth of a thick salve from it, forced that finger into Chriani's mouth and onto his tongue. It tasted of summer herbs and burned sugar, sweet and dark.

As the warmth of the salve's magic washed through him, Chriani felt the pain at his shoulder ebb. Against the waves of nausea coursing through him, he had stopped noticing that ache.

Breathing deep, he waited for the nausea to end, waited for the shadow to lift from across his sight.

It didn't.

He saw the black arrow then.

It was hanging on a rough wooden rack alongside a dozen other Ilvani relics — arrows, long-knives, what looked like a horse's harness and reins. He recognized it without knowing how, other arrows of grey alongside it looking nearly as dark beneath the haze that covered his eyes.

Standing, he lurched toward it. Had to fight to do so, feeling the magic of the arrow repelling him, forcing him backward beneath the weight of a spasm that made his limbs ache.

"The arrow," he whispered. He had to look around to find Derrach, standing still and pale behind him. "Do you feel it?"

But it wasn't the power of the arrow that had frozen the acolyte, Chriani realized numbly. It was the way the talisman's blood-red light was pulsing crimson, suddenly too bright to look at where the frantic Magus Milyan had left it on the table.

"It wasn't doing that before," Derrach whispered. "It wasn't doing that…" She stumbled back to the table and dug frantically through the papers there, scattering them to the floor in her haste and coming up with two scrolls in hand.

Chriani heard her words as a dark hiss as she cast her spell, an empty echo in his head. The talisman was tugging at him, the arrow's power feeding into him like the burn of a scorpion's sting.

He was standing in front of the arrow in its rack, couldn't remember the three strides that must have taken him there. He could hear Derrach shouting at him, but her words were lost in a shrieking wind.

Seeing it close up for the first time, Chriani could mark the black arrow as an Ilvani shaft only by its fletching. He thought at first that its head must have been snapped off when it was drawn from Kathlan, but the arrow bore no head. Only a steel cap at its gently pointed tip. It was designed to pierce leather, to strike and stick, but not to kill. He might have mistaken it for a practice shaft, if not for the red-black stain of Kathlan's blood that still clung to it, speaking to a strength in its magical construction that would have shattered wood.

With all his strength, Chriani seized the arrow in both hands. He felt it burning him, felt it impossibly heavy as he drove it down into the platform of the floor. It stuck there hard, the dark steel of its tip disappearing into the wood.

He tightened his hands around it and pushed. He felt the shaft bend, heard it splinter.

There was only darkness after that.

He awoke to the sound of Milyan looking at him.

The magus wasn't screaming. Wasn't speaking. Just staring through the storm of wind-sound that was slowly fading from Chriani's mind. He was on the floor, the red-faced mage looming above him. One half of the black arrow was embedded in the floor where he'd sunk it. The other half lay beside his numb left hand, the shaft black to the core where it had shattered cleanly, cracking more like stone than wood.

The pain was gone. The nausea had passed like it was never there. Like it had passed when Chriani walked away from Kathlan and the arrow earlier that day. Easy to see that now, even if he still didn't understand.

He sat up slowly, so weak that it took all his effort to move. Milyan took a step back as if to give him space to rise, but the staring didn't stop.

"Attuned to him… An offering of blood…" It was Derrach's voice, but Chriani thought she might have said something more. It was hard to focus.

There was a long silence before Milyan spoke. "Remarkable."

Chriani sat there for a long while, unable to do anything but watch. He thought he saw Derrach grinding something in a stone bowl, saw Milyan drink wine from that bowl when the acolyte was done. He heard the whispers of incantation, saw both mages vanish to reappear across the room. Fear twisted through him before he realized dimly that this wasn't magic he was seeing, but his own senses slipping momentarily to darkness. The scene before him blinking in and out.

He forced himself to move, rising to stumble to the magus's chair. Not asking permission to sit, but determined not to slip to unconsciousness on the rough wooden floor. Milyan was at the dark table, two leather-bound books open before him. He arched a gnarled eyebrow at Chriani but said nothing.

Where the larger of the two tomes half-faced him, Chriani saw not just words but illustration. An intricate sketch of black trees washed with green. A gleaming light broke like lines of fractured glass through shadows that masked the forms of swirling crows. He tried to focus on it, but his vision blurred, his stomach churning.

The Ilvani had called his name. *Chriani irnash…*

An offering of blood.

"The arrow," Chriani said at last. "What is it?"

"Broken, you half-wit. And its magic all but dispersed, thanks to you." Milyan slammed one of the books shut and threw it at Derrach. The acolyte caught it awkwardly, passed another to the magus. "You make my work difficult. I do not forget…"

"…a dweomer of seeking," Milyan was saying. He had moved again, Chriani losing the thread of his senses. He squeezed his hand tight to dig his fingers into his palm. A point of pain there to concentrate on.

"Say that again." Chriani focused on the pain, focused on the edge of anger threading his voice. Not an ideal reckoning, but he'd take it.

Milyan sighed, waving Derrach in as he returned to his books. The acolyte stepped close to Chriani, thrust a flask of water into his hand.

"The Ilvani enchanted a dweomer of seeking," she said quietly. "Attuned to a singular living essence. Your essence. The magic is shaped with some aspect of the creature to be targeted. An offering of blood made."

The chill that rose up Chriani's spine was like a cold blade caressing his back. Slowly, he stood, holding onto the chair back for the moment it took his head to clear.

"Sergeant Thelaur," Chriani said. "She was shot. They hunted her too."

"No." The timbre of Derrach's voice spoke to a level of anxiety in her that eclipsed even her day-to-day fear. "The arrow taken from her was magic, to be sure, but of the simplest kind. It was a lucky shot, no more."

"How did they pick me? In the middle of combat like that? Why was I marked?"

Derrach made to answer but Milyan beat her to it, giving a bark of laughter as if he might be correcting a child's grammar lesson. "You were marked before the battle started, master Chriani. Such weapons are crafted over long days, prepared with rituals that would finance my retirement could I recreate them."

"But why?" Chriani said. The memory of the raid was twisting through his mind as fragmentary images, each one frozen into place.

"He shot at me from a dozen strides away. Why magic an arrow to seek me for a shot any good archer could have pulled off?"

Milyan laughed again. He whipped his spectacles off, polished them absently on his filthy robe. "Did you listen to none of what's been said here tonight? Or are you simply as obtuse as every captain and most of your fellow rangers report you to be? The talisman's magic was to seek you, soldier, and would have done so from across the Ilmar if need be. The Valnirata call the relic *gavalirnon*. The hunter's heart."

Chriani felt the mage's words slip into place in his mind, the weight of the day's events assembling around it. All the images locking in tight.

"The arrow's magic," the magus continued. "That was to bind you once the hunter's heart had found you. Its magic is a dweomer of domination that has no breaking, making you little more than a puppet. Your will and spirit, consumed and controlled by another."

The expression on the face of the Ilvani who had shot at him was sharp in Chriani's mind suddenly. Hair of grey and gold torn on the wind, a wild light in his golden eyes.

"When you fell," Derrach added. "When I gave you the unguent because I thought you'd been poisoned." Her look told Chriani this was a story she had already told Milyan, for whatever it was worth. "The pain you felt. Even at a distance, the arrow's magic was tearing at your mind and essence."

Chriani irnash! Lóech arnala irch niir!

Chriani made the moonsign. Didn't realize he'd started until his shaking fingers were already tracing the crescent above his heart.

For a moment, he tried to remember whether he had paid Derrach for the healing. It was strangely important suddenly, though he wasn't sure why. He absently felt his coin purse, found it lighter. Understood that she had taken care of it while he was insensible.

He nodded thanks to her, but she had already looked away. Then he headed for the door.

"Master Chriani!" Milyan barked from behind him. "You will attend. I have questions..."

Chriani stepped outside, letting the tent's door flap close behind him as he went. A part of him hoped that Milyan would call guards on him, the night air filling his lungs, clearing his mind. He felt the anger rising, felt it push his hands to his belt, the dagger and longsword there, steel cold against his fingers. But he heard only silence behind him as he paced away.

— CHAPTER 4 —
CHRIANI'S PROMISE

THE NIGHT WAS BRIGHT with stars as Chriani walked the perimeter of the camp. He followed the well-worn access trails but stayed within the sentries' patrol lines, not feeling up to facing a challenge or having to lie about why he was there. The pathways he walked were bright to his eyes, the passing sentries loud against the quiet of the night, giving him ample opportunity to avoid them.

He heard griffons more than once, heard the cries go up along the patrol lines in response. From his own nights on perimeter watch, he remembered hearing those warnings, and the long bouts of holding his bow drawn and nocked that followed. He had no chance of ever hitting a griffon, he knew, the gavaleria flying well above the range of bow and spell alike. But some captain had embraced the false show of force long before, and so it was standard procedure in the camps. A hundred archers aiming at faint shadows soaring across the dark sky.

He didn't know how long he'd walked, but the slender Clearmoon was high by the time he finally stopped. He was atop a low rise, the bright-lit tents of the barracks behind him. He stood staring at the darkness of the distant Greatwood for a long while. Not actually seeing it, the wall of the forest a league away. But sensing its shadow as a dark stain along the horizon, swallowing the light of the stars beyond the shimmering that marked the pale reflection of the grasslands.

He felt that distant darkness as much as saw it. Felt the threat of that shadow this night in a way he hadn't since he came to the frontier. He'd done countless patrols and sorties over five months, remembered isolated exchanges of bowshot across the great expanse of the Locanwater as it wound its way close to the forest's edge. But even as he stared into the night, Chriani understood that the fear he felt now wasn't coming from the forest.

This was the fear that came from within.

He'd been the target of an attack that had no precedent he'd ever heard of. The Ilvani tracking him. Marking him with magic that had made a ranking war-mage's eyes go wide with wonder.

Kathlan had stopped that attack. Had saved his life, he was sure. *A dweomer of domination that has no breaking, making you little more than a puppet.* The pain he'd felt when he drew close to the arrow, tearing at his mind and essence, Derrach had said.

For a long time, Chriani had told himself there was nothing he feared. If a thing threatened him, he would fight it. If it had no value to him, he would ignore it. Eight years a tyro he'd won for that ambivalence.

Things were different now. More complicated. If the mark at his shoulder was ever seen, it would be understood that Kathlan had known the truth of Chriani's life and said nothing. He could die fighting all he liked. Not caring about anything except who he took with him, making a timeless reminder of how good he had been before he finally fell.

A year and a half before, he hadn't known what his life was worth. Hadn't cared about how long it was set to last. Today, he knew that leaving that life meant leaving Kathlan behind, and that thought struck a cold dread in him like nothing Chriani had ever known before.

Too many secrets. Too many truths he carried within him now that were greater than he was, but Kathlan was more important than all of them in turn. A bond between them that he had pledged at the end of the path leading from Rheran to Aerach and back again. The storms that had remade his life. No secrets from her. Not anymore.

No.

Because he was lying to himself, as always. Too many truths buried inside him. Too many lies that wrapped those truths up tight.

The secret of what the Prince High Chanist truly was. Of what he had done. Chriani had never told Kathlan. Could never tell her, could never share the bitter sting of that truth and the madness that lay beneath it. But that was for her sake, he could tell himself. A lie told to protect, to guard against an ache he would carry for her sake.

No.

He felt the fear cut through him, felt himself shaking. A wave of nausea hit his gut like the arrow's magic burning in him, driving through him like a slow knife.

No...

Eighteen months ago. It had been the first real cold Brandishear had seen that year, High Winter a month and a half gone. Chriani had taken that path that had changed everything, and had left the Princess Lauresa on the path she'd chosen for herself.

Nine months later, there were birth celebrations in Aerach, and every courier and merchant across the Clearwater had shared the tale.

He remembered that the Prince High Chanist had been in the field then. The ranger camps were moving along the frontier, marking Ilvani skirmishes outside the Greatwood, near Addrimyr. Echoes of the events of the winter before.

Not all of it...

He shook his head to clear it. He buried that shard of truth, those broken threads unraveled from his life, drawn to a net of tight knots that held the past trapped beneath them.

An offering of blood, Derrach had said.

The Ilvani had called his name.

The secret of what the Prince High Chanist had done was worth more than Chriani's life.

There it was.

The thought circling unseen, shifting through the darkness of his mind as the truth so often did. His mother's patience, waiting for the light to break, for the pieces to fall into place.

He felt the chill air, saw that the lights within the barracks tents had dimmed. He focused on the emptiness he carried at the deep center of his thought and memory. His father, his mother. Barien now. Lauresa. The things gone from his life and never coming back.

He placed the secrets there, felt them vanish back into the shadow that he'd shaped for them. He would hold them there, keep them close. Protect Kathlan from the steel edges of the truths she had no need to bear.

If the Prince High Chanist was making a challenge to what Chriani knew, he understood what he had to do, where he had to go. He heard the call of griffons to the east, the gavaleria winging their way back across the forest as he turned toward the camp.

When Chriani returned to his tent, Kathlan was sleeping. Not surprising considering the lateness of the night, but it felt like an unexpected boon all the same. Along the paths from the perimeter, he had tried to think of what he was going to tell her, coming up with nothing but silence each time.

At her neck, he saw a pulse of green that warmed him with the memory of its color. It was a silk ribbon that had been her mother's, one of many that had tied Kathlan's hair all the time Chriani had known her. She hadn't been able to use those ribbons since taking her tyro's writ, the uniform regulations going on for half a page on the acceptable styles and colors of hair ties. So she'd woven one through a knotted silver brooch, wore it always now as a pendant on a leather cord, where its green reminded Chriani of the late-summer fields outside Rheran when they'd met. Of rain in the green spring that followed the winter of his coming back to her. Of Kathlan's eyes, and the peace of waking with her watching him.

He found paper and inkpen in his footlocker, lit a candle and took the time to write a detailed account of the events of the previous day. His hand was cramped by the end as it always was. When he received his commission, the interminable amount of report writing required of the rangers of the prince's guard was a thing that had taken him by surprise. He folded the report when he was done, would file it in the morning.

As he stripped down to smallclothes and slipped onto the cot behind Kathlan, he realized how chilled the walk had left him, feeling how warm she was even through tunic and loose leggings. She didn't wake as she pressed herself to him. Didn't wake as she shivered, gave him the heat of her body that quickly lulled him to sleep.

He didn't stay that way long, starting awake again with just the first edge of dawn shimmering through the tent. It was still dark to anyone else's eyes, but Chriani had enough light to see by as he slipped from the blankets, crawled silently across the floor to the footlocker. He found a field pack, stuffed it with clothing as he dressed.

At the bottom of the trunk, he found a wooden dagger. He'd packed it carefully away before the journey south from Rheran, then had all but forgotten it. He felt it shift back now into the space of memory where all the things he'd forgotten would eventually be claimed.

It was a child's practice blade, carved by Barien when he took the eight-year-old Chriani in off the street and under his wing. It was the first blade Chriani had ever practiced with, working day and night with it until he made tyro under Barien's guidance, gaining the right to train with steel that came with that. If anyone had asked him why he kept it, Chriani was quite certain he wouldn't have been able to answer. So he kept it hidden, hoping the question would never be raised.

He closed the footlocker, latched it with a click. When he looked over to the cot, Kathlan was watching him.

"You know I wasn't serious last night about finding you a horse."

Chriani tried to find the words he needed to say, but the silence still filled him. He forced it aside to say instead, "I need to ride for Rheran. Business at the Bastion. I can't talk about it. Not yet."

Kathlan swung herself from the cot, the languor of sleep still on her but her eyes bright, focused. "I'll pack, then."

"No," Chriani said. He shifted across the floor to stroke her shoulder. "You can stay."

"I'm your adjutant, Chriani. I serve under you. If you're ordered to the Bastion, that's what it is."

"I don't want you making the trip, Kath. I'll be..."

She struck him on the same cheek she'd hit the night before.

"Listen, don't..."

She struck him on the other cheek, harder. Chriani felt a sharp spike of pain in his jaw as he wrapped his hands around both her wrists.

"Unless you've got a third hand to get in front of my knee, your next words will get you in more trouble than you know," she said sweetly.

Chriani was silent a moment. Slowly, he let her hands go.

Kathlan kissed him on both his flame-bright cheeks. Then she pulled her uniform and leather from beneath the cot, dressed quickly. "What do we need?"

"I need you to stay..."

"This is not a debate, lord."

In her tone, all the jest was gone. This was the seriousness that stopped his own voice when he heard it in her. Not anger. A conviction that he loved, even as he felt himself breaking against it like the waves of winter against Rheran's steep stone shores.

Whatever was going to happen in the Bastion, whatever Chriani meant to discover there, he didn't want it to become part of Kathlan's life. He would save her from the truth if he could, but doing so meant feeling himself bend beneath the weight of yet another lie.

"Prepare the horses," he said finally. "Be ready to ride after mess. I need to talk to Rhuddry."

Kathlan kissed him, held him for a long while before she left.

The camp was just coming to life as Chriani made his way toward the captains' pavilions, their banners tight in a chill breeze from off the mountains. He had donned his spare uniform jacket, washed himself before he set out. He saw Umeni in the distance at one point, arguing with a sergeant Chriani didn't know. He slipped along a side track to avoid him, quite certain that his overdue audience with Captain Rhuddry would involve as much of Umeni as he could take.

He caught the captain at her breakfast, as he'd expected. The look she gave him as her door guard ushered him in carried a dark lethality, as he'd expected. She was dressed casually in sleeveless tunic and leggings, but no one who met with Rhuddry would ever ignore her military bearing, in or out of uniform.

"Captain Rhuddry." Chriani nodded gravely to her, tall and sharp-edged where she sat alone behind the pavilion's map table, dressed now with more food than maps. Boiled eggs and cold beef, brown bread, honey, and fruit were set out before her, a cup of steaming wine at hand.

"Your absence in my pavilion last night was noted, master Chriani. And reported." She made no move to ask Chriani to join her as she crunched her way through an egg, shell and all. He tried to feel slighted but failed.

"Forgive me, lord. I was ordered by Guard Second Rank Makaysa to report first to the war-mages, where I was struck down by Ilvani magic. A side effect of the ambush and assault incurred by second squad yesterday, during which Sergeant Thelaur was killed." As he'd walked that morning, Chriani had spent time thinking on how best to get all the pertinent points of yesterday's events across to the captain as efficiently as possible. His delivery hadn't been perfect, but it would do.

Rhuddry split a blood orange with care. Her fingers were long, her complexion pale in the manner of Holc and the mountain folk of Aerach and Brandishear. "I have heard from Milyan, though his volume makes his conclusions a challenge to follow. Moreover, he has little to say on events in the field, given his presence three leagues away from the field. Ranking Guard Umeni has also made his report..."

"And Umeni was also not there, lord. I was. I caught Sergeant Thelaur as she fell. As noted."

He stepped forward, nodded again as he set his written report down before the captain. She glanced at it but made no effort to scan it.

"Umeni wants your head, soldier. And all I've been able to think of since yesterday dusk is whether my life would become simpler if I handed it to him."

"I have no doubt that it would, lord. But to make it easier on all of us, and to spare you the embarrassment of later admonishing Umeni for his incompetence, this was a targeted raid. Seek the report of Guard Second Rank Makaysa."

"I have. It was less earnest in its conclusions than you seem to be."

"I urge you only to look to it for support of my conclusions. First squad was targeted with a ride-by ambush, designed to draw second squad…"

"Is there anything else?"

Chriani did his reluctant best to square his shoulders. As he did, he realized that when he slipped his spare jacket on to avoid the new stains on the first, he had forgotten how long it had been since the spare had been cleaned. He saw Rhuddry grimace as she looked from him to her food.

"I request furlough to Rheran, effective immediately."

A slice of orange slowed halfway to the captain's mouth, but it found its way in the end. She chewed thoughtfully for a moment. "Am I to assume this is proof against Umeni finally taking the revenge you deserve? Or are there other factors at play in this asinine request?"

"Any ranger who suffers injury in the course of field duty that requires the magic of the healers may request detached duty," Chriani said simply. "According to the regulations of the prince's guard, as I recall them."

"Chriani, wiping your ass in the field is the only use you'll ever have for any copy of the regulations of the prince's guard."

"Perhaps that's where I read the regulation in question, lord. Magus Milyan can confirm my injuries, and the healing administered by…"

"Spare me, please." Rhuddry spread honey to bread with a knife far too sharp for that task. The muscles on her arms stood out as she watched Chriani, as if she might be thinking of other uses for the blade. "Your escapade with Milyan last night has already been brought to my attention, even as he insists I appoint you squad leader. Something about leading a force of war-mages into the deep wood."

"Magus Milyan can use Makaysa or any of her squad to lead him to the trail he needs to find."

"Thank you for that, master Chriani. Your tactical advice means the world to me. Milyan also recommends I have you subjected to divination, with your will or against it, to determine why exactly the Ilvani would make what he describes as a significant investment in arcane resources to locate and claim you on the battlefield."

Chriani made no reaction, but the fingers of his left hand squeezed shut to still a moment of trembling.

"My own opinion," Rhuddry continued, "is that I trust Milyan's divination slightly less than I trust my horse to sing. And that the Ilvani's urge to target you with any weapon can be easily explained by them having met you."

A bell sounded in the distance, calling the morning mess. An unfamiliar ache was twisting through Chriani's newly healed shoulder as a result of his standing at attention. The magic of healing did that sometimes, he had found. As if even while it knit torn tissue, it drew from some greater reserve of strength to leave a weakness in its wake.

Rhuddry popped a slice of beef into her mouth, thoughtful. "Master Chriani, it occurs to me that since you joined my company, you spend half your time attempting to prove you can take on responsibility you haven't earned. And the other half of your time acting as though any responsibility is too much for you."

Chriani said nothing. Simply waited, understanding the importance of that.

Rhuddry took a long drink from her wine mug before setting it down. "Furlough denied," she said with a thin smile. But before Chriani could react, she spoke again. "Instead, I'm placing you on courier detail to the Bastion. You'll start by taking the report Milyan is to have prepared this morning. His thoughts on the Valnirata's magic will keep Chanist's mages entertained through the High Winter, no doubt."

Chriani nodded. "Thank you, lord."

"Thank me by leaving your adjutant here. She's worth at least three of you."

"And two more for her horse," Chriani said. Before the captain could question his response, he added, "Forgive my humor, lord. Kathlan will accompany me, but we will return as quickly..."

Rhuddry interrupted him with laughter, in a way that set Chriani on edge. "You have absolutely no idea why I would deny you furlough but send you to Rheran just the same. Do you, soldier?"

"Because you enjoy every captain's love of doing the things others ask of you, but in a way that makes it seem like you ordered it, lord?"

Chriani enjoyed the moment it took for Rhuddry's surprise to shift to anger. Only a moment.

"Because on courier detail, you'll spend the rest of your assignment with the rangers on the trade roads and out of my sight." Rhuddry drained her mug. "I don't want you back in my camp or my command, master Chriani. You are dismissed."

He stood there silent, just long enough to make her uncomfortable — partly for the sake of doing so, and partly because the anger that rose in his heart, in his throat made him very aware of how important it was that he not speak.

Making a captain uncomfortable was one small thing he could do, Chriani realized. One small thing he had done, and which had just gotten him exiled from the rangers as a result. He felt the blood hot at the back of his neck as he turned from her, his hand trembling again as he walked away.

When he made a stop at the war-mages' pavilion, he found Derrach working, even as Milyan was apparently off seeking an audience with Makaysa. The overstuffed satchel that contained the magus's reports for the Bastion was waiting, though, as were the orders to deliver them. A glowing rune set into the satchel's clasp guaranteed that Chriani had no thought of opening it. He had the acolyte wrap the case in oilcloth before he would even touch it.

"You owe me healing," he said evenly as he checked the wrappings, making the moonsign because it seemed warranted for once.

"I'm sure I don't know what you're talking about," the acolyte said.

"What I'm talking about is I counted what you left in my purse last night."

"I can't..." Derrach said.

"I'm being reassigned. Sent back to the Bastion." Chriani felt nothing in saying it, knowing that word of his effective demotion would be spread across all corners of the camp by day's end. "It'd be a shame if word of your private sales got out some short time after I was too far away to be connected to them."

Derrach's expression was dark as she fished once more in the voluminous pockets of her robes. She pulled out the same jar Chriani had seen the previous night. Black glass sealed in wax and paper, reset now with a wire ring, tightly wound.

"No draughts," she said, "but this will do you. Heal your wounds, proof against poison. One fingerful. Probably two doses left after last night, but I can tell Milyan I used it all on you. Take it and go."

Chriani nodded thanks as he slipped the salve to an inside pocket of his jacket. He took the satchel, held it more carefully. "What's in here, anyway? What's Milyan sending to the Bastion for?"

"How would I know?" Derrach asked indignantly. She tossed her head to sweep her black hair back as she turned away. Then she turned back a moment later to see Chriani still waiting. He had scooped a handful of Ilvani blood gold from his purse, tossed one to her.

Derrach sighed in ill-concealed spite, though she caught the coin. "He's sending for more resources. Reporting what he's learned from the weapons taken from the Ilvani. Screaming about how you and the others failed to return those coins you saw."

"And what are they?"

"He has no idea, even after a night awake with his oldest histories. Hence his interest in being the one to find out."

"What else?"

"That's all, and a fair sight more than you have any business knowing."

Chriani tossed a second coin to Derrach. She scowled. "Military intelligence, or so Milyan deems it. He claims that his divinations can read the origins of the Valnirata weapons, and not just those taken on your raid. He calls them dweomercraft of the north. Says the Ilvani of Calalerean are using magic of Crithnalerean. New alliances, or so he reads it."

The politics of the Ilvani was complex and unclear, and a thing Chriani had always been happy to know as little about as possible. Calalerean was the northwest corner of the Greatwood that bordered Brandishear, and one of the provinces of the Valnirata lands. Crithnalerean was the Ilvani exile lands, north of the Greatwood and marking the expanse of the Clearwater Way — the path Chriani had taken a year and a half before. The exile lands bordered Calalerean and Laneldenar adjacent to it, along the frontier of Aerach to the east. That part of the Valnirata that bordered the Duchy of Teillai, where Lauresa had been delivered to her new life.

"Anything in Milyan's notes about me and divination?"

Derrach snatched a third coin from the air without looking. Her expression showed what Chriani took to be a thankfully honest puzzlement. "Not that I saw. Are you taking a sudden and unexpected interest in your future, soldier?"

Chriani smiled as he turned to go, was almost through the tent's door flap with the wrapped satchel before he turned back again.

"The drawing," he said, remembering. "In the book Milyan looked at. Crows against dead trees. What was that?"

Derrach was at the table, her long hair framing her face as she hunched over a carefully arrayed selection of scrolls. Her eyes narrowed as if she was suddenly wary of Chriani's powers of observation.

"Field notes," she said. "From one of the Imperial surveys. Assessments made of old magic of the Ilvani."

"You speak the old Ilvani? The tongues the Valnirata use?"

"Of course." Derrach's tone gave the impression that she might have been hurt by Chriani's lack of insight.

He tossed a fourth coin to the table, watched it roll off and to the floor. With a flick of her fingers, Derrach had shifted it somehow to her hand. She smiled as Chriani made the moonsign.

"Lóech arnala irch niir. Lóech niir." He spoke the words from memory, tried to shape the accent properly.

"*Three coins for the truth of revelation*," Derrach said. "*Reveal your truth.* Or perhaps *Three coins for the truth of confession* would be better. It's from an old word, *lóecharinna*. A revelation of personal faith." Her eyes narrowed again. "How do you know this?"

"The Ilvani we pursued into the Greatwood were saying it," Chriani said. Not entirely a lie. "Tell Milyan I remembered it. Figure out what it means yourself and impress him. Help take his mind off you stealing from his stores."

Chriani nodded a farewell in response to Derrach's dark look. But he was thoughtful as he walked away.

When he found Kathlan at the stables, she had packed food for a good day or two. No need to sit mess, which suited Chriani fine. If she wondered at his silence as they made their way out of the camp, she didn't ask about it. If she had any guess as to why he chose the quickest trail, wanting to minimize the number of people who would see them go, she didn't voice it.

They headed south and around the perimeter, circling the camp at a distance before returning to the track that would take them to the well-guarded ford on the Locanwater, then to Alaniver and the trade road north. Two couriers passed them along that west-leading track at a fast canter. The morning patrols were heading out as well, but bending off to the east, toward the distant forest.

Once they had slipped beyond the camp, it didn't take long to lose all sight of it within the rolling swells of scrub grass. The only sign of its four thousand soldiers was the faint traces of smoke from the kitchens and the captain's pavilion. Rhuddry was probably still finishing her breakfast, Chriani thought.

The day was bright around them, with blue sky and scudding cloud blowing east. The morning sun held the dark stain of the forest wall along the eastern horizon behind them. That shadow didn't fully fade against the pale hills until they had made the road, the sun just past its height. Through a spread of tilled fields and pasture, they pushed east and north alongside wains and farm traffic.

Only then did Kathlan speak. "You'll tell me what this is about when you can." Not a question.

"Of course," Chriani said. He saw her nod like that was enough.

The road from Alaniver to Rheran was a week of riding with good weather and long days, but even with the need to deliver Milyan's satchel in a timely fashion, Chriani found himself in no particular hurry. In Kathlan, Chriani could feel the same excitement she had exhibited on their initial journey south to the ranger camp, the same sense of wonder as when they had ridden the patrol roads around Rheran when her leg was first healed. To one who'd spent a lifetime dreaming of riding, every day on horseback carried a sense of contentment that Chriani knew was beyond him. He drew on Kathlan's contentment, though, especially as the journey wore on and all he felt by the end of most days was sore.

The world beyond the Bastion was nearly as new to him as it was to her, but he didn't see it as she did. He had traveled some of these roads before and more than once, but only as a child. Riding with Barien while the sergeant served as warden to Lauresa, he had seen the southeast steppes of Brandishear and the seaside forests, had traveled west and north to Elalantar. On his own, he had gone east to see the farmland of Aerach spread beyond the end of the Clearwater Way.

Still, the land carried a sense of sameness to his eyes that he couldn't shake. He couldn't embrace it in the way of Kathlan, who would seek out the stories of every town and village in which they stopped. She marked the days that way, Chriani instead noting the landscape's slow progression of grasslands to farmsteads. Great flocks of sheep dotting the hillsides gave way eventually to terraced fields following the river valleys on their meandering way north to the sea.

They stayed most nights in billeted lodgings, their insignias of the prince's guard enough to earn them a pallet by the fireside or the soft dryness of a hayloft. Even a spare room and a clean bed twice, stopping at farmsteads north of Alaniver and south of Cadith, where the last harvests were in and the seasonal laborers had already headed north to the forests for the winter.

The respect for the uniform was a thing Chriani wore with less comfort than Kathlan, even though he had worn the uniform far longer than she had. Most often, their offers to pay for their meals were refused with grace and admiration, the folk of the frontier knowing the job the rangers did and showing their respect for it as they could. In even those cases, Kathlan would leave a clutch of silver siolans on hearth or windowsill before they departed in the morning.

Another difference between them — Kathlan could sleep easy in those strange beds, or sharing rooms with strangers. But for Chriani, each night on the road took him into the deep night wide awake, whether in Kathlan's arms or sleeping separate in shared bunkrooms. When he did sleep, the strangeness of traveling brought him back even before the first glimmer of dawn. Listening to the sounds and the silence.

He was thus growing more tired as the journey wore on, using the excuse of rain to add a day to that journey, and to spend much of that day in taverns among the close-set farm villages that spread south from Rheran. They had taken an inn in Glaeddyn, Chriani talking up the prospect of a bath to Kathlan, but truly more interested in a solid night's rest for himself behind a locked door. It had worked to a point, the city's noise and traffic putting him in mind of the more familiar clamor of Rheran. But as it had each day along the road, with any thought of that city where he'd spent most of his life, Chriani found himself dwelling on the thought of why he was returning to Rheran, and of what he hoped to accomplish there.

He had no idea what he was doing, what he was searching for. Only the dark and unspoken knowledge that he could think of just one person in all the Ilmar who would want him destroyed. A person who knew the risks of having him killed, and so who might have conspired instead to have him taken by the Ilvani and never seen again.

When he had returned to Rheran in the deep winter of a year and a half before, taking the last steps along the path that had changed him, Chriani had said words alone to the Prince High Chanist. A newly appointed squire with a promise of commission still to come, no note of distinction in his record.

"You would serve me after all this? To what end, master Chriani?"

Eight years a tyro, held back by a sullen anger that became a point of pride in him. As if he might have had nothing else to be proud of. He had stood alone in the Bastion throne room, a place where not even ambassadors and nobles walked unescorted, to issue a challenge.

"To watch you, my lord prince. To remind you of the price of your ambition."

That Chanist was behind the Ilvani attack that targeted him was an easy guess, though Chriani still had nothing like a full sense of what had forced the prince high's hand. He had challenged Chanist. Had used Irdaign as a threat to warn the prince that the truth would come out if anything happened to Lauresa or him. But that knowledge would be undone if Chriani could be undone, Chanist manipulating events to his own ends. The Ilvani claiming Chriani, controlling him. Making it appear as though he had turned traitor, perhaps. Making sure that if the truth ever did come out, that truth would never be believed.

As he'd taken up his commission to the guard and the responsibilities that came with it, Chriani found himself set into a position from which he could make good on his promise to watch the prince. Circling Chanist from a distance, like an outrider on long patrol. Never a word between them, as was proper. Rarely in the same room at the same time, Chriani's new duties taking him across the Bastion and on patrol around it.

As a ranked squire and then a commissioned guard, he was part of a more complex power structure. The business and appointments of the prince high, the security and operations of the Bastion, became things he was made aware of, was asked for comment on. No longer information overheard at the mess table or traded as secrets, incomplete and half-heard. But even as he used his new position to make good on his promise, Chriani felt himself falling back under the weight that position imposed.

As a tyro, his skill with the bow had seen him named a braggart. A liability, always trying too hard to make his betters look bad, and so his betters had responded in kind. A guard with Chriani's skill at arms was seen as an asset, though. A disciplined warrior, a potential leader in the field. Except each time Chriani demonstrated his lack of discipline and leadership, it only underlined to those around him how their first impressions had been correct all along.

In all important ways, Kathlan was Chriani's opposite in uniform. As Chriani's tyro, she had fallen into life in the guard with an ease that required him to hide his jealousy. She took to the rigors of rank, took to her duties with the same forthrightness and honest effort that had been the foundation of everything else in her life. And so he found his attention split. Upholding the dark duty of his private promise to the prince high, made in deep night and the shadow of an empty throne room. Upholding the brighter obligation of the pledge he had made to Kathlan the very next day, waking in her loft to find her watching him.

Over his first year as a guard, Chriani had made good on his promise to watch the prince high. To remind him. But in the end, it had been Kathlan whose presence in his life reminded Chriani of more significant obligations.

He had slipped from the bed that first morning after his return from Aerach. Had crossed over to where she sat on the floor, wrapped in a blanket. He sat with her, let her wrap it around him too. It had been cold that morning.

"Do you remember what you asked me before?" he said. "The night I left?" It was a question from the previous night, before Chriani's challenge to the prince high closed off the path that had taken him to the exile lands, to Aerach and back. But the question looked back further to the beginning of that path, when he'd stolen a horse with Kathlan's aid and set himself back into the life of the princess he had loved once. The princess he had watched ride away in the end.

"I asked you what you could possibly know if you didn't know what you wanted for yourself. I asked you your ambition."

"I want you to be mine," Chriani said. "I want to speak oaths with you. Take the marriage rites if you'll have me..."

"Slow that talk down," Kathlan said to interrupt him. No look of surprise in her, though.

He had expected surprise. He felt an unfamiliar warmth flood through him when he saw acceptance instead. Then he felt that warmth redoubled as she pulled herself onto him, sat astride him and pulled the blanket tighter around them both.

Eighteen months since he pledged himself to her, and Chriani had felt his threat and his promise to the prince shift over that time. The implicit pledge of mutual destruction he and Chanist made, tempered by his commitment to Kathlan. Not softened. Just made smaller, Chriani feeling his world expand around him in a way he had never expected.

On special dispensation from Guard Captain Ashlund, Kathlan had been assigned half time to remain in the Bastion stables where she'd spent her whole life, caring for the horses of the prince high's own regiment. She had two other stable hands working under her, spent every other day at Chriani's side for weapon and hand-to-hand training.

It wasn't enough, though. Chriani had known it from the start.

"I'm going to ride with the rangers," Kathlan had told him, more than once. When the orders came, the ranger captains having watched her for a year, Chriani was ready to set aside the secret truths he knew. Give himself over to the greater truth of what Kathlan meant to him, for a time at least.

He was thinking about the truths he knew when the walls of Rheran came into sight late on their ninth day out from the camp. Those last days of the journey had taken them into High Autumn, passing the nights at the celebrations of harvest fest in small towns along the long, straight road from Glaeddyn. He was thinking about all the questions Kathlan hadn't asked him over those nine days, content with small talk on the road, and sharing songs with the farmers and merchants whose paths ran alongside theirs for a time.

Kathlan's voice was good in its own right, but it was the way she sang a story that truly caught the ear. Her love of tales, her appetite for lore, had been well sated since she and Chriani rode south. She would share stories in the mess each night, reading the old histories and seeking out the knowledge of the veteran sergeants in her off-duty time.

For his own part, Chriani had no real interest in tales, though he had been forced to learn his share of them from Barien. The lore of the Incursions. Stories of soldiering from the rangers and the Rheran guard. The history surrounding the Empire's fall more than sixty years before, and the rebuilding of the Ilmar in the aftermath of that fall. But the story he was a part of was the only one he knew well. And he had been fighting for a year and a half against the need to tell it. All the things he needed to say to Kathlan before it was too late.

It was a strange feeling, Chriani had come to realize, to care for someone enough that their pain cut you more than your own. Understanding how important it was for them to never hurt, to never fear because of you. He had never experienced that before, not even with Barien. And from the first day of his pledge to Kathlan, of coming back to her and understanding the truth of what he was meant to be, Chriani had set himself up to hurt her on the steel-sharp secrets kept close in his heart and mind.

On that bright blue-white winter morning when he'd pledged himself to Kathlan, he told himself he would free those secrets in the end. He would dull their edges, would leave them to the light and air and let them rust away like cheap iron. Instead, he had sheathed them in silence and honed them with more silence still. Had added to them, in fact. Rhuddry's last words to him, effectively exiling him from her camp, were something he'd spent much of the nine-day journey thinking on. Wondering how he'd explain it to Kathlan. He could apologize for all he was worth, but that was only half the battle, he knew. The main thrust would be convincing her to let him release her as his adjutant, so that she could go back alone. Knowing she'd have no problem doing so as long as Chriani was no longer her unwanted baggage.

She would be all right without him. He could convince her of that. Maybe even set her on that path before he stepped onto the path of whatever his return to the Bastion would bring. Easier that way.

For nine days on the road, Chriani had felt the prince high's words in the throne room that night wedge into his thoughts like an always-shifting sliver. A part of him had expected to die that night in the throne room, surprised that it hadn't happened then.

"A man might die many ways, squire."

Nine days on the road, and Chriani had felt the memory of the black arrow's magic burning in him over nine mornings of waking in the faint light of promised dawn. Wondering over each of those mornings what had made the Prince High Chanist decide he'd waited long enough.

Darkening cloud the morning they sighted Rheran had turned to rain by the time they reached the south city-gate, well before sundown but the day already gone to gloom and shadow. Traveling the main road, they had passed Bastion guards and couriers at regular intervals throughout the day, Kathlan returning their nods of salute more quickly than Chriani did.

He felt the faint chill at his neck, down his back, that told him he was expecting trouble. He found himself turning to watch the retreating backs of the guard patrols they passed, more than once. He chastised himself for his paranoia each time, even as the memory of the black arrow burned in his mind once more.

The harvest fest celebrations in the Brandishear capital tended to expand around the seven days of High Autumn without restraint, starting in the last days of Patalis and running well into Tarcia. As such, the trade streets were crowded despite the weather. Where Chriani and Kathlan rode steadily toward them, the walls of the keep were slabs of shadow pocked with torchlight, marking off the extents of the walled fortress that was the heart of the city. Within the keep, the central stronghold of the Bastion rose on its low bluff of dark stone, but Chriani could barely make out the lights of its towers through the haze of rain.

As they passed the market court, they saw it packed tight with tents and wagons, crowds of city folk and travelers moving shoulder to shoulder through the spaces between. Bonfires were burning at the centers of the wider intersections, sending off as much steam as smoke, but their warm light helped cut the gloom where shuttered lamps were straining to fill the falling dark. Beyond the market court, they would approach the wall of the keep and circle around to the north gates. Those were the main entrance to the center of the city, opening out to the steep slope leading down to the harbor and the seawall.

As they drew close to the keep's south wall, though, Chriani slowed to bring Kathlan close beside him. "We should get a room," he said. "One last night." He heard the words come out wrong even as he was saying them, but if Kathlan heard any extra meaning in them, she gave no sign.

"What about your Bastion business?"

"It can wait a night. Same for Milyan's reports. Whoever they're marked for can read them by daylight tomorrow as easily as lamplight tonight."

Kathlan laughed. "Whoever they're marked for will be Chanist's mages. Nothing I can think of would make me keep them waiting."

"I'll keep them waiting for you." Chriani leaned across in the saddle to kiss her, feeling their horses bump shoulders and blow their displeasure. "We report tonight, it's straight to cold showers and the barracks. I say we got caught an extra day on the road with bad weather. Private room. Hot bath, warm fire."

"Is that an order, lord?" Kathlan's tone was mocking but her expression was serious.

"Do you know the penalties for disobeying a superior, tyro?"

"If they don't already involve physical punishment, let me know what else I need to do, lord."

Kathlan made a full salute with a flourish, Chriani laughing. She clasped his hand as they rode.

The inn they steered to was the Trickster, two steep lanes south of the keep along a high side street. Chriani knew the inn more by reputation than custom, with that reputation built primarily on its proximity to the keep's secure southwest gatehouse. That proximity made it a preferred locale for Bastion guards needing a place for private trysts off duty, or for sleeping off debauchery whose aftermath would be too trying even for the barracks.

Mud-soaked and dripping, almost half a year gone from the Bastion, Chriani wasn't worried about either of them being recognized at the inn stables or the common room, both of which they passed through in short order. A single Ilvani blood-gold paid for the inn's best room and dinner besides — lamb stew and well-aged cheese, bread with fresh butter, a jug of ale and two mugs that was all carried with well-practiced skill by the eager serving boy who escorted them.

The room was an oversized top-floor turret, clean and simple. A fire along the inside wall was already burning hot, copper kettles steaming on the hearth. "The lord's suite," the boy proudly named the room. "Fire burning all the day, just waiting for you, weary travelers." The tub the kettles filled was pocked but watertight, Kathlan already stripping off her riding clothes even as the boy filled it. To Chriani's eye, he looked like he was taking his time, and spending less of that time watching the tub than he was watching Kathlan. A clutch of copper cinches set him to finish and sent him packing, though.

Chriani made sure the door was locked before he set his own clothes out to dry, hanging his cloak to cover the room's single window. Holding back its edge for a moment, he saw night falling in the city beyond, heard the ringing of the evenmark bells in the keep. Hand to the glass to block the room's reflection from his eyes, he marked off the tavern's second-storey roof spreading below him. The hiss of water was loud at the gutters, rain hanging like a curtain of dark grey.

As he slumped in front of the fire, he listened to Kathlan singing as she soaked. It was a barracks hall song whose lyrics could make the strongest sergeant blush, but Kathlan's interpretation was even more stridently lewd. He assumed that was for his benefit, felt the stirring of his hunger for her even through his fatigue. A familiar feeling, and welcome, but shrouded this night by the darkness that traced through Chriani's mood and mind.

"A man might die many ways, squire."

Eighteen months before, the Prince High Chanist had threatened his life. Chriani in turn had dared him to take it.

Chriani irnash! Lóech arnala irch niir!

We hunt Chriani. Three coins for the truth of confession.

In thinking through it, Chriani found that it made a kind of sense, as much as madness could make sense. Eighteen months before, Chanist had wanted all-out war with the Valnirata. Had committed acts to accomplish it whose darkness Chriani wouldn't think on. For the prince to have struck any bargain with the Valnirata would have seemed inconceivable in the aftermath of those events. But Chriani remembered what Derrach had said about Milyan's intelligence.

The Ilvani of the western forest were using magic of the exiles of Crithnalerean. It had started there, perhaps, with Chanist able to more easily conspire with the exiles than with the war-clans of the Greatwood. His troops had far more contact with the Crithnala, who themselves hated the Valnirata of the Greatwood nearly as much as Chanist did. The prince high seeking out unlikely allies. Setting Chriani at the center of some duplicitous bargain that would leave him free to seek his war with the Ilvani once more.

It was all guesswork, though. Still too many things that didn't make sense. Chriani eyed his saddlebags where they sat beneath the bed, the mage's satchel inside. He remembered the glowing sigil on the latch. Information there, no doubt, but he wouldn't be the one to claim it.

Kathlan's song had changed, but he hadn't noticed when. The lines of a romantic lay hung sweet and mournful against the splash of water, the crackling of the fire. Chriani fed more wood to the grate from the ample supply at the hearth, then watched Kathlan as she finally stood. Water flowed from her, skin gleaming dark in the shadows. Hands running along arms and legs to dry herself, wringing her hair.

Chriani irnash...

The Ilvani had called his name.

"Water's still hot," Kathlan said as she crossed to the bed, drying herself with the extra woolen blanket the boy had left. Chriani washed but didn't soak long. With his boot knife, he shaved and trimmed his beard, then stood at the hearth to dry. By the time he slipped in beside Kathlan, the bed was already warm.

Their lovemaking was slow but sudden, a product of the fatigue that both were feeling. But in the time after, they were both equally content to simply inhabit each other's arms, feeling the warm glow of the room wrap around them as the fire died to flickering shadows.

Chriani felt Kathlan's fingers along his shoulder, marked her tracing out her name in the Ilvani script as she sometimes did. He had shown her the lettering that morning of their pledge, had carefully explained the four names and as much of his reasons for scribing them as he was able. She had gone quiet when Chriani showed her Lauresa's name there. He told her half the truth of the path that had brought him back to the side of the princess he had once loved, even as he pledged his love for Kathlan again. Saying what he needed to say to make her understand.

He told her the story. The princess attacked along the Clearwater Way while under guard and bound for Aerach. She and Chriani escaping, fleeing ahead of Valnirata war-bands and the order of assassins who would eventually be exposed as the dark force behind the attempt on the life of the prince high and his oldest daughter. Chriani was caught up in it, taking up Barien's duty of protecting the princess with his life. Learning things about himself he had never thought to know. Finding the strength that Barien had always known was in him.

It was a good tale, as tales went.

As Kathlan's hand found his, her fingers touched the steel ring that Lauresa had given him. Chriani had told her of the ring's magic on that bright blue morning of a year and a half before, and had shown her the magic of the black iron band. Two secrets he had eagerly shared to show her he had nothing to hide anymore.

The lies came too quickly sometimes. Too easily.

The steel ring was one of a matched pair, the power they shared putting the thoughts of two people in connection when both rings were worn. Before they parted, the princess had told Chriani to wear his always, and he did. She told him she'd put her own ring on if she ever needed him. Kathlan hadn't been pleased to hear that. Chriani had set her mind at ease, though. Telling her truthfully that when Lauresa said it, he was certain he would never hear her voice in his mind again.

"When I came back from Aerach," Chriani said quietly, "we talked about taking the rites."

The words hung quiet in the silence and firelight of the turret room. No sense that they were even in him until Chriani heard himself speaking them. Remembering that morning of deep winter. Remembering the truth he shared with Kathlan, and the truths he had kept hidden, and the promises he'd made because he felt the ache of those hidden truths as a wound he needed desperately to close.

"I remember," Kathlan said sleepily. "Do you remember me saying no?"

"I remember you saying to slow it down. You never said no."

"So slow it down." Her fingers had walked up his hand and across his chest beneath the blankets. Chriani shifted to put his arms around and beneath her. He kissed her gently.

"It's been more than a year. I go any slower, we're running backwards, Kath. We could take the rites."

She extricated herself from him, leaning back on one elbow to assess him in the shadows. Not angry. Not upset. Just curious, her green gaze bright to Chriani's eyes.

"We could," she said at last. "In the sense of it being a possibility. But there being no point or purpose to taking the rites makes it an open question of why we should?"

"For the sake of doing it. Showing everyone else what it means for us."

"We've got no family for either of us, Chriani. Who's the *everyone* you're so concerned for suddenly?"

"That's not what I mean. It's just that as much as it means already, as much as we mean to each other, it gives us something else. Shows the world what we are."

"It'll show the captains as well. You know the regulations. Separate assignments. You'll lose me as your adjutant. I'll never be able to serve under you."

Chriani laughed, but it rang hollow in his ears. "I'll be the one worried about serving under you when it comes to that, Kath. And we don't need to make it public. Find a justice in some market town where no one's watching. Take furlough to Elalantar and come back with it done."

"So you're going from everyone knowing what we mean to each other, to no one knowing, to only us knowing in the space of fifty words. Except we already do know. Or I do, at least. So why is this so important to you?"

Because Chriani had no answer he could give her, he kissed her in reply. He felt her warmth, realized how cold the room had become.

"Fire's dying," he said as he slipped from the bed. He crouched low to the hearth, banking coals and lining the grate with kindling and fresh wood. He was stoking the flames from their slumber when he heard Kathlan pad naked across the floor behind him. From the mantle where she'd set it while she bathed, she took her pendant brooch, slipping it over her head. She dropped down to sit in Chriani's lap, her back to him as she pulled the blanket around them both. As he wrapped himself around her, she rocked against him gently, breasts and belly hard against his arms.

"Why is this important?" she whispered to the shadows. "The truth."

Beneath the blanket, Chriani caught a glimpse of green and silver at Kathlan's neck, the brooch and its silk ribbon that was the color of her eyes. And with that came all the memory of the first time he'd seen himself in those eyes. All the understanding of how the question of the rites was important because he had hurt her. Over and over again, the thought hammered against his mind like it might be hoping to break the silence of his tongue. It was important because he had lied to her, had let each new lie settle on the foundations laid down by the truths he still couldn't tell her.

It was important because he had stood in front of Umeni, stood in front of Rhuddry, and lost everything he and she had both worked for. A stupid thing to do. Courier duty, and needing to tell Kathlan that if she wanted to finish out her assignment with the rangers, she'd have to do it without him. They would be together in time, but for now, he had no right to keep her with him. Had no way to tell her why.

"I just want us to always be," he said. "I don't want it changing. I want to think about the future and know what's to come..."

"I don't want children," Kathlan said.

Something cold twisted inside him. Not where he'd been going with the conversation. Not where he'd wanted to push her, not what he wanted to hear.

Not that, not now.

"I didn't mean..."

"We're soldiers, Chriani. That's our life, while we're young at least, and I hope for all time. I was daughter to two soldiers, and I watched them both buried in uniform. I can't put any child through that. I won't leave any child to page at the Bastion, and wondering each time you and I ride out whether we're coming back."

He let the silence hang for a long while. "I didn't want this talk," he said. "It's not what I meant."

"I know. But it's been on my mind, and I should have said it already. No secrets."

Chriani shivered with Kathlan's warmth, clutched at her hand to stop himself from trembling. She lifted her other hand, shifted the blanket to set her fingers to the war-mark at Chriani's shoulder.

"You lost your father for this," she said quietly. "I know what it means to you. I know what he means to you. And I can't have your children never knowing you. I just can't, Chriani."

Not that. Not now.

The late autumn of the year before, he'd heard first word through the Bastion's protocol office. Had been waiting for it. A week later, it was in the markets, and then for that month that followed with every courier that came in across the Clearwater Way.

There were birth celebrations in Aerach.

No secrets, they had said, and so Chriani let the shadow settle in his mind that hid the thoughts of a child in Teillai, daughter to a duke, and to his wife Lauresa. A duchess who had been a princess once. The child's name set down in royal proclamation in Aerach and Brandishear, but the space of that name was a darkness in Chriani's mind.

"Come back to bed," Kathlan said at last. The fire was blazing again, Chriani with no idea how much time had passed while they sat there.

He followed her numbly, felt her drape herself across him as he fought back the shivering. Felt it fade at long last, Kathlan's warmth drawing it out and away like pulling poison from the wound that was his heart.

She slept before he did, Chriani watching the play of firelight across the ceiling for a long while, seeing faces in that light as he slowly drifted off to darkness. His father. His mother. Barien and Kathlan both. And as much as he wanted not to, as much as he tried to push it down, slip it safe beneath the armor of dark thought, he was thinking on the face of the daughter of a duke as sleep finally took him. Imagining the features of a child he would never see.

CHAPTER 5

BELLS IN THE NIGHT

THE MEMORY OF THE black arrow brought Chriani back to waking, barely into the deep night and the fire not yet cold. It was quieter, though. The rain had stopped finally, but a wind had risen from the north, its steady hiss augmented by a staccato pattern of dripping along the eaves above the room and the guttered roof below.

He lay and listened to Kathlan's slow breathing in the dark beside him, feeling her foot moving against his. Even lost in a dead slumber, she would do that, some awareness of their contact stirring always in her sleeping mind. It was her right leg, once injured and now restored. Some subconscious sense of the pain she had once carried there, perhaps. Making up for all the small pleasures of movement she had lost for so long.

After all the days of waking early along the road, Chriani had hoped that being back in Rheran would give him the sleep he needed. But instead, he felt the last strains of his stomach churning, a kind of visceral memory of the nausea that had taken him outside the forest that day, in the war-mages' pavilion by dark. Not just the memory of the black arrow's magic, of the fear that had accompanied it, but something stronger. An echo, like the pain that flares from time to time in healed joints. The strange play of nerves that endured in the scars of the deepest cuts. The itch at his finger.

For most of his life, Chriani had slept in fits and starts, rarely making it through a night without some matter of annoyance, some private rage driving into his sleeping mind like an awl punching new leather. But he had lost that, most unexpectedly, when he returned from Aerach. Sleeping that long first morning in Kathlan's bed, before they spoke. Spending that day at her side, then each night thereafter, feeling himself slip into a sense of calm he'd never known before. Waking at dawn into the same dream of being at her side that had carried him through the night.

When I came back from Aerach. He had said it to Kathlan earlier in the fire-bright dark. It was the only way he ever spoke of those days now with her. A kind of convenient code for things he had promised her were told and done, gone to memory. All the things he still couldn't say.

Barien had never slept a full night through that Chriani could remember. Official duties as warden to a princess. Plans and protocol to execute as a sergeant of the Bastion, unofficial duties as Chanist's right hand and adviser. Sitting through tactical councils and trade talks, drinking with counselors and dukes, had seen Barien out of his chambers at night as often as he was ever in them. Late meetings would take him to the mess or the armories, advising captains and tyros alike. His even later meetings with Marjir, the princess high's tailor, were of a more personal nature and in his own chambers, requiring Chriani to find his own place to sleep on those nights. Even returning at dawn, though, he would often find Barien already awake, a low murmur of voices and laughter answering his knock at the door.

As Chriani got older, when his own duties and outside interests began to push him to later nights and earlier mornings, he realized he had no idea how Barien managed. At less than half his mentor's age, Chriani understood that he was as good as any soldier at going two days without sleep, or making do with three or four nights of short and interrupted slumber when he needed to. But he remembered long nights of Bastion intrigue and war council meetings with Chanist that would keep Barien on his feet for a week or more. The warrior would catch moments of short slumber before dawn and in the heat of the day, even as Chriani and the other tyros serving those meetings inevitably dropped to a dead sleep at the mess table.

While he slept this night, Chriani had dreamed of Barien. He remembered it suddenly, the half-remembered sense returning of he and the warrior riding side by side along the seacoast rode that ran from Rheran to Sudry. Dawn was breaking above the Clearwater Sea spreading before them, its perfect brilliance setting bright fire across the waves. Kathlan was riding with them, and her presence told Chriani that this was the wishful vision of dreams rather than a real memory. Though Barien had been a friend to her, she had never ridden with him while he lived, her leg holding her back.

Chriani had dreamed of Barien more often since going to the frontier, not fully understanding why. When he came back to the Bastion after Aerach, he had expected to feel the press of all those memories as he picked up the pieces of his life. But that life had left his dreams blissfully filled with thoughts of Kathlan, as were his days. In the camp, though, he would often wake with a sense of Barien's voice in his mind, the warrior's words forgotten but the feeling of his presence still sharp.

In this night's dream, Barien had been somber. Talking in dark tones of betrayal, of treachery coming from the highest places. Chriani knew what he was speaking of and was trying his best to talk over him, trying with the power of his own voice to keep Kathlan from hearing. Barien talked of loyalty and of choices as Chriani shouted back at him. Arguing of how the idea of loyalty should make things easier, but knowing how his own loyalties had been shattered on the Clearwater Way. Not sure if they would ever come together again.

When Barien finally stopped speaking, Chriani saw blood fleck the warrior's lips, and he knew in the dream that his friend and mentor was dead. He felt that thought burning in his memory, forcing him as it always did to think on whose hand it was that had struck Barien down.

He was breathing hard, he realized, a familiar anger twisting through him as he slipped carefully from the bed to piss in the commode closeted in the corner past the hearth. Then he set tinder and wood to the barely smoldering coals, fanned them till they caught and crackled. Pacing to the window, he drew back his cloak to see a haze of stars through shredded cloud. The slates of the roof were gleaming, dark edges limned with moss and starlight.

Where the curtain of rain had pulled back, he could see the Bastion. Just the barest view over the keep wall, the inn and its uppermost window marking out a high point on the upward-sloping streets to the south. Dark against an even darker night sky, the castle's towers and turrets rose within the walls of the keep that were a symbol of strength and the center of the city — just as the Prince's Bastion was the even stronger center of the keep. A heart of political power and military strength, beating within a body of ancient stone.

For most of his life, Chriani had lived within the pulse of that power. A brightness to his memories of those times. Magical evenlamps and hearth fires burning in the barracks mess hall, shining steel and bright sun on the training grounds. The mottled rage gleaming on the faces of the many, many guards, sergeants, lieutenants, and captains he had insulted, inconvenienced, and thwarted over long years.

All of it was shadow now. The Bastion and the keep that surrounded it were a cold stain that drained the light, that had drained the brightness from his memories. Like the darkening image that stayed with you when you sighted too long toward the sun.

It was a place Chriani had dreamed of once. A place he had yearned to find his own way into, to find a way to belong to. The bright past seeming to promise a brighter future for a time, but his past and future now seemed to be cut and unraveling from the same skein of shadow.

As Chriani was pacing back toward the fire, footsteps sounded out on the slate of the roof above his head and around him.

He felt it as much as heard it over the hiss of wind, the faint sound of rainwater dripping from tile to tile. Drops building to rivulets that twisted and washed their way through encrustations of moss and guano, pigeons swarming the black tiles of the city's rooftops for the heat they held on a winter's day. He had been listening to the sound while he slept, had felt it as the gut-echo of the black arrow woke him.

A kind of song rang out within the steady repetition, the endless cascade of rills spilling down past the window. So that he heard it, understood it in a moment, when that song was interrupted.

Footsteps above him, shifting almost silently but blocking the flow of water as they did. Chriani marked them in his mind as if seeing ripples spread out across a still pond, noting the points from which they spread so as to judge the movement of the creature beneath the water. Five figures were above them, moving toward the window that was the room's only point of outside entry.

He woke Kathlan with a touch, thrusting her sword belt into her hands from where she'd set it on her pack beneath the bed. His own hands ached for his bow, but that was in the stables, stored with the saddles and tack. His longsword hung from the bedpost, a habit Barien had ingrained in him by example and relentless reminder, the scabbard hissing silk-silent as he drew it. While he lived, Barien had been less successful in training Chriani to actually use a blade, but in the time since the warrior's death, Chriani had tried to change that. A thing he had done in Barien's memory, bringing him to the point where he could call himself skilled but still largely untested.

That was about to change.

Kathlan wasn't a warrior. Not by nature. Not like Chriani, trained at the side of the best sergeant in the Bastion from his eighth summer. She was the best rider in their troop because that had been her passion, but the blade and the bow were still new to her, even after training at Chriani's side for a year and a half. She had the instincts, though. The things that couldn't be taught. From the second she seized one of her daggers, she was ready. Locked to Chriani's eyes, following his movement as he pointed to the roof and window. She was out of the bed and shifting silent across the floor, as naked as he was, crouched low to the ground.

They were both ready as a sharp splintering of wood and glass sounded, the window torn outward to shatter and slip to the roof tiles. Whoever was attacking would keep the floor clear of broken glass, not wanting to risk slipping as they pushed inside. A ripple of shadow unfolded as Chriani's cloak was torn free. Then even as he took the measure of the first figure to slip inside the room, Kathlan's dagger left her hand to bury itself to the hilt in the Ilvani's chest, her rapier already drawn before the intruder staggered and fell.

Firelight shimmered across the floor, meeting faint starlight from the window and the still-clearing sky. Chriani's eyes split the shadows, saw the gleam of gold in the eyes of the Valnirata warrior as he dropped. The edge of the war-mark was visible beneath the figure's vest of grey-green leather, arms wet and bare, a long-knife in each hand clattering loudly to the floor.

Above them, the footsteps shifted again, reacting to the unexpected sound and movement. A figure dropped down in front of the window, slipped back out of sight as if trying to draw attack. Chriani waved Kathlan to hold. When the figure appeared again to force its way through, they met it from either side, cutting high and low. A second Ilvani in leather and cloak. He staggered as Chriani's blade took him through the back of the leg, Kathlan's rapier punching through armor and bone as it took him dead center in the chest.

In the moment it took Kathlan to work her blade free of the body where it had fallen, Chriani pushed to the window, drove his sword down to anchor it in the floorboards. He grabbed the top of the sill and punched his feet straight out, the Ilvani who had just dropped to come through taking the full force of his strike. The warrior was shunted backward, slipping on the tiles before pitching backward to the wide roof below.

Voices sounded out faint from the floor below him. A wash of light in the darkness outside showed a lamp lit at someone's window, the fight heard.

"I need to draw them," he hissed to Kathlan. "Keep them on the roof, away from the other rooms. You go downstairs, get to the guard, sound the alarm..."

"I won't leave you."

"I can hold them…"

"This is not a debate." Kathlan's voice was cold.

Chriani could only nod, no time for anything else. One long moment to grab his leggings, pull them on and tie them quickly. No time for his boots. Another moment to seize his tunic where he'd hung it at the fireside, then pull it on. A wet pain flared at his shoulder, as he realized he must have torn it on splintered wood at the window. The warmark was covered, though.

Kathlan was dressing just as quickly behind him as Chriani pushed out through the window, hitting the freezing tiles with bare feet. The wind was rising, a shock of cold taking him as he dug hard with his toes to hold himself, swung up with his blade by instinct to catch the thrust of the Ilvani backsword hacking down from above him.

The warrior swinging that blade was perched on the turret's sloping roof like a bird of prey, long hair shrouding her face. The backsword favored by the Ilvani was a single-edged blade, curved and tapered. Sharp enough to slice bone like passing through paper. Chriani made two quick feints against it, forcing it high. Then he grabbed the Ilvani's hair and pulled hard, pivoting off his hip to drive her over him and down to the tiles. He tossed away a handful of that hair as she scrabbled to hold on, almost slipping to the roof's edge before she found her feet. Her sword clattered past her and over into darkness, but she had long-knives already drawn from scabbards at her thighs as she paced carefully up the slope of the roof toward him.

Chriani felt Kathlan come through the window behind him, reached out to touch her as she stepped close. He watched the movement of the Ilvani on the roof around them, measured the shifting of their slow approach. They'd expected an ambush, not sure what they were dealing with anymore.

"Four of them," he whispered. "Straight and left, two behind."

"I see them."

"Stay close."

It was a useless command by virtue of the roof offering no real alternative, but Chriani said it anyway. He had to fight the urge to turn all his attention to Kathlan, keep himself between her and the Ilvani as they closed. Remembering the feeling of seeing her struck by the arrow meant for him.

"Ilvani attack!" Chriani shouted to the night sky. "Call the guard!" But he heard only fast footsteps from the street below. From this high vantage point, the curtain of rain gone, he could see the keep's south-west gatehouse. The lights of its windows were burning bright against the cold. No movement there, though. No reaction to his warning, his voice muted by the rising wind.

The eyes of all the Valnirata were burning gold in the shadows. They were watching him as he stepped away from Kathlan, his sword and dagger sweeping the air. The Ilvani's first strikes were tentative, assessing them both. Chriani and Kathlan kept them moving, shifting along the slick tiles. He felt her close beside him, let all his senses expand to wrap around her, listening for movement beyond.

He heard two quick strikes of steel, saw from the corner of his eye as she parried and deflected a two-handed knife fighter striking from the upslope. His own attention was focused on two warriors pushing in to his front and right, timing their movement to strike at once, give him no chance to parry. He surprised them by going wide, hooking the long-knife attack so that it sent the sword strike past him by a finger's breadth.

He felt the Valnirata focused on him. Trying to get past Kathlan, but they weren't attacking to kill him. He could read it in their movements, in the timing of their strikes. Like in the woods, when they had waited for the moment to unleash the magic of the black arrow. They had something else in mind for Chriani if they took him down this night.

The Ilvani kept their silence as they fought, but the leather of their boots was loud against the tile. Swords and knives flashed in the starlight, pressing harder now as Chriani and Kathlan shifted beside each other, using the inn's three broad chimney stacks as cover and backing. Chriani drew first blood, taking advantage when an Ilvani knife fighter slipped on the slates and went down to her knee. A moment's distraction, but enough for him to punch his sword through armor and breastbone with a full-body thrust.

They weren't attacking to kill Chriani, but as long as Kathlan was at his side, that wasn't a courtesy he could afford to return.

He heard her behind him as she tagged a second warrior, the crunch of bone and cartilage that said she'd taken him through the hand. He spun around to refocus on that same target, catching him off guard and off balance. His sword cut deep into the warrior's neck on the backswing, sending him crashing to the tiles, then over the edge of the roof to the dark street below.

He heard shouting from that street, but it wouldn't be enough. Rising from the rooftops adjacent to the inn, he counted eight more figures in the shadows, saw them take measured steps and leap the arms-wide gap across the alleyways that surrounded them. Two pressed quickly toward the window, cutting off that route of escape.

"Chriani!"

Kathlan's voice was his only warning as a figure shot up out of the shadows behind him. A lithe warrior in a shimmering cloak of ilvan-weave, helping to mask her movements as she'd crawled prone along the far slope of the roof, coming up from the dark alleyway behind the inn. She hammered at him with a succession of two-handed backsword attacks, Chriani blocking them but gaining no chance for a counter-strike. But it wasn't the Ilvani's sword he was focused on — it was the horsebow hanging across her back, the combat quiver at her hip.

As another sword thrust came for him, he let it slip by him, heard it hiss past even as he twisted in toward the assailant. He took an elbow to the side for his trouble, but he'd expected that. With his bare foot, he kicked down to smash her knee, felt her crumple at his feet. He fell with her, rolling twice along the slates before he released her, letting her carry on over the edge of the roof and down to the street below.

When he came up, his longsword was gone but he'd yanked her bow free, had a single arrow in hand.

He forced the bow's lower limb between his feet as he flexed and strung it. He had time to set the arrow and pull, feeling the weapon's draw and tension, sensing and assessing its curve and balance in the single instant of aiming.

He twisted to sight the gatehouse. The windows were still bright, but a smaller point of light was the lantern hanging above the locked gate on its black iron bracket, hooded against the night. Chriani judged the distance at three hundred paces, a long shot for an Ilvani bow even if he'd had full light.

He let his fingers flick from the string, saw the arrow arc up and over the nearest rooftops, disappearing into shadow. He saw the gate-house lantern shatter where it was hit dead center, heard a shout go up as the door was thrown wide.

"Attack from the Greatwood!" Chriani screamed it to the black night, hearing his voice echo even against the wind. "The prince's guard in combat! Sound alarms!"

Tile shifted at his back. He spun to bring the bow down hard, cracking it across the face of the Ilvani slipping across the roof toward him, sending him off balance and onto his back. Chriani dropped to the warrior's chest with both knees, tearing the long-knife from his grasp as he heard ribs break.

Off at the gatehouse, the rise of a tolling bell told him the guards had heard him. Three strikes, then a silence. Then three strikes again, echoing. The alarm call of the prince's guard.

Chriani rolled off the body beneath him and was running for Kathlan. She was caught between knives and sword, two Ilvani pressing even as a third loomed up out of the darkness.

He shouted. "Lóech arnala irch niir!" It was a moment's instinct, nothing more, when a moment was all the time Chriani had. As his voice rang out across the rooftops, golden eyes flashed toward him, two of the Ilvani at Kathlan momentarily distracted.

The third Ilvani was bare-armed in black leather, dark hair hanging wet to shroud her face. She had a dagger in one hand, a handaxe in the other. Taking advantage of the distraction in her two companions, she lashed out with both blades, taking each of the other Ilvani across the throat.

Chriani faltered. Stared.

Kathlan was scrambling back as the two warriors that had pressed her tumbled to the tiles, clutching vainly at their necks as their life left them. She had her rapier and dagger up, watching the figure in black, but the new arrival looked past her to meet Chriani's gaze. Dark eyes flashed in the starlight, the figure twisting as two more Ilvani rose from the slope of the roof.

In the brightness that his eyes revealed, Chriani saw the tangle of black and red that was the war-mark at the dark figure's shoulder.

As the warrior slipped toward Kathlan, she twisted to go back to back, fighting with her. In the four steps it took Chriani to get to the two of them, rapier and dagger, dagger and axe flashed out. The Ilvani pushing in were forced back as Chriani jumped into the fray, let himself slide along the slates as he spun. With the long-knife he'd claimed, he cut through the warrior closest to Kathlan. The other tried to step back, stumbling as her boot caught the edge of a tile.

The black-armored figure tumbled forward and up, both arms crossing over as she rose. The Ilvani who had stumbled keeled over backward, his leather parted across his chest in a bloody X.

A long moment of silence hung. Mist twisted along the rooftop, caught by the rising wind. Chriani sensed no movement, no life in the scattered bodies, though he knew his senses were distracted by his focus on the figure before him. He recognized her face, though he had never expected to see it again.

He recognized the dagger as the warrior slung it to a scabbard at her back. It bore a thin haft of steel and bone, its cap and spiked guard gleaming dully with the look of mottled silver. A scalloped blood-edge marked the base of the blade, which was acid-etched with markings Chriani recognized as a match to the war-mark at the dark figure's shoulder. A match to the mark at his own shoulder, and to memories he wanted desperately to forget.

The unexpected ally was smiling coldly. "No greetings for old friends, half-blood?"

In the brief time in which Chriani and Lauresa had been captives of the Ilvani exile leader Dargana, he had seen her smile only once. She had called for his execution as she did so, the expression carrying no mirth. Only a sense of malevolent power.

"Not the time or the place," he said at last. As if in answer, the guardhouse alarm was echoed, a deeper tolling sounding out from inside the keep, then again from farther out toward the city walls. More bells sounded out in the night, the guard across Rheran on sudden alert.

"More true than you know."

Chriani stepped close, long-knife raised, his bare feet sensing faint warmth on the tiles. He glanced down to see that he was standing in blood, washing away from two Ilvani where they had fallen.

He saw the gold of their eyes flash in the starlight as the bodies lurched with unexpected movement.

A trace of fear ran up Chriani's spine as the Ilvani began to convulse, one by one. Their limbs contorted, chests heaving as if something might be driving into them from the roof below. Their dead mouths moved as though trying to speak, spitting red-black froth but making no sound.

"Blood and moonsign..." Kathlan made the moonsign as she said it, stumbling back. Chriani shifted across the tile to stand beside her. The crescent was scribed across her heart in red, her tunic marked by the blood on her hands.

He watched Dargana's expression as the movement of the bodies slowed, then stilled. No surprise there. Just a cold recognition.

Even in the faint light of the cloud-streaked sky, Chriani saw the flash of gold at each of the bodies' swollen tongues, the clasp of their fingers. Three coins for each of the dead, not there a moment before.

The Ilvani fallen closest to him had twisted her head over, the coin slipping from her mouth to spill to the black tile. An instinctive revulsion twisted through Chriani as Dargana crouched to carefully collect it, then just as carefully pulled the other coins from mouths and fingers, one by one.

"Chriani?"

He heard a dozen different questions in Kathlan's voice. She was shivering, but whether more from the chill of the rising wind or the aftermath of the fight, he didn't know. This wasn't the first time she'd killed. That had been on their third patrol into the Greatwood, when a perfectly placed bowshot had taken out a rogue Ilvani who had leaped from the trees overhead onto the back of their squad's lead rider. Chriani had seen the same look in Kathlan's eyes then that he saw now, but he could only shake his head to her in an awkward call to silence. No way to answer her. Not yet.

"Does she speak Ilvalantar?" Dargana scooped rainwater from the roof to her hand, sifting the fistful of bloody coins within it as she called to Chriani in that language of the Ilmar Ilvani.

Chriani responded in the Ilmari tongue. "Anything you say to me, say to her." He had no idea whether Dargana spoke anything other than the Ilvani tongues he had heard her use in the past, but the exile leader shrugged to tell him she understood.

"You're being hunted," she said in Ilmari, only the slightest trace of an accent catching at the words.

Chriani caught Kathlan's look from the corner of his eye. "And?" he said.

"And you'd be in their hands now if not for me."

Kathlan spoke up, an edge of defiance and distrust in her voice. "We didn't need your help to deal with this lot…"

"You needed me to deal with the six I left in the street south of here. The ones set to come through the inn and take you while you were distracted by the attack from the roof."

Kathlan's response was cut short by Chriani's hand in hers, squeezing it gently. Dargana shook the coins dry before she slipped them to a pouch at her waist. From another pouch, she pulled something, tossing it to Chriani. He grabbed it without seeing it, half-closed his fingers to hold it. Saw a pulse of red light welling up within a chunk of bloodstone set within a golden claw.

It was the same talisman he'd taken from the dead Ilvani in the forest, but the leather cord that strung this one was sliced through and dark red. As he had before, he felt the power of the hunter's heart calling to him. The stone was oily even to his wet fingers, its magic seeming to seep into his skin.

His hand convulsed in response, the talisman falling to the slates. Dargana nodded as she stepped to scoop it up, slipped it to her pocket. "Something you've seen before," she said. Not a question. "They'll find you, half-blood. You need to get to somewhere safe. But in exchange, I need your aid. I need your prince…"

The exile's words were cut to silence as the rooftop around them flared to the brightness of full day. Mage light pulsed from one of the chimney stacks, shedding deep shadow behind it and bathing the rest of the rooftop in light. The prince's guard had moved even faster than Chriani expected, but the presence of war-mages was an unexpected and dangerous turn.

"Hold attack! Chriani of the prince's guard with one tyro!" He looked to grab Kathlan but she was already moving, seizing him by the hand and pulling him toward the nearest chimney stack. She drew him down flat behind it as he called out again. "Regiment of Rheran and the Bastion, on assignment from Konaugo Post. The Ilvani are down, hold fire!"

"Half-blood!" Dargana hissed from the shadows, unseen where she'd dropped down into the narrow well of darkness the mage-light hadn't touched. "To me!"

"This is the guard," Chriani called back, as quietly as he could. "We won't make it…"

"Show yourself and your insignia!" The voice from below had moved, shifting closer. Bootsteps rose over the wet wind as Chriani saw figures clambering up to the rooftops adjacent to the inn. He twisted to see the path to the window lit up bright and wholly impassable. Beyond that window, everything that marked him and Kathlan as members of the guard was out of reach.

Footsteps struck the edge of the roof as three figures in the insignia of the Bastion garrison leaped across, following the same path the Ilvani had taken to land before Dargana. Cursing, the exile pushed backward, trying to stay low in the light. Chriani saw her twist, saw the war-mark at her bare arm pulse as stark shadow against her skin.

They gave no warning. No call for surrender. From the edge of the roof, three crossbows sang out. One bolt shattered off the chimney a hand's breadth from Chriani's head, forcing him to duck down under a hail of splintering brick, the long-knife slipping from his grasp as he held on.

The other two took Dargana in the back.

She tried to rise. Stumbled. Her boots slipped on the wet slates and she went down, sliding to the edge of the roof, then over it. Chriani heard her hit the stones of the street below.

She'd fallen to the narrow alley behind the inn, away from the roof's edge from which the balisters had shot. Chriani was moving by instinct, seizing the too-brief moment it would take them to reload. He pulled Kathlan with him as he pushed off down the tiles, sliding back and away from the guards, lying flat against any follow-up attack.

He grabbed at the edge of the roof as he slipped over it, felt his blunted nails torn as they scraped the slate. He hung on with one hand, the other around Kathlan, but she was latched to the roof even tighter than he was, clinging to the gutter and scanning the darkness below.

Chriani saw the questions in her eyes still, understood that she was following him without asking them. He squeezed her hand to make the only thanks he could, then swung out over the edge of the roof and down. The inn wall along the alley side was all rough stone and plenty of handholds. Kathlan was a faster climber than he was, dropping down in three smoothly swinging motions. Chriani pushed off to catch her, close enough to the ground that he could roll.

The alley was dark, but beneath the veil of starlight, he could see Dargana on her side, fighting to breathe. She had fallen beside the Valnirata that Chriani and Kathlan had killed together, blood pooling on the rain-slicked tiles from the jagged gash at his neck. His lifeless eyes were dark, the bright gold that had filled them gleaming now in the coins set in his slack hands, his open mouth.

The bolts that dropped Dargana were bloody stumps in her back, shattering where she'd rolled as she hit the ground. No sign of their heads at the front of her armor likely meant they had hit ribs, dug into the lungs beyond. A bad wound.

Kathlan had lost her rapier, but she drew the second dagger she'd tucked into her belt. Chriani was weaponless, felt the urge to seize the dagger sheathed at Dargana's back. His hand stayed where it was, though. Afraid to touch the grip of the bloodblade. The *narneth móir* of the Valnirata, a weapon as ancient as it was deadly.

"Who is she?" Kathlan whispered. "Chriani, what in fate's name is going on?"

"She's Ilvani of the exile lands," he said simply. "She helped the princess and I get free and to Aerach." Most of the truth there. Too much else to explain in the moment. "She's on our side. Dargana."

As if in response to her name, the exile's eyes flickered open, scanning the darkness around her as if she wasn't sure where she was. Chriani's hand at her shoulder brought her arm lashing out against him, but she stopped it short when she recognized him. The hand went instead to the bloodblade, Dargana drawing it with a grimace of pain.

"And what side is our side, exactly?" Kathlan was circling, wary, dagger held toward Dargana on the ground. "The Ilvani are hunting you, but she saves you. You call the guard, and now we're running from them."

On the narneth móir, Chriani saw again the acid-etched glyph that marked the name of Halobrelia. The same glyph at the center of the war-mark that he and the dark Ilvani both shared.

A shadowed doorway stood near the dead-end wall of the alley. Chriani ignored Kathlan's questions as he pointed her to it. "In through there. Kick it open if you need to. Get to the room, get your insignia. Get Milyan's satchel with our orders, and the glass jar from my jacket pocket."

"The guard..."

"I'll deal with the guard, but Dargana's breathing blood. She'll die if the bolts stay in, but she'll die faster if I draw them without healing. Go, Kath. Trust me. Please."

Kathlan's eyes were cold as she turned from him and sprinted away. He heard two kicks take her through the door, but his focus was on the bootsteps coming from in front of him, out along the darkened street. Shouts of challenge rose, Chriani not knowing if other Ilvani were fleeing the scene. Not knowing if they were still coming for him.

The Valnirata warrior that had fallen still wore his bow. Chriani pulled it from the body's back, strung it quickly. He had nowhere to take cover in the alley, but he could keep whoever was approaching from closing if he needed to. He collected the arrows that had spilled from the dead warrior's combat quiver, spread across the rain-slick stones.

"Half-blood..." Dargana whispered through flecks of red-black at her lips.

"Stop talking," Chriani said.

"Your prince... Chanist..."

Dargana spat the name, an enmity in her voice that Chriani felt reflected in his own heart. A heat twisted through him that shook off the chill, pushing even into his numbed feet.

"What do you know of the prince?"

"I bring intelligence to him… a message you need to send. You need to get clear from here… send word to Chanist…"

"Save your strength," Chriani said coldly.

It wasn't something he'd hoped to be right about, he realized. Even having made the decision, having returned to the Bastion, his suspicion of Chanist was nothing more than gut instinct. The quick reaction that his mother had warned him of, tried to teach him to look past.

At the open alley mouth, a pulse of mage-light appeared, flaring from the stones. Figures pushed in from both sides, balisters crouched low with crossbows at the ready. A guard squad from the Bastion. A better option than facing the Ilvani, but Chriani understood how much trouble he was still in.

"Chriani of the prince's guard," he called again. "Hold fire."

"Stand clear with your hands out and show insignias." A deep voice rang out from behind the balisters, whatever sergeant was in charge hanging back.

"My insignia and uniform are in the inn. My adjutant and I were attacked inside and took the fight to the roof. There's no threat here, stand down…"

"Lord, I see him. I recognize him."

It was one of the balisters who spoke. Chriani had to squint to see her face, remembering it as he did. She was a tyro alongside him. Two years his junior, she'd made rank as a squire two years before him.

"It's good to see you," he said. In the chaos of his thoughts, he couldn't recall her name.

"Sergeant Eliana, it looks clear," the balister called to the darkness behind her. Chriani heard no sense in her voice that she shared his sentiment.

From the shadows behind the balisters, four more figures approached. A tall sergeant in full uniform cloak led them, Chriani guessing that he'd been on duty at the gatehouse. He recognized the longtime master of the gate guards, would have forgotten his name as well if the balister hadn't said it. Another officer he'd spent much of his life annoying.

"Stand," the sergeant called.

Slowly, carefully, Chriani stood. He spread his arms wide to show he had no weapon, but the only thing the balisters focused on were the dead Ilvani behind him and Dargana at his feet.

A look of grim satisfaction twisted through Eliana. "How many with you? How many dead?"

"My adjutant in the inn, fetching insignia and credentials. One Valnirata dead here, at least four dead on the roof. Possibly six dead on the street nearby. One other here, under my protection. An Ilvani who fought against the others, alive but injured."

In response to his words, the balisters sunk down. Eliana barked a command. "Step away!"

"She needs healing," Chriani said, ignoring him. "There's no threat..."

"Take them both!"

Chriani swung his arms behind him even as the guards began to move. The balisters had only just shifted to the side to allow Eliana and his three swords to step forward when Chriani revealed the dead Ilvani's bow in hand, an arrow already nocked and drawn.

He had stood carefully so the guards wouldn't see the bow held behind him as he rose. Balanced against his leg, out of sight. Wouldn't see the arrow he'd slipped to his sleeve, unseen and ready to drop to his hand. That hand was rock-steady now, taking dead aim at Sergeant Eliana's heart where he stopped short.

No one moved.

"You'll hang for this, squire." Eliana's voice was ice.

"That's *soldier*," Chriani corrected him. "And not unless any of your squad are stupid enough to shoot me first and send my fingers off the string. In which case, it'll be a hanging you won't live to see."

Eliana was quick to motion the balisters to lower their aim, but they stayed in firing position, weapons locked and ready. Chriani noted a faint disappointment in the one who'd recognized him. Brinta was her name. He remembered it now.

"Chanist..." Dargana's voice was a whisper from the ground, thick with pain. "Half-blood... if I don't make it..."

Chriani couldn't look down, but he heard Dargana slip to unconsciousness. Each breath she took was a wet rasp.

"This Ilvani has intelligence for the Prince High Chanist." Chriani said it loudly, making sure everyone in Eliana's squad heard. "Send a runner to the Bastion, tell them what's happened here. Wake the prince and inform him that we need an audience."

Even as the words came, he wasn't entirely sure why he said them. An instinct, perhaps, that it was a thing that might just save him in this moment. Taken to the prince high even in irons, he'd have a chance to talk his way free. Challenge Chanist with what he knew, with what he suspected. His career in the guard would be done, but he'd have his life at least. But standing off against other guards, armed and with threats made, he knew it was a short leap of assumption to see Dargana as Valnirata herself, and to see Chriani as being complicit in the night's attack. If that happened, he'd lose his life in a heartbeat.

Eliana spat. "You don't get to decide how this ends, treason-bastard."

"Send a runner to the Bastion, lord. Give the prince high the following message, from me. This Ilvani agent was with me on the Clearwater Way."

The coldness of Eliana's gaze matched Chriani's own. He felt an ache starting in his arm, felt the chill press in around him as he stood motionless. The wind was low in the alley, but even still, he didn't know how long he could hold the shot. Didn't want to find out.

With a nod to a guard beside him, Eliana gave the order. The runner slipped back out of the haze of mage-light, vanishing as fast footsteps in the shadows.

Kathlan's footsteps followed a moment later, coming back down to the broken door. "My adjutant approaches behind me," Chriani said evenly, "bearing insignia and healing. Your squad will please remain standing down, lord."

Eliana said nothing as Kathlan appeared at the door. She had her dagger down low at her side, Magus Milyan's oilcloth-wrapped satchel under her arm. Both her and Chriani's insignias of rank were held high in her other hand. She approached slowly, Chriani hearing her footsteps stutter as she got close enough to see the bow in his hand, realize what was happening.

"It's all right," he said quietly. "Open the jar. A fingerful to her mouth, then pull both bolts as fast as you can."

Kathlan needed no more instruction than that, dropping to Dargana's side. She rubbed her hands briskly, fighting the cold before she slipped Derrach's salve to the exile's lips. Then she seized the remains of a bolt in each hand, Dargana waking with a scream as Kathlan pulled them fast, focused like she might be executing a field exercise. The healing power of the salve closed the wounds, though it did nothing for the surge of pain as they were remade. The Ilvani was fighting to breathe, teeth set, but the job was done.

Dargana rose slowly to a sitting position as Kathlan stepped back. The exile carefully reclaimed her bloodblade where it had fallen, Eliana and two of his balisters tensing in response. Chriani stayed where he was, stock-still.

The exile assessed the situation as she slowly stood. She stepped around Chriani to where he could see her from the corner of his eye, even as she kept her own gaze on the guards at the end of the alley. "You certainly know how to impose order in the ranks, half-blood," she whispered.

"You're welcome," Chriani whispered back. "And stop calling me that within earshot of anyone else unless you want us both dead. We're waiting on word from Chanist. Try not to kill anyone until then."

Dargana shook her head. "I can't say I was surprised a year past to hear that your prince had somehow stayed alive. I knew you didn't have it in you."

From behind him, Chriani heard a change in Kathlan's breathing. Not understanding what Dargana said, not knowing what it meant. A tremor rocked his hand at the bow. He felt the pressure of memory seething, tried to push it back into shadow.

He remembered darkness in the Ghostwood that stood at the heart of Crithnalerean, the Valnirata exile lands. Dargana could have killed him and Lauresa both that night, but Chriani had stayed her hand. Had told her the truth.

"If Chanist were the father of one I loved," she had said when he was done, *"I would cut his living heart from his body."*

"Not now," Chriani said quietly. "Or not even I'll be enough to save your life in this city."

"Show them your shoulder, half-blood." Dargana smiled, lips still showing blood. "They'll forget all about me."

Footsteps from the darkness beyond the alley mouth filled the silence that followed. Eliana's guards fell back, their lack of response telling Chriani it was a runner returning. A Bastion sergeant by her uniform, no one Chriani knew. Not the guard Eliana had sent.

She was breathing hard, took in the scene before her with a perplexed look, but her surprise didn't slow her orders. She nodded to Eliana. "Word from the Prince High Chanist. Under escort, Chriani of the prince's guard is to bring the prisoner to the throne room at once, and to be given all necessary support."

With a look of dark reluctance, Eliana motioned for his balisters to stand. Chriani waited until they had unlocked their crossbows before he lowered the Ilvani bow, feeling an ache twist through his arm and shoulder. He tried to fight the tremor that seized him. The cold that numbed his body was finally settling in as his bitter surge of strength faded.

"Sheathe your blade and stay between Kathlan and I," he said to Dargana. "Keep your hands together and in front of you. Don't say a word until I tell you."

Dargana smirked again, but she nodded as she slipped the blood-blade to its scabbard. She set herself in position between Chriani and Kathlan behind her, keeping her eyes down, matching their pace as they advanced.

Chriani felt eyes on him — the questioning look of the Bastion sergeant and the other guards, the dark hatred that came off Eliana in waves as the squad fell in around them. As they stepped clear of the mage-light and into the shadow of the street, he saw the wall of the keep looming in the distance, light flaring to life in the darkness above it.

He oriented himself toward that light as it filled window after window of the Bastion, burning bright. Drawing him on like stars used to chart a sea course by night, but which were never bright enough to show what might be lurking within the endless dark.

— CHAPTER 6 —

LEGENDS ONCE TRUE

THE KEEP WAS IN LOCKDOWN, both it and the Bastion as alive as Chriani had ever seen them by night. Sentries were thick at the southwest gatehouse when the doors were opened to them, and even thicker along the walls of the keep and the Bastion outwall. Uncounted eyes watched their group closely as he, Kathlan, and Dargana were escorted across the keep's broad courtyard, toward the staging ground and the Bastion gate ahead.

Those gates were open as they passed within the fortress, with guards stationed there and at every corridor intersection beyond. Chriani even saw young pages flitting along the edges of the great hall where it angled into the servant's quarters, papers or packages in hand. Not much chance that they had been ordered to actual duty, he knew, but they would keep busy and out of the guards' way while they kept their eyes and ears open for the story of the night.

They walked as a procession along the central court, Chriani and Kathlan in dry uniforms courtesy of the captain of the Bastion. That was Ashlund, a close-shaven veteran who towered over Chriani, and whose bulk blocked the light of evenlamps along the corridor where he paced ahead of them now. Ashlund had held the captain's commission for the same year and a half that Chriani had held his commission in the guard. His promotion had come only weeks before Chriani's own, in response to the death of Captain Konaugo. Before Chriani had left the Bastion, he and Ashlund had honed a mutual hatred over long years.

The captain had been waiting beyond the gatehouse for them, a squad of six guards with him. His expression suggested that Ashlund already knew it was Chriani he was waiting for. The way that expression soured even further told Chriani how bad he looked, still barefoot and barely dressed in the aftermath of the fight.

"A wet sack of shit would have made a better fit for commission in the prince's guard than you right now," Ashlund said evenly.

"Remind me, lord, what the penalty is for compelling an officer to keep his own counsel by breaking his jaw." Chriani's voice carried a dark earnestness that translated to shock on the faces of the other guards and Kathlan alike. Where she stood at his side, he heard the quick change in her breathing. A subtle warning to watch himself, but she said nothing.

Ashlund smiled, the ruddy skin of his wind-burned face tightening in a wholly unattractive way.

"You think to present yourselves to the prince high like this?"

"I was thinking I wouldn't be attacked in my sleep and driven half-naked to the street by a war-band within Rheran's walls. Captain Konaugo had his faults, but he stopped well short of giving the Valnirata free run of the city."

Ashlund's color rose to a deeper red to tell Chriani he'd won that round, and that he should stop while he was ahead. He had thus acquiesced when the captain ordered clothing brought to the gatehouse, giving him, Kathlan, and Dargana time to dry themselves by the fire while they waited for the courier to arrive. He and Kathlan dressed quickly, their borrowed uniforms a reasonable fit. Her silent glare calmed him, just a little. Chriani's tunic was still wet and showing blood at the shoulder, but he kept it on beneath an overtunic and jacket to keep the war-mark covered.

Ashlund said nothing about Dargana's appearance, nor did she speak any word to him as they walked. He only stared darkly at her belt, and at the bloodblade still sheathed there. No one had tried to take it from her, which told Chriani how important the events of this night had become. He was glad for her silence, but was conscious of the Ilvani's eyes burning into his back all the while they walked.

Crossing the interior courtyard to the entrance to the throne room, Ashlund ignored full salutes from four guards at the great doors as he ordered a halt to their group's movement with a wave of his hand.

"I'm to guard the three from here," he said to Sergeant Eliana. "On the prince high's orders." A handful of words, but they neatly dismissed the sergeant, established Ashlund's authority, and wrapped two members of the prince's guard within the same cloak of distrust that marked an Ilvani of the Valnirata treading through the deepest corridors of Brandishear's best-guarded fortress. It was a subtler insult than Chriani would normally have expected from Ashlund, who had always typically refrained from calculated rudeness in favor of direct physical threat.

Sergeant Eliana scowled as if he'd been hoping for a front-row view of whatever was in store for Chriani, but he only nodded. His squad turned with him as he did, Ashlund pushing open the throne room doors.

The garrison called it the throne room, but in fact, it had been long years since any ruler of Brandishear had used the cavernous space as anything but a primary council chamber. Chriani knew that the throne had been long gone even before Chanist took the crown, replaced with long tables and a huge central fireplace, tall shelves along the walls stacked with books and maps. Not a place for false praise and nobles' deference, but where a prince with a reputation for fairness and an eye for skill and dedication in others would meet, eat, and drink with captains and ambassadors, merchants and tradesfolk as equals.

It was a good tale. Chriani had believed it once.

They were alone as they entered. No other guards, the main doors closing behind them. The smaller doors far across the chamber, leading to the private entrance hall outside the prince high's quarters, were shut. Ashlund stepped past the three of them to take up a position next to the great meeting table that dominated the room, the fireplace burning brightly. Maps were strewn across the table, as they almost always were. Two flagons were set among them, beside a dozen goblets.

"We await the prince high," Ashlund said, but he gave no orders as to where or how Chriani and the others should wait. He simply watched, his gaze ignoring Kathlan but flitting from Chriani to Dargana with the same cold revulsion.

In Kathlan, Chriani saw a rapt expression as she paced slowly across the throne room floor. A great mosaic was set in the open space between tables, showing the falcon of Brandis that was the standard of Brandishear, its wings unfurled, tight knots of blue and white tile marking a great circle around it. He realized he didn't know if she'd ever actually stepped within the throne room before, but he could feel her reaction to the power in the chamber, seemingly clinging to the walls even when the great room stood empty.

He remembered his own first time staring down at the great falcon that marked the floor. A child of ten years, only two years past being pulled off the street by Barien when Chriani's attempt at cutting the sergeant's purse had gone very wrong. He remembered being presented to Chanist, feeling the power and the authority that resonated within him. He remembered the ceremony and the writ that had made him a tyro and Barien's adjutant, the prince high's hand on his shoulder, the ice-blue eyes watching him.

A jumble of images and impressions that could be recognized from his own life were circling him at a distance, shuffled and faded in his mind, like he might be having that life told to him by someone else. Too many of those images were Kathlan, reminding him that he had brought her into this. He had used what little power he had to get her the chance she had always deserved. Letting her step away from the stables, letting her be what she could be. He was hoping desperately now that her closeness to him wouldn't make her pay for his mistakes.

The prince high was on his way. Chriani would know soon enough.

"Who is she?" Kathlan's voice was a subtle whisper at his ear where she had made her way over to him. Chriani knew what she was asking, looking to see Dargana pacing around the fire, staring to the flames and seemingly deep in thought.

"I'm sorry you're angry with me," he said quietly. He turned himself to keep his back to Ashlund, not wanting to worry about whether the captain could read the movement of his lips as he spoke.

"I'm not angry, Chriani. But I'm tired and I'm cold, and I don't know what's going on because you haven't told me."

"I did tell you. She's the Ilvani who captured Lauresa and I, who helped us in the end. She led a war-band, and the last I saw of her was in the Ghostwood. I promise you, if I had any thought I'd see her again, I'd have given you her name."

"She captured you? You said she saved you."

"She did save me. Me and the princess both. Tried to kill me first, though. You know what that's like."

It was a calculated attempt at humor, but Kathlan's expression didn't warm. "What was she saying on the street? About the prince high still being alive?"

The cold of the question seized Chriani, held his mind tight. It was something he should have been thinking on, he realized. Using the time of their walk to the Bastion to come up with an answer.

"The Valnirata hate Chanist," he said simply. "They call him the Ilvani Scourge for besting them in the Incursions like he did. The exiles are no exception."

"She said you didn't have it in you. What in fate's name does that even mean?"

Chriani took a quick glance over his shoulder at Ashlund, saw the captain focused on Dargana. A fear twisted through him that he had to fight to speak over, his whispered words carrying an impossible weight in this place. "She and I are kin somehow. My father was of her war-clan, and an exile like her. I'm a traitor to both sides in her eyes."

It was a good tale. He found himself almost believing it, even as Kathlan shook her head, incredulous.

"And you brought her here?"

"She brought us here, Kath. She told me while you ran to the inn that she's got a message for the prince high. I don't know what it's about, but we'll see it through."

Chriani heard his words hang heavy in the silence. He had no idea whether Kathlan believed them, no idea what was happening. He had brought her into this, and there was no sense how it might end.

From under her arm, Kathlan thrust Magus Milyan's satchel into Chriani's hands. Then she stepped away from him without a word, suddenly intent on the bookcases along the east wall. Chriani glanced behind him again, saw Ashlund watching him this time.

He made his way over to Dargana by the fire, half expecting Ashlund to call him back, but the captain maintained his stony silence. The exile was still staring to the flames, but she raised her head as he approached, her dark eyes bright in the firelight.

"How are your wounds?" he asked her.

"Healed clean and numb as a week-old horse's kick, no thanks to your mud magic." The magic of animys and the healers was an Ilmari tradition, and so the Ilvani shunned it. The Valnirata had their own traditions of herbalism and alchemy that were said to be nearly as effective, though few among the Ilmari had ever seen such healing. Eighteen months past in the Ghostwood, Chriani had become one of those few.

"You're welcome," he said coldly.

"As are you, half..." Dargana checked herself in response to the coldness of Chriani's gaze. She smiled. "As are you, lord. That's right, isn't it?"

"Why are you here?" Chriani shifted to put his back to Ashlund again. "The truth, and quickly. I have my own business with the Prince High Chanist, and I don't want us at cross purposes. It's a short walk in here under guard, but you need to follow my lead if you want to walk out again."

"The Ilvani hunt you for the bloodblade, Chriani."

Dargana's words caught him by absolute surprise. A darkness had slipped into her expression that Chriani didn't understand, but whatever game the exile was playing, he had no time for it. "Answer my question."

"I just did, lord. The blade you carried in the Ghostwood. The narneth móir wielded by Caradar, the exile warlord, who killed your Prince

High Chanist's father and put the son on the Brandishear throne. The blade that Chanist seized from Caradar when he cut him down and ended the Incursions. The Ilvani want it. I'm here so that you and I can make sure they fail."

For the eighteen months since Chriani had ridden back from his long road to Aerach, the dagger that had killed Barien had been far from his thoughts. Never forgotten, but set aside in that place within his mind where it could be hidden from sight. But even as Chriani tried to process what the exile was saying, the side doors opened at the far end of the throne room.

As if he might have heard Dargana speak his name, the Prince High Chanist was there, stepping quickly into the room as the doors were closed by guards standing watch in the hall behind him. He was dressed in grey beneath a uniform jacket of the prince's guard, as he almost always was. His head was bare, the prince having never worn a crown to the best of Chriani's knowledge. His only symbol of rank was the armband of his own company and regiment, the falcon of Brandishear set in gold thread at his shoulder.

Chanist looked older. It was Chriani's first thought upon seeing him.

He had expected anger. He had expected to feel a surge of the cold threats that had carried him from the throne room the last time he and Chanist spoke. But all those thoughts were muted suddenly beneath a sense of unfamiliarity, of a year and a half during which the prince high seemed to have aged more than Chriani would ever have expected. The shoulders were stooped, the pale hair gone more to grey. He had a picture of a stronger Chanist in his mind but couldn't find it for some reason. A memory of a memory.

Ashlund turned to face the prince, as did Chriani and Kathlan, both of them approaching to where Chanist's path toward the table would take him. Ashlund and Chriani both stopped five paces away, as was custom for those who bore arms in the presence of the prince high or his family. Kathlan held back farther. Chanist ignored them all, crossing to the table and the flagons set there. He poured wine for himself, well mixed with water, draining his goblet before he turned.

"My lord prince," Ashlund murmured. Chanist finally nodded, as if only just noticing that the four of them were there.

No other guards had come in with Chanist, as would have been customary. Chriani remembered his own words on the street, spoken from haste and fear in the hope of forcing Eliana's hand. *This Ilvani agent was with me on the Clearwater Way.* This was the result, then.

"You are an unexpected visitor, master Chriani." The prince high's voice carried its familiar weight, but Chriani sensed a weariness in it. "And bringing even more unexpected guests."

Chanist's blue eyes settled on Dargana, who hadn't moved from her place by the fire. Chriani felt himself moving toward the prince high as if by instinct, cautious as he tried to plan how this encounter would play out. He stopped a suitable distance down the table, setting Milyan's satchel down to the dark wood.

"My visit was as ordered, my lord prince, and to pass these reports to your war-mages."

"I'm not accustomed to being asked to do courier service. Next time, deliver your documents directly."

The mocking tone in the prince high's voice was a thing Chriani remembered from their last meeting. Only the two of them then, no one else around, and Chanist revealing a kind of truth of his nature that Chriani suspected few others had ever seen. He recalled the rage in the prince high that night. His hatred of the Valnirata that had killed his father, his brother and sister, flaring as a fire in heart and mind that threatened to burn the Greatwood to the ground.

"Do you think to stop me, master Chriani?"

Chriani spoke quietly. "Are you sure you want Ashlund here for this, my lord prince?" A quick feint, as much to antagonize the captain as to remind Chanist of what had passed once between them.

"That's Captain Ashlund to you, soldier." Chanist spoke without answering the question, but Chriani saw his eyes flick from him to Kathlan, standing behind him. A kind of challenge there, like the prince high suspected that certain of the things he wouldn't want spoken in front of his captain, Chriani would likewise be loath for Kathlan to hear.

Chanist turned his attention to Dargana. She was smiling again.

"You may all approach, as you wish." The prince high poured for himself again before pushing the flagons toward Chriani, who noted the subtlety in the prince's tone. An imperious attitude, but cautious. Not giving Dargana an order that he knew she would simply refuse. Masking how important she might be by showing as little interest in her as he could.

To Chriani's surprise, the exile did approach the table, stepping up beside him. He shifted instinctively, tried to keep himself between her and Chanist as if he was worried about what she might do. She simply poured herself wine from the flagon, though. Drank it unwatered.

"Three months past," Dargana said, "the Crithnala lands were invaded by forces of the Calala Ilvani." She gave no preamble or warning to the subject matter, her tone suggesting that she and Chanist were somehow continuing a conversation they had started long ago. "They attacked into *Nyndenu*. The Ghostwood. Horse troops of Calalerean province pushed across their border in a fast assault, and the exile tribes in Nyndenu were routed. There's been fighting to the north since then, with folk fleeing the Ghostwood and the tribes of the Kelerin Hills trying to take the fight back to the invaders. The Calala move by stealth, though. Attacking by night to avoid the notice of your patrols when they cross the Clearwater Way. Not wanting to attract Ilmari attention before their conquest is done."

Chriani tried to conceal his surprise, even as he saw Ashlund doing the same. At the center of the table, a large map showed all the Ilmar. Its faded colors marked it as old, Chriani judged, its corners held down by steel weights. It was upside down from his position, but he could read the names of the Ilvani provinces of the Greatwood well enough.

"These matters are known," Chanist said. "What of them?"

"You know far less than you think, prince," Dargana sneered. A tension twisted through the room, Ashlund taking a step toward her, but Chanist waved him back. "You know that bandit activity on the Clearwater Way has increased in recent weeks," the exile said. "You know that carontir patrols along the frontier with Calalerean have pushed out to attack Ilmari farmsteads. They hold you to the frontier, keeping your own patrols from pushing too far into the forest. But you don't know why, and you won't know until I tell you."

Most folk of Brandishear saw Calalerean and the Valnirata nation as synonymous, focused on the Ilvani of that northwest province where it abutted the most populous reaches of the principality. Even for the loremasters of Brandishear and the other principalities, though, the politics of the Valnirata remained a subtle and secretive subject.

The treaty of the Ilmar, which Chanist had forged in the aftermath of driving back the Ilvani Incursions, held the Ilmar nations together in a pact of mutual animosity toward the Valnirata. All four princes had made agreement that should any future incursion come from the dark forest, all four of their principalities would respond as one. But there had been no formal contact or treaty between the Ilmar nations and the Ilvani of the Greatwood in a hundred generations. No ambassadors, no heralds. Few opportunities for spying, with the xenophobic Ilvani taking little trade from outside the forest and allowing no Ilmari within it.

As such, even the prince high's best sages could only guess at the structure of and struggles for power that went on in the Greatwood.

"I know the minds of the Valnirata well enough, exile." Chanist began to pace around the table, Dargana holding fast. "I know every troop count, every sortie fought on both sides of the Greatwood, as I know how those sorties increase steadily, month by month for more than a year now."

Ashlund stepped closer as well, and Chriani could see the captain's attention focused sharply on the bloodblade at Dargana's back. For her part, she kept her hands in front of her and firmly on her goblet as Chanist approached. "Your call to war has been answered," she said coldly. "Do you expect me to believe you hoped otherwise?"

"The exiles are the best fighters of the Valnirata," Chanist said, complimenting Dargana even as he ignored her question. Weary or not, the power of the prince's statecraft was as sharp as ever. "Calalerean rises to foment war along the Brandishear frontier, as you say. So why waste resources and risk distraction on forays to the north?"

"Because the Calala came into possession of magic in the Ghostwood. Ancient rites, and powerful. They seek to bind all the Valnirata as one, drawing on the power of the past."

"The Ilvani live their past in every waking moment. What power could the Calala hope to seek…"

"They seek the narneth móir of Caradar, the exile king. Lost to the Valnirata in the aftermath of the Incursions. A potent symbol of Ilvani rage against the Ilmari. And a sign that war will return."

Chriani saw Chanist pale. The prince high stepped past Dargana, Ashlund flinching. He poured himself more wine, but as he did, his gaze traced across Chriani's. A question there.

"I believe you know that blade, prince." Dargana smiled.

Chriani felt lightheaded suddenly. A chill was rooting beneath his still-damp tunic, though the room was warm. He felt the truth lurking beneath the animosity that swirled between Chanist and Dargana like a rising storm. He saw Kathlan from the corner of his eye. The things he hadn't told her. The lies he carried, still.

Not that, not now.

Ashlund snarled as he pushed forward, two strides putting him between Dargana and Chanist. "You show respect to the prince high of Brandishear, Ilvani, or so help me…"

"Why a prince?" Dargana cut Ashlund off as if he wasn't there. Ignored him as she stepped past to look at Chanist, thoughtful.

"Enough of your insolence…!" Ashlund was actually going for his sword before Chanist put a hand to his back to stop him.

The prince's blue eyes flashed in the captain's direction to force him back a step, still seething. Chanist then returned his attention to Dargana, as if her question had some compelling interest to him.

"What do you mean, Ilvani?"

"I mean, Ilmari, why are you prince? Brandishear, Elalantar, Aerach, Holc, each with its prince. Aren't there usually kings above princes in what passes for history among your people?"

"There were kings before the Empire." Chanist said it with a hint of amusement in his tone, as if he might be talking to a child. Speaking lessons of the Empire of the Lothelecan, which had spread across the world, then vanished from the Ilmar and all other lands more than two generations before. "And war between them that never did more than die down. Someone always wanting to rule all the Ilmar lands. Under Empire, the kingdoms were regencies, split among the four provinces. When the Empire fell, there were calls for a king again, but the four regents saw the chance for war and took the titles of prince high. They agreed that none would be king, crafting alliance instead of war."

"And allowing them to make war against the Ilvani instead."

Chanist's cold smile matched Dargana's, the sight setting Chriani on edge as he watched.

"Ilvani and Ilmari were kept at peace through long years of Empire," Chanist said. "But by the Ilvani's fear of the Imperial Guard and nothing else. The Ilmari were content to leave the Greatwood alone…"

"While staking claim to stolen land beyond it. All the Ilmar was Ilvani once…"

"Thirty centuries ago, yes. During which time the Ilvani warred on each other until the migration of our tribes gave them something else to fight…"

"The Migration Wars…"

"Were won by the Ilmari, who forged their nations and were content to let the Valnirata live in peace. Then when the Empire fell, the war-clans of Calalerean and Laneldenar set their eyes on Brandishear and Aerach before the ink on the Ilmar treaty had dried."

"You think you know the history of the Valnirata, old man…"

"I have made the history of the Valnirata, exile! I have lived it. And you and your kin should hope and beseech whatever fallen gods still dwell in the Greatwood that my time for shaping history is done…"

"Enough!"

It was Chriani's voice that cut the steel-sharp tone of Chanist's anger and the reply Dargana had been set to make. He forced them both to silence, as much from surprise as anything. It was a surprise he shared, no idea what he was meant to say now.

He felt the change overwhelming him, as it so often did. Unseen pieces of the puzzle coming into view, but as they moved, they shifted all the other pieces into new positions. Set them to new shapes. New patterns.

"The Ilvani seek the dagger that once belonged to Caradar," Chriani said, as much for his own ear as anyone else's. Feeling the understanding falling into place. "They hunt me because they know I took it from the assassins who meant to use it against the Princess Lauresa."

He was watching Chanist as he said it. He saw the prince high try and fail to mask his surprise. The dismissive gaze was shaken by uncertainty, only for a moment. It was enough, though.

Chriani had been wrong. Chanist wasn't behind the attack in the forest, and he certainly wasn't responsible for bringing the Valnirata into Rheran. That fact alone of the second attack should have given him something to think about. Too much else going on, though. Too many things he didn't want to see.

"Sit. All of you." When Chanist spoke this time, it was an order. Chriani stepped up slowly, taking a chair at the prince high's left hand. Kathlan followed to sit next to him, her face a mask. Ashlund moved to the right, between Chanist and Dargana. He sat only after the Ilvani exile had slipped to a chair.

"Chriani. Where is the blade that was Caradar's?"

The Prince High Chanist's voice was pitched low to leave the question hanging. An evenness to its tone that Chriani understood the reasons for.

He remembered the morning he gave the dagger to Lauresa, the last time he saw it. Knowing that she would take it a principality away, protected behind all the stone and steel of a duke the Ilmari called *the Lion of Aerach*. A duke whose legendary campaigns against the Valnirata gave them every reason to avoid him. Its safety was thus assured by its being under the protection of one who had no business holding it. One who didn't even know he held it, Chriani trusting Lauresa to keep it hidden. No one ever thinking to seek it there.

"It's safe," was all Chriani said. All he could say.

Ashlund was up from the table like a shot, his chair scraping stone as it pushed out behind him. "Your prince orders you..." he snarled, but Chanist raised a hand to stop him.

"Master Chriani has my leave to keep his own counsel in this matter if that is his wish. You do not need to know my reasons, captain."

Ashlund nodded, but the fury in his eyes didn't fade. Chriani felt himself scoured by it, set his gaze on Chanist to try to refocus.

"This intelligence is why you returned to Rheran," the prince said to him. "To speak these things directly to me."

"Yes, my lord prince." An easy lie. Chriani nodded to Milyan's satchel at the far end of the table. "The reports from Magus Milyan concern magic used by the Ilvani in their attack against me. However, Captain Rhuddry expressed skepticism as to the goals of the Valnirata. I thus decided to return to Rheran myself to report."

"Do so now, and quickly."

Chriani told the story, beginning with the attack in the forest that had begun it. Sergeant Thelaur's death and the black arrow. The deep wood and the finding of the dark shrine. The events in the war-mages' pavilion. The coins. Even as he was speaking, he sensed the holes in the story left by his now-unspoken assumptions about why the Ilvani had targeted him. Chief among those was why he had felt compelled to report to Chanist personally, Ashlund's expression and Kathlan's alike telling him they were wondering. Chriani hoped that Chanist not caring would cover it in the end.

The prince high turned his attention to Dargana when Chriani's story was done. "You talked of Calalerean controlling magic of the exile lands," he said. No sense given of whether the things Chriani said had meant anything to him. "What manner of spellcraft have they seized? And what power do they claim by it?"

"Not spellcraft. Rites older than spell magic. Lóech arnala irch niir. Three coins for confession. What Chriani talked of seeing in the Greatwood. In the city tonight. Your guards will find coins on some of the Valnirata dead. Your mages need to see them."

The chill that had settled in Chriani pushed deep along his back, digging in like his spine was being stitched up tight. He shivered, tried to hide it.

"The rites of confession..." Dargana continued, but Chanist cut her off with a wave of his hand.

"I know the Ilvani lore as well as anyone. The rites of confession are superstition. Golden warriors bound by magic and dark oaths, able to see and hear a half-world away. Children's stories."

"If you know Ilvani lore, you should know we have no stories, prince. Only legends once true, and long memories. Longer than all the life and history of the Ilmar. The warriors of confession were real. The *lóechari*. The rites of confession were spoken before the first Ilmari crawled over the peaks of Ursumma and out of the Black Fens, but were lost by the time the Migration Wars were done. The Calala seek to rebuild that lost past, and they'll use the power of the rites to do it. The unity of the Migration Wars. The bloodshed of the Incursions. And all the Ilmari dead that will come with it."

"You hold perhaps too high an opinion of your people's prowess of magic, exile." Chanist showed no more than a mild thoughtfulness toward the doom wrapped up in Dargana's tale. He mixed wine and water in two goblets, pushed them carefully across the table toward Chriani and Kathlan.

"You'll change your story when you've seen that magic, prince. I have. The Calala have rebirthed a cult that's been less than a memory for a hundred generations. They use ritual magic to bind warriors to the Ilvani cause and specific missions. If those warriors fail in their missions, they die."

"Making it sound rather like the Valnirata are doing our job for us."

"Except that the rites allow shared knowledge," Dargana said, ignoring Chanist's thin smile. "Those bound by the power of the coins can share thought and memory while their minds are at rest. No legend, prince. The Ilvani that attacked in the city tonight had knowledge of Chriani but had never seen him before. They knew where to find him, using magic attuned to his life and blood."

"Master Chriani is hardly a legend among the Valnirata," Chanist said, dismissive. "How much of his life and blood do you suspect the Ilvani have access to?"

Dargana's gazed shifted to Chriani. Her dark look softened, a sense of misgiving there that seemed entirely out of place. A flicker of something like guilt flashed in the exile's dark eyes, Chriani finding it a wholly unnatural look.

"When Chriani escaped the Ghostwood," she said to Chanist. "When I let him go. He left something behind."

Her eyes shifted down to Chriani's hand on the table, the full complement of fingers there. Chriani felt the familiar itch rise against the tremor of cold still pushing through him. He squeezed his hand shut, saw Chanist watching.

It was quite literally the last thing Chriani had ever expected to think about. "How did the Ilvani get hold of my finger?" he asked. "For that matter, how did they know whose it was?"

"Abrindra," Dargana said, and Chriani felt a vague recollection of the name from the frantic flight he and Lauresa had made across the exile lands. He remembered riding behind Dargana's second, then nearly dying at his hands before Valnirata griffon riders had encroached on the Ghostwood and attacked.

"He kept the finger," Chriani said.

Dargana nodded. "As a token. To go along with a promise to kill you one day for bringing the gavaleria down on us. The Calala captured and tortured him, though. They killed him before he had the chance."

"Why would he have any reason to tell them it was mine? And why would the Calala care?"

"Because Abrindra told them you were the Ilmari who carried Caradar's bloodblade, stolen from Chanist, who stole it from the exile king before."

"Which brings us here." Prince Chanist's voice carried a thoughtful tone, his blue eyes bright. He had taken in everything that had been said with no hint of a reaction, but Chriani felt the full weight of the prince's focus and attention. "Or which brings Chriani here, at least. Your presence, exile, requires a bit more explanation still."

Dargana smiled again. She drained her goblet, then slid it down the table to stop in front of the prince high. He poured for her, wine unwatered. Ashlund slid it back to Dargana, stiffly.

The exile sipped slowly. "Elalantari red. From the islands."

"You have an excellent palate," Chanist said. "Istilnean, in fact. The princess high's family has vineyards there."

"The vines stolen from the Ilvani, along with the islands' names."

"As you wish. Your story, please."

The exile pushed her chair back to stand, stepping away from the prince. She looked down to the maps on the table. Ashlund responded by shifting in his own chair, but he stayed seated.

"When the Calala crossed north into Crithnalerean," Dargana said, "we fought them. I fought them alone when none from my war-band were left. Then I fled to Laneldenar when the fight was lost. I fell in there with a faction that seeks peace with the Ilmari. They sent me here to talk to you, prince."

The crackling of the fire was the only sound for a long while. Chanist's face, a mask through all the talk of frontier attacks and cult magic, showed genuine surprise. Ashlund's reaction was more direct.

"Speaking as a captain of the prince's guard and responsible for the security of the Bastion and Rheran, allow me to invite you to fuck yourself, Ilvani."

"Captain..." In Chanist's voice, Chriani heard the weariness again. Ashlund seemed to hear it too, taking advantage of it to press.

"I beg forgiveness, my lord prince, but this tale is beyond insult. I don't know what game this one plays..."

"My game is yours for the asking, warrior," Dargana said sharply. "The Ilvani of Laneldenar recognize the danger in Calalerean's quest for ancient magic. They want to avoid the total war across the Ilmar that too many others want. As do I."

Ashlund laughed. "If war comes again to the Ilmar..."

"You'll be the first one I kill, laóith, as a promise. Up till then, these games of war that you and the Valnirata play are fun enough. Even in the Crithnalerean, I've killed my share of Brandishear rangers. You've probably done your best to kill friends of mine. But I came to understand a while back that total war means the Greatwood destroyed. And even if the Calala turn Brandishear to one endless charnel field before the last of them fall, it's not a price I'll pay."

Dargana didn't need to look to him for Chriani to know who she was speaking of. He had made that plea to her in the Ghostwood. One last, desperate chance to save Lauresa. One chance to stop the war that Chanist had meant to start.

"The Ilvani in Laneldenar want to meet with representatives of the Ilmari," Dargana said. "In secret. No word to get out to Calalerean. Too many things that might go wrong. They want envoys from Brandishear and Aerach, east and west. I'm to take the envoys to a meeting across the Hunthad in Aerach."

Ashlund seemed dangerously close to the point where his blood would kill him before any Ilvani had the chance. His face was fire-red, his knuckles white where his hands were flat against the table. Dargana ignored him as she nodded deep to Chanist. The acknowledgement of station and respect. The gesture was awkwardly done, but Chriani felt how much effort it had taken her.

"I offer you my service, prince," the exile said. "Now be smart enough to take it."

To Chriani, it felt as though the room was shifting around him. He was a bystander, watching as others tilted through some complex game whose moves he had seen before but never truly learned. Like all his other times in the throne room, he watched while those with power conducted the rituals that power demands. It had never been his game, though. Never his fight.

But that was changing, it seemed.

Ashlund was the one to break the silence, speaking through clenched teeth. "If your mission is to Aerach, why not begin it there? Take your children's tale to Prince Vishod and see how long an interrogation among his war-mages it takes to pull the truth from you."

"Because I knew Chriani," Dargana said. "And I knew that he gave me access and approach to the Prince High Chanist. As I knew that Chanist could bring Vishod to this undertaking, and because when Chanist does so, Chriani will lead the envoy of Brandishear. I came for him."

Ashlund's expression held a furious darkness as it was, but at Dargana's words, that darkness pushed to a place Chriani had never seen before. Under other circumstances, he would have tried to enjoy it, but he was distracted now by too many things shifting past him like fast-moving targets. No way to focus in on them, no way to understand. Not without asking questions of Dargana that he couldn't ask in front of the prince high. Saying things in front of Kathlan he couldn't say.

"How did you get to Brandishear?" Chanist asked. His voice carried no real interest in the question, which made Chriani assume he might simply be trying to keep Ashlund silent for the sake of the captain's health.

"I was ordered from Laneldenar to work my way into Calalerean. Find the forces seeking Chriani and follow them."

"And the Calala Ilvani accepted you?"

"As they accept hundreds of the Crithnala. Calalerean prepares for war. They'll take any blades they can, though they limit entrance to their cult to their own warriors for now. I pursued the lóechari force that entered Rheran tonight, all of us passing over the dockside gates. Your patrols pass at intervals far too regular."

"At long last," Ashlund snarled, "a part of this tale I believe. You did enter the city with the Valnirata tonight, because you're one of them. And so, caught and cornered, you throw yourself on the weakness of this one…" — the captain jerked a massive fist at Chriani — "…to walk you past the noose. Have him stand for you when you ask for a Brandishear honor guard to escort you back to your war-band, laughing every step of the way!"

As if she knew it would make Ashlund's anger worse, Dargana stayed cool by contrast. "The leaders of the war-band that struck tonight knew of the failed attack against Chriani in the forest the moment he turned it back. They knew he was riding north. They knew this because of the magic they track him with. The magic of the coins, linking every Ilvani bound by the rites of confession."

"Why not attack him on the road, then?" Ashlund said, a note of triumph in his voice as if he'd caught Dargana in a lie.

"Because a dozen riders moving fast along the trade road will be noticed, even by dark. A dozen entering the city among your merchant wains are all but invisible."

"But you followed him along that trade road, or you never would have found him here!"

"No. They didn't."

Dargana reached into her pocket, Ashlund tensing, two steps away. She moved slowly, kept her other hand on the table. Carefully, she set out the Ilvani coins she'd claimed on the rooftop, the talisman beside them. Its stone pulsed blood-red in a steady rhythm.

At Chriani's side, Kathlan made the moonsign, Ashlund following her. The prince high and Chriani sat silent, but Chriani alone could feel the steady pulse of the hunter's heart in his head. Recognizing it as the beating of his own heart.

"You'll want your mages to look at these," Dargana said to Chanist. "The magic of the cult connects the minds of those who take the rites. Binds their memories, allows intelligence to be spread and shared between them. As the cult's power spreads throughout Calalerean, Laneldenar and Brandishear and Aerach alike will be exposed…"

"To Ilvani deception and nothing more." Ashlund spat to his hand, wiped it to his leather in a gesture of dismissal. "Brandishear fears no seer's magic. Will you tell us that the shades of the Incursions rise against us next?"

In the defiance of the captain's tone, Chriani understood something. Though his anger was his own, Ashlund was speaking for Chanist now. It was a subtle shift in his language, in his posturing. But a well-practiced one. Taking that role because he was used to doing so, the prince high's weariness pushing him to silent reflection in a way Chriani wasn't used to seeing.

He sensed the age in Chanist again. Saw the once-straight back bent as the prince high stared at the coins and the talisman across the table.

"You Ilmari have your seers," Dargana snapped. "Your spells of sending. This is different. The moment the Ilvani of the cult in Crithnalerean knew Chriani through the blood magic they used on his finger, every cultist of the lóechari knew Chriani as well, like they might have known him his whole life. For every sortie you fight, for every scout party that engages the cult, every cult commander in the Greatwood will know your troop movements at once. You'll set your companies along the forest wall and the Valnirata will slip between them, because a single lóechari scout making contact tells every cult commander where you are."

She leveled her gaze at Chanist, cold. "Imagine the battle at Welbirk, prince. The day Caradar slew your father, with your brother and sister already gone. Imagine that every Ilvani of the Greatwood had known that day that the prince high of Brandishear and both his heirs had fallen, his company lost, Rheran in chaos. Imagine all the Valnirata mobilizing at once to take advantage of..."

"Enough," Chanist said. His voice was quiet against the exile's, but the strength in it was enough to stop her.

A long silence held, Ashlund breaking it. "My lord prince, I ask your permission to arrest this agent of the Valnirata..."

"This Ilvani will be given free leave to journey to Aerach, captain." Chanist stood slowly from the table, a decision made. Chriani and Kathlan were on their feet at once. Dargana took her time rising, Chriani noting the calm in her expression. No sense of triumph, though, not even in response to Ashlund's fury.

"My lord prince, I beg you..."

"A captain who cannot hear my orders is of little use to me, Ashlund."

As the prince paced along the table, Chriani saw the strength surge in him. He was taller somehow, the grey hair turned to gold again in the firelight as he stepped forward to scoop three of the coins into his hand. The pulsing talisman he left where it was.

Ashlund nodded, his face a mask suddenly. "As you order, my lord prince."

"A squad will accompany this exile as Brandishear's envoy, to meet with an envoy of Aerach. I'll see that the message is sent to Vishod's seers myself. You will deliver Chriani's documents and the Ilvani artifact to Varyn in the tower, captain. That is all."

"With your permission," Ashlund began, "I will lead this envoy myself..."

"Chriani leads the envoy of Brandishear," Dargana said again. "There's no negotiation on that."

Chanist was staring to the magic in his palm, the coins glowing gold with their own light. "I am sure Captain Ashlund will have no problem having Chriani in his company…"

"Chriani leads the company and this captain comes nowhere near it. Or I'll return alone to tell the Laneldenari that the Ilmar is lost."

Chanist looked up from the coins, a flash of gold playing across the prince's blue eyes. "Why?" he said simply.

"I trust Chriani. Unlike you or this by-blow of a blacksmith and a prize pig." She glanced to Ashlund. "When those I don't trust get too close to me, they end up dead."

Chriani heard the evenness in her tone, saw the prince high assessing it. The way Dargana had spoken told him she'd chosen the words carefully.

Beneath that care, he knew she was lying. Some other reason, some other game playing out here. Things she wasn't saying.

Chanist simply nodded. "So ordered. Captain Ashlund will name the squad but Chriani leads it. He can treat you with whatever degree of trust he thinks is warranted."

The prince high's words hung in the silence of the throne room. Chanist's hand clasped around the coins as he paced toward the smaller doors leading to the private entrance hall and his quarters. Watching the prince go, all of Ashlund's anger drained from him in an instant. The captain stood now with an expression of absolute confusion, as close to fearful as Chriani had ever seen him.

"My lord prince, why…?"

"Because I share this Ilvani's fear of what I do not understand, captain. And I would hear what the Laneldenari have to say before I pass judgement on it. And because I will serve my people at any cost…"

Chanist faltered, two steps from the doors. He turned back, his gaze finding Chriani, and he was old again in the pale light of evenlamps that lined the walls above him. Something lost in him.

An unfamiliar feeling twisted through Chriani. Pity for the prince high. Then he pushed it down again, felt it break against Barien's memory and the sharp pain it made.

He remembered holding Barien in the empty hall of records, feeling the warrior's life ebb from him. He remembered those last moments of life, remembered the wound that had dropped the Bastion's best sergeant.

He remembered, would always remember, that it was Chanist's hand that had done it.

Lauresa had begged him not to go after her father for what had happened. Irdaign her mother had bade him let Chanist live, seeing the anger in Chriani and knowing what it might do. And though Chriani had found in the end that he could forget what the prince high had tried to do to Lauresa, could forget the destruction his madness had attempted to wreak, he would never forgive him for Barien.

"Captain Ashlund will make whatever arrangements are necessary for your departure." Chanist said it to Chriani, but Chriani was looking past the prince. Wouldn't meet his gaze. "This meeting is done."

The prince high pulled the doors open, Chriani seeing guards on the other side stand to attention. They pulled the doors sharply closed, the echo of brass and wood hanging for a moment in the silence.

Chriani felt Kathlan's hand find his where she had stepped up behind him. She was shaking.

He waited for Ashlund to speak, confident that anything he said first would do nothing good.

"Chriani of the prince's guard," the captain said at last. "By order of the Prince High Chanist, I award you temporary rank and the commission of acting sergeant, and command of a squad to be named by me. Your commission and orders will be written up. I assume your adjutant will join you."

Chriani nodded but Ashlund wasn't looking at him. "Yes."

"See yourselves to guest barracks. Keep your Ilvani assassin under control and out of my sight. You are dismissed."

Chriani felt a spike of anger rise, but Ashlund turned to snatch up the talisman, the remaining coins, and Milyan's satchel from the table. He strode quickly toward the main doors, pulled them open with a bang and stood waiting. Chriani moved to follow, motioning Dargana to fall in behind him, Kathlan behind her.

As they passed along the interior courtyard, the doors slammed shut again behind them. Chriani glanced back to see Ashlund standing in the shadows. The captain was watching as the three of them made their way toward the great hall and the barracks beyond. When Chriani turned back again at the great hall doors, Ashlund was gone.

— CHAPTER 7 —
A DIFFERENT FEAR

IT WAS A TEN-DAY JOURNEY from Rheran to Aerach, and even with good weather, Chriani knew they'd be spending five of those days along the Clearwater Way. It was a journey he had never made before the winter road that had taken him east a year and a half before. A journey he'd had no intention of ever making again.

On their way to the guest barracks that Ashlund had ordered them to, Chriani cornered three pages and directed them to clear out two rooms with doors that could be locked and watched. He sought out the sergeant on duty, a veteran named Gredia, and asked her for four guards. It took dropping Ashlund's name and repeating Chanist's orders to force her to action, but the length of time it took for the guards to arrive made Chriani suspect the sergeant had double-checked those orders first.

The guards were to watch Dargana — not for her own protection, but to make sure no one else in the Bastion had any ideas about coming for her. Too many soldiers there had lost friends and comrades along the Clearwater Way. As such, Chriani worried at how the amount of ale that typically flowed in the mess halls in the off-duty times might collide with word that a Crithnalerean war-band leader was presently the guest of the prince high.

Waiting for the guards to arrive, he heard word that supported his instinct to keep Dargana and the soldiers of the Bastion away from each other. Six more Ilvani had been found dead near the site of the unprecedented attack in the city, spread across a lane approaching the Trickster's front doors. All of them had been killed by a bloodblade, most with weapons drawn that did them no good in the end.

One of the dead Ilvani had been carrying potent magic, someone said. A single black arrow. The war-mages would be examining it.

Chriani and Kathlan took the second room once Dargana was safely locked away. Kathlan held him in the dark, and only when he felt her shaking did Chriani realize how hearing the full story of the attack and the black arrow had affected her. Knowing now that the Ilvani hunted him. She asked no other questions, though, for which he was grateful.

He wasn't sure he'd even managed to sleep before the dawn came with Ashlund knocking at the door and handing him his orders in angry silence. The single terse page was masterfully vague and suspiciously lacking in direction, making Chriani suspect that no matter the outcome of the mission, Ashlund was already planning how he could deem it a failure.

A promotion from first-ranked guard to acting sergeant was almost unheard of outside a combat zone. It was a remarkable sign of the promoted guard's expertise, and of the trust enjoyed in the eyes of superiors. Or it would have been, at least, if the promotion hadn't been Chriani's, and if Ashlund hadn't already spread word across the Bastion that it was a promotion wholly unearned. The rangers assigned to his squad were five veterans Chriani didn't know — another sign that the captain was taking steps to ensure his first command was also his last.

They set out eight strong from the Bastion just after high sun and the daymark bells, after a rushed morning of preparation, and with Chriani still feeling the fatigue of the previous eight days in the saddle. Kathlan looked better rested by far, though he was fairly certain she hadn't slept any more than he had.

The service records for the squad's rangers accompanied Ashlund's orders, but even though Chriani heard their formal introductions in the stables before they left, he suspected he would struggle throughout the journey to match faces to names. Walaric was the youngest member of the squad, which made the number of misconduct citations in his record that much more impressive. Daellyn and Wilric were sister and brother from the southern mountains, having made rank there before their combat skill brought them to the Bastion. Jessa had made her name as a tracker. Beah was trained as a healer, and could work a bit of magic.

That last note had been marked as confidential. Many among the guard were so fearful of spellcraft that even healing magic was something to distrust — a feeling Chriani understood all too well. He had never known the magic of the healers before the dark path he'd set out on a year and a half before. He had gotten well used to it since then, though.

Because he didn't know the new rangers, Chriani had no sense of who to pick as his second. As such, he chose Kathlan, rationalizing that as long as making a wrong pick from among the others offered a chance of insulting the better choices, he was better off insulting all of them in the name of making a choice he knew he could trust.

Most of Kathlan's duties as second involved overseeing the horses, which she would have done anyway, and guarding Dargana. She managed to get the exile into the leather and uniform jacket of the prince's guard for at least the march out of Rheran, but Dargana had the insignia torn free even before the south city-gate was fully behind them. When they made camp that first night, she used her bloodblade to cut the sleeves from her armor while she sat by the fire. She left her tunic sleeves intact, though, the war-mark well covered. She also kept her hair tied back at Chriani's instruction, hiding the Ilvani peak to her ears.

The shorter days of autumn saw them on the road by dawn each day as they made their way from Rheran to Caredry, and the start of the Clearwater Way. Then through the guard post citadels of Gleoran and Durrant, Talimeth and Rhercyn. They were traveling quietly, attracting no attention. Along the trade roads, they had stayed away from inns and private houses to set camp each night. Now, within the stockade walls of the Clearwater fortresses, the rangers pitched their tents away from the tents of other squads. Whether soldier or civilian, all those who crossed the Clearwater Way did so with the fear of Ilvani attack on their minds, making Chriani understand the importance of keeping Dargana out of sight.

The exile clearly wasn't a prisoner. She rode free, and in addition to her bloodblade, Chriani had outfitted her with an Ilvani handaxe looted from the Bastion's store of captured weapons. But he recognized the importance of at least making it look as if Dargana was being kept under guard, including having her and Kathlan share a tent at night while the other rangers took watch.

At first, Chriani was glad of the excuse to keep a distance from Kathlan. He had no idea whether anyone else in the squad knew of their relationship, but he hoped that distance would ensure it never became an issue. However, as the journey wound on, he quickly realized that the nights of that journey were the first since his return from Aerach that he and Kathlan hadn't spent at least a brief time beside each other, locked tight in each other's arms. The sense of emptiness that accompanied those nights alone was a feeling Chriani found far too familiar. Another journey he had hoped to never make again.

Before they left the Bastion, Chriani had discovered that the promotion to a sergeant's commission came with a new uniform jacket and insignia. The falcon of Brandis was at his shoulder in gold now. He and the rest of the squad wore the regalia of a detached patrol, heading for foreign lands. Marked as the prince's guard but losing their regimental sigils. However, far more important to Chriani than the change in insignia was the badge he wore within his belt — a golden disk set with moonstone, which glowed faintly in the absence of all light to show its dweomer.

The badge had been given to him with great antipathy by one of Chanist's war-mages, a venerable scarecrow named Varyn. His sun-dark skin was laced with scars whose lines were suspiciously straight. Self-inflicted, some rumors said, in the administration of secret blood rites condemned by Ilmar law and any sense of self-preservation.

"You have use of this relic on the prince high's orders," Varyn had said dismissively after summoning Chriani to the prince's tower along the Bastion's northern flank. That was the domain of Chanist's court wizards and healers, and home to the library and collections of arcane regalia they kept on the prince high's behalf. The reputation of its magic and its half-mad keepers made it a place Chriani was glad he had seen only once before.

"The relic will aid you in your... problem with the Ilvani," Varyn explained, "masking you from divination and related sorceries while you wear it. So there is no misunderstanding, the relic is worth far more than you are now or will ever be. It remains my property and will be returned. Should you not return it, I will hunt you down and discipline you in ways that will shatter all your previous conceptions of just punishment. If you happen to be dead at the time, it won't help you."

Varyn had also returned the talisman Dargana claimed, its severed cord of red leather retied. Chriani noticed as he hadn't before that most of that coloring appeared to be bloodstains. It gave him even less interest in taking it, but the outraged Varyn was most insistent.

"This is your test and proof of the badge's power, simpleton. As long as the talisman shows no light, you are safe. If it glows again, then the badge's magic has failed and the Ilvani can find you. Seek out one of Prince Vishod's war-mages if you can. Though finding one of any competence will be a challenge."

Chriani had worn the badge day and night since then. It had started around his neck on a chain, over tunic and under armor, but the disk pulsed with an unnatural warmth that quickly unnerved him. He had clipped it within his belt in response, its gold not as well hidden from sight but its warmth not as noticeable.

Each night and morning since, alone in his tent, Chriani had held the talisman and stared at it in the darkness, confirming to his own satisfaction that its blood-red light was nowhere to be seen. The oily sheen of the stone had disappeared, gone now to a layer of dust that wouldn't rub off.

He had shown the disk to Kathlan and Dargana before they set out, wanting to put both their minds at ease about the Ilvani's pursuit of him. Kathlan showed the greatest relief, the exile simply shrugging. "You put Ilmari magic against the sorcery of Muiraìden, you'll lose eventually," Dargana had said. "Stay moving either way."

The longer they traveled, the more focused Chriani became on the questions he had for Dargana. Questions he hadn't been able to ask yet, having had no chance to speak to the exile privately since the throne room. With Kathlan riding at her side, Chriani had been forced to limit their conversations to signs of Crithnala activity and other dangers of the road. More worrying, though, was the relative closeness of the other rangers, all of who kept one wary eye on the Ilvani exile as they rode. Chriani had no idea what their relationship to Ashlund was, but he was certain that anything they saw or heard would reach the captain's ear when the squad made it back to Rheran once more.

They had met Ilvani bandits three times since joining the Clearwater Way at Caredry. The frequency of those skirmishes was enough to trouble the veteran rangers, but the attackers had dispersed quickly when shown any resistance.

"They're Crithnala fleeing Calala war-bands," Dargana advised the rangers after the first brief encounter. "Seeking supplies and coin, but not willing to die for it." She didn't seem to care that most of the rangers ignored her, or seemed more than happy to talk of killing the Crithnala no matter what their intent. "If we meet the Calala they're running from," she told them, "it won't be so easy."

That Calala attack came in the morning along the final leg of the Clearwater Way. They were nine days in, the fortress of Rhercyn behind them and the border of Aerach one last day's ride ahead. The skies had stayed clear across the exile lands, but that was changing. The Ghostwood and the Greatwood alike were too far away to be seen from the Wayroad, but the southern sky above them was shimmering gold and green along the horizon. Not so to the north, where the air was streaked by cloud that thickened as it rolled in from the sea.

At a point where the Wayroad twisted between a low pine bluff and sand to the north, they found themselves facing sudden bowshot from behind them, and the cries of Ilvani warriors coming through the trees.

It was an ambush, obviously. A feint that might have taken a squad of new-made guards by surprise, or one of the privately guarded merchant caravans that braved the Wayroad when time was of the essence or sea passage around the Sandhorn was made hazardous by seasonal storms. A trap that would have caught Chriani as a tyro, before he'd faced the Ilvani and their deadly silence in battle.

"Ambush west!" he called, but the rangers were already scattering. Two drove back along the trail, flat to their horses' necks and shields up to protect against the arrows that continued to arc out from the trees. The other three cut hard around the bluff, pushing off the road with bows drawn and firing into the six Ilvani hidden in shadow and scrub beyond. The main force that would have attacked from cover if any of the rangers had panicked and bolted away from the token attack from the rear.

"Calala!" Dargana shouted, but Chriani knew the rangers wouldn't need the warning. The Ilvani war-band reacted to the failed ambush with a single-minded purpose, pushing their horses back along the treeline in an attempt to draw the Ilmari riders in. Taking cover but not retreating. Looking for the fight the exile war-bands had hoped to avoid.

Chriani had his bow out, was following the three riders that had fallen back. "Get to the trees for cover," he called to Kathlan. "Keep Dargana out of sight."

Even as he shouted, though, the exile called out. "Three riders fleeing!" Then with a flick of her reins, Dargana turned her horse and charged the side of the bluff, twisting onto a narrow trail through the trees that Chriani hadn't seen. He cursed as he slewed to a stop, turned his horse to follow her. Kathlan was two strides behind him.

He hadn't seen the riders Dargana was following.

Chriani watched the scrub to all sides, wary. He heard bowshot to the east, steel on steel to the west where the rest of the squad had disappeared. The Ilvani had gone silent again. He lost sight of Dargana at one point, needing to check his horse's speed on the rough trail. He had given Kathlan specific orders in Rheran to not sit the exile on any steed that would let her run, but the chestnut mare Dargana rode was flying somehow under her light touch, drawing steadily away.

He rounded a corner where the trail opened up to a broad clearing, the scrub trees there overgrown by a lone limni whose branches reached for the sun. Dargana had her reins loose, was letting her horse crop pale grass between the trees. Waiting for him.

"Where are your riders?" Chriani said coldly as he reined to a stop.

"Must have lost them. We need to talk."

The unfamiliar urgency in her tone caught Chriani off guard, but he was too angry to care. "Not your decision to make," he said coldly. "And not at the expense of endangering my squad..."

"We're in Aerach by dusk and fallen in with another squad in the morning. Unless you can call down another Calala attack at your whim, we'll have no other chance but here and now."

Before Chriani could respond, he saw Dargana's dark eyes flash to shadow as Kathlan raced in behind him. She slowed her horse quickly, ignoring Chriani as she stepped past him to stop at Dargana's side.

"You ever think to race one of my horses again where it might break a leg, I'll break both of yours first so you can judge what it feels like." Kathlan's voice carried a dark fury that Chriani recognized. To her credit, Dargana didn't laugh in response.

"I take my responsibility to a mount as seriously as you do, horse master. But this one is more fleet than she lets you know. She was in no danger."

"You'll walk her back all the same."

"As you wish."

From the scrubland behind them, they heard a horn. Two short blasts, a call to return. Chriani caught Dargana's thin smile.

"The others will be looking for us," the exile said. "Someone should ride ahead and round them up before they scatter."

"Someone should have thought twice about breaking off from the squad in the first place," Kathlan said coldly. "So what are we going to talk about?"

She was watching the exile, Chriani understanding that Kathlan had heard what was said even as she rode up. Dargana's smile grew colder.

"You don't need to concern yourself in these matters, girl..."

Kathlan spat. "I'll concern myself with what I choose, and take on anything you or your Ilvani can throw at me. You doubt it, try me."

"That's enough." Chriani had to angle his horse between the two of them where they were pressing, Kathlan the first to back away. Beyond the tangled scrub, the horn sounded out again. "Go," he said to Kathlan. "Tell them Dargana and I followed outriders and are cooling our horses on the way back."

It was as close to an order as he'd ever given her, but there was no hardness in his voice. Kathlan's green eyes showed a sudden chill, though, flicking once to Dargana as she spurred away.

Chriani set out ahead of Dargana, holding his horse to a walk. He scanned the trees around them, saw no sign of any movement. "Have your words," he said. "And quickly." A report featuring rangers coming under fire while Chriani and the exile were off in the woods would sit well with Ashlund, he knew.

Dargana followed along the same route, a half-length behind. "I spoke the truth to your prince," she said, "but not all of it. The rest is for you alone. I fled to Laneldenar and heard factions there talking peace. But it meant nothing to me. I only wanted to kill Calala for what they'd done to Crithnalerean. I had nothing else to care about by that point."

"And what changed your mind?"

"Veassen. That's a name you need to remember. A seer of the Laneldenari. Blind since birth, they say. He seeks the heir of the exile's blade. He told me it was you."

The words, the title, meant nothing to Chriani. But as Dargana spoke, he felt a chill settle at the back of his neck. He kept his eyes on the scattered groves around them, the shadows glimmering beneath their branches. "Am I supposed to know what that means?"

"You carried the blade, half-blood. You tell me."

"I'll tell you if you call me that one more time within a league of any Ilmari, I'll have your tongue."

Dargana simply shrugged. "Caradar's line broke with the Valnirata at the end of the Migration Wars. He invoked the history of a forebear named Daronnon when he claimed power in Crithnalerean and named himself the exile king. But the legends are older than even Daronnon, talking of how a narneth móir called 'the exile's blade' will be key to the final fate of the Ilvani of Muiraìden. When Caradar's power was rising, many thought he would turn out to be the prophesied heir. But when he fell to Chanist, the legend fell with him. Veassen thinks that's changing. So do the Calala and their lóechari. That's why they hunt you."

The absurdity of it almost inspired Chriani to laugh. He only shook his head, though. "Whatever superstition the Ilvani chase, it's got nothing to do with the dagger. It's a blade no different than yours. And it's got less to do with me..."

"Veassen was the one who told me to go to Calalerean and work my way into the war-bands there. He told me to find you and confirm that the blade of Caradar was safe. He didn't say to find you and the blade. Didn't say find out if you have it. Because he already knew you weren't carrying it."

"An Ilmari of the prince's guard not carrying a bloodblade? Give me whatever odds your seer was offering and I'll take that bet."

"Veassen told me I'd find you in Rheran," Dargana hissed. "He told me when the lóechari would set out in pursuit of you, when they'd arrive in the city. Third day of your High Autumn, he called it. Two days of rain, then the clouds would break by night. He told me the name of the inn where you'd stay. Told me to watch for you on the roof. Told me what to tell your prince when we met. Told me that you're the key to everything the Calalerean Ilvani want."

Chriani felt the exile's earnestness. The same dark honesty with which she had threatened to kill him a year and a half before. Despite all his best instincts, though, he did laugh this time.

Dargana's anger showed as she pushed her horse forward, pressing close. "Veassen sent me to help you against the lóechari. Then I was to bring you to the eastern border of the Greatwood, where the Hunthad crosses into Valnirata lands."

"So you show up to save me from one group hunting me, only to deliver me to another? How many others are out there waiting to lay down bids?"

"You're a fool, half-blood."

Chriani felt the oath grate on him, but he was too weary to warn the exile off speaking it again. "So it's been said, and by better than you."

"If the blade of Caradar is the exile's blade, it holds power beyond its symbolism," Dargana said. "You claimed it, half-blood. You brought it back to Valnirata."

"This is sotting children's stories. Do you mean to tell me this is why you dragged me into...?"

Chriani's horse faltered. Its ears pricked up, head pulling to the left in a way that told Chriani it had sensed something in the silence.

He had his bow out, an arrow drawn and nocked. Guiding the horse with his knees as he let his senses slip out to seek any sound, any movement. The scrubland was breaking around them, the edge of the pine bluff ahead. No real screen of trees to worry about, but the grass could hide vipers or scorpions. Wolves and lions also prowled the exile lands, though they seldom ventured this close to the Wayroad.

He saw nothing. Heard nothing. Only the sound of hoofbeats rising where Kathlan and one guard were running an outrider pattern toward them.

"Discard some arrows," Dargana said quietly. "Anyone who can count will know you haven't shot today."

She was right. A faint anger twisted through Chriani as he let six arrows drop unseen behind him before he spurred ahead.

When they had drawn close enough, the ranger hailed him. Walaric, Chriani remembered.

"Well met, lord. We were worried when we lost you on the road."

"Three riders fleeing," Chriani said. "No way to catch them in the scrub, but we made sure they didn't circle back."

"Understood, lord. Our concern was more for the status of the Ilvani envoy."

Chriani felt the challenge left hanging in the words. Knew the best way to deal with them. He rounded on the ranger, summoning up a rendering of Ashlund from any number of his own memories. "Dargana rode out into fire, same as you, Walaric. If I ever need your assessment of the loyalty or effectiveness of anyone in this squad, you'll know it first. Is that clear?"

The guard stared coldly for a moment. "Wilric, lord. Walaric waits for us at the Wayroad."

Chriani sat his horse in silence a moment. Then he spurred past. Wilric took up a position to his left, Dargana and Kathlan on his right. As they rode, from the corner of his eye, he saw Dargana smile.

They passed from the Clearwater Way just after dusk, a haze of faint light ahead marking the transition from the exile lands. The Wayroad ended in Werrancross, the great fortress city that marked the start of the defended western frontier of Aerach, and whose place at the mouth of the Hunthad River made it a gateway for ship trade to Brandishear and Elalantar beyond.

The cloud gathering over the past two days had turned to a haze of cold rain well before sunset, behind which the lights of Werrancross were veiled. The city wasn't their destination, though. Among the few clear details of Chriani's orders were the need to maintain a low profile in Aerach while they met up with a squad of rangers out of the capital at Aleran, arranged by the Prince High Chanist's magical messaging. Even with their Aerach escort, they would be traveling as a group of most unofficial emissaries, making their way into the Greatwood quietly. Any contact with the Ilvani would be made with no direct connection to either crown.

Against that secrecy, they would at least be able to travel more openly in Aerach. All four nations of the Ilmar had their share of Ilvani, many of them generations removed from the Valnirata and the Migration Wars that had pushed the most warlike of their people back to the forest that had been their greatest domain. As such, for Dargana to be seen riding with the rangers would raise fewer glances along the trade roads than it would have among the patrols of the Clearwater Way.

At a tumbled series of stone cairns that marked the edge of the first of Werrancross's many outskirts villages, Chriani called a halt. The rangers were all hunched under their cloaks, the lead and rear riders bearing lanterns that set a rippling light around them, the road a meandering slick of mud that vanished before and after them into shadow.

"Time to find shelter for the night," Chriani called. "Head out by twos for the nearest lights, two groups east, one north. I'll take the south. Try to find a roadhouse that can hold us all, then return here. We'll compare notes and choose if there's a surplus, but I doubt there'll be many empty rooms in this weather."

The rangers nodded their understanding but kept a sullen silence as they lit more lanterns. The looks and tone of their whispered conversations had been darker than usual over the last of the journey, Chriani's inability to remember Wilric's name still burning in his mind. Hopefully, they would find accommodation with ale on tap so he could make amends. Or at least drink himself to the point where he no longer had to dwell on what the others thought.

"You'll ride with master Kathlan and I," he said to Dargana. His voice was louder than he liked, but he felt the need to create at least the illusion of authority over the exile. "Stay close." She was the only one of them riding uncovered, soaked to the skin and dark hair streaming behind her, but showing no sign of discomfort or care. She raised her hand in a bad mockery of the full salute. The last of the guards watched darkly as they spurred away.

Chriani had spotted a circle of distant firelight to the south, almost from the moment they'd crested the last of the hills that marked the transition from scrubland to the broad fields and terraced slopes of Aerach's northwest frontier. He hadn't called it out to the others because he worried about whether only his eyes had pulled the flicker of flame out of the darkness. He judged it as the closest possible stopping place, though, hoping to be back to the meeting point before the others if he could. Not wanting to give them time alone, standing in the rain, to grow even more dissatisfied with his leadership.

As they spurred toward the light, they found themselves following a track whose mud-filled ruts would have wallowed any wagon on the road this night, but which the horses navigated with ease. As they drew closer, though, Chriani quickly came to understand that the firelight he'd seen wasn't a village as he hoped but some kind of wagon camp.

A broad grove of trees was lit up brightly by colored lamps, Chriani catching sight of a dozen or more horses sheltered there. Six traveling wagons were pulled in tight to the edge of the wood, where a hollow marked out a grove alive with the light of a huge bonfire. He could make out at least three dozen figures sitting there, safe from the rain beneath trees or arrangements of colorful sheets of canvas staked out and extended from the wagon roofs. He saw children dancing, mugs passed around the fire. The smell of roast meat and the sound of singing hung on the air.

Kathlan and Dargana slowed up, Chriani taking the lead as they approached the fire. It wasn't the shelter he was looking for, but if the search for inns failed, it would make a better fallback than sleeping rough or seeking out other forest shelter in the dark.

From the shadows at the back of one wagon, a figure dressed in brown and green stepped into the light. An older male, greying hair tied back beneath a broad-brimmed hat, and a peaceful expression on his face as he approached. Chriani slowed to a stop a few strides away, nodded in greeting.

"Chriani of the Prince's Guard of Brandishear," he called. "Traveling with a squad of seven and seeking shelter."

"Maron," the figure replied. He reached out his hand to touch Chriani's, grasping it in an unfamiliar gesture. Different customs in Aerach, he guessed, but he matched Maron's firm grip.

"I have guards checking the local villages for inns, but if we come up empty, we would be grateful to join you here. Shelter our horses in the wood, share your fire. We can pay for…"

Maron shook his head emphatically. "You and yours are welcome, friend, if you wish. But please, you're drenched. Come and warm yourselves before you turn back to seek your companions."

His accent was odd to Chriani's ear, but he couldn't place it. Not an Aerachi dialect, but still familiar. A faint hint of the soft lilt of Ilvani to it somehow. "You are gracious, friend, but we should…"

Chriani's voice was cut to silence, his throat closed off by a sudden tightness. He was looking past Maron, idly scanning a trio of children that had pressed close to the edge of the firelight to watch him.

A figure stepped out from behind the children. Chriani recognized her even in first silhouette. The spill of bronze hair caught the gleam of lanterns behind her, the grey that touched that hair turned to an even deeper red by the light of the fire. She stepped toward them, smiling a greeting.

"Chriani?" It was Kathlan's voice at his shoulder, wary. Alert. He heard the rattle of steel that was her hand on the hilt of her rapier, Chriani's own hand shooting up to stop her.

"It's all right," he said, but he made the moonsign in spite of himself.

Maron laughed to see it. "You won't need that here, friend. Come. The night's too cold for waiting."

Chriani had wanted to kill the prince high. The memory in his mind now, coming unbidden. Breaking through the shadow, forcing itself up like bile, like water from the lungs of the near drowned. He was bound to kill the prince high. Had ridden back west across the Clearwater Way with no other thought in his mind, knowing it was his fate and the end to everything he was. Knowing he had no reason to turn away from that fate.

In the end, he had found his reasons. Two of them, turning him from that path. Lauresa's grief, which he'd felt in three days of her opening herself to him after what seemed a lifetime of yearning. A heart so perfect, so pure in her that she couldn't hate her father. Not even after knowing what he was. She was Chriani's first reason.

The figure who stood within the circle of lamplight, who had pleaded with Chriani for the life of the prince she had loved once, was the second reason. She was watching him now. Irdaign. Mother to Lauresa. Princess precedent of Brandishear. Wife to the Prince High Chanist before she was set aside a dozen years before.

She beckoned to him now. Then she turned and walked back into shadow.

"Kathlan. Stay with Dargana and the horses," Chriani heard himself say.

"Chriani, what...?"

"It's all right. I won't be long." His gaze flicked to Dargana, saw her watching him intently. Questions there, but none of Kathlan's uncertainty.

He swung down off his horse, heard Kathlan and Dargana do the same. With a nod, Maron led the two of them and the horses toward the wood even as Chriani paced away. Following Irdaign where she had disappeared from sight.

The Leisanmira. The accent he couldn't place. The wandering folk of the Ilmar, crossing all four principalities but never at home in any of them. The spell-singers, whose magic Lauresa had channeled in secret.

Magic her mother taught her. Chriani had heard the accent only once before, in a song Lauresa sang. Irdaign bore no trace of it that he had ever heard, though these were her people. Her past carefully reshaped by Chanist's advisers when she had married the prince high and left that life behind a generation before.

She was sitting on dry ground at the side of a small fire, set back from the larger central blaze. The other members of the wagon camp nodded to Chriani as he passed, smiling greetings but not speaking. He heard their voices ringing out in melodic whispers beyond him, though. Building songs in the shadows.

"It is good to see you, Chriani." Irdaign beckoned him to sit, Chriani nodding to her as he did. She offered him wine in a steaming mug, heady with the scent of fruit and spices. He shook his head, though. Already enough uncertainty to his thoughts.

"Why are you..." He took a breath, tried to focus. He fought the urge to make the moonsign again, knowing the insult it would seem to her. The fear of things he didn't understand. "How did you know I would come here? Or did you make this happen?"

"No one does my bidding against their will or knowledge, Chriani. Or at least not except by craft more subtle than what you would call magic. But I do have gifts, which speak to me at times. Small gifts that tell me of things that might come to pass."

Irdaign's tone was even as she spoke, the musical quality of her voice joining somehow with the songs rising around her. But to Chriani's ear, it carried an edge of something else as well. A thing he couldn't quite place.

"Do you know why I'm here?" he asked.

"I know some of it. I have no need to know all of it, if you worry that I have brought you here for questioning."

"I don't know what need for questioning you'd have so long as you can see what I do. See what I am with your sight."

Irdaign shook her head with a sad smile. "My sight does not see into you or any other, Chriani. And even if it did, overhearing word of secret envoys from Brandishear from couriers in the halls of Castle Osthegn is more dependable than the sight by far."

Chriani nodded, but he felt the shift in his mind that came with new knowledge. Something changed. "We were to be met by troops of Prince Vishod's from Aleran. What does Osthegn know of our mission?"

"Vishod has made his own alterations to Chanist's requests, I gather. He finds a measure of power in being able to accept a plan, then to alter it with impunity so as to not seem like Chanist's servant. The games princes play."

It sounded strange to Chriani's ear to hear her speak Chanist's name. A darkness to it as it churned his thoughts of what bound her and the prince high together. He couldn't look at her, stared to the fire instead.

"I have been told you travel south?" she asked.

Chriani nodded, not sure what he could tell her. Not sure what he should tell her.

"I warn you that the duke was not entirely happy with Vishod handing off Brandishear's request. But the rangers he has assigned to you know the southlands well, and they are blindly obedient to the duke. As he likes them."

"So why are you worried?" Chriani looked up again to meet her gaze. Saw acknowledgement there in the blue eyes. That worry was the edge he had heard in her voice before.

"The trinket you wear," she said. "At your belt. I sense its dweomer. New magic, and powerful. It seems out of character for you."

He thought for a moment of how to explain it. Decided in the end for the truth. "The Valnirata are hunting me," he said. "Because of... things to do with what happened before." He saw a flicker of pain in the blue eyes that told him Irdaign knew what he spoke of. "The badge keeps them from finding me."

"How long will you wear it?" Irdaign asked, and the question caught Chriani by surprise simply because it hadn't yet crossed his mind.

"I don't know." The fire was warm. Chriani's cloak had been soaking wet when he sat down, his clothes damp beneath his jacket and armor. They were almost dry now. "Why are you here, Irdaign?"

When she laughed, Chriani heard the sound spread around her. Unseen children picked it up as if it were some kind of game, their own laughter echoing back and around him as Irdaign spoke.

"I am here because I saw you here, Chriani. You are the reason, if reasons are something you feel compelled to pursue. I saw you seek me here, whether you knew it or not, and sensed that you had need of me. So speak that need, and I will help you if I can."

As Irdaign's words slipped through him, Chriani felt the moment seize around him. Against the firelight, the voices seemed to congeal like mist, hanging as echoes whose colors reflected the lamps shimmering in the wood. A child's voice rose above all the others, singing words he remembered.

Cal lun tau seryan ede to maynd
Lun tau seryan neld to caynd...

It was part of the only words of Leisana he would recognize. The language of the Leisanmira, and a song Lauresa had sung while he traveled with her. The "Ode of Seilonna" was a lament of leave-taking, the princess had said. It spoke of the road that leads endlessly away from home, never leading to what the traveler truly seeks.

Until Irdaign spoke, Chriani wouldn't have understood what his need was. He knew now.

"When I last saw the princess," he said carefully. "I gave her a gift." Irdaign made no response. Waiting. "No one knows where it is. Not even those few others who know of its existence. But some might try to find it. Tell Lauresa..."

The princess's name sounded wrong on his tongue. He felt a weight to it as he spoke, realizing how that weight came from the length of time since the princess had truly left his heart, left his thoughts. And even as she had left his thoughts, Chriani realized how those thoughts were clinging to a version of her that no longer existed.

Lauresa was a duchess's name now. Not a princess anymore.

"Make sure she understands that it's safer where it is now, safer with her, than it could be anywhere else."

"And those who seek it...?"

"Are my problem," Chriani said.

The degree of resolve in his own voice surprised him. The fear of having been hunted, the fear that came with magic he didn't understand, had been riding alongside him like an unseen companion since that day of stumbling upon the shrine in the deep wood. But Dargana's sudden interest in her Ilvani children's tales had muted that fear somehow. Reminding him that it was easy to be afraid of what you didn't know, but that simple fear would never stop him from fighting.

Irdaign nodded. "I understand. And what else?"

Chriani stared to the fire. He felt a different fear twist through him, of the weight of assessment and expectation in Irdaign's voice. He knew his fear of that voice and the power of the mind behind it, even as he hated himself for it.

She wouldn't need the sight, he told himself, to know his mind right now.

"Is she happy?" he said at last.

"As she can be, yes. Her daughter is a blessing in all ways, though a son would have suited the duke better. All things in time, though."

Chriani noted the subtle shift in Irdaign's voice. A sudden brightness to her words. A moment of a mother speaking of a daughter and granddaughter, setting aside other concerns.

There was no sign in that voice that she knew the truth, but Chriani couldn't look at her. Didn't know if he could accept seeing the recognition of that truth in her eyes.

The rain had lessened, he realized. The songs had shifted around him, punctuated by laughter. He felt an unexpected lightness threading his mind, and a warmth that was more than the fire.

He was happy for the fact that Lauresa could be happy. Knowing how that was all he'd ever have.

"I need to go," he said.

Irdaign stood as he did. "I'm sorry to have kept you, Chriani. But I am glad we spoke."

He nodded as he turned for the wood and the horses, but Irdaign stopped him with a hand to his shoulder.

"Do you trust me, Chriani? Enough to set aside your fear for a time?"

I'm not afraid of you. The urge to lie came quick and instinctive, but the words went unsaid. Only three meetings he'd had with Irdaign, and she had seen through to the truth of his heart from the first.

"I do."

"I would leave you with a charm of song. If you will allow me."

Chriani forced himself to nod. Knew he couldn't give himself time to think about it. Then Irdaign sang.

A warmth spread from her hand where it still touched him. Chriani felt that warmth trace its way across his shoulder, down his chest. It rested there for what seemed a very long time to the reckoning of his fear, though his distant consciousness counted out the song Irdaign sang in a measure of moments.

When she took her hand away, he looked down to see a mark at his armor. A sigil of light whose lines were Ilvani but not Ilvani traced themselves around the outline of a flower, five white petals ranged around a brilliant point of pure light. The mark vanished, but as it did, Chriani sensed its brightness follow the warmth, pushing down through armor and tunic to his skin. He felt it spread inside him, surround and press against the other magic he held. The steel ring worn openly at his finger, the golden disk hidden but exposed. The black ring tucked within its secret pocket at his belt, the dead talisman next to that.

"We would have you be safe in all things," Irdaign said when the sensation had passed. "It is a small magic that flows in me. A personal magic. But it might help you in time. Until our next meeting."

The question forced its way from Chriani's mind to his voice without him being able to focus it. He heard the words twisted by the fear still settling in him. "Have you seen that already? Our next meeting?"

"No. I only hope it."

Irdaign stretched up to kiss him on the cheek, Chriani realizing how slight the princess precedent was when she stood at his side. At all other times, he felt a power in her that made her presence seem larger. He walked away from her but glanced back once to see her standing tall again, drifting back into the shadows.

He touched his chest as he walked, felt nothing there but the warmth of the fire traced into his leather. He didn't make the moon-sign, though. He felt a kind of false pride in that as he found Kathlan and Dargana at the bonfire, motioned that it was time to go.

The horses were dry and suspiciously well rested, Chriani recognizing Kathlan's handiwork but suspecting that the Leisanmira who waved their goodbyes as they saw them off had some part in it. All of Kathlan's questions showed in her expression as they set off, lanterns deployed against the night and the rain that was starting heavy again. Chriani said nothing to her as they rode.

At the cairns, he saw light waiting that told him they were the last ones back. He ignored the rangers' dark looks, heard from Walaric — the real one this time — that they had found a roadhouse that would suit. Only two rooms left, but the innkeeper had promised to hold them and offered a stable with loft space for the rest.

"We were worried at your absence, lord," Wilric called out as they rode. Chriani heard the same challenge in his voice that he'd heard in the forest earlier that day, but he made a more measured response this time.

"I had arranged to meet with a messenger from Teillai. Word on our mission. I apologize for the secrecy."

When he spoke, it was with the clear purpose of Kathlan hearing, so Chriani wasn't surprised when she responded.

"Why Teillai? I thought our orders were to meet with Vishod's force out of Aleran?"

"Vishod changed the order," Chriani said. "Sotting princes playing games." Even as he said it, he felt himself hoping that Irdaign's information was correct.

The run-down condition of the roadhouse made it clear why two rooms had been open so late on a night of rain. However, the stables were dry, the stew piping hot, the bread fresh, and the ale better than Chriani had hoped. He ordered the squad off duty at once, letting them eat while he oversaw the stable grooms tending to the horses. He paid for two rounds at the bar in advance, the dark looks of at least a few of the rangers softening even as he left.

He arranged for Kathlan and Dargana to take one of the two rooms, then assigned the three rangers who would do watch for the night to share the other. It was part of the routine for any patrol, though Chriani doubted it would be necessary this deep into settled lands. He was fine with the stables, anxious to not undo whatever peace he'd made with the squad by taking the best for himself.

But at the back of his mind, lurking where he didn't want to have to see it, Chriani understood also how anxious he was to not talk to Kathlan. Not now, not tonight at any rate. He needed time for rest and silence in the aftermath of what Dargana had said that morning, and his conversation with Irdaign. Gathering his thoughts before the questions he knew were coming.

But as he entered the stables after eating, he saw Kathlan look up from where she was tending his horse.

Chriani had watched her go upstairs with Dargana at the end of the meal, was positive she hadn't slipped past him in the common room while he ate by himself. Out through the window, he guessed. Knowing she needed to catch him off guard. He made a note of the proximity of the two other rangers bunking in the loft, heard them talking quietly to each other. He tried to find the appropriate tone to ask what Kathlan was doing, but she beat him to it.

"I wanted to check his feet before I slept, lord." She spoke just loud enough for the rangers above her to hear. "A lot of running in the woods today."

"You should be with Dargana." All Chriani could think to say.

Kathlan's voice quieted, pitched only for his ears now. "We'd best make this quick then."

Her dark eyes met his, Chriani silent a moment. Then he nodded as he knelt beside her, made it look like he was inspecting her handiwork as she used a hooked awl to pick debris from his horse's hooves and shoes.

"What did you and the Ilvani talk about today? What is it she doesn't want me to hear?"

"The same as you already heard in the throne room, plus some thought on where we're headed and what we might meet there. She won't talk in front of Chanist's rangers or Vishod's. Doesn't want to give up what she knows of the Ilvani in case the others turn on her before this is done."

"Who was it you met with tonight?" She asked the question almost before Chriani had finished speaking, no sense of how she had judged his first answer.

"I said it true before. An agent from Teillai. She wanted to tell me about Vishod's change of plans so I didn't look a fool when we meet the escort."

"She didn't look much like any guard scout to me."

"She wasn't. She's with the duke's household, came to us of her own accord. It's not important."

"Then how did you know to look for her there? The middle of a rainstorm, the middle of nowhere...?"

"The badge the prince's mage gave me does other things. Court magic. Messages."

The lies came too quickly sometimes. Too easily. Chriani saw Kathlan glance to the steel ring at his finger. He saw the question in her mind, was relieved when she asked another instead.

"So why did the message not come from Vishod himself?"

"I said before, it's princes' games, Kath. It's not important."

"Chriani..."

"I said it's not important."

His voice was barely a whisper, but the sharp bite of the command in his tone brought Kathlan's hand to a stop. She stared at the horse's hoof for a time as if searching for something. She picked at it a while longer, then collected her tools.

All of it was wrong, Chriani knew. He felt the anger churning in him. Recognized the particular darkness released in the act of him hating himself.

Kathlan needed the truth. He owed her the truth.

"Thank you, squire," was all he said as he stepped to the stable doors and slipped outside.

He shifted into the shadows between the stables and the inn's dark front door, so that he was waiting for Kathlan when she emerged just shortly behind him.

"Kath…"

"Sleep well, lord."

"Kath, don't do this." Chriani caught up to her fast pace, tried to slip in front to slow her but she was having none of it.

"Get out of my way…" Her elbow in his ribs came at full force, his boots digging in as she drove him back in the mud.

"Then stop and talk to me…"

"I can't talk when you've got nothing to say, Chriani."

"That's not fair. I've got things I can't say because I'm under orders, and I don't know what you want…"

"I want the truth!"

She stopped dead in the faint light from the inn's front windows. Chriani checked that well-fogged glass, scanned the shadows around them. No one there.

Kathlan's hands were locked to her side, one of them still holding her awl. Chriani fought the urge to step close to her, fairly certain how that would end.

"In the throne room…" Kathlan stumbled with the words, as if she was trying to sort them as she spoke. "You told the prince that you came to Rheran because Captain Rhuddry didn't believe Milyan about what happened with the Valnirata. Only you decided you were going to Rheran that night before you ever talked to Rhuddry or set eyes on Milyan's reports."

Chriani felt a chill settle in his heart. He tried to force his mind back to the events of that meeting with the prince, to remember exactly what he'd said. It was all shadow now, though. Too many lies told that night. Too many lies since.

"When you lie to me, I know it," Kathlan said. "Not always right away, and not always understanding the truth you won't tell me. But I can tell the lies, Chriani. You've given me far too much practice over time."

"Kath…"

"You can tell me there's things you're not allowed to say. I'm not asking for your secret orders or the sotting Valnirata's battle plans. But when you tell me you can't say it, I know when the truth is you can say it but you won't. So what do you want to say to me right now?"

She needed the truth. He owed her the truth.

"There are things I can't say to you now, Kath. I just need…"

She shook her head, pushed past him and was at the door in three strides.

"I love you, Kath."

Kathlan slowed for a single step but didn't stop. She didn't look back as she slipped inside.

That was the truth. But it was the only truth Chriani could offer her, and he had always known it wouldn't be enough.

That was the truth, and had been true even throughout everything that had happened. The dark path. His return from Aerach. Because all the while he had walked that path, every step he'd taken along the road back, Chriani understood that it had been Kathlan he'd been walking back to.

He had known then that if he lost her, he'd have nothing left. Had always known it. And so he lied to her, because he knew in his heart that if he ever told her the truth, it would take her from him. Force her away and push her to a place of hating him. No way to ever bring her back.

He made a circuit of the inn yard, checking on the first watch. Not a thing he needed to do, but he had to walk. When he was done walking, he returned to the loft, the other two rangers asleep. He set his bedroll as far from them as he could, waited in the darkness for a time while he listened to their steady breathing. He pulled the hunter's heart from his belt then, saw it still dark. He stared at it for a long while before he slipped it away again, then let himself sleep.

— CHAPTER 8 —

FOUR DAYS SOUTH

THE RAIN BROKE BEFORE dawn, the squad already awake and fed and ready to ride. Chriani had been the first one up, relieving Beah on last watch and telling her to take more sleep if she could. When he heard the first stirrings in the stables, he waited out of sight behind the inn. As expected, Kathlan was outside a short while later, Dargana in tow as she went to check the horses' morning feed.

The rangers were in good spirits as they ate, the general mood of the squad having improved over a dry night and with the promise of better weather ahead. Kathlan's mood compensated, though, when she appeared in the common room just long enough to snatch up bread and cold beef to take back with her to the stables. Her silence was knife-sharp, her gaze ignoring Chriani with great dexterity. Dargana was close behind her, Chriani catching the exile's dark eyes on him as she went.

They made good time on the road despite the mud, Chriani leading them along the main trade route for Aleran as Ashlund's orders had indicated. The capital city wasn't their destination, though. Instead, they were seeking a sprawling market village called Dunacha, a half day's ride into the farmsteads outlying Werrancross to the east. They followed merchant traffic to find it, the sun just past high as they rode through. Chriani spotted a tall league marker at the center of the village's broad central green. Three roads led off and away from it, heading back west for Werrancross, toward Aleran east and north, and to Teillai away to east and south.

Standing to the side of the Aleran road, away from the wagon traffic but still within easy sight, the Aerachi squad was waiting as expected. Six rangers and a lieutenant, all in green and grey. The eagle of Aerach was embossed on black leather at their shoulders. But on their saddlebags, Chriani saw the lion that was the sigil of Teillai and Castle Osthegn.

The games princes play, Irdaign had said. He likely wouldn't have noticed without her warning.

As the Brandishear rangers approached, a tall figure at the head of the Aerachi squad nodded toward the far edge of an adjacent willow copse. The two groups converged there, farther from the crossroads and well out of earshot of any traffic. Chriani saw eyes on him from the Aerachi side, felt the gaze of his own rangers just as strong at his back.

He had no idea what to do, he realized. No idea of what official greetings he should be making, no idea of the Aerachi salute. Thankfully, a lack of knowledge had never slowed him down before.

"Well met," Chriani called. In the absence of a salute, he gave a full nod. "I'm Sergeant Chriani. I trust the weather on the road from Teillai was drier for you than the Werrancross road was for us last night."

He caught a flicker of surprise in the Aerachi leader's expression as he reined to a stop. "Well met to you, and Lieutenant Venry at your service." He returned Chriani's nod, though not as deep. "Duke Allenis Andreg sends his favor, and his apologies that the squad of the Prince High Vishod's guard meant to meet you were unexpectedly reassigned."

Chriani gave a shrug of well-practiced indifference. "On the contrary, I welcome it. The rangers of Teillai know the Hunthad lands better than any. I'm sure you would have been Prince Chanist's first choice as escort if he hadn't known that seeking out the duke directly would have vexed your prince to no end."

From the corner of his eye, Chriani caught the Brandishear rangers' surprised reactions to his diplomatic tone. He knew that only Kathlan would recognize it for what it was, though — a blunt mimicry of Barien. It was the sergeant's voice he was using, and the appearance at least of his deft statecraft.

"Indeed," Venry said. "I understand that you are in command?" An unexpected emphasis on the last word.

"I am. And am surprised, frankly, to see a lieutenant sent out as escort for a sergeant's squad."

"As surprised as the duke was to hear that an acting sergeant had been entrusted with such a mission."

And so the diplomacy ended. Chriani smiled. "I appreciate, then, what manner of punishment the duke must have felt you owed for him to have set you the assignment."

From the dark looks that flashed between the Aerachi rangers, Chriani guessed that he had hit close to the truth. Venry simply nodded. "My squad is at your command then, sergeant. And we would appreciate you naming our destination."

"Seeing as I've never been there, I've got no way to know the name, lieutenant. I'll be trusting you for that. I can give you directions, though. We follow the Hunthad along the frontier and into the Valni-rata lands."

"To arrive where?"

"We'll know when we…"

Chriani was interrupted by a shout from behind Venry, catching both him and the lieutenant by surprise.

"Blood and fucking moonsign… They ride with Ilvani!"

One of the Aerachi riders bolted forward. The only female in their squad, she was tall and imposing, scale mail at her neck and shoulders over well-worn leather. Before Chriani or Venry could so much as move, she had pushed forcefully ahead and into the Brandishear squad. The rangers pressed back in alarm, horses blowing their agitation as the Aerachi warrior's steed pushed in tight against Kathlan and Dargana.

"Jeradien!" Venry called. "On me, now!"

The ranger made no sign that she heard him. Chriani caught a flash of blades as he wheeled around, Dargana and Jeradien both drawing as one. They were a kind of mirror image with their black hair and eyes, and a matching ferocity in those eyes that Chriani could see. Dargana slashed axe and bloodblade across each other and into a defensive pos-ture, the Aerachi's longsword angled to block her body.

"What treason is this?" the ranger Jeradien shouted. Her gaze dart-ed from Dargana to her lieutenant, her rage palpable. "The orders said nothing about an Ilvani…"

"Your orders are the same as our orders," Chriani said, cutting her off. "To be envoy to the Valnirata. Were you not expecting to meet Ilvani along the way?"

Jeradien drew herself up to her full height. For one long moment of uncertainty, Chriani was certain she would have tried to cut him down if Dargana had been close enough to catch on the backswing.

Unlike in Brandishear, it was unusual to find females in the guard of Aerach, Chriani knew. Eighty leagues from Rheran as the hawk would fly it, but this land might as well have been a world away. Though not specifically excluded from service, women remained rare in uniform be-cause the principality's laws favored a strict political patriarchy. Most who sought out military service were found in the ranks of the healers when they were found at all. Among the officers of Aerach, women were all but nonexistent, with those holding the necessary combination of as-piration and connections set for marrying instead. More valuable to their families as tokens of alliance than as champions of real power.

Chriani had ignored the affairs and customs of Aerach and the other Ilmar principalities for most of his life, and been happy while he did it. Then the proclamations came to say that the Princess Lauresa was to marry in Aerach. He had learned a lot since then.

He worked himself closer to Jeradien, to keep her from focusing on Dargana if nothing else. "Back away now, soldier, or your hand becomes a trophy."

"You dare…"

"I won't be the one taking it."

In all the tension of the standoff, Dargana hadn't moved. Hadn't spoken. She was watching Jeradien, eyes wide and unblinking. Breathing slowly. Her mare likewise stood motionless, even as the other horses felt the rising tension and attempted to shift away from each other, not wanting to be crowded if the command came to fight or flee.

Chriani's own horse started underneath him. Venry was pushing between the two of them, both horses shifting back, heads up to show their wariness. "Jeradien," the lieutenant called, "you will stand down now." It took a long moment of waiting before the Aerachi ranger flicked the reins to send her horse stepping back. At once, Venry had turned on Chriani instead.

"My squad, sergeant." The lieutenant's voice was pitched to carry to Chriani's squad and his own. A challenge issued. "My ranger. If you presume to give orders to her or anyone else under my command again…"

"If you want my silence, Venry, then keep your squad under control."

"I'll have respect from you, sergeant…"

"You'll have what respect you earn, lieutenant. And you're spending far more than you're earning right now."

The look of outrage on Venry's face was steel-hard as Chriani slipped his horse past him, facing off against the Aerachi rangers where they stood still circled. His eye swept the road to see a pair of horses being walked there, a line of farm ox-carts heavy with late hay working their way through the mud.

"I'll say this once." He pitched his voice to carry to both squads around him, but so that no one else would hear. "This is Dargana of the Crithnalerean. She rides with Brandishear because she hates the Valnirata Ilvani with as much passion as any of you. She's likely killed more of them than have any of you. She has my trust and the trust of the Prince High Chanist. That's my first and last word on this."

In the words, in his gaze as he met the eyes of the Aerachi one by one, Chriani felt all his memories of Barien twisting through him. The strength of the warrior's voice, the evenness of his tone. Always careful to never let an order turn to anger, even as anyone who heard Barien's orders understood the anger the sergeant was capable of if those orders were ignored. Chriani had heard those orders in the dust of the training ground, on short patrol around Rheran. He had heard them on the longer journeys that had taken him across Brandishear with Lauresa, Barien guarding the princess with a single-minded determination, Chriani at his side.

As a child, not long after he'd been taken in by Barien, Chriani had asked the sergeant why he'd never made higher rank. He was surprised when the warrior told him he'd never tried. "You could have title," Chriani had said. "You could have all the soldiers taking your orders, not just some."

Barien had laughed at the time. "The power to give orders don't come with title, boy. Power comes from others having your back when the title stops meaning anything. When you're captain in the barracks, you've got whole companies saying they'll stand behind you. But pushing through mud on a battlefield, cut off from the front line and nowhere to run but into swords, plenty of captains find out just how far behind them their troops are standing."

"But why can't you do both? Be someone who can make others follow you first? Then get your title when you know you're good enough?"

The warrior had grown more thoughtful then. "Because by the time you've become good enough to be someone others will follow, you've learned that the title isn't important anymore."

Chriani waited until he heard Venry moving at his back before he wheeled his horse, stepping it forward to block the lieutenant's path.

"I know what your orders are," he said, still speaking loud enough that the other rangers could hear him. "I know the duke who gave them to you, and I can guess how it rankles him to have to play Vishod's games. Denying Chanist's request for the prince's own escort so he can distance himself from our effort if it fails. But your duke commands you, and any of you who can't fulfill that command, anyone who doubts the importance of this mission, ride back to him now and make your excuses."

He remembered Irdaign's talk of the obedience of Andreg's troops to their duke. He understood the difference of how far they'd stand behind him or that duke in the battles Barien had spoken of.

Dargana still had her weapons drawn. Chriani met her gaze, slapped his own scabbard as a warning. Slowly, she returned the axe to her belt, sheathed the bloodblade behind her. As she did, Venry jerked his reins to spin away from Chriani. He took his place at the head of the Aerachi contingent, Jeradien falling in behind him.

"How long to the Greatwood along the river?" Chriani called to the lieutenant.

"Four days south from Werrancross," Venry said coldly. "If your squad can keep up."

Chriani ignored the insult as he found Jessa in the Brandishear squad, waved her toward the Teillai road to the south that was their first course. Then because he didn't know any of the other Aerachi's names, he called to Jeradien, spurred close to her. "Our best scout is Jessa, but you know your frontier better than any of us. Take point with her, keep a good pace."

The tall ranger made no eye contact with Chriani, looking to Venry for his nod before she spurred ahead.

The squads fell into two lines behind their respective scouts, Venry riding the outside as if to put as much distance between himself and Chriani as he could. Chriani let himself fall back like he was watching behind them, but it was Kathlan he rode up to where she brought up the rear.

"I need you to keep an even closer eye on Dargana. Stay between her and the Aerachi if you can."

"As you say, lord."

The distance between the two of them gave her voice the crispness of new ice underfoot. Chriani tried to soften his own tone, tried to focus. Conscious of a sudden brittleness to his thoughts. "It's not her I'm worried about, mind you. It's any Aerachi that gets close enough to her…"

"As you say, lord."

Dargana was riding outside on the Brandishear side. Kathlan spurred ahead to slide in beside her, not looking back.

The weather stayed clear for the remainder of the day, though cloud from the north came and went as the rangers rode. They made good time with Jeradien and Jessa leading them, the landscape not much changed from Brandishear but wholly unfamiliar all the same.

Though the Greatwood was still too far away to be seen, its green darkness loomed along the horizon to the south and west. But the juxtaposition of sun and forest created along that horizon seemed wrong to Chriani somehow. A lifetime in Brandishear had fixed the impression in his mind of the Greatwood standing always south and east, far out of sight but gleaming green along the horizon with the light of each rising sun. Here, though, the sun slowly falling marked the unseen wood as they rode, a line of shadow spreading to the west. No glimmer of mountains seen as the day was swallowed by the distant trees.

They set camp the first night well past dusk, a good distance from the road and out of sight of the last farmstead village they had passed. Both squads ate field rations over a shared fire, but there was precious little conversation between them. Jeradien and Dargana both stayed in their tents.

Chriani's only conversation with Venry involved the setting of the watch, the lieutenant's tone cold. He ignored that tone as he offered to take the first watch himself with one of Venry's rangers. Knowing he wasn't likely to sleep anytime soon. He hoped the tangible tension in both squads would settle during the next day's ride, but expected that he was hoping in vain.

The Hunthad River marked their movement toward the frontier starting on the second day. They crossed its muddy waters as the sun was reaching high, taking a broad stone bridge that arced up and over a rushing narrows, just past where the trade road curved east for Teillai. Chriani knew from experience that the river could be forded in winter when its waters were low, though he was happy to not have to do so now. But it was that memory that caused him to feel the landscape's sense of strangeness shift to an unexpected and unwelcome familiarity.

As the less-traveled track they followed twisted south, he recognized the wild meadowlands through which he and Lauresa had emerged from Ilvani territory. The unmarked and shifting boundary between the exile lands of Crithnalerean and their current destination of Laneldenar to the south. Memories of that flight were a year and a half old but still fresh in his mind. Not like the memories of the Bastion, wrapped now in their own sense of distance. These were raw as yesterday's thought, even as much as Chriani wanted to push them away.

As he'd expected, the angry silence hanging over both squads the first day had worn on and grown even heavier by the time they stopped for the second night. Jeradien and Jessa led them to a collection of farmsteads whose stables were large enough to accommodate the horses of both squads. The rangers pitched their field tents in the adjacent just-mown meadow, Dargana and Kathlan's set at a distance and the exile kept well out of sight.

It took the farm families inviting the rangers to share their communal meal for the animosity of the Brandishear and Aerachi squads to finally melt. As they were in Brandishear, patrols were commonplace through the frontier farmsteads of Aerach, and as the rangers gathered around a large firepit for spit-roasted pig and the last of the season's sweet corn, their hosts showed a profound lack of curiosity about their presence. The uniforms of Brandishear were noted, with Chriani having briefed all the rangers to explain that they were traveling to the great southern citadel at Doniver to exchange training with the Aerachi. However, the farm folk were more interested by far in tales of raids and Ilvani slain, and the rangers of both principalities were more than happy to share them.

Chriani spent the meal drifting back and forth between the fire and the tents, bringing food to Kathlan and Dargana while explaining to the farm folk that one of his rangers was resting an injured leg. While at the fire, he spent more time listening than talking, hearing the tales turn bolder as the spiced wine began to flow. He was surprised to find that he had heard of more than a few of the Brandishear rangers' exploits, including Daellyn and Wilric's part in defending the southern city of Kaeralith from wolf-rider raids out of the mountains the previous winter.

He was more surprised by far to hear the tale told by two of the Aerachi rangers. A daring raid into the Crithnala lands in deep winter of the year before, they said. Perhaps the local folk had heard of it? When the Princess Lauresa of Brandishear had been taken by mad monks along the Clearwater Way, it was the rangers of Teillai who brought her home.

Chriani said nothing as he listened. He marked the names of the two rangers doing the talking — Nyduri and Tenry — and made a point of following them back to the tents as the fire burned down and the watch was set, the farm folk already returned to their homes.

The Clearmoon had been waxing full since the rain passed, almost daylight bright to his eyes now. He approached the two quietly from behind while they pissed at the edge of the tents' field of lantern light, trusting to the warmth of the wine and their murmured laughter to cover any sound of his approach. He listened to their talk turn to Dargana, as he'd hoped it would.

"Too long since I rode the exile lands," one of them said, Chriani not sure which. "But I'll tell you true, I'll see one less Crithnala on this side of the Hunthad the first time Sergeant Sackless lets his Ilvani scut off the leash."

Chriani sent his foot between the speaker's legs, then twisted to drop him. He took advantage of the second figure's surprise to spin, driving in with a roundhouse kick that sent the Aerachi to the ground beside his friend. Both the rangers staggered to their feet, fumbling the laces of their leggings as they backed up, screaming profanities that Chriani didn't know. Different customs in Aerach.

Both stopped shouting when they saw it was him, but he felt quite certain that their silence had more to do with the footsteps racing in from all sides. Rangers of both squads were bringing light, slowing as they circled. In the glare of lanterns, he could see where both Nyduri and Tenry had pissed themselves when they fell.

Chriani saw Daellyn and Wilric before him, didn't look to see who else was at his back or how far behind him they stood. Waiting only until the crowd had settled before he spoke.

"You're a peace envoy and you'll act like it. Whether it's in your nature, whether you like it or not, whether you can even spell *peace* with all the letters given to you. I hear another word from either of you on Dargana, or on your exploits in Crithnalerean, I'll send you both back to Teillai slung over the same horse. You have anything to say back to me?"

A long silence hung. From the corner of his eye, Chriani saw Venry pace around him to draw the two rangers' line of sight. The lieutenant's look carried a white-hot rage, but whether it was inspired more by his troops or by him, Chriani didn't know.

"I have a question, lord."

Jeradien called out from behind him. Chriani turned back, one eye still on the two rangers, wary.

"You didn't share much in the way of your exploits at the fireside tonight." The tall ranger's voice was ice. "I would have liked to hear of your experience in the field, vast as I'm sure it is."

"If there's ever a day I feel the need to impress you, you'll know it," Chriani said. The words were Barien's, a favorite saying of the sergeant's when dealing with those he had no interest in dealing with. But before Jeradien could speak again, another voice rose from the shadows.

"Sergeant Chriani took command of his squad outside Alaniver, on the Calalerean frontier, two weeks past when our troop sergeant took an arrow to the heart." Kathlan stepped into the circle of light. She was in loose leggings and a tunic, like she might have been sleeping, but her hand was set on her sword belt, her rapier hanging there. "He took her off her horse as she died, led two squads out of the Greatwood at speed, firing all the way. Dropped back to lead a sneak attack on their flank that got us clear in the end."

She ignored Chriani as she stepped up to Jeradien, green eyes flashing like emerald fire. If she cared that the Aerachi ranger towered almost a full head taller than her, she made no sign. "We left a half-dozen Ilvani dead that day, but Chriani went back for more. He led the capture of four of them, then captured magic in the deep wood that the war-mages are still looking at. Nine days later, he and I were fighting a Calalerean war-band that struck inside Rheran itself. He killed four that I saw, but it was dark. I might have missed one. Later that same night, Chriani sat with the Prince High Chanist and Captain Ashlund of the prince's guard in private meeting in the Bastion throne room. Now he's here. You have any other fucking questions?"

No one spoke. Jeradien's dark eyes flicked from Kathlan to Chriani with undisguised hatred, but her look cooled when she met Venry's gaze.

The lieutenant broke the silence to relieve Chriani of the awkward obligation. "We have two more day's hard riding ahead of us at least. We should all take our rest."

The way he spoke, it wasn't an order, Chriani noted. Though it looked like doing so had cost the lieutenant significant effort.

He nodded. "Troop dismissed," he said.

Kathlan was the first to turn and go.

Chriani wandered the edge of the makeshift encampment for a while, wanting to give tempers time to cool and needing to be nowhere within earshot until they did. In the moon's-light, his eyes had no trouble spotting one of the two he'd attacked — Nyduri or Tenry, he still didn't know which — slipping into Jeradien's tent. The tall ranger's anger made more sense suddenly, even as it suggested that anger wasn't likely to flag anytime soon.

From his own rangers, Chriani was surprised to receive actual salutes as he passed Wilric and Jessa on first watch. A subtle change in their attitude toward him, though how much of that was his standing up to the Aerachi and how much was Kathlan's impassioned speech, he didn't know. As he slipped to his tent and beneath his bedroll, Chriani found himself suffering from the faint hope that whatever other complications were bound to come his way, leading the Brandishear rangers might have become easier at least.

He just had absolutely no idea what he was leading them into.

They crossed the loop of the river again just after setting out the next morning. That second crossing was a military ferry, two squads of guards stationed at either end. They would keep the water on their right now, following it for fifteen leagues more and watching as they drew closer to the wall of the forest, rising to the west. The field maps he had obtained from the Bastion libraries showed that where the river met the Great-wood, it would turn due south. Crossing over into Valnirata territory, and marking the meeting place Dargana had said they were bound for.

Beyond the ferry, the cart roads grew sparser. The farmsteads began to cluster tight around fortified towns protected by patrols from Teillai and Doniver, the river winding on toward the still-unseen forest. They shadowed that water throughout the day, stopping the night at a hilltop farmstead whose houses sat behind a stockade wall that was brightly lit by watchfires even before dusk. As with the previous night, they slept in a quickly assembled camp but ate with the farm folk, then paid for the gift of the meal by purchasing oats for the horses, replenishing the stores that the Brandishear contingent had used up along the Clearwater Way.

The mood at the evening meal was a great deal quieter than it had been the previous night. That suited Chriani fine.

As in Brandishear, the folk of the Aerach frontier made no secret of their respect for the patrols of the prince's guard. Most of the frontier farmsteads held back a fixed portion of their harvest and goods, whether root crops for storage, smoked meats, oats or autumn fruit. They kept it set aside and ready for when the patrols passed, selling it for minimal cost, or sometimes just offering it in thanks.

Close by the farmstead stood one of the leaguestones Chriani had noticed for the first time that morning, just beyond the ferry. These were border markers consisting of unadorned standing stones, whose weather-beaten look spoke to how long ago they'd been placed there. From time to time throughout the day, he had also noticed ash-grey Il-vani arrows shot into lone trees well on the wrong side of those stones.

The Brandishear border held no such formal markers, but Chriani recognized that the true frontier on both sides of the Greatwood was marked off not by stone or trees, but by a near-identical swath of open rangeland that fronted those trees. An empty space into which the set-tlers of Aerach and Brandishear knew not to tread, understanding that as much as anything else, the border of Valnirata stood where the pa-trols of Ilmari and Ilvani alike said it stood.

Their fourth day out from Werrancross, Chriani's troop sighted that unseen border with the sun at its height. The rough track they had been following broke at last from the Hunthad, curving off east toward the Doniver townships, so they left that track to follow the river across open grassland. League after league, they watched the shadowed wall of the forest slowly appear, curving out and across their path. The muddy course of the Hunthad twisted its way toward those trees, distant and bright beneath clear sky.

Jessa and Jeradien were riding point, two others from the Aerachi squad up front to keep them in sight. As Chriani watched the dark stain of the forest ahead, Lieutenant Venry spurred up to his side.

"Is there a meeting point to be recognized?" he asked. "And will we reach it before dusk?"

"The Ilvani will find us," Chriani said, remembering Dargana's words from the throne room. "Hopefully tonight, but I don't know exactly." He glanced back to the exile, riding behind him with Kathlan close at her side. "We cross the frontier and wait."

Venry's snort of frustration was audible, but Chriani didn't bother with a response.

"With no messages run, how do you expect them to know where we are?"

"I expect them to be watching from the far side of the river. I expect they've been doing so since we left the ferry behind, marking our progress."

Venry shook his head with a certain amount of satisfaction. "I've had my best outriders watching. They've seen no sign."

"Neither have I. Which is what makes me think they're out there. When the carontir along the Brandishear wood want you to see them, you see them."

A smirk touched Venry's lips as he slipped back to the side rank. "Your tactical acumen is impressive, sergeant. I thank you for sharing it."

Chriani was hoping, in truth, for contact before dark. But as they advanced along the river and the wall of the Greatwood rose ever higher, he judged the press of wet grey cloud following them from the north and called a halt well before dusk. They had more than enough daylight left to enter the Greatwood, but setting a camp within the darkness of the forest wasn't something he had any urge to try.

He sent one of the Aerachi riders forward to call Jessa and Jeradien back. Jeradien returned but sullenly reported to Venry, so Chriani talked with Jessa about potential sites for a camp.

"We saw just the place," the scout said. "There's a ruin, top of a rise due south. Be there in good time, and plenty of view to all sides as long as the weather holds."

Chriani gave the order and Jessa led the way. The site was as she described it — a broad, smooth hill with a rough circle of foundation stones a dozen paces across, set with crumbling mounds of rock poking out from under overgrown turf. It made for an excellent observation point and defensive position, even as its tumbled stones would create a break from the wind, rising now from the north. They were still a good distance from the forest, but Chriani could hear that wind stir the sentinel trees of the Greatwood to a steady droning hiss.

The horses were tended within a narrow poplar grove, the tents pitched on open ground. As the rangers set camp, Chriani wandered the hillside to gaze out at the forest, the swells and valleys of its canopy shifting beneath the light of the falling sun. He was thinking hard about what their next move would be if the Ilvani didn't make their presence known. Wondering how long the rangers should wait for them, or whether to enter the forest at once. How to set patrols, how far to press into the wood. He would need to talk to Dargana in private, but he knew that any approach to her involved talking to Kathlan first. Not sure it was a conversation he was ready for.

Along a narrow ridge to the north, the encircling rubble of the hill was punctuated by three larger standing stones. Part of the gatehouse, perhaps, of whatever fort or frontier guard post this had once been. The stones were too old by far to have been raised during the Incursions. However, many older sites had been rebuilt or repurposed as staging grounds and watchtowers during that conflict, then torn down by the Ilvani as Aerach and Brandishear pulled back from the frontier in its aftermath. Despite their proximity to the forest, there was no mistaking the plain construction of the stone slabs as Ilmari work. Though cracked with age and weather, their original construction was still visible, clean and plain. None of the dangerous beauty the Ilvani imbued into all their craft.

"We're ripe for ambush here."

Venry's voice sounded out from behind him, Chriani turning to see the lieutenant pacing his way up the hillside, hand at his scabbard.

"You know a place half a league from the Greatwood and a day's ride from the nearest city that isn't ripe for ambush, I would have been happy to hear about it earlier."

"Quick with mockery." Venry took on a distracted tone as he circled Chriani, creating the sense that he was talking to someone else. "Even quicker to anger from what I've seen. No real sense that you care whether it's guards or officers at the wrong end of your invective."

"You have a point to follow the talking, lieutenant? Or is the talking really the best you get up to?"

"My point, Sergeant Chriani, is that if you're a sign of the caliber of commission in Brandishear of late, I have great fear for the Ilmar's future. This close to the Greatwood, when the Ilvani come calling, I don't plan to be sleeping."

"We could set a watch," Chriani said brightly. "That would show them something. In fact, set the schedule yourself, and make sure you're on it."

Venry stepped closer, voice low. "Pretend to authority all you like. But you're a simple-minded mercenary with an insignia you haven't earned, boy…"

Chriani drove forward and down, slamming his head into Venry's chest. It was a well-practiced move among the Bastion guard, granting the advantage of leaving your hands and the target's face unbloodied when the counterattack came. It didn't help with the beating you'd take, but it looked good when you told the officers later how you'd been jumped without provocation.

Venry nearly lost his feet as he stumbled back, fighting to breathe and with murder in his eyes.

"Only one person called me *boy,*" Chriani said evenly. "And you're not him. That's a warning…"

"Fuck your warning, sergeant, and watch your back. There are a thousand ways to come to harm in the Greatwood."

"Is that a threat, lieutenant?"

"Just advice, lord."

"Thanks for that. I've seen a few of those ways myself, but I try not to get killed as often as I'm guessing you do…"

"Lords."

Kathlan's voice clipped Chriani's to silence, saving him from escalating his taunt in a way he knew he would have regretted. She had slipped up along a narrow track that swept the hillside, a rainwater rill carving a narrow channel through the grass. Her dark look told Chriani she was still focused on what had passed between them outside Werrancross, and that she had been listening to him and Venry since their exchange began.

"What is it?" Chriani said as he paced away from Venry. His hands were shaking, he realized.

"With understanding that you both clearly have more pressing personal business, I wish to report that we're being followed."

Dargana was already waiting for them, lying still and alone on a pitched rise to the north of the camp. She glanced back to see the three

— 161 —

of them approach, but said nothing.

"Dargana's the one who spotted it," Kathlan said as she motioned Chriani and Venry to follow her down to the ground. "First morning after Werrancross. So much traffic on the road then, I didn't think anything of it. Until the next morning, and the next. We've been watching. Making sure it's not just coincidence."

Chriani scanned the horizon from the adjacent forest to the more distant meadowlands. He saw nothing but the faint shimmer of the wind in the grass, but his silence gave Venry a chance to make his thoughts known.

"Ilvani." The lieutenant spat to the ground beside him, ignoring Dargana's dark look. "You've led us straight into…"

"No, lord," Kathlan interrupted. "And begging your pardon. We're followed not from the west but from behind. Were they to mark our movement, the Ilvani would be observed across the river or in the shadow of the trees."

At the echo of his own words to Venry, Chriani saw the lieutenant's expression darken. He refocused his gaze to the north, though.

"This is something else," Kathlan said. "They're square behind us, almost due north tonight. Following our path exactly. You can see them best at dawn when the light's off the meadow, but with the cloud breaking and bright sky…" She pointed. "Look there."

Chriani focused, unblinking. Beside him, Venry shaded his eyes. Before them was the flat of the river valley, a twisting course that faded quickly to become no more than a mud-brown stain against the green. The sky above was bright, though, the cloud to the north torn to threads by brisk winds. Caught side-on in that brightness, showing the gold shimmer of the sun setting now behind the forest wall, faint shapes marked the horizon.

"I see them," he said quietly.

"I don't." Venry's tone was cold, but Chriani had no doubt he spoke the truth. "You'll forgive my skepticism, sergeant."

"I would if I cared. Don't trust me, though. Trust Kathlan. Something's there."

A year and a half into service and Kathlan was already one of the best riders in the prince's guard. Called to the rangers as a tyro. Likely to make rank before the next High Summer unless Chriani held her back. Even if he hadn't loved her, Chriani understood that he would trust Kathlan with his life. A thing he vowed he would tell her before this night was done.

"Lack of traffic behind us notwithstanding," Venry said, "it could still be anything."

Dargana spoke then. "Not three days running by dawn and dusk, it couldn't. They're always a horizon away. A league, I'd mark it now. As far away from us as they can get while still seeing us ahead of them. Not trusting just to tracking. They're watching."

Chriani saw and felt a dark wave of animosity flicker in Venry's eyes. He realized this was the first time Dargana had spoken in the presence of any of the Aerachi rangers.

They were losing the light. He had no time for this.

"Venry, get your best rider. Kath, that's you for me. Pick the five freshest horses, get them ready to go. We need to take a look."

Kathlan's expression was still cold, but she met Chriani's gaze at least as she nodded. She rolled off the ridge and out of sight from the distant horizon before she stood, raced back to the camp at a run.

"Dargana, you'll come." Chriani still had no idea how much he could give the Ilvani in the way of orders, but he wasn't anxious to make it appear in front of Venry that he was begging her for favors.

"This is too much. I will not ride..." Venry started, but Chriani had his counter ready.

"You leave her here unguarded with your squad, you'll come back to half a squad and a nightmare's worth of reports to make to your duke, lieutenant. But more important than that, we're losing the light. We can make use of her eyes, especially if it is Ilvani watching us. If it's a ruse meant to split our forces, set a full watch with fires every twenty paces, archers at the ready behind the stones. Anything that comes in, they'll be able to see it before it reaches them. If it's us coming in, tell them to listen for the horn but not to drop their aim till they count all of us off. Call your rider, and quickly."

"Jeradien," Venry said coldly, his contempt for Chriani's orders clear. But he followed Kathlan's lead as he slipped back along the hillside, not rising until his body was blocked from sight to the north.

When the lieutenant had gone, Chriani spoke to Dargana. "Anything else I need to know that Venry can't?"

"How about your eyes being all the sight you need, half-blood?" Dargana smiled.

Chriani said nothing as he fished the talisman from the pocket of his belt. He cradled it in his hand to shade it from the light but saw it still quiescent. No pulse of red within its gold-clasped stone. He slipped it back as he motioned Dargana to follow him, shifting back along the hill, then away.

Kathlan had wrapped all the moving points of the horses' tack with felt to keep them quiet. However, the wind blowing strong from the north as they set out would do a better job of masking not just their sound but their scent as they made their way up and away from the river. Without the wind, it would have been impossible to range as far on horseback as Chriani knew they needed to without being heard. On foot, he wouldn't have liked their chances of reaching the target before full dark, the Clearmoon shimmering bright to east and north but not ready to rise.

He took them on a wide course off the track they'd followed through the day, looping south first, around the campsite hill and into a light screen of scrub trees that provided additional cover in the fading light. They were riding blind, shadowing the track they had followed during the day and hoping they didn't overshoot the resting place of the party behind them.

Chriani had no idea whether their pursuers would have moved off the track, but it was a safe assumption that they had no fire burning, for fear of it being seen from the rangers' camp. That camp was a bright distraction behind them now, watchfires lining the hill to crown it with bright points of flame in the gathering dark.

Venry made the ride in silence but stayed at Chriani's side, just behind Dargana on point. Jeradien shared her lieutenant's sullenness, but she kept well back even of Kathlan in the third rank, like she was obeying some need to stay as far from Dargana as possible.

They came in from the west, circling around through tangled groves of witchwillow between the trail and the river. When they had measured off a distance near to a league in Chriani's mind, they approached to within clear sight of the water, tethering the horses within the trees.

He used the fact of the pursuing party watching the rangers to his advantage, keeping the fires of the camp in view behind them. Just as those fires were nearly lost to sight, Chriani signaled for the others to slip forward in a single line. They moved with bows and blades at hand, crouched low and with Dargana leading. Chriani was behind her, the falling shadows bright around him, as he knew they were for her. Meadow grass muffled their footfalls, the wind still strong from ahead as they approached.

Dargana spotted the horse track through the trees, signaling a stop as she fell back. She motioned to the north, Chriani seeing a low rise set with moss-crusted rock that would have seemed only a smudge of darker shadow against the falling night to the others. He nodded, Dargana leading again as they dropped low to the ground to advance.

The crest of the rise provided a good vantage point, the last light of the sun sinking now beyond the looming forest behind them, setting a muddy haze against the cloud-streaked sky. Dargana scanned the shadows for a long while, Chriani trying to not make it obvious that he was doing the same.

"There," the exile hissed.

Chriani had spotted them even as she spoke. A faint blur of bright movement, barely visible even to his eyes. Horses at tether, figures moving around them. Two hundred paces away, he judged, and screened by scrub trees where the unknown pursuers had pushed back from the track but kept themselves within sight of it.

"Riders," Dargana whispered. The wind was rising, Venry and Kathlan pushing close to hear her. Jeradien stayed where she was. "A camp. Eleven horses that I can see."

"Ilvani?" Chriani was focused, trying to bring the glimmering shadows of the distant camp into detail.

"Ilvani don't make camp in the open while within sight of their own wood."

"We need to get closer," Venry whispered. "Or get some light on them. Startle them."

"And accomplish what?" Chriani asked.

"Let them know their secrecy's undone. If they're bandits, they'll break. If they're not…"

Chriani heard an unspoken thought left hanging in Venry's words as the lieutenant's gaze found his. "You think you know who this is," Chriani said flatly. No more than a guess, but Venry's expression told him he was right.

"The Prince High Vishod prides himself on his intelligence. He likes to keep his hand in all things. Especially where political advantage might be gained."

Chriani stared at the lieutenant a moment, incredulous. Then he looked out to the dark camp again, felt the pieces of his understanding shift. "Vishod sending to Teillai for this mission lets him keep his distance from it if it fails," he said darkly. "But he won't let the Duke Andreg take all the credit if it succeeds. You knew this, and when told that we were pursued, said nothing?"

"I suspected," Venry said sharply. "I already know which of my squad Vishod has paid to be his eyes and ears here, and how my orders will be mysteriously rewritten depending on the outcome of this futile exercise. But for him to take a more active stance is as much a surprise to me..."

"I don't doubt that the sun rising comes as a surprise to you..."

"Pardon me again, lords." Kathlan's whispered hiss from behind silenced them both. Even without the sharpness of his eyes, Chriani would have been able to read her annoyance. "It's getting dark. Whatever we're doing, it needs to be done quickly."

Chriani nodded. A decision made. "Return to camp, break at dawn. We set out south again, away from the forest. Find a good spot for a squad to hold back and out of sight. Wait for them to catch up, then surround and deal with them." He waited for Venry's nod, which was terse when it came. "Fall back," he whispered.

Jeradien and Kathlan began to slip down the ridge and into shadow, Venry after them. Chriani motioned Dargana to follow him.

The exile didn't move.

She was still flat to the ridge, still staring to the darkness ahead. No sign that she had heard or cared about the whispered conversation around her. A look of absolute fury was in her dark eyes. A look of recognition.

"You'll need light," she called, loud enough that Chriani knew she was talking to all of them above the hiss of the wind. "Don't let them ride." Then she launched herself over the top of the ridge and was running for the dark camp ahead.

"Treason-bastard!" Jeradien's cry sounded out like steel on steel. Chriani tried to grab the warrior as she hurtled past him, but he wasn't fast enough. Venry was shouting behind her, calling her to stop, but the Aerachi guard was gone after Dargana.

With a look back to Kathlan, Chriani was up and running, down the slope and into darkness.

— CHAPTER 9 —
ALL THERE IS

SHADOW WAS DROPPING around them, uneven ground threatening to send Chriani stumbling as he ran. He heard Venry and Kathlan behind him, felt the urge to give them an order, but he had no idea what to say. No idea who they were facing, no sense of what was going on. Knowing only the raw hatred he'd seen in Dargana's eyes, but the list of people the Ilvani exile hated was likely a long one.

He was running flat out, but across the distance of two hundred paces that Chriani had measured in his mind, he could only watch as Dargana and Jeradien pulled steadily away from him. Movement shimmered in the shadows ahead, the figures in the camp in motion, horses snorting as they heard racing footsteps approach through the darkness.

He was close enough now. He saw what Dargana had seen. Ilvani in dark cloaks, slipping like ghosts through the trees.

"Valnirata!" he shouted. "Keep them from the road!"

He slung his bow off his back and nocked an arrow as he dropped to one knee and slid to a stop, needing to anchor himself. Kathlan broke to the right beside him, Venry going left. Chriani fired two shots into the darkness, picking the closest target, a tall Ilvani still slinging his quiver on. He fell with both Chriani's arrows in his chest.

Then he was up again, running left for a dozen strides, then cutting hard right. The hiss of bowshot rose around him, arrows flashing past. He dropped again, shot twice more, taking another archer in the arm. As the Ilvani stumbled backward, he made no sound.

A pulse of light came from far right. Kathlan had a torch lit, hurled it into the camp where it flared to daylight brightness. She hit the ground and rolled hard as three arrows streaked her way. From the left, Chriani heard Venry shooting, saw the Ilvani he'd tagged stumble back. As the figure twisted away, Chriani saw the war-mark gleaming dark at his shoulder.

One down quickly, and two more hopefully out of combat. Unless the Ilvani were riding doubled or Dargana had miscounted the horses, he and Venry had taken the fight to slightly better odds. If the

Ilvani spread out beyond the light, though, the battle would turn in short order.

As the clash of steel rang out ahead of him, Chriani rose to sprint forward again. He shot on the run, no accuracy to his aim but intent only on hemming the Ilvani in, giving himself a chance to get close before it was too late.

It did him no good. By the time he got there, it was done. He was able to watch it, though.

Jeradien had been pursuing Dargana when she took off down the slope like a shot. Most likely thinking the Ilvani was fleeing from them, meeting up with compatriots in the woods. Chriani had no idea what might have happened if the Aerachi warrior had reached Dargana before Dargana reached the camp, but the exile got there first. She drove straight into the closest sentry as Kathlan's torched landed, axe and bloodblade in hand. Their steel gleam flashed to blood-red as she spun in and hit hard.

The Ilvani sentry fell. Jeradien saw it from three paces behind. She shifted left, her focus off Dargana as her longsword arced up and over. It carried all the momentum of her run as it hacked through mail and bone, dropping the Ilvani who had been pushing forward to strike at Dargana's back.

Three more Ilvani were pressing. Chriani watched Jeradien and Dargana cut into them as if they were standing still.

Movement at the edge of the light, three figures scrambling back from the brightness and the flurry of steel at the center of it. Bowshot rang out, arrows arcing through the light. Dargana spun to knock one shot aside with her axe, dropped to let a second pass. Jeradien wasn't fast enough, struck in the leg. Chriani tracked the shooter as he pushed forward, slowing long enough to shoot. He heard Venry shooting from his left again, saw the figure fall.

Two Ilvani still uninjured if the count was right. One of them appeared behind Jeradien as if melting out of the shadows of the trees. Even wounded, the Aerachi warrior slashed a backsword attack away from her left side, carried through and swung up to get a piece of the Ilvani's leg. A fast counterstrike, Jeradien's blade coming up just in time as her wounded leg gave way. Then the Ilvani warrior fell as Dargana rose up behind him, sunk the bloodblade deep into his shoulder as he tried to twist away.

"We call for quarter!" The voice of the wounded Ilvani rang out in Ilvalantar as he fell to his knees. Dargana was above him, ready with a killing stroke. But as the warrior dropped his backsword, both she and Chriani saw the clear blue of his eyes at the same time. No sign of gold there. Dargana snarled as she stepped back, but her blades stayed where they were.

Chriani was ten paces away. He saw those Ilvani who were still moving respond to their companion's call as if it was an order. Weapons down and arms spread, no hesitation. The golden light of the cult was nowhere to be seen in any of their eyes.

One of the Ilvani was still moving, though, not hearing or not caring that the others had submitted. Going for the horses. Chriani sighted his shot carefully, arced it through the trees and into the target's leg. He heard a muffled cry as the figure fell.

"Watch them," he called to the others. Though it was reported from time to time along the frontier, Ilvani offering free surrender without being beaten completely down in combat first was outside the scope of Chriani's own experience. He wasn't sure what was going on, but he wasn't going to run the risk of one of them escaping while he sorted it out.

He dropped his bow, drawing his longsword as he sprinted for the horses. The figure he'd tagged was cloaked but barefoot, head shrouded as she tried to stand. All the Ilvani warhorses but one had stood stock-still through the noise of combat, but the injured figure was fighting for some reason to clamber bareback onto that single nervous steed. Chriani was there to haul her off, drop her to the ground.

He saw the blade flash in her hand, almost too late. As he rolled, it caught him in the shoulder instead of the stomach, punching in clean on the left side. He smashed her arm free of the grip, grabbed and twisted to force her down in front of him. He rose to his knees over her, the tip of his sword at the back of her neck.

The cloaked figure didn't move. She was face down with hands at her side, breathing slowly.

Setting his teeth, Chriani pulled the knife from his shoulder. It was a jagged blade, meant for striking and tearing at the soft flesh of the belly, for punching up under the ribs. He was lucky to have rolled with it, watching the Ilvani darkly as he tossed the knife away.

It was quiet around him. He saw Venry with the surrendered Ilvani, tying their hands behind them while Dargana and Kathlan circled slowly around them, blades at the ready. There were five of them, clustered tight together now. All wounded but none in danger of dying, Chriani judged. Jeradien was watching the prisoners as well, sword drawn but not moving. She had cloth stuffed into the broad gash in her leather where the arrow had tagged her.

All of the Ilvani's eyes were bright in the torchlight. Blue or green, brown or violet. Still no trace of gold to be seen.

"Let us know if you need assistance with that one, sergeant," Venry called, his tone cool.

Chriani shrugged off the pain at his shoulder as he ignored the lieutenant. "Kathlan, Dargana," he called. "Check the fallen. Watch yourselves."

Kathlan nodded as she slipped back into the shadows. Dargana hit Chriani with a dark look, but she did the same.

"What happened to the Valnirata not making camp outside their woods?" Venry called coldly. He tied the last Ilvani prisoner, stood and wiped his hands on his leather like he might be rubbing some stain from his fingers.

"These aren't their woods," Chriani said as he carefully stood. "These are the Calala." He hadn't known it before, but he could see it now. Reading the war-marks on the surrendered Ilvani.

"And you're telling me you recognized them from where we sighted them?"

"I'm telling you Dargana did." Chriani put pressure to his shoulder but kept his sword at the neck of the wounded Ilvani at his feet. "These are the same as attacked inside Rheran two weeks back. Enemies of the Laneldenari we're meant to meet. They'll have been avoiding the eastern Ilvani, same as they've been avoiding..."

Chriani's voice cut off as he kicked the wounded figure to roll over at his feet. He stared at the face looking up at him from the ground. Not an Ilvani. Ilmari, young. An unhealthy pallor to her, hair of dirty gold, cut rough. Eyes of palest blue. It was no face he'd ever seen before, but he knew her all the same by the grey tunic and leggings she wore, the straight-line ritual scars that marked her cheeks.

The wind was rising again, cold. Twisting through Chriani with an ache sharper than the pain at his shoulder. Venry was beside him suddenly, staring down as he paced around the Ilmari. Chriani tried to speak, tried to explain who it was at their feet, but his voice was gone.

Venry said it for him, though.

"Uissa." The lieutenant spat to the ground. "Working with the Ilvani. What the fated fuck is this?"

From the ground, the prisoner smiled.

Venry had recognized her by the scars, just as Chriani had. The same markings he'd seen on the assassin who had followed him in pursuit of Lauresa. The assassin he'd killed in the Ghostwood, that past closed off behind him. Or so he thought.

"I will tell you of that one." From where the Ilvani knelt, one of them called out in the Ilmari tongue. "And of our purpose here." His accent was sharp but his voice was clear. The warrior who had called the surrender. His silver hair fell to frame his face, shrouding eyes that were the deep blue of a summer sky.

"Speak then," Venry said as he paced back toward the prisoners, angry. Chriani stayed close to the Ilmari, ignored that it should have been him giving the order.

"We are of Calalerean," the Ilvani said. His tone showed strength but not defiance. "Ordered across Crithnalerean to meet with that Ilmari agent. Ordered to pursue rangers of Brandishear that she had followed across your Clearwater Way."

Chriani looked toward the horse the Ilmari had been trying to reach, realized as he should have before that it wasn't an Ilvani steed. A stark difference in its lines and bearing.

"And what were you meant to do when you found them?" Venry asked.

"To observe only," the Ilvani said. "On my word. To watch interactions between the Ilmari and the Ilvani of Laneldenar. We are trackers, not carontir."

The statement made a certain amount of sense to Chriani, given how easily the Ilvani had been overcome. Seeing them now in the light, only the leader was in full leather.

"Why did you surrender yourselves?" Venry said. His voice carried a note of disappointment. "Why tell us all this? What do you hope to gain?"

"Because I have no cause to act in secrecy against my kin of Laneldenar. I spoke against these orders from my captains and failed, but I will not die for them. I would return with my riders to our folk, with your mercy."

Chriani could see the strength in the Ilvani's blue eyes even from where he stood. A stark honesty there. He and Venry exchanged a glance, Chriani happy to see that the lieutenant seemed to have no more idea how to proceed then he did.

When he looked down again, the Ilmari was watching him. Staring with cold blue eyes.

"One more wounded," Kathlan called out as she and Dargana approached from the shadows. She had an Ilvani warrior in front of her, hands tied and blood at his shoulder where he'd torn an arrow free. "Found him blacked out. The other four are dead."

She pushed the silent Ilvani to his knees alongside the others. He dropped with no resistance, made no sound. Dargana took up a position around the prisoners again, Jeradien glaring as she stepped away. The exile ignored the Aerachi warrior. Chriani saw blood still wet on the dagger and the axe in her hands.

"That's no Ilvani," Kathlan said as she stepped up to the Ilmari prisoner. "Is she from Vishod?"

"The order of Uissa, squire," Venry said. "She's a mercenary, and most definitely not from Vishod. Not that they haven't tried to worm their way into his court. Political intrigue and assassination is their specialty. My Duke Andreg has routed out their hidden holds for years, along the Hunthad close to Teillai. Whatever we do with the Ilvani, that one won't tell us anything. You'd be best to kill her now."

He said the last to Chriani, who felt his sword shiver in his hands. The Ilmari smiled again.

"Kathlan, rope." Chriani sheathed his blade as he grabbed the Ilmari's hands, rolled her onto her stomach again. She stifled a cry as he tied her tight, the arrow still in her leg and shifting each time she moved. It was a straight-through wound, painful but not life threatening. Chriani broke the shaft clean at both ends, pulled it through carefully. The prisoner shook with the pain, but the bleeding wasn't bad.

"They tried to kill your princess. Uissa." Venry said it almost as an afterthought. "My Duchess Lauresa. Before the wedding, they thought to settle old scores with the duke. He smashed their main hold at High Summer last as retaliation, sent them running for the frontier."

Chriani saw Kathlan nod, remembering that story. A good tale, as tales went.

"Laóith irnáera!"

Dargana's voice shattered the hiss of the wind, the clash of weapons following. *I kill the laóith!* Chriani stood to see her gone from the prisoners, all of them watching her instead where the exile faced Jeradien at the edge of the torch's shimmering light. The two of them were hammering at each other with bloodstained steel. Dargana pressed hard, swinging from both sides, but Jeradien countered with blinding speed.

Chriani saw the same look in both their eyes. Both striking with deadly intent, each of them ready to kill.

Venry was running for them, shouting for both of them to stand down, but not even Jeradien seemed to hear him. Chriani sprinted in, his shoulder flaring with pain as he drew his sword and swung between them to crash off their blades, throwing off the timing of their strikes. He dodged Dargana's furious counter, twisted in to hook her leg and send her down. Jeradien lunged in but his own sword flicked up to her chest, forced her to a stop.

They stood frozen that way for what seemed a long while. Venry was at Chriani's left hand, his own blade out as Dargana slowly rose.

"The two of you fought back-to-back a moment ago," Chriani hissed. He heard the anger in his voice that matched the cold fire in Jeradien's eyes. "What in fate's name..."

"Chriani..."

He glanced over to Kathlan, saw her nod to the ground. A bloody display there. An Aerachi dagger, close to the two archers Chriani and Venry had first dropped. Jeradien had been collecting their ears as trophies.

Dargana spoke up from behind him, words for Jeradien. "Touch these bodies again, laóith, and I'll carve out your heart."

"I invite you to try."

"Enough!" Chriani lowered his blade and pushed Jeradien back. She responded with a lunging forehand blow to his face, Chriani barely managing to roll with it in time. The backhand follow-up would have caught him, but Venry stepped in to grab his ranger. It looked like it took all his strength, his voice cold at her ear.

"That was your troop sergeant you just struck. This ends now. Stand watch on the prisoners."

Chriani rubbed his chin as Jeradien went limp in her lieutenant's grasp. She nodded as he let her go, ignoring Chriani as she scooped up her dagger and stalked off toward where the bound Ilvani still kneeled. All of them were watching darkly, Chriani saw.

"For the actions of my guard, you have my apologies, lord." Venry's voice carried a sense of formality, but Chriani had no idea whether it was for Jeradien having hit him or for the trophies she'd been attempting to collect in the first place. "I trust I'll have your apology at some point for all of us being forced into this battle despite your order to fall back."

Chriani ignored Venry as the lieutenant paced away, calling to Kathlan instead. "See if the Ilvani have a store of arrows. We can make use them."

"Yes, lord."

Chriani couldn't tell what she was feeling as she turned away.

"Dargana," he called. He stepped to the bodies, pushing one onto its back with his boot. Their sightless eyes looked up at him, green and amber.

"Dargana!" His voice was cold as he called her again, saw the exile step up through the shadows. A faint sense of relief twisted through him in response to the lack of gold in the Calala Ilvani's eyes, but it vanished quickly under the weight of an uncertainty that was channeling anger now. The familiar feeling of losing control. "Do you feel like telling me why we just attacked an Ilvani band of superior numbers in the dark? I ordered you to fall back…"

"I don't take your orders, lord." Dargana's voice carried a degree of venom Chriani hadn't heard since the time she'd tried to kill him. "I saw them well enough to recognize their war-marks as Calala. Them following us meant your plan to engage them by daylight might have brought every Ilvani of the lóechari down on us."

"They're not the cult. You saw their eyes."

"I see them now. I wasn't taking chances then."

"Not your decision to make…"

"I don't wait on your decisions either, laóith. At the first sign of the feint you planned for tomorrow, they would have run. Kathlan's the only one in either of your squads who can ride, but an Ilvani of the Muiraìden will outride even her by day or night. Coins or no, these are the Calala that hunted you in the Greatwood, and in Rheran. Your prince's magic isn't hiding you as well as you…"

"Lieutenant!"

Jeradien's strangled cry rang out over the hiss of the wind. Chriani heard a stark terror twisting through her voice.

By the time they got to her, Venry was already there. Jeradien was a half-dozen strides from the Ilvani prisoners, scrambling back and on her knees. Her sword had fallen at her side, both hands shaking as she scribed the moonsign against her breast, over and over again.

Three of the Ilvani were on their feet, twisting their arms behind them, tearing futilely at their bonds. The other three were convulsing, their limbs twisted with a violence that drove them across the ground, arched their backs and legs as they thrashed.

"Chriani irnash!" The Ilvani leader screamed it, the muscles of his arms and shoulders knotted tight. Chriani heard his wrist break as he tore through the ropes that bound him. "Lóech arnala irch niir!"

In the eyes of the leader and all the Ilvani, a golden light blazed.

Chriani had time to step back before the Ilvani reached him, charging full speed and hitting hard. He had no weapon in hand but managed to get his arm around Chriani's throat, choking him as they both struck the ground. Chriani's longsword came up, stabbing in hard to take the Ilvani in the shoulder, force him off. It took two more strikes, hammering awkwardly from the ground, to end him.

Movement at the edge of his vision. Dargana was attacking, the Ilvani shrieking as she cut them down. He heard a bow sing, saw Venry shooting. Behind them all in the darkness, the dead moved. From the two archers that Jeradien had cut, a voiceless rasping rose as their lungs emptied, a dread tattoo beaten on the ground by their flailing limbs.

Then all was quiet again.

"Blood and moonsign." Venry still had an arrow nocked, but he raised his bow so he could roughly scribe that sign himself. Kathlan came in from the shadows at a run, a clutch of Ilvani quivers stuffed with arrows in her hand. She stopped short, stared.

Chriani stepped over the body of the Ilvani leader, looking down to where the bright gleam of gold still filled his eyes. In his hands and mouth, he saw the flash of coins, the same golden light gleaming in the hands and mouths of all the dead around them.

Chriani had listened to the leader. Had heard his words and the honesty in them. It hadn't been a trick, he told himself. He knew that with a certainty he couldn't understand. The power of the cult was in all the Ilvani's minds, but they hadn't known it until the magic of the coins claimed them.

Chriani remembered the Uissa prisoner, spun around as if he expected her to have fled during the chaos. She was still on her side, though. Staring at the dead Ilvani with a rapt expression. A fascination in her gaze that set a chill in Chriani's heart.

When he looked back again, Venry was staring at him, dark eyes blazing.

"He called your name," the lieutenant said. His gaze shifted from Chriani to Dargana, then to Kathlan. None of them showing the anger or the fear that marked him or Jeradien. "You know this. You've all seen this before."

Chriani nodded. "It's magic of an Ilvani cult. We've seen it in the western Greatwood, and in Rheran."

"And you thought to say nothing…"

"I'll say what I have to say when I call it time to speak."

"This is a trap, you fool! You lead us into Ilvani territory with their agents following. Ready to surround us the moment we enter the wood."

"They've been following for three days, Venry. If ambush was their plan, they could have done it at their leisure. We're in empty frontier. Plenty of cover, no witnesses. This is why we're here. These are the Calala that the Laneldenari oppose. This power is what they fear. Why they want peace."

It was part of the truth at least. Venry's reaction said it wasn't enough, though, even as Chriani saw a flicker of insight in the lieutenant's eyes.

"He called your name," Venry said again. "Pursuing rangers of Brandishear, he told us. You fought Ilvani in Rheran, your second said. A war-band in the Brandishear capital." The lines of connection were tightening in the lieutenant's thoughts, Chriani seeing it. "The Ilvani are following you."

"Yes."

"You will tell me what's going on here..."

"When I call it time." They were all the words Chriani could summon up, his thoughts scattered as points of darkness in his mind.

Venry spat to the ground as he turned away. He helped Jeradien to her feet, directed her toward the horses. "Cut the Ilvani steeds free, but keep the horse the assassin tried to flee on. We ride back now."

The horses of the Ilvani took no other riders, and all rangers knew of the peril in attempting to rebreak them. Tales were told of warbands pushing as far as the outskirts of the frontier cities to reclaim horses stolen by the Ilmari — and to kill those who had taken them. Chriani nodded his agreement to Venry's order, but the lieutenant wasn't looking at him as he paced away.

"Help Venry," he said to Kathlan. Dargana had already disappeared into the darkness.

"Chriani..."

As Kathlan stepped close to him, Chriani heard the fear in her voice. However, the surge of nausea that whipped through him told him it wasn't just the fate of the Ilvani that had affected her. He looked to the quiver she held out to him, saw a single black arrow set in a side pocket.

He motioned her to drop the quiver to the ground. He had to send his foot into the black arrow three times to shatter it, but the dark touch of its magic passed like shadow before sunlight when it was done.

"Help Venry," he said again. Kathlan nodded as she slipped away.

Alone, Chriani dropped to his knees beside the dead Ilvani leader. His shoulder was aching again, the spill of blood cooling there. He searched the body carefully, a kind of numbness settling across his mind. He saw his fingers moving but wasn't really conscious of it, feeling them trace out the seams of pockets and compartments, slip within the lines of the Ilvani's light leather.

Beneath a closed flap within the warrior's gauntlet, Chriani found the hunter's heart hidden. This new talisman was strung on a chain of thin steel links rather than leather, but like the talisman Chriani carried, its rough-edged bloodstone was dark within its golden claw.

As he watched, the golden light in the Ilvani's eyes faded. Left them the same bright blue as before.

He tried to make sense of it, tried to shuffle the pieces rearranging themselves to unknown patterns in his mind. In the deep winter of his journey to Aerach, the order of Uissa and the Ilvani of Calalerean had attacked each other. Their animosity had saved Chriani and Lauresa, in fact, the Calala taking vengeance for Uissa's forces donning the livery of Valnirata warriors to pretend that the Ilvani were behind the attempt on the princess's life. A bond between both factions now made no sense.

They were tracking him. He felt the truth of that. Someone else in the troop might have been their target, but if they were seeking someone else, the hunter's heart should have shown light. With the talismans dark, they must have pursued Chriani by stealth and observation alone. But for how long? Or was there other magic at work here now, powerful enough to overcome the protection of the badge at his waist?

Chriani slipped the second talisman to one of the pockets of his belt, made the moonsign absently. When he glanced over, he saw the Uissa prisoner watching him.

The sound of hoofbeats rose to mark the Ilvani horses set free, then faded quickly as they disappeared into the darkness. Kathlan came back through the center of the camp, scooping up her torch. Chriani saw Venry and Jeradien circling past the edge of the light to head toward the distant rise and their horses beyond. Venry was leading the prisoner's horse at a run, Jeradien making the moonsign behind him. Chriani stalked over to lift the Ilmari to her feet, pushing her ahead of him as he followed Kathlan's light.

They raced back along the same track they'd taken by day, Jeradien and Kathlan carrying torches to front and rear. Chriani kept his bow drawn, Venry leading the Uissa prisoner's horse with the prisoner slung across and lashed tight to its saddle. No one spoke.

When the light of the watchfires came into sight, Jeradien sounded the horn to warn the camp of a squad returning. Chriani's eyes marked the rangers beyond the firelight, hunkered down behind the upthrust stones and with arrows nocked. A heightened sense of wariness didn't pass until all the riders had slowed within the defensive perimeter.

They walked the horses to the grove, whereupon Venry untied the Uissa prisoner and pulled her to the ground. While the lieutenant's horse was unsaddled and rubbed down, he hauled the prisoner off, disappearing with her beyond the trees. Chriani knew it should have been him dealing with her, but he was content to let Venry have his moment. He needed the time to focus, trying to slow his frantic thoughts. Remembering how the prisoner had watched him. Trying to understand what her presence among the Ilvani might mean.

As he rubbed down his horse, Chriani saw two Aerachi rangers crouched around Jeradien. One was tending to the wound at her leg but she was talking low to both of them, all three glancing in his direction at different times. He knew there'd be no need for a formal debriefing.

As Kathlan walked past him carrying her saddle, he called her over. "Where's Dargana?"

"Went to the tent, lord. I told her to stay out of sight." Though Kathlan's response held the formality that told Chriani she was still angry, he heard a break in its chill tone.

"Go see our rangers," he said. "Tell them what's happened."

"I can't tell them much until I know myself," Kathlan said. She didn't wait for a response as she turned away.

When Chriani went in search of Venry at last, the lieutenant was at one of the western watch fires, conversing with another ranger from his squad. They had the Uissa prisoner staked to hold her, the ropes at her wrist attached to a heavy horse hitch driven deep into the rocky soil. Her pale face was streaked with dust, her dark eyes bright. Watching Chriani in silence as he approached.

At a whispered word from Venry, the other ranger made a quick exit. The lieutenant turned to Chriani, his attention caught by the blood at his shoulder. "You should see the healers," he said absently. He was calmer than he'd been in the Ilvani camp.

"It's fine for now," Chriani lied. He had been feeling the pain spreading steadily throughout the ride, reaching well down his arm and across his back now. His left-front shoulder, which no healer could ever see.

"This one is a problem," Venry said. He prodded the Uissa prisoner with his foot, forcing a wince in response. Though she shared the seeming reluctance to speak that Chriani had seen in the assassin he had faced and defeated when defending Lauresa, there was none of the Ilvani's silent stoicism about her.

"I doubt we'll gain any information from her," Chriani agreed, "but we have enough rangers to watch her while we decide what's to be done."

"Uissa's importance to Aerach has made that decision for us, sergeant. The dealings between the order and the Ilvani must be brought to my Duke Andreg at once."

Venry's voice carried the same conviction Chriani had heard that first day in the road. He felt a subtle shift in the lieutenant's attitude, the anger tempered now with something stronger.

"The news will get to him in good time. Or send two of your riders as courier if you can't wait..."

"The troop sets a course for Teillai at dawn. A day and a half's hard riding will get us there, though there'll be a fair bit of open country to cross."

"We'll have plenty of time to get the prisoner to Teillai once we've met with the Ilvani."

"That plan has changed, sergeant, owing to recent events. I'm taking command."

There it was. Chriani's original tactic of using obedience to the duke as incentive for Venry to follow his lead would naturally fail in the face of a better use of that obedience.

"Take command of whatever you like, Venry. My squad will ride for the Greatwood without..."

"The assassin will be questioned." Venry's dark eyes burned now with a cold light. "You will tell the duke about the Ilvani magic we saw. And about why the Calala have followed you across two principalities and the exile lands."

"I'll say what I have to say..."

"You'll say it when I order it, sergeant. Or the prince's mages will find the answers in ways you might not like."

The watchfires had wrapped the crown of the hill in a streaming wreath of smoke, spilling off south as the wind pulled it away. Chriani looked up to the light of the Clearmoon, waning but still bright. He couldn't remember the last time he'd seen the Darkmoon, passing through new and gone from a night sky that seemed brighter somehow without its blood-red stain.

He felt a lightness to his thoughts. The weight of responsibility had lifted from him, even if it took Chriani's familiar sense of failure to do it.

"I've given the order," Venry said. "I've called for double watch through the night. No way to tell what else might be out there. Assuming that's not something else you know but haven't bothered to mention."

"Permission to seek the healers, lord?" Chriani met the lieutenant's gaze, holding it fast.

"Acting Sergeant Chriani, as long as it involves leaving my sight, you are free to do as you like."

Chriani turned without a word. He felt Venry's eyes on him as he tracked across the top of the hill, heading for his tent.

It took an effort to seal the tent's door flap with one hand, the pain in Chriani's shoulder radiating through his fingers now. He waited a while, listening for footsteps. The wind made it hard to pick out the fainter sounds on the hilltop, but when Chriani was certain he was alone, he carefully stripped off his armor and the blood-soaked tunic beneath.

He had no light, seeing by the faint glow of firelight through canvas walls. With brandy and clean cloths, he wiped and flushed the wound, the knife punching deep into muscle but missing bone and tendon. He tried for stitches, but the torn flesh flared with an agony that went white-hot behind his eyes. He drank the brandy instead, waiting until the pain had passed.

The troop was riding for Aerach in the morning. He didn't have much time.

From a distant corner of his mind, Chriani felt the thought of how reassuring uncertainty must be. He found himself wishing he could lie to his own mind as easily as to everyone else in his life, tell himself he wasn't sure what his next move should be. But he did know his next move. He always knew, following a course of anger and instinct his whole life.

He and Dargana would head into the Greatwood alone. He would wait until the deep night, mark the movement of the sentries before he set out for her tent. They'd have to leave their horses for the sake of quiet, but that would work to their advantage in the end. In the thick of the forest, they would move slower but it would be easier by far on foot to evade pursuit.

Kathlan was his only point of uncertainty, burning in his thoughts as his shoulder was burning now. She'd be in danger if she came with him. Would lose everything she'd ever wanted, everything she'd worked toward for a year and more. But she might just as clearly be in danger if she stayed behind. They might question her in Teillai. Assume that she knew the things Chriani knew — or that Venry thought he knew, at least.

"Chriani…"

At the door flap, he heard the urgency in Kathlan's voice. Word of Venry's orders had spread.

He winced as he pulled his bloody tunic back on, unsealed the tent, then sealed it again behind her. She took over for him on the last pegs, his fingers fumbling in pain.

"You've heard…" Chriani began, but she put a finger to his lips. She lit a candle from his pack so she could see, lifting the tunic to assess the bloody mess beneath.

"First things first."

More carefully than Chriani thought he deserved, she washed the wound out a second time. She stitched it tight as Chriani drank again, a fear rising cold and dark from his gut, twisting up to his heart. Each beat of his blood was reflected in the pulsing pain at his shoulder, but that was fading with the wound closed.

"Here," Kathlan said. From an inside pocket on her jacket, she pulled the glass jar with Derrach's salve.

"Keep it," he said. "The stitching will do fine." The magic of healing could mean the difference between life and death in the field, but Chriani's wound was nowhere near that serious. He was trembling, though, Kathlan noting it as she slipped the salve back to her pocket.

It was a different kind of pain he was feeling now.

Kathlan spoke as she gathered up bloody cloths from the tent's ground-sheet floor. "I need you to tell me what's going on, Chriani. I need the truth."

"You know what's going on, Kath."

"I know what you've told me. I know it's not all. The Ilvani hunting you. These mercenaries. The one who went after the princess…"

"I killed the one who went after the princess," Chriani heard himself say. "This one's different. I don't know her…"

"But she knows you, Chriani. I saw the look on her when you were standing over her."

He could have told Kathlan he didn't understand that any more than she did. That much was the truth at least, his mind fragmenting as the pieces of the puzzle reshaped and resized themselves.

"Why was the princess marked for this? What did they want from her?" Kathlan's voice as she spoke held a clarity that made Chriani understand she'd been thinking the question for much longer than it took to ask it. Much longer than just this night.

"Like Venry said. They hate the duke. Wanted to hurt him…"

"Then why attack her before she even gets to Aerach? Venry said they work at court."

"I don't know, Kath."

Chriani had to look away from her, staring down to the war-mark at his shoulder. The tight black of Kathlan's stitching was all but lost already in its dark ink.

"When you lie to me, I know it, Chriani."

He could tell her about Chanist. He knew that in the moment. Had known it since the night he rode in through the Bastion stable gates on his return from Rheran. He could find the strength in himself, find the will to tell her who was behind the attempt on Lauresa's life. Who had held the blade that slew Barien. Tell her the truth of all the prince had done, what he was.

He knew he wouldn't, though. Something stopping him tonight as it had stopped him a year and a half before. Not the unexpected feeling of near-pity he had felt for the prince high in the throne room two weeks past. Not the understanding that in telling Kathlan, he would force her to share the pain he carried for Barien, for Lauresa, knowing all the while that there was no end to that pain now.

If he told her the truth about the prince, Chriani understood that it would be only as a distraction from deeper truths. Darker truths. An excuse written down in blood and memory, to let him keep hiding the thing he did need to tell her. The truth of what he had done. What he was.

"I need to get to Dargana without anyone seeing," he said at last. "The two of us need to run for the Greatwood tonight."

"The three of us." Kathlan's voice held a tremor that cut through its normal strength. Still defiant, but breaking. Something chipping away at it.

"No, Kath. It's my commission I'm throwing away, but I never earned it to begin with. I won't let you fall with me…"

"I make my own choices, Chriani…"

"But you can't make my choices, Kath. You can't share in this. Not this time."

A long silence. Kathlan's hand touched his bare shoulder, trembling. "Then just go to Teillai. It's two days ride, we'll come back when it's done…"

"I can't go to Teillai," Chriani said.

He felt light-headed. A sense that the ground was opening up beneath him, the tent and the black sky both falling.

"Because of her," Kathlan said. The clarity again. A thing she had been thinking on for a year and a half now, but the words were breaking even as she said them. Chriani grasped her hand, tried to squeeze the tremor from it but he was shaking suddenly. Couldn't stop himself.

"Not for her. There's something… there's someone else…"

Not that, he thought. *Not now.*

Something broke in him, finally. He felt the weight of this one last truth crush every lie he'd ever crafted. Felt it push aside every other thing he might have said, like wind-whipped grass breaking before a cavalry charge.

From when he was younger, he remembered vague dreams of running, and of never being fast enough to escape the unknown darkness he feared would catch him. He felt that same sensation now, felt it close around him. Felt it force the words from him that he knew would be the end of everything.

"There's a child, Kath…"

The trembling in her hand stopped. Her fingers slid from his shoulder. The chill of the tent was at his bare back where she shifted away.

"Lauresa's child…" Chriani whispered. "The duke of Teillai's first-born is mine. Or so she told me. On the road, before I left her to ride back to you."

He heard Kathlan's breathing quicken from behind him. When he turned to face her finally, the pain in her expression cut through him like flame-hot steel, eclipsing the pain at his shoulder.

She was silent a long while. "Why?" was what she said in the end.

"Because it was all we had." A clarity in Chriani's voice as he said it. A thing he'd been thinking on for too long. "The first time I was with you, Kath, I knew how I felt about you. I knew I loved you, even if I couldn't say it then. And if I'd known that first night with you was the only night we'd ever have, I'd have given you anything you asked for."

"You still love her." Not a question.

"No," Chriani said, and it was true. He'd known that truth since the night he'd ridden back into Rheran a year and a half before. Feeling the faint pain that healing had left behind at his fresh-severed finger, and realizing that the pain in his heart that had been Lauresa was gone. The pain he'd felt since the day he met her, a tyro twelve years old.

"But you did."

Chriani tried to reach for Kathlan's hand but she pulled away, green eyes fixed to his. "I did," he said. "I loved her once before I ever set eyes on you. I loved her a second time even as I loved you. And I love you now, and that's all there is."

"All there is except your secret daughter of a duke."

The thing that had broken in Chriani was breaking in Kathlan now. He heard it in the tremor that threaded her voice, felt it as heat and cold coursing through him, saw it as the shaking in her arms, her hands clenched to fists now.

"She's not... Her parentage won't ever be an issue, Kath. Aerach's titles go father to son..."

"So glad you worked all that out beforehand, then."

As she shifted toward the front of the tent, he tried to hold her. Kathlan drove her fist into the stitches at his bare shoulder in response, Chriani crumbling beneath a storm of pain that flared white-hot in his mind.

"Don't touch me..." Kathlan whispered. She fumbled at the door flap, tearing the pegs free. "Don't ever..." Then she was outside and gone.

Chriani lay there for a long while, waiting for the pain to subside before he could push himself to his feet. He stared at the candle, still burning. Its light was shimmering where the walls of the tent rippled in the wind.

From what seemed a lifetime ago, he remembered Barien telling him that Kathlan was the best thing that would ever happen to him. He remembered ignoring the warrior. He might even have laughed. Turning so that Barien wouldn't see the flush at his face to tell him Chriani already knew he was right.

He remembered Barien singing with Kathlan at that harvest fest that was the first night for her and Chriani. An emptiness rooted deep inside him, reminding him that another piece of Barien's memory had been broken off tonight. A kind of living thread that ran from him to Kathlan to the warrior, vanished into shadow.

"Sergeant Chriani."

Jeradien's voice came from outside the tent. Chriani felt the breeze cold at his bare back.

The door flap was still unsealed. The Aerachi ranger should have waited for his response, asked his permission to enter. Proper protocol when seeking out a superior.

She pulled the flap wide instead. "I am to offer apology for striking you, lord." Angrily stated, making it clear she was doing so only because Venry must have ordered it. She had pulled the tent open without asking leave for the same reason, leading with her sense of sullen defiance.

Her eyes were downcast to counter the insolence, giving Chriani time to stumble backward, grab his cloak to hide himself. Almost quick enough.

Jeradien looked up. She saw the war-mark at Chriani's shoulder an instant before he covered it. A thing they would kill him for one day.

From her crouch at the entrance to the tent, she shot forward in a rising charge. Chriani had never moved faster in his life as he rolled out of her way. It wasn't enough.

He fell beneath the weight of her as she struck like a mule's kick, taking him into the back wall of the tent and tearing it from its moorings. She was locked tight to him, the two of them trapped in shadow as the tent wrapped around them. Then she'd torn it free with one hand, Chriani gasping cold air as her other arm wrapped around his throat.

"Treason!" she screamed. "Aerachi rangers! All on me!"

Chriani put everything he had into the elbow he drove into Jeradien's face. Part of it was caught by the mail she was still wearing at her shoulder, but he felt her stagger back, managed to slip out of her chokehold.

As he twisted away from her, she spun for a side kick. Her boot struck him squarely in the shoulder, dead center in the Uissa warrior's knife wound.

The world flared white around him for an endless moment. Then it was done.

Chriani was on the ground and on his knees, Jeradien kneeling in front of him with her dagger at his throat. Two other Aerachi were at his side, pinning his arms behind him. He couldn't move, could barely breathe through the pain. He heard footsteps, voices shouting.

Jeradien had blood at her lip where Chriani had tagged her. "Treason," she whispered, like it was all she could say.

Chriani looked past it all, over Jeradien's shoulder toward Kathlan and Dargana's tent. He saw no sign of Kathlan, but the exile was there, escorted between Daellyn and Wilric. The expressions of the Brandishear rangers told Chriani they had no idea what was going on.

Dargana saw it, though. She drew her axe and her dagger, launched herself toward Chriani through the crowd of rangers gathering. He wanted to shout for her, tell her to stop. Wanted to tell her to run, but he knew she wouldn't.

She tried to fight her way through to him, but the Aerachi were alert, ready for her. Steel on steel rang out, Chriani seeing a flash of blood where the dagger slashed a glancing blow against someone's hand. Then Dargana was down beneath a wall of blades, arms behind her and held to the ground.

"Hold her!" Venry's voice sounded out as he approached at a run. He had a bow in hand, must have come in from perimeter watch. He took in the scene before him with a single glance, his expression freezing to well-controlled rage. He stepped close, knelt to inspect the mark at Chriani's shoulder.

A deeper fear twisted through Chriani. Kathlan's name was part of that mark now, set down there on his long winter ride to Rheran. Chriani didn't know who among the Aerachi could read the Ilvani, but he trusted that someone would. He forced himself to look down, his heart hammering in his chest. The four names were obscured, though, a dried crust of red-black blood shrouding them.

Venry didn't touch the mark. He shuddered as he stood, as if even being in its proximity was too much to bear. "Bind them and set a guard," he said. "One Aerachi. One from the Brandishear squad, master Kathlan."

The lieutenant turned to look behind him. Kathlan was there, standing with the Brandishear rangers around her. She was Chriani's second. Was in charge now.

She wasn't looking at Chriani. She nodded deep. "Understood, lord," she said.

It was good, Chriani knew. The Brandishear rangers needed to protect themselves now. Make sure the Aerachi, pushed to the edge of battle madness in a heartbeat, knew that they'd known nothing of Chriani's secret.

"The Ilvani tried to get to him," Jeradien hissed. "They're working together…"

Venry cut her off. "I said bind and guard them. We'll settle this in Teillai."

The Aerachi dragged Chriani and Dargana to their feet. The exile tried to break free, managed to strike someone, so they forced her to the ground, then bound and carried her. Two of the Brandishear rangers stepped up to help.

Kathlan had disappeared but Chriani hadn't seen her go. Venry was talking to Jeradien, both of them watching him coldly as he was dragged away. He made no attempt to resist.

His hands were tied but they let him walk to the watchfire where the Uissa prisoner was still bound and on the ground. In the assassin's dark eyes as he and Dargana were dragged up, Chriani saw no surprise. She nodded to him as he was pushed to the dirt face first. One of the rangers was looping rope around his feet.

"Be ready," the Uissa assassin said.

Her voice was slight, carrying an impression of someone younger than she looked. Barely a whisper against the wind.

The other rangers made no response, as if only Chriani had heard her. They made no response either as the hiss of the wind shifted, something faster moving within it. A sound he recognized.

"Arrows!" Chriani shouted. "Get down!"

A moment of confusion and cold looks. Then the space around the watchfire was shredded by a hail of grey shafts from the darkness.

The Ilvani arrows tore up the ground where they struck, the rangers scattering with shouts of alarm as they dropped and rolled clear. Venry's voice and Kathlan's both rang out from somewhere far away, screaming for the rangers to get to cover, return fire. Chriani's hands were behind him, his shoulder in agony as he rolled into the shadows, tried to get out of direct sight. But as he did, he felt his understanding shift. Sensing something beneath the frantic fear scouring his mind.

The rangers were returning fire now, but whatever force of Ilvani was attacking stayed well out of sight in the darkness. Another flight of arrows arced in, striking across the hillside. Three of them landed within an arm's length of Chriani, quivering with the force of impact.

There were no bodies. The rangers had all fallen back behind cover. Dargana had twisted to her knees, trying desperately to slip her bonds. The Uissa assassin was still on her side, smiling. She hadn't moved.

The Ilvani were missing with every shot. Pushing the rangers to behind cover, away from the watchfire where the three prisoners had been left alone. Three arrows within easy reach.

The pain at Chriani's shoulder tugged him toward darkness again but he fought it off, stifling the scream that tore through him as he pulled his legs up tight, forced his arms down and under. He grabbed the closest arrow, awkwardly wrenched it from the ground. A hunting shaft, its serrated steel head gleaming in the firelight.

He had to kneel on it to hold it, thrusting his bound hands against the blade and sawing hard. He felt his hands cut more than once, blood flowing freely as the ropes finally parted.

The Ilvani fusillade shifted. The sound of steel on stone rang out across the hillside as shaft after shaft shattered against the tumbled foundations behind which the rangers were sniping. They were pinned down suddenly, no way to return fire.

"To the horses!" Venry's voice was fear and raw fury, sounding out against the wind and the endless Ilvani assault. "Torches up! On my mark, ride!"

The order to flee. They would leave the tents and most of their gear behind, only their weapons going with them. A desperate move, but Venry had no way of knowing what was out there.

Chriani fumbled the black ring from the pocket at his belt. He almost dropped it as he scrambled toward Dargana, grabbed another arrow from the ground. He saw her look of surprise as he vanished from sight, the view around him fading to a deeper shadow.

"Don't move," he whispered as he dropped to Dargana's side.

"You're full of surprises, half-blood," she murmured back. But she stayed still and low as Chriani sliced through the bonds at her hands.

The sound of hoofbeats rose. The rangers were mounted and moving, holding on the far side of the hill. The horses were in soft harness and unsaddled, the sign of an emergency retreat. Venry and one of the Brandishear rangers broke off, racing toward them.

Dargana's hands were free, but Chriani hissed in her ear to keep her down. "They'll see you. Don't move." He shifted to her feet.

Venry swung down from horseback to hack through the stake rope holding the assassin down. The ranger leaned over, grabbing the Uissa prisoner and throwing her over his saddle as if she weighed nothing. He looked around, though, frantic as Venry regained his horse.

"He's gone! Bastard Ilvani traitor!"

Venry swiveled in the saddle to scan the hillside. "Leave him to his war-band, then. If it's him they want, they'll let us go."

"What about the bastard exile…"

Venry's face twisted to a grim smile as he turned his horse, charged toward Dargana.

Her feet were free. Chriani grabbed her, tried to pull her with him as he rolled away, but she shrugged him off. Dargana shot to her feet, the horse balking as she sidestepped. She had the arrow in hand that Chriani had used to free her, punched it straight into Venry's thigh as she pulled him off the horse and to the ground.

A shout rang out from behind Chriani. Even without being able to see him, Jeradien almost accidentally rode him down. He struck at her horse by instinct as he rolled away, felt the world around him shimmer to tell him he had broken the dweomer of the ring in doing so.

The Aerachi ranger saw him this time. She turned her horse hard, tearing up the turf as she cut around, a dagger in her hand. Moving at speed, twisting awkwardly with no saddle, she was still good enough to catch Chriani on the run as she threw. A bright point of pain flared at the back of his leg as he went down.

Jeradien was off her horse, sword in hand. Chriani hadn't seen her leap off, must have blacked out. He tried to rise but his leg, his shoulder, were agony. The hatred he saw in the Aerachi warrior's eyes was all-consuming, all-final.

A horse came in fast from behind her, a booted foot lashing out to catch Jeradien in the side of the head. The warrior convulsed once, then slumped to the ground, the sword spilling from her hand.

Kathlan pulled to a frantic stop, leaped from her horse and dropped to Jeradien's side. Chriani managed to get to his feet, found a fast-bleeding wound at his leg. Kathlan was checking the blood at Jeradien's neck as she fumbled in her jacket, pulled something out that she threw to Chriani. The healing salve.

"Go," she said quietly. She wouldn't look at him. Raising her voice, she called out, "Jeradien's down! Chriani's headed for the trees!"

Other horses were racing in behind her now, pushing toward Venry where he'd fallen. The lieutenant was moving, though, trying to calm his horse. The Ilvani arrows had stopped, but no one seemed to notice.

Venry's saddlebags had been torn open, Chriani saw. Then he saw Dargana running toward him, her bloodblade in hand. Kathlan was lifting Jeradien from the ground, the Aerachi ranger's eyes flitting open.

"Go," Kathlan said again, louder this time.

Chriani turned and ran.

Dargana was close behind him, the hail of arrows starting up again as they cleared the firelight. A screen of bowshot fell behind them, blocking any pursuit. Chriani was limping, fighting darkness with each step as he fumbled his fingers to the jar, took the last dose of the salve as he ran. Healing magic filled him with its empty warmth, the pain at his leg and shoulder fading as he let the jar drop.

A sharper pain was at his chest now. He ignored it as he ran.

At the point where even Chriani's eyes lost the last haze of light from the watchfires, he heard horses. But from ahead, not behind. Grey shapes loomed, starlight seeming to shimmer on their flanks. He was still running, felt light hands reach to grab him under the arms. Then he was in the air, frantic as he found himself dragged up and suddenly sitting a white horse, a slender figure in front of him.

There was no saddle beneath them, Chriani's legs struggling to lock to the horse's lean flanks. The figure in front of him grabbed his arm, pulled it around to lock tight to a well-muscled chest, smooth skin flecked with fine scar lines.

In the faint haze of starlight, Chriani saw the war-mark at the bare shoulder of the Ilvani he rode behind.

Other horses shifted in the shadows around them, all running flat out. He saw Dargana astride another horse, sitting behind an Ilvani warrior at the far side of the troop, but he couldn't count that troop's total numbers as they moved.

A shadow loomed. The stars flickered, then faded, then were gone. Chriani felt the change in the air, a warmth and a closeness settling in around him. The echo of the horses' hooves was muffled, the droning of the river rising to his right.

A burst of light came from before and behind him. He looked forward, twisted back to see two of the riders with glowing disks in hand. Magical light, something like the evenlamps of the Bastion, but these glowed a pale green that set black ground and shadowed sky into sharp contrast.

They were in the Greatwood. The life Chriani had built was gone.

It was all he could think of, his mind shutting to all other thought. Just like that. Kathlan and his commission, a place in the prince's guard. All of it vanished behind him as the thunder of hoofbeats carried him into the night.

He held on tight. Nothing else he could do as the Ilvani plunged into the darkness of the forest, leaving the world behind.

— CHAPTER 10 —

THE HIDDEN CITY

THEY RODE THROUGH the night, but Chriani remembered little of the journey. The well of pale green hung around them like swirling mist, making their frenzied flight seem even faster. He had no idea how the Ilvani horses were holding to the twisting paths they shot along, maintaining a running pace as they did so. In the darkness and the shifting pool of light that passed within it, he had no way to even guess at the passage of time. But he became conscious at some point that the speed of the horses would have to flag eventually, the exhausted steeds needing to rest.

The horses didn't flag, though. The troop raced on.

As on the Brandishear side of the Greatwood, the trails they traversed were a complex series of half-seen paths. An uncountable number of side trails split off from the main, Chriani knowing even from his minimal exploration of the forest that fully a third of those would mark false starts and dead ends. He couldn't comprehend of the lifetime it would take to learn to navigate the wood as well as these Ilvani were doing it.

He was riding with the carontir. The elite ranger patrols of the Valnirata. No mistaking their skill as they raced their horses through the night.

The sound of the Hunthad came and went for what seemed a long while. Then at some point, the troop forded the river at speed, plunging in without slowing. Chriani nearly fell off, his rider needing to clasp his hand hard. Freezing-cold water washed across his legs, the horse feeling to him like it might be swimming in spots, even with two riders on its back. Then they were on the far bank and running again.

More than once, Chriani found himself wondering how anyone would ever hope to fight a war in this endless green darkness. More than once, he remembered the Prince High Chanist's promise to make a war against the Ilvani that would burn the Greatwood to the ground.

When they stopped without warning, the forest was still dark. The Ilvani reined to a halt in a sheltered clearing where a small stream twisted through a tight mass of overgrowing vines, its water shimmering in the pale green of the riders' magical light. As they slowed, Chriani felt a dull ache in the muscles of his back and shoulders, the steady rhythm of the horse's back beneath him driving a wedge of pain up his spine.

His Ilvani escort slipped off first, pushing up and swinging one leg over his horse's head. He silently offered a hand to help Chriani down. Chriani needed to use it, his legs all but collapsing beneath him as he hit the ground.

Beneath the arching roots of a great limni, the stream had etched a pool out of loam and sandstone, the horses shifting forward to drink there. They were eleven in number, the Ilvani riders and their mounts. The fleet warhorses of the Greatwood, barely winded despite having run what seemed half the night. A troop of war-marked Ilvani, half in green-grey armor, half naked to the waist except where leather protected them at the shoulder or stomach. Six female, four male, lean bodies ridged with muscle. A wide belt pack was the only gear the carontir rangers wore except for bow and blade, and the almost-empty quivers of arrows slung at their backs and hips.

Chriani was still wearing the steel ring at his finger. No one had searched him in the chaotic aftermath of Jeradien's attack. A sense of relief twisted through him as he turned it absently, not sure why it was important anymore. He checked his belt, felt the black ring in its pocket, the golden badge, the two talismans, his lock picks. The only things he had carried with him. The only things left to him now.

Dargana was across the clearing, Chriani catching her gaze as she paced away from the horse she'd been carried on. Until he did, he realized that he had assumed her to be complicit in whatever had happened at the camp. Some kind of plan that she and the Laneldenari had hatched in case of trouble. But seeing her expression now, he understood that she was as shaken as he was.

As their horses drank, the Ilvani stretched and paced but were silent. All of them were watching Chriani as he made his way to the water, crouched down to drink. He was still shirtless and barefoot, blood-crusted and in leggings as Jeradien had found him.

He washed his shoulder carefully, the pain and the gash of the cut healed over by the salve but the black crust of blood remaining. Kathlan's stitches were looped tight and useless now across smooth flesh. He broke them with his fingers, pulled them painfully. He washed away a trace of new blood when he was done.

"Are you all right?"

Dargana's voice came soft from beside him as she knelt at the water's edge. She spoke low and in the Imperial tongue, no trace of an accent.

Chriani responded in kind, noting dark looks from a few of the Ilvani close by. "I'll live."

Dargana's knowledge of that common trade tongue caught him by surprise, though he thought he understood her purpose. The Valnirata Ilvani had been bitter blood enemies of the Empire of the Lothelecan. As such, even as relatively few of the Valnirata spoke Ilmari, even fewer had any proficiency in the language that had been the Imperial standard across the Ilmar for more than a thousand years.

"I'm hoping you know what's going on," Chriani said evenly. "Because I don't."

"I know some of it," Dargana said. Then, as if predicting his question, she added, "Though I don't know what happened last night. I was told to bring you to the Greatwood by following the Hunthad. I wasn't expecting this."

Chriani nodded. "Do you know where we're going?"

"If it's the place I think, a city. They'll hear the name if I say it to you."

"And why is that a problem?"

"Because knowing anything of one of the hidden cities of the Valnirata can get a stranger to the Greatwood killed."

A ghostly whistling rose from across the clearing, the horses reacting to it with excited snorting, shaking out their manes. The signal had come from the warrior Chriani rode with, who was watching him.

"We ride," the warrior said. He seemed to be using the Ilvalantar that Chriani knew, or the words were the same in whatever forest tongue he was speaking. He spoke slowly either way, as if concerned for Chriani's ability to understand him.

"I'm sorry about Kathlan," Dargana said as she stood, turning for the other side of the clearing. "She'll be all right, though. She's got strength the Ilmari will never understand."

Chriani nodded, even as he felt himself trying to force thoughts of Kathlan from his mind. Too much fear there. A thing he couldn't think on yet.

She would be fine. She had to be. He didn't know what story she'd tell, but he knew there'd be one. She'd called out when she told him to flee, had set up the idea that he was the one who struck down Jeradien. It would look like Kathlan had saved the Aerachi warrior's life.

Kathlan would lie as much as she needed to, Chriani thought darkly. He had showed her how.

His reflection was pale in the pool as he rose, showing him his shoulder, clear to see. The war-mark there echoing the marks the other Ilvani wore.

The Ilmari, Dargana had said, as if excluding Chriani from their number. As he reached the horse, he felt the expression ring empty in his mind, feeling a distance from it that told him she was right. The threat of being killed for who you were would do that.

The white horse that had borne him was a stallion, strong but compact. Still, Chriani needed an arm from its rider to boost himself to its bare back. He felt as much as heard a flicker of dark laughter drift through the troop. Across the way, Dargana clambered up to her rider's horse without difficulty. With disbelief, Chriani noted how that horse was among a few in the troop that carried no reins in addition to no saddle. Its rider had her legs high up on the horse's flanks, her knees and bare feet alone guiding the creature as it shot ahead.

Dargana had no need to hold onto her rider, Chriani saw. He kept his own hands back this time, locked his legs to the horse's sides. He set his arms to either side of him for balance as they set out again at a run.

The troop stopped once more past dawn for an equally short rest, the horses and their riders all taking water again. The light through the trees was a shadowy haze by now, bright enough to see by. The light disks winked out, disappearing into belt packs before the Ilvani set out again.

Riding on by daylight, Chriani found that his balance improved. So too did his ability to take the measure of the warriors they rode with. Their riding style at least was familiar to him, even in the short time that he had patrolled the frontier. The Ilvani rode as if they were born on horseback, mount and rider sharing one set of senses, a singular focus. No fear in them. Nothing existing outside the space of the vine-swept trails, the towering limni growing in tight ranks, raining down pale sunlight and a drift of green-gold leaves as the horses passed.

Chriani had never seen the Valnirata of the Greatwood outside combat, he realized. Never had the chance to watch them riding except across the long spaces that separated Ilvani and Ilmari as their riders shadowed each other along the frontier. Never seeing them except through the haze of frantic expectation and the hiss of arrows back and forth through the trees.

In their unbridled ease as they rode, in their instinctive sense of control, the Ilvani reminded him of Kathlan. An unwitting observation. A single moment of stray thought, but Chriani felt a pain hammering at his chest, a darkness to his vision. He had to hang on to his rider escort momentarily, fighting to regain his balance as they raced on.

One more stop saw the horses take water and engage in standing rest, but the halt was so brief that Chriani had no time to do anything but stretch his legs. Then just as he was getting to the point when he feared he might fall off the horse from exhaustion, the troop slowed its pace, slipping along a narrow trail that entered a broad glade tufted with pale green grass. The great trees rose up to frame a narrow circle of sky above, the forest around them a shimmering aura of gold and green.

Though the sky was too bright to scan, Chriani guessed that the sun was high in the world above and around them. He was steadier this time as he dismounted, watching as the horses were led to an area of flattened grass near a spring-fed pool. The glade had the look of some kind of tended way station. Thin silver ropes marked the edges of nets strung within a framework of low branches, the Ilvani unfurling them to reveal sacks of feed and forage. This they scattered to the grass, the horses eating as the Ilvani looked them over, rubbed them down with their hands.

With nothing else to do, Chriani sat, feeling the weight of exhaustion push him down as if the ground might be swallowing him. Dargana approached with a silver flask in hand, its sides etched in a bewilderingly complex pattern of leaf-curved lines.

"Mead," she said as she knelt. By her movements, she was nearly as stiff as Chriani, though she didn't look as tired.

"From where?" he said.

Dargana nodded toward her own rider where she was gently massaging her horse's left hock, working it with long fingers. "It'll give you strength."

Chriani sipped at the flask and felt an unexpected rush of warmth twist through him. He caught the familiar meadow scent of Ilmari mead in the liquor, but mixed with unfamiliar flavors and fragrances. He drank deeper, feeling the pain in his back lessened, the light around him burning brighter as his fatigue was seemingly drawn away.

One by one, the horses lay down, collapsing to the ground and settling into position for a deep slumber. As they sat down beside and between their mounts, the Ilvani were talking to each other. Whispering in the shimmering silence. More than once, Chriani saw them glance in his and Dargana's direction.

"Are we prisoners?" he asked quietly.

"We don't need to be. You want to run, you know as well as they do, there's nowhere you'll get to in the wood where they won't catch you."

Across from them, Dargana's escort rose to her feet with a paper-wrapped package in hand. She shared Dargana's darkness, her eyes black beneath a shroud of tangled hair set with streaks of night-blue. The same color as the edges of her war-mark, wrapping her shoulder and sweeping down to encircle one breast.

She stopped before them, tossing the package to Dargana. The exile nodded as she touched right hand to left shoulder like some gesture of thanks. Chriani wasn't sure what underlay the exchange, noting only that the Ilvani warrior seemed to be doing her best to ignore him, but he mimicked Dargana's gesture as best he could.

The Valnirata warrior responded by spitting, catching him on the cheek.

Chriani was on his feet before he realized he was moving, Dargana up just as fast, trying to step in front of him. She was whispering words in the forest tongue, talking too fast for Chriani to catch her meaning. A flash of blue steel erupted as a bloodblade appeared in the warrior's hand.

"Taelendar!"

The Ilvani who was Chriani's escort called out from across the glade, his voice shutting the whispered conversations of the other Ilvani to silence. Even the faint wind tracing through the trees above them seemed to slow. Chriani didn't know the word the Ilvani had spoken, but from the way the warrior snapped to attention and spun around, he guessed it was her name.

Chriani's rider said nothing else. Just held the angry warrior's gaze for what seemed like a timeless moment. Chriani's hands were locked to fists, but he realized it only when he felt Dargana's hands against his, pushing them down.

The warrior Taelendar swung her bloodblade behind her to sheathe it in its back scabbard. The way she held her hand meant that Chriani got to see the dagger for a long moment before it disappeared within well-worn leather. He was fairly certain that was as she'd intended it.

She stalked back toward the horses, making a wide arc around the clearing as Chriani's rider stepped forward. He was tall and dark, hair and eyes the grey-black of charcoal ash. Though Chriani had seen the war-mark on the Ilvani's shoulder for most of their ride, its full effect was visible only from the front. It was in black and grey, a stark shadow where it plunged down and across his chest, encircling breast and navel as a cascade of razor-sharp lines.

"I am Farenna," the Ilvani said. He spoke the common Ilvalantar, though his accent was sharp, enunciating clearly as if he had guessed at Chriani's lack of practice with the complex tongue. "I am captain among this troop. You are Chriani, and friend to us. Taelendar is young. She is angry, but you are in no danger. Please, eat and rest."

"Our thanks," Dargana said. She made the same gesture as before, but Chriani didn't follow her lead this time.

"For our security," Farenna said, "I must search you, friend Chriani." His tone was even. Almost apologetic.

Chriani felt the absurdity of the statement, standing before the Ilvani half naked and weaponless. "Search me for what...?" he started to say. Then he saw the flare of a blue-white light in Farenna's hand.

Against the shimmering of that light, the steel ring at Chriani's finger pulsed with an unnatural warmth. Before he had any chance to react, Farenna was nodding as if he could read something in the ring's dweomer, the light dancing as he traced his fingers along Chriani's belt.

Chriani's hands were locked to fists at his side. Dargana caught his eye, shook her head ever so slightly.

"You have gold within your belt, Ilmari." Farenna's hand shifted along the leather as if he was testing it. "I sense the shadow my spell casts against it. Please. Show me."

The eyes of all the Ilvani were on him, Taelendar standing with arms crossed upon her chest. Carefully, Chriani slipped his fingers to the belt's hidden pockets. He pulled forth the black ring, his lockpicks. The golden badge, the two talismans. The Ilvani captain touched them all, one by one. But at the sight of the talismans, his hand slowed.

"The hunter's heart," he said quietly. *Gavalirnon*. He plucked one of the talismans from Chriani's hand. "How do you come by these?"

Chriani made no move to stop him. "I took them off the Ilvani hunting me." He had no energy in him to even try to lie. No reason to anymore. "The gold disk is Ilmari magic. It masks me to the tracking power of the talismans. That's why they're dark."

He expected more questions but Farenna simply nodded, thoughtful. He returned the hunter's heart to Chriani's hand. "My thanks."

"Where are you taking us?" Chriani asked as the captain turned away toward the horses.

Farenna glanced back. "You must wait for your questions, friend Chriani. As we have waited for you."

Chriani watched the captain darkly as he paced away. "What does he mean by that?" he asked Dargana.

"Eat," was all she said. She slipped to the ground and opened the paper-wrapped package, some sort of flatbread revealed within. "You need to rest, and badly. The Ilvani don't need the sleep you do. They won't wait for you."

Chriani felt the weight of his exhaustion hit him again as she said it, but he shrugged. "The horses will be resting a while. I'll manage what I can." He broke off a bit of the bread and tasted it, sensing a sweetness like the draught Dargana had shared.

"The horses of the Valnirata rest no longer than their riders do. We'll be up and gone again before the sun has moved halfway to dusk. Rest every time you can, or they'll be carrying you in."

"Carrying me in to where?"

Chriani saw an answer in the exile's dark eyes, but she said nothing in response.

He ate half the bread in short order, washing it down with more mead and finding his hunger strangely satiated. Dargana shifted away from him when she was done, settling back against the upthrust root of a limni nearly as broad as she was. Chriani heard her breathing deeply, settling into the strange posture of sitting half-sleep that the Ilvani favored.

The trancelike manner of Ilvani rest was no secret among the Ilmari, but Chriani had never actually seen it. He had no idea what specific gifts of their Ilvani parents others of his mixed blood inherited, but the secret of waking sleep wasn't a thing he had ever known. Not sure why that aspect of his father's lineage hadn't been passed down to him. Across the clearing, the riders had gone silent, most of them likewise sitting cross-legged with eyes closed. Farenna and two others were doing a sentry's walk along the perimeter of the glade.

"You didn't kill him," Chriani said to Dargana. "Venry. Last night." He remembered the lieutenant trying to run the exile down, her hauling him off his horse in the chaos of the Ilvani attack. He hadn't expected to see the Ilmari get up again.

"I guessed right that he'd claimed my blade. Getting it back was more important."

"You threatened to kill me once for even having touched a blood-blade. I would have thought him stealing yours would be worth something."

"The Laneldenari weren't shooting to kill," she said. "I assumed they had a reason for that, so I accepted it."

"I remember you saying you don't wait on other people's decisions."

Dargana's black eyes held Chriani's gaze for a long moment before she closed them again.

He found a relatively soft patch of ground, but he also felt a knot of tension in his gut that told him sleep would be impossible. He had no tunic or cover, felt the chill of the breeze and the pain in his back. He was thus surprised to find Dargana calling his name what seemed only moments later. He sat up to see the light had shifted, the haze of the sun slanting in from ahead of him now. The horses were on their feet, the Ilvani rubbing them down again, a few already mounted.

Though Chriani's head was clearer, the weariness of his body felt as though it had settled in to turn his bones to brittle glass. He stretched as he followed Dargana, excising the trembling from his limbs.

He swung up behind Farenna without assistance this time. The horses set out slow to start as they left the glade and the haze of sunlight behind. Then they plunged into shadow and picked up speed, Chriani sitting straight, staring ahead like all the rest as they pushed deeper into the forest.

Along the narrow tracks of the Greatwood, the Ilvani horses made speed as if they might be riding along the smoothest Brandishear farm road, alternating between a gallop and a jog without ever becoming winded. Over two days of riding, the carontir kept the same schedule of short rests at intervals to drink and stretch, with two longer rests in clearings stocked with food and sweet mead.

That draught seemed like the only thing keeping Chriani on his feet. He would collapse to a dead sleep during those longer rests, once more by light, once by dark, but his exhaustion never truly broke.

By night, they rode within the shimmering veil of the Ilvani's mage-light. By day, the grey-green light shone dim through the towering screen of branches above them. Birds and insects were the only sounds, obliterated beneath the drumming of the horses' hooves over trails of moss and loam, but rising each time they stopped. Chriani heard wolves howl more than once, and a single time, a screech something like an owl, but louder than any bird should ever have been able to make.

The call was thin and distant, but even then, the Ilvani showed almost as much alarm as Chriani felt. For a time, they slipped into an outrider formation, four rangers flanking the main body of the troop with bows drawn. Eventually, though, the forest returned to its familiar stillness.

They saw no settlements as they rode, and this lack of signs of life began to weigh on Chriani. No cleared farmsteads, no villages. No woodcutters' shacks, no tree fort watchtowers. Just the endless expanse of forest, and an emptiness that pressed down on him like all the world might well have disappeared beyond the Ilvani rangers and the endless wall of green.

Midway through the third day since the attack on the Ilmari camp, that changed.

Chriani had heard the tales of the Ilvani cities. It was part of the training that had taken over his life when he unexpectedly made rank and was offered commission in the same day. History and warfare. Battle tactics and best practices in the field. An endless discussion of the mysteries of the Greatwood and the bloodthirsty Valnirata war-clans that dwelled there. Eschewing smaller permanent settlements that couldn't be defended, the Ilvani were said to center themselves in vast cities impossible to attack or siege. Even if you guessed correctly as to where they were, it would be three days hard riding to reach the nearest of those forest cities from the edge of the Greatwood. And you'd make that journey with the Ilvani fighting you every league of the way.

All of what Chriani had learned of the interior of the Greatwood in the past year had the feel of legend to it, for the simple reason that no Ilmari had ever seen it. Exiles' reports alone told the story, along with sparse accounts from seers and scryers among the war-mages of Brandishear and Aerach. Even during the Incursions, the forces of both principalities had avoided pushing into the deep wood. Fearful of what they would find there.

Chriani saw the change first as a light. The forest canopy was still bright above them, his eyes having long grown accustomed to the Greatwood's ever-present daylight gloom. This was something else, though. Something dead ahead, shimmering like a distant signal fire as the horses surged through the shifting screen of the trees.

He saw the archers next. Darker shadows within those trees, clinging to broad platforms. Those were set against the great trunks of the limni, suspended from thick branches by twisted rope-cables crawling with pale green vines. Bows were nocked and following them as they rode, each rank of sentries they passed replaced by another rank ahead.

The riders crested a rise where the trail broadened, then abruptly ended in a road paved with white stones. These glowed with a pale light, the horses slowing as they came near. Farenna was in the lead, Chriani leaning past him to see as their horse turned sharp into the light, the road ten strides broad and curving away to both sides ahead and behind them. A vast paved circle cut through the forest, the great limni looming to either side.

Within that circle, the city of the Ilvani rose.

From ten paces farther away, it hadn't been there. Following the trail that should have given him direct line of sight, all Chriani had seen was trees and vines, the shifting shadows that played out across the forest floor as the distant wind shifted through the canopy above. Some manner of magic. An incredibly elaborate illusion. He fought the urge to make the moonsign.

A sea of light played out before him, spreading from the tangled undergrowth up to the first tier of branches standing high over his head. Then it rose even higher, climbing upward in long, swirling strokes like frost against winter glass. It clung and clustered like spiderwebs, radiating out from central points. It hung like drooping nets, parallel lines of green-white radiance that glimmered gently as the horses drew near.

The spires and platforms of the city were ranked in endless rising tiers. Huge disks extended out from the edges of the limni, anchored by buttresses and rope cables that twisted past and through each other. A pattern of light and shadow was wrapped from tree to tree, connecting uncounted limni as a vast living loom. Chriani saw ladders and rope bridges, saw uncounted Ilvani passing along them like they might have been walking an Ilmari city's main streets.

He tried to grasp at the size of the settlement before him and couldn't. No way to see through to its far side, the light fading, flaring, blurring out to an endless haze of green-white ahead. And even if he had seen the city's far side, could have compared it to the spread of Rheran or Glaeddyn, Welbirk or Athegwyn or any of the other cities he had seen, the life and the light here expanded upward in way no Ilmari city could ever do.

Even at the edge of the Greatwood, the limni rose easily to six times the height of a tall warrior. As high even as any tower of the Bastion. Here within the forest, pushing closer to the heart of that endless green, Chriani felt a sense of unsettling awe at the thought of how much taller still the great trees might be.

Even before the apex of that height, great winged shapes flitted between the trees, slipping onto and off the tallest platforms with a screech that sent a chill up Chriani's spine. Griffons. Hundreds of them, swirling like starlings across the shimmering sky.

"This is Sylonna." Farenna's voice from in front of him brought Chriani's thoughts back to sharp focus. "This is the nearest city of the Ilvani to the Hunthad River. Nearest to the place where you were met."

Though Farenna still spoke slowly, his Ilvalantar was shaped by his accent, pushing the boundaries of familiarity. The word he spoke wasn't *city*. Not exactly. The closest translation in Chriani's mind was *forest-home,* but with a sense of connection like the two words were one. Not a paired description, but a statement of a single concept, no boundary to break it.

He felt light-headed suddenly. Entranced by the vision before him and unable to look away, even as he felt a weight in the Ilvani captain's words. *Knowing anything of one of the hidden cities of the Valnirata can get a stranger to the Greatwood killed,* Dargana had said.

Chriani remembered the Ghostwood, where he and Lauresa had been led by Dargana's band. He remembered the rotting platforms clinging to the limni there like some leprous shadow, anchored by fraying ropes and shot through with uncounted years of decay. But even through that decay, he remembered the ageless beauty that still clung to the ruins. The vague sense of all the history that must once have stood there.

He remembered wondering what it all might have looked like once. He knew now.

Ilmari and Ilvani were one folk once, his mother had told him. But that had stopped mattering long ago to the generations raised on the ancient history of the Migration Wars, and who had lived the more recent history of the Incursions.

Chriani knew the Ilmar Ilvani who had turned away from their forest kin. They were artisans and crafters, horse masters and foresters. Most were skilled with bow and blade, though precious few of them ever took service with the guard. Those who did were used as translators and loremasters, mapmakers and scribes. Kept away from the patrols of the Greatwood, and from the ranks of the war-mages for fear of the innate sorcery that all Valnirata Ilvani possessed — at least so far as Ilmari superstition held.

The blood of his father flowed in Chriani's veins. He had been told the tales that all Ilmari children knew, and other tales from his mother that his father had told her. He had met the exiles, had seen the ruins of the Ghostwood. He had fought against the Ilvani of the forest, skirmishing with their patrols for five months. He knew their ancient grace, respected their deadly power, or so he thought.

He had told himself he understood this world.

He'd been wrong.

Along the curving road that marked the boundary of the forest-home, other roads opened up at right angles, curving inward toward the center of the circle like twisted spokes. Farenna turned the troop down one of those roads, Chriani seeing other horses, other figures ahead. Ilvani moved and ran along the white stones, even as they descended and climbed along rope ladders twisting up into screens of overhanging branches.

As Farenna's riders approached, the Ilvani of the city slowed. Chriani saw them fall back against the edges of the road, then saw more of them moving in from adjacent paths, a network of white stone trails crisscrossing through the shadows. They stood without speaking, but he could hear unseen voices calling out in an ethereal song that twisted around him and away on the wind.

The Ilvani were waiting. They were watching him.

From out of the crowd, a dozen children slipped forward with no command, running up as the horses stopped. Farenna slipped to the ground, Chriani not waiting for an invitation to follow him. In his entire life, he had never wanted a weapon in hand more, though he knew how utterly useless any blade or bow would be against the crowd massing around him.

The Ilvani of the city wore a mix of fabric and leather, robes and armor, tunics and leggings. The tones of their clothing were earth and leaf, or dyed bright colors that seemed to pulse within the forest-home's pale light. They were dark or pale of complexion, hair braided or hanging free, eyes of every color of gem and flower, faces clear or marked with pigments in sweeping lines. No sense of sameness to them, except for the war-marks at all their shoulders. All of those marks were visible, children and adults alike either bare-chested, or wearing tunics or leather cut away to reveal the center of those tight-spiraling knots of dark line.

Four of Farenna's riders fell in to either side of Chriani, staring coldly ahead. He glanced back, saw Dargana likewise flanked.

"Follow me," Farenna said. He caught Chriani's gaze, held it as if he knew his thoughts. "You are the first Ilmari to set foot in Sylonna in long generations. Do not be afraid."

Chriani felt a dozen different responses he wanted to make, but his mind couldn't focus enough to shape any of them. He asked a question instead. "Are we guests or prisoners?"

Farenna smiled, catching him by surprise. No malice in it, though. "As long as you do not refuse our hospitality, friend Chriani, you will have no need to find out."

The area around the path Farenna led them on could have passed for any Ilmari settlement overgrown by nature. Chriani saw stables where the horses were led, heard more singing at the stalls of a leatherworkers' adjacent to it. He saw what looked like an apothecary's shop, next to a wide bazaar at which cloaks were on display in all the colors of nature. He saw what could only have been a tavern on the platform above them, its edge crowded with Ilvani looking down at him.

A broad stair loomed ahead, Farenna making for it. It shifted as the Ilvani leader climbed, Chriani realizing its rungs were tightly woven rope that looked barely able to hold a child's weight. It carried all of them, though, Chriani moving carefully as he climbed. The limni that the stairs ascended was the largest tree he had ever seen, its bole as broad across as the Bastion courtyard.

On the platforms hanging around that tree, the Ilvani had gathered to watch Chriani's approach, as below. Staring at him with a specific intensity that seemed to go beyond the sheer novelty of his presence. There was more uniformity to the dress of these figures, with most of them in gleaming armor or robes, gold and silver at their necks and fingers. Nobility by their look, if the Ilvani had such things. Military leaders perhaps, though they bore no more sign of insignia or rank than Farenna or his riders had.

Chriani let his gaze pass across the Ilvani as he climbed. Challenging them, not looking away. But at the feeling of the rope stairs shivering like a boat twisting into the wind, he risked a look behind him. The Ilvani that had watched him were stepping out behind the last sentries and Dargana. Following them.

When he shifted his gaze back to the crowd, Chriani saw white eyes staring sightlessly back at him.

A seer of the Laneldenari, Dargana had said. *Blind since birth, they say.*

The Ilvani was silver in the tone of his shadowed skin, in his robes, in the hair swept off his head and braided down his back. His hands were laced together around a thin staff of gnarled wood, his milky eyes staring without blinking. No sign of any pupil in them.

Veassen. That's a name you need to remember.

As he met those white eyes, Chriani saw the seer nod to him. Then he blinked and the face was lost within the crowd.

The stairs ended at a broad platform spreading into darkness. Farenna continued straight on, Chriani following even as his escort shifted to either side of him. Losing the tight formation that had brought him there. He felt a closeness to the air, saw the familiar tone of the green mage-light through the screen of leaves above him. They were inside an arched dome of dark canvas, stretched over wooden ribs. The platform was encircled by it. Closed off to the world outside.

A single tolling of a deep bell sounded out from somewhere. Farenna stopped, Chriani a step behind him. A pulse of light washed out of the shadow to either side, revealing a raised dais of dark wooden steps spreading around a central platform a dozen strides across. Along the edges of that dais, the Ilvani who had followed Chriani were moving in from the stairs, his escort shifting past him now as Dargana stepped up beside him.

He stopped because he didn't know where else to go. At his side, Farenna turned and nodded.

"I will be here," the captain said. "I will help you if I can."

Too many questions were running through Chriani's mind, but he knew he would waste his time in asking them. He only nodded in return as Farenna walked over to slip into the crowd, make his way up to the dais with the others.

Standing still, alone with Dargana at the center of the platform's emptiness as the tiers filled, Chriani felt the exhaustion settle across him again. He had never ridden so far, so fast, in his life. Pushed to the limits of waking and endurance, even as the Ilvani rangers had barely shown any sign of fatigue. He needed to move, he realized, worried that his legs would seize up if he stood too long. He began to pace around the open space, looking back to see Dargana following him.

In the crowd along the first tier of the dais, the blind seer was watching him.

The Ilvani's white eyes stared straight ahead, his staff held out before him. Chriani hadn't seen him walking in, didn't know whether he'd needed to be escorted. The other Ilvani were shifting around him as if the seer had picked that spot and stopped, oblivious to the movement to all sides.

As he kept the seer at the corner of his eye, Chriani assessed the faces of those others. They were watching him intently, meeting his gaze openly as they filled the dais from edge to edge. The same anger was showing in too many of their eyes.

He tried to assess this place he was in, tried to assess how the unseen pieces of his own future were pressing down around him. But there was no understanding here.

You must wait for your questions, friend Chriani, Farenna had said. *As we have waited for you.*

A silence fell across the platform hall. Chriani paced back to something like the center of the open space, Dargana stepping up to his side. He was conscious of his bare feet slapping loudly on the wooden floor as a voice sounded out from the crowd. The speaker was a tall Ilvani of autumn brown, hair and skin a match to the robes he wore. He spoke one of the Valnirata tongues — the distant source of the common Ilvalantar that was different enough that Chriani couldn't follow it. He felt certain that was as intended. He was only a spectator here, meant to remain ignorant of what was said. Dargana was at his ear, though, whispering a translation into Ilmari.

"That's Laedda, master of Sylonna and speaker of this gathering of elders. He names you as the Ilmari they call Chriani, of Brandishear and Rheran. You should acknowledge it."

Chriani nodded as he called out in Ilvalantar. "My mother was the Ilmari. My father was of the Crithnalerean and House Halobrelia."

The words came by instinct, and from a sense of defiance against the wall of unseen animosity shifting around him. It wouldn't have been news to any of them, of course. The Valnirata could read the central glyphs of the war-mark at his bare shoulder better than he could.

One of those Valnirata stepped closer. She was a tall and pale warrior in gleaming green leather, a golden circlet set atop her head. Her emerald eyes flashed with a dark indifference as she spoke.

"A child," Dargana translated. "Even by the standards of the Ilmari mongrels." But before Chriani could respond, she broke off her whisper to speak for herself. "This warrior you call a child has the ear of the Brandishear prince. A personal relationship. He is hand-picked for this mission of peace."

From across the chamber, a whispered chorus rose to send a chill up Chriani's spine.

Ilvalachna...

It was the name the Ilvani had for Prince Chanist, inherited from his father Goffree, fallen in the Incursions. The Ilvani Scourge, who had destroyed Caradar the exile king and driven the Valnirata back to the forest.

Chriani resisted the urge to look at Dargana, to try to get some sense from her eyes and expression of what was going on. Her mention of the diplomatic mission to Laneldenar caught him by surprise, in that he had all but forgotten about that mission in the chaos and exhaustion of the past three days. He had assumed that original purpose had been burned to the ground by the events at the camp and the Ilvani attack.

Some of the Ilvani had apparently assumed that as well.

"Reports of the Ilmari's conduct among his own riders dismiss any claims of rank and privilege." A pale Ilmari warrior in leather and chain mail spoke the words that echoed in Dargana's voice. Her black hair was oiled and tied back tightly, gleaming like her armor. "He is disgraced and distrusted. Likely to be subject to incarceration or execution if he returns. What use is the laóith to us now?"

"He must be returned to Aerach at once. We waste time on this folly."

"He has seen Sylonna!" someone shouted, rage sharpening each word. "He cannot be allowed to take even that name back to his murderous kin."

Chriani quickly began to lose the thread of what was said as other voices rang out in succession. Not overlapping each other, so that Dargana's voice at his ear still sounded out clearly. But creating a continuous stream of argument and antagonism that went by too fast for him to follow her translation.

"...take advantage of this prospect..."

"...another feint from the west. The prince's power fails..."

"...other envoys, other chances..."

"...distractions and false hope. Slay the laóith now..."

If the encounter had been intended as some form of debate, the Ilvani executed it with the same ruthless efficiency as their skirmish tactics. No speaker was ever interrupted, no one was shouted down. Even so, Chriani heard the anger in their voices, heard the disappointment. He understood as he hadn't before how Dargana had spoken truth, in saying that at least some of the Ilvani wanted this peace. They had wanted and expected an envoy who could deliver it.

Tell them who you are...

The words came like a whisper in Chriani's mind, pressed in close and echoing. A male voice speaking the Ilvalantar, each complex syllable ringing out clearly. He forced his hand down where it shot up by instinct to scribe the moonsign over his heart.

You know what this is, Chriani of Ilmar and Halobrelia. You know where to see me, but be wary. Others are watching.

Chriani turned slowly as if assessing the crowd, voices rising and falling around him. Their words faded for him, though, his perception shutting down. Closed in and focused on the sensation of having another mind in his. A sensation he had felt before.

His gaze passed over Veassen but didn't linger. He saw the blind seer nod.

Someone was shouting. Dargana's voice at his ear repeated it, but Chriani heard it only as fragments of sound. The tall warrior in grey-green leather again. "…folly to even attempt…"

He clenched his fist to stop it trembling. The steel ring at his finger was tingling, but whether the sensation was real or just the panic of his mind, the seer understood.

Yes, he said. *The ring.* The voice was strong in Chriani's head, even as it carried a weight of age and understanding that gave it a hollow quality. *I have no relic to match it, but I can make use of your ring's magic. In my lifetime, I have learned and forgotten more spells than are known among all the Ilmari. Trust me, Chriani.*

I have problems with being asked to trust people I don't know, Chriani thought. He was speaking the Ilvalantar in his mind, but it came easier to him somehow than it did as speech. Some power in the link between them that let him focus his thoughts.

There is no time for the explanation you deserve, Chriani. But know this. I am the one who sought out Dargana and bade her seek you. I am the one who saw you pursued by the Ilvani of Calalerean, as I saw you standing here today. We are connected in your being here. And in what must happen here today.

Even over the scant few times he had used the steel ring with Lauresa, Chriani had quickly learned how difficult it was to focus his thoughts, keep them from turning to words that could be heard at the other end of the link. He found that focus now, though, because the seer's words in his mind had summoned up a single thought in reaction, and it wasn't one Chriani would share.

Kathlan was gone.

His whole life, he had willfully — often gleefully — distanced himself from everyone around him. The street children he had lived among after his mother and grandfather died, before chance and Barien's kindness had taken him to the Bastion and a new life. His peers among the tyros from the day he'd been granted his insignia. His superiors among the squires and guards, the captains and lieutenants of the prince's guard. Lauresa, the two of them drawn together and driven apart, not once but twice.

Chriani had driven himself even from Barien when the darkness that shrouded his mind became too much sometimes to hold back, and even as Barien had known the reasons why. Only Kathlan had ever been truly absolute in his mind, his heart. Three short years, during which Chriani understood only now how much he had hoped that his mind and heart had changed.

Only Kathlan had ever been set above his instinct to push everyone and everything away, given enough time. And now he had managed even that, and his life was done.

"...feed into the Ilvalachna's plots to dominate all the Ilmar..."

He still heard Dargana's whisper, but Chriani didn't need her translation anymore. The seer in his mind had sharpened his ear for the tongues of the Ilvani somehow, granting him insight even into the fast-spoken words passing back and forth across the chamber floor. The green-armored warrior was shouting down Farenna now. She was taller even than the rider was, lean like a wolf, her golden hair beneath its circlet woven as a screen of braids. She slapped the hilt of a backsword at her belt to punctuate her words, other Ilvani scattered through the crowd striking right hand to left shoulder in time with her. Some kind of show of support.

If all this was your plan, then your plans were finished before they began, Chriani said darkly. *Now get out of my head.*

He was already pulling the steel ring from his finger when the seer spoke.

Chriani, I know what happened on the Clearwater Way.

He let the ring stay where it was. Something in the voice, in the way it slipped through his mind, created a sense of calm that spoke to the truth of the statement. Chriani wondered suddenly if it would even be possible to lie through the link the rings created.

Not a tough claim to make for things Dargana could have told you, he said in his mind.

The exile spoke no word of these matters, the Seer said. *Nor would she, as you who know her true character would understand.*

Then you read it through my thoughts...

No, Chriani. I saw it before it happened. Your pursuit of your princess. The assassin of Uissa slain as you flew in the Ghostwood, the narneth móir in your hand. I saw you claim that blade from beneath stone where it was hidden. My magic might read the thoughts of your mind in the moment, but memory is hidden even beyond the reach of spellcraft. Tell me the last time you thought directly of these things?

A silence fell. The brown-robed Ilvani who had spoken first, Laedda, had command of the chamber again.

"This council renders its judgement," he called out. A sense of endings, of lost opportunity and anger, was in his voice. "Chriani of the Ilmar will be returned to his homeland, and will carry with him this doom of the Valnirata. That having seen this one of the hidden cities, his life is owed to us. Should he ever again set foot in the Muiraiden, that life shall be forfeit…"

Tell them of what Dargana told you, Chriani. There is little time.

"I would speak," Chriani called.

Laedda's voice and Dargana's echo cut off in abrupt astonishment. From the speaker's indignation, Chriani might have guessed that he'd never been interrupted before.

"I am Chriani of the Ilmar and House Halobrelia," he said again. He spoke the Ilvalantar carefully, but felt it come easily to his mind. The ring was warm upon his finger. "I am the envoy chosen by Chanist, who you name the Ilvalachna, but who has trusted me…" Though his voice remained clear, Chriani's thoughts of Chanist distracted him. He felt his tongue seize up. "I will carry your intent back to him."

And try to avoid getting shot on sight or hanged for treason while I'm at it, he thought. He could sense the words made real in the seer's mind.

You must call yourself one of fate's chosen, Veassen said in response, *and bonded to the Ilvani and Ilmari realms.*

Are you mad or simply drunk?

Quickly, Chriani. Tell them of what you did on the Clearwater Way. The story as it is known. The war that would have begun if not for you.

"The trust of your prince carries no weight here," Laedda said evenly. Chriani waited for Dargana to translate, not sure what might happen if the sudden upturn in his fluency was noticed.

"Then trust me for what I've done," he said finally. "I am one of fate's chosen, and bonded to the realms of Ilvani and Ilmari alike." Chriani felt himself flush as he said the words, but the Ilvani were strangely rapt as they watched him. "I fought the assassins of Uissa and rescued the princess of Brandishear on the Clearwater Way."

Not the biggest lie he had ever told. Certainly not the worst. As a matter of instinct, though, Chriani understood that the stakes of his lying had never been higher.

"I stopped Uissa's plot to blame the Valnirata for the murder of an Ilmari royal heir, and to incite war to east and west that would have seen the Greatwood burn."

You have done well, Chriani. Now tell them the last.

"I know the Calalerean Ilvani seek the heir of the exile's blade."

He shouted the words, hadn't meant to. No idea where the defiance that filled him had come from. He heard the silence that hung in the aftermath, turning to take in the assembled crowd. His gaze passed over the seer as he went. Veassen was standing expressionless, no sign that he had even heard what was said.

Among the other Ilvani, something had changed.

"This gathering of elders ends," Laedda said. "A council of masters meets the rising of the pale moon."

No one argued. No one spoke in response. Chriani saw a restless anger in the gaze of the tall warrior with golden braids as she turned from him, but the seething emotion that had filled all the platform space just moments before was gone as quickly as it had come. The Ilvani turned to file out along the tiers of the dais again. Chriani stood where he was because he had no idea what else to do.

He glanced to the side once to see Dargana watching him. She looked relieved as she nodded. It was an unfamiliar expression on the exile.

The blind seer was gone. Chriani hadn't seen him leave. His mind was clear, no sense of any voice there but his own.

Farenna lingered to the end, approaching Chriani and Dargana as the last Ilvani filed out.

"You will follow me, friend Chriani," he said. "Accommodations will be made for your rest. As a guest." He smiled, but Chriani was too weary to return it. A chill twisted through him as he and Dargana followed Farenna to the stairs. Pieces of the puzzle slotting into place.

The seer had sought him out and bade him speak to whatever council this was. He had told them things Veassen already knew, but which the other Ilvani clearly didn't. Chriani's thoughts were scattered, fighting their way through two levels of shadow.

The games princes play, he thought. The Ilvani had very different ideas of power and leadership, he knew, but some things stayed the same.

He had no idea what he had gotten caught up in. No idea how he was meant to get out.

He remembered the seer's voice in his mind. Remembered how his own voice had shouted out in the end.

The Calalerean Ilvani seek the heir of the exile's blade...

He had said it, but even now, Chriani had no idea where it came from. Veassen's voice had been in his head, but he couldn't remember those words spoken by the blind seer. Only in his own mind.

It must have been an echo. The seer thinking, Chriani speaking, as one. It had happened that way sometimes with Lauresa in his mind.

Why couldn't he remember it, then?

Outside the council hall, Farenna led Chriani and Dargana to a wide bridge that arced away and up from the great platform, twisting through a screen of branches into unknown heights above.

"Follow," the warrior said, stepping onto what looked like a path of thin wooden dowels suspended in empty air. The corded ropes they were strung along were so thin they could barely be seen, the bridge shifting with Farenna's movement as he stepped on. There was no railing, Chriani saw as he followed carefully.

The nobles and captains who had filled the hall had already scattered, but the platforms around the bridge were thronged even more thickly now with the other Ilvani of the forest-home. All of them were watching Chriani as he and Dargana followed Farenna up and into shadow.

— CHAPTER 11 —
THE LÓECHARI

THE LOFT WAS SCREENED by curving walls of white cloth, wrapping a broad platform whose ceiling was successive layers of the endless canopy of the Greatwood above. It had the look of guest quarters, with water and mead, flatbread and some sort of cheese set on a low table. Blankets and cloth cushions were scattered about, no other furnishings to be seen. Chriani had no idea how high above the ground they were, but as he lay back now on a rough bed of cushions, grass-stuffed by their feel and their scent of meadow hay, he could feel the platform shifting gently with the wind, could see the haze of sunlight bright through the leaves.

In the aftermath of the gathering of elders, Farenna had led him and Dargana along two more gently swaying rope bridges to a twisting ladder lashed to a tall limni's split trunk. "To the top," he said, indicating that they should climb. Chriani felt a dizziness take him as he swung onto the loose-hanging ladder, forced himself to focus as he clambered up carefully, rung by rung. At the top of a high series of platforms stacked like so many shelves, he and Dargana emerged through the hole in the center of the loft's floor. Farenna didn't follow them.

Dargana had prowled the platform for a short while, staring into the leaves above as if to make sure they weren't being watched or guarded. Chriani was too weary to do anything but sit, pulling a cushion under him as he felt along the edges of the cloth walls. Though they were tied tightly, he wasn't sure he trusted their strength, shifting away so there was no chance of leaning back against them. A raised dais set off behind screens revealed a washbasin and a low commode, but the loft had no place specifically to sleep. The Ilvani had no such need.

"Are you all right?" Dargana brought bread and two flasks of mead from the table, then sat across from Chriani. When he simply ate in silence, the exile shrugged and drained one flask on her own. Then she moved to the far side of the platform to sit cross-legged, closing her eyes.

Chriani was more tired than he thought possible. His mind was a storm of shadow, his back and legs and shoulders aching in previously unimagined ways. He gathered cushions in an attempt to make some sort of makeshift pallet, but succeeded only in scattering them when he lay down. He settled in the end for laying two blankets folded on the smooth wood of the floor, then wrapping another around him. He set cushions beneath his head and legs, trying to quell the ache in his back. Fatigue washed over him like warm water, his vision blurring as he closed his eyes.

Against all logic and reason, though, he couldn't sleep. Not all at once, at any rate. He felt the light above him shift from time to time, felt a new stiffness in his back or legs that told him he had drifted off, but only for a short while. He wasn't sure how long he'd lain there, listening to Dargana's slow breathing and feeling the exhaustion of almost three days hard riding course through him, until suddenly both Dargana and the light were gone.

Chriani shot upright, wincing as he did. The platform was empty, his eyes taking a moment to adjust to the green glow that filled it. The canopy of leaves above was dark, a pale light coming instead from glyph lines scribed along the outside edge of the floor. Though he had no idea how long he'd slept, his head was strangely clear, the ache in his legs and back subsiding. And he was ravenous. He ate the rest of the bread, distrusted the taste of the cheese but ate that as well. He was working on his second flask of mead when he heard movement at the ladder, looked over to see Dargana scramble up and over onto the floor.

"You're awake," she said, and Chriani saw that she had changed. The black armor she had refitted from her Brandishear-issue gear was gone, replaced with a loose-fitting robe of dark blue. Her hair was shining and tied back to a thick tail, the peak of her eyebrows and ears even more noticeable. If she hadn't spoken, Chriani might not have recognized her at first.

"It's close to the time of the council," she said. "Take the ladder to the first platform below. There are baths there. Be quick, though."

Chriani responded by drinking more slowly. Dargana noted it but made no response as she sat down to eat. Chriani's mind was clear enough to sort through every question he wanted to ask her, everything he needed answered. He kept his silence by instinct, though. Knowing somehow that it wasn't time for the questions yet.

When he was ready, he slipped down the ladder, swinging off it at the first of the platforms below, vaguely remembered in passing from when they had ascended earlier. A landing of dark wood dropped down along four steps that turned around a tall screen of lacquered paper. Beyond the screen, the platform was broader than the loft and open to the air around it, a gentle wind blowing. Other screens surrounded a pair of commodes and two low pallets covered with folded blankets, like some kind of healer's table.

At the center of the space stood three oblong wooden tubs, each filled with steaming-hot water that poured out from a brass globe set at its head. Chriani saw no pipes to carry the water, no source of heat, no drain in the tub. Just whatever magic was set into the globes, or perhaps the water itself. Flowing endlessly, high above the ground.

A similar lack of plumbing was in evidence at the commode, speaking to some magical function within it, and inspiring Chriani to make the moonsign as he used it. He was fairly certain he'd never done that before.

Low shelves around the edge of the platform were stacked with blankets and towels. Chriani took one of each as he warily stripped, leaving leggings and smallclothes in a filthy heap on the floor behind him. He took his belt with him. Not wearing it, but simply wanting to keep the things held in its secret pockets close by as he slipped to the water.

He felt a delicious heat thread its way into tight muscles, let his fingers work into the stress points on his legs, the knots in his shoulders. There was no sign of soap or oil at the tub, but its water washed the sweat and grime of the long road from him all the same. It had the scent of spring rain and lilac. Chriani made the moonsign again, more than once.

Even as his body relaxed, though, he felt his mind drawn down tight beneath the uncertainty that was the aftermath of the council of elders. No idea what he had gotten caught up in. No idea how he was meant to get out. His thoughts were clearer than they had been in long days, but that clarity only let him see how hopelessly tangled those thoughts were. At his core now was an emptiness he'd never felt before. As if everything he'd ever been — everything he might ever be — had been drained from him. He had disappeared from the world that once held him, like the power of the black ring had somehow consumed him. All history, all possibility, gone.

When he stepped from the tub, his leggings and smallclothes had disappeared from the floor where he'd left them. Chriani felt a spike of tension as he let his senses slip out around him. No one there, no one watching. Someone had come, though, and he hadn't heard a thing. Just the wind in the trees, blowing colder now with the heat of the bath still in him.

Hanging on a wooden rack where the clothes had been, he found Ilvani garb. Undertunic and smallclothes in some manner of white linen, soft. Leggings and tunic of a light, tight-knit wool, warm but airy as he pulled them on. Boots of felt and leather, stitched in gold. A robe of green and black, tied at the neck. Another tie for his hair, white cord, woven as tight Ilvani knots. Both the robe and the tunic had the shoulder cut away, the war-mark standing out like blood and shadow on Chriani's skin.

A curved finger-knife and a steel mirror had been left with the clothing. The water of the tub had left his beard unnaturally soft, the knife's razor edge cutting effortlessly as he trimmed and shaved. When he was done, he slung his belt on, even though the Ilvani leggings had no need for it. Then he tied his hair high, as he had never done before. Pulling it up and back, trailing down his neck and exposing the slight peak of his ears. Not as sharp or pronounced as the ears of the full Ilvani, but still something he had been taught from the time he was a child to never show to the Ilmari world in which he lived.

In the space of a single night, that world had become a thing he had no reason to think of anymore.

When he slipped around the screen, Dargana was perched on the landing and waiting for him. She stood as he approached. "It's time."

"Not quite," Chriani said.

With her hair back, Dargana's eyes seemed even darker than they did when that hair framed her face. Her gaze tracked to Chriani's own hair, his ears revealed. She smiled. "I'm not the one to answer your questions, half-blood."

"You brought me here. You know why I was brought."

"Yes," Dargana said. "And no, I don't. I was told to bring you here and I brought you. That's all."

She swung onto the ladder, sliding down it in a way that made Chriani's stomach lurch. He thought of how far down the ground was if she slipped.

"What did you tell him?" he called, too loudly. Dargana pulled herself to a stop below him, looked around quickly as if watching for anyone else who might have heard. It was silent around them, though. Just the whisper of the wind through leaves and veiled walls.

"I told him nothing." The exile said it in the Imperial tongue, as if fearful of being overheard. Chriani's thoughts had to shift to make sense of her.

"Veassen knew…" Chriani started, but Dargana cut him off.

"Veassen told me. You following the princess. The Clearwater Way. He told me how we found you near the scorpion sands, how the pale assassins were following you. The bloodblade given to Uissa by Chanist's hand before you claimed it. He knew it all."

Chriani was silent a moment. He heard the truth in the exile's tone, and something else. An unfamiliar fear. A sense that the blind seer was as much an unknown to her as he was to Chriani.

"And what did he say it meant?"

"It meant that you were meant to be here."

"My fate's my own," Chriani said darkly. "No one else calls it for me." But he heard the tremor in his voice as he said it, saw the thin edge of a smile stray to Dargana's lips.

"That night in Aerach," she said. "When Kathlan and I followed you to that wagon camp. Who was the Ilmari who knew you were riding there before you did?"

Chriani felt a chill as the memory came back to him like something from another lifetime. He heard Irdaign's words as a whisper in his mind. *Small gifts that tell me of things that might come to pass.* He felt them shift into place alongside the echo of Veassen's words, lurking deep within his mind. Words Chriani had tried and failed to still.

I am one of fate's chosen…

Dargana didn't wait for his response as she continued her descent.

Chriani followed her down past two side platforms, watching her swing off the ladder at the third level below their quarters. It was a platform they had passed on the previous climb, higher than the first council chamber. Clambering off, he found her waiting. Two sentries in white lacquered ring mail stood three paces behind her, backswords at their hips. They stepped aside for the two of them, Dargana leading as they ascended a solid stair that arced out from the platform and into open air.

Chriani had to focus to find his balance, keep his footing as he stepped out into the empty night. He could see the half-full Clearmoon just rising through the screen of trees, the ground dark below. Their footfalls were all but silent as they went.

The platform wrapping around the limni that was their destination was split into three terraced sections, wrapped with vines and screens of silver cloth. A blue light filled the space, shining from a fountain that bubbled on the middle terrace — a central spire like a spiked lance, rising from a pool edged with smooth stone.

Dargana stepped aside as she reached the first terrace. Chriani moved past her, seeing the Ilvani waiting. Twenty of them in total. He recognized the speaker Laedda, who stood with Farenna a short distance behind him. The Ilvani captain had his grey-black hair tied back, a sash across his chest that left his war-mark visible. A backsword was at his belt, naked steel with no scabbard holding it. Within the blade, a faint blue gleam spoke of some dweomer in the steel.

At the farthest side of the third tier stood the tall warrior with the golden braids from the previous council. The same dark fury she had showed when arguing with Farenna was in her eyes. Other faces were vaguely familiar to Chriani from that earlier council, but the inscrutable expressions of the Ilvani were all but impossible to read where they watched him.

Even as he noted that the blind seer was nowhere to be seen, he heard footsteps behind him. Veassen was there, had appeared from nowhere. Chriani flexed his fingers in the pattern of the moonsign but kept his hand at his side.

The blind seer made no sign of sensing Chriani, who had to step out of his way as Veassen pressed forward. As he did, he tapped his staff to the platform's wooden floor with a steady ticking sound, mixing with the chiming of the fountain in a strangely musical way.

The lack of any sort of table or meeting area across the three tiers of the platform gave Chriani a moment to wonder how a council worked among the Ilvani, and how it differed from the standing scrutiny of the previous day's gathering. He got a sense of it quick enough, though.

"We are met," Laedda called. "This council of masters begins." He spoke the Ilvalantar this time, eschewing whatever Valnirata tongue he had used at the gathering of elders. He met Chriani's gaze as he did, his expression suggesting the change was intentional. Not caring yesterday whether Chriani understood him or not, but knowing it made a difference now.

"This council is corrupted..." The tall Ilvani warrior called out from the third tier even as Laedda's voice faded. Her grey-green leather was overlaid with silver scale today, shimmering as she stepped forward. She spoke one of the Valnirata tongues, so that Chriani lost the thread of it after those first few words.

"That's Contáedar," Dargana said at his ear where she'd shifted up beside him. "War master of Laneldenar."

"We met yesterday, thanks," Chriani whispered back.

"This'll go easier the less you talk for now. Let them say what they have to say."

"And when they're finished talking?"

"Veassen knows."

The blind seer was the length of the first tier away, having tapped his way to a place near the broad stairs that rose to the second tier. Dargana's voice was barely a whisper, no way for him to have heard her. Chriani saw the seer's head shift in seeming response all the same, the milk-white eyes finding his.

"...all Valnirata's purpose is known..."

Contáedar was still speaking. Chriani tried to focus as he looked away.

With no seating, no fixed positions or even any sense of rank or order, the Ilvani paced as they spoke and listened. Contáedar fielded responses from two others, Dargana once more translating at Chriani's ear. It was questions about troop movements in the Ilmar, and the strength of the treaty forged in the aftermath of the Incursions. 'The feint,' the Ilvani were calling the events of a year and a half before, talking as though both Brandishear and Aerach had been too quick to take advantage of the rumors of Valnirata involvement in those events. Chriani was one of the few who knew how dangerously close to the truth that was.

The war master had two backswords slung across her shoulders today, and a bloodblade in a scabbard set across her stomach. She slipped her hand to that blade as she shouted out something that sounded like a warning. Chriani saw her dark gaze fix on him.

"She says that the Valnirata are destined to march on the Ilmar," Dargana said, "reclaiming it for the sake of past and future. That war against the Ilmari is the only way."

"...Brona Coebann..." Chriani heard. Contáedar was calling the Clearwater Sea by its Ilvani name, still used by the mariners who traversed its coastal cities.

"She says it is the Ilmari's destiny to be driven like rats to the sea."

As at the larger council of the previous day, the Ilvani never interrupted each other, employing an instinct for response and a patience that would have seemed like weakness in any Ilmari dispute. In the range of anger and animosity they expressed, though, the Ilvani and their cold and methodical concentration would have put any diplomat or merchant lord in Rheran to shame.

Away from whoever was speaking, the Ilvani drifted together individually to whisper unheard words. Commenting or criticizing in secret as the dialogue shifted from place to place, voice to voice. An Ilvani in black robes flicked his fingers to create a pulsing sphere of light before him, as if to accentuate his words. "In Calalerean," Dargana translated, "they embrace the power of the past and the old faiths. We acknowledge the strength of that past, but fear it for the strength it grants the Calala. We ignore that by the act of embracing that past ourselves, the strength of Laneldenar would be greater still."

For long years, one of the things that had kept war between Ilmari and Ilvani a distant threat was the schism and conflict within the Ilvani themselves. The Valnirata were perpetually divided by the war-clan structure at the heart of their culture. Never openly skirmishing against each other, but distrustful. Content to build four individual powers in their own lands, and to hone their blades when they needed to against Ilmari to east and west, humanoid tribes to the south, Crithnala exiles to the north.

Chriani remembered it all as a vague blur of memory. More of the field training for his assignment to the rangers. Kathlan had been the one with the head for history and lore. She would have understood it all far better than he.

"We dream of the Ilvanghlira unified," Contáedar was saying through Dargana at Chriani's ear, using the name the Ilvani employed to refer to themselves. "We dream of the divided Ilmar splintered beneath the single wedge of our might..."

"Lóech arnala irch niir!"

Veassen's voice rang out like the echo of an iron bell, cutting off Contáedar and Dargana at once. A musical tone twisted through his words, Chriani feeling an echo of the voice he'd heard in his mind at the previous council.

It was the first time any of the Ilvani speakers had interrupted to shut down another's voice. By the way all movement stopped across the stepped platforms, Chriani could guess at the weight of such an action.

"Three coins for confession," Dargana whispered, but it had become the one phrase of the Valnirata tongue Chriani knew best.

The blind seer spoke the Ilvalantar, and slowly. Contáedar's expression darkened as if she knew it was for Chriani's benefit, though he continued to focus on Dargana's whispered translation at his ear.

"We speak of the old faiths rising in Calala, but the wise among us know that Calala seeks not the faith of the past but power. Power that means destruction to all Muiraìden, no matter the hand that wields it. The wise among us know the reasons why the Ghostwood of Nyndenu was left to shadow. The cult of the confessor are the lóechari. Their power is an ancient poison, and the Ilvani's dark dreams of war against the Ilmari are the honey that masks its taste."

"You should speak of whatever poison has taken your mind, seer." Contáedar's response came as a sneering hiss, but Dargana's translation at Chriani's ear was even. "The only histories of concern to me are the records of war, which is the dream the Ilmari made. The Ilmari who breach our borders, slay our scouts. The Ilmari who slew our forebears, claiming the lands they walked. Staining the woods our people settled in the dawn of the world."

Four Ilvani circled close behind Contáedar as she spoke, striding across the platform while they followed like some kind of support train. The war master's anger was razor sharp in the strength of her voice. The knuckles of her hand were white where she gripped her sword. "The Ilmari scar our lands with the filth of their cities, the roughness of their stone, the lumber of forests cut and burned with every new generation. As long as we hold Muiraìden, the terms of the Ilmari and their envoy will ever be demands of surrender."

It was a familiar anger, Chriani realized. A rage he had seen before. In Prince Chanist. In Ashlund, in Grus, in too many others. All consuming, never ending. Something carried for long years, like a wound that would never fully heal. Festering, feeding itself.

"Do you think to stop me, master Chriani...?"

Veassen spoke up, his voice clear. "You speak of what terms this envoy brings without hearing his words, war master."

A chill twisted through Chriani as the seer's voice rang across the chamber, a silence following. The Ilvani that had been moving were still. Veassen's were the only eyes that didn't shift toward Chriani where he stood.

They were waiting for him to speak, and he had no idea what he was meant to say.

Be calm, Chriani. Tell them why you are here.

Veassen's voice rang clear in Chriani's mind again, a subtle presence that made him wonder how long the seer might have been listening. He took a few steps forward, pacing parallel to the edge of the first tier. Playing for time.

I'll need to know why I'm here first.

You know who you are, what you have done. Speak it here, so that all may know.

Is there truth magic on me?

Such spellcraft can be easily unwrought. These are the masters of Sylonna. Their judgement of your words will be based on instincts far more difficult to deceive.

In the seer's tone in his mind, Chriani heard a strange and sudden reflection of Barien. A kind of gentle condescension, breaking through the sullenness that seemed to cling to Chriani sometimes like a protective shell.

"The Ilmari do not seek war," he called out. He tried to find Barien's voice and its gift for diplomacy, but the need to speak the Ilvalantar pushed the warrior from his mind somehow. He spoke slowly, but felt the same ease with the tongue that he had felt at the previous council. Veassen's understanding in his own mind. "We have our soldiers, and we have our history. But the people of the Ilmar crave peace. They need and want peace, despite what your war master tells you here today."

With a hiss, Contáedar turned her back and paced away from him. The four Ilvani closest to her did the same.

Well done, Chriani. Speak now of Calala. Of what you have seen.

"But we will stand against destruction if it is promised. And if destruction is promised from the Calala Ilvani, it must be put down. I have seen the magic that the seer spoke of. The three coins for confession. I've seen what it does, and I fear it as you should."

Silence hung across the chamber, Chriani conscious of his heart beating fast. Too many of the Ilvani were smiling, even as the expressions of others settled in beneath a grim uncertainty.

They don't know. A realization coming to him, spoken to Veassen in his mind. *They don't think any of this is real.*

No, the seer replied. *Many of them do not. To the Valnirata, the history of the cult of the confessor is known and forgotten. One legend among thousands, lost in the days of wild magic when all the Ilmar lands were ours. We must convince them otherwise. Calalerean's theft of that ancient power must be shown. We must convince them of the truth.*

And how does that become my task?

Because they will believe you are a part of that truth, Chriani. Whether you believe it or not.

Chriani realized he'd been standing in silence longer than he wanted to. Some of the Ilvani were whispering as Laedda called to him.

"Speak, envoy, of what you know."

Dargana had stepped back, Chriani catching sight of her watching him.

He told them. Spoke of that first encounter with the war-band that had tracked him, and of the Ilvani prisoners. He told them of the shrine and the dead warrior. He told them of the coins. At Veassen's prompting, he described the shrine in as much detail as he could remember. And as he did, he saw the same dark look flash through the expressions of the Ilvani closest to him. The ones who had been smiling before, each of them watching intently as he met their eyes in turn.

He told them of the war-band that had pushed into Rheran in pursuit of him. *Now tell them why,* Veassen said in his head. The seer's tone was even, but Chriani felt a sense of expectation in the words that he didn't like. He ignored it as he continued.

"I was pursued by the Calala of the cult, both in Muiràiden and in the Brandishear capital. The Calala knew me. They heard of what happened when I pursued the Princess Lauresa on the Clearwater Way, and their agents shared that knowledge through the rites of the cult. They work as one."

He pulled what Dargana had told him in the throne room of Rheran from memory, tried to assemble it into something that would make it sound as if he knew what he was talking about. He told of being pursued along the Hunthad, and of the strangeness of the cultists they had seen there. "The Calala Ilvani who pursued me in Aerach, who we killed the night that Farenna came for us. Their eyes were clear at first. The cult rites showed in them only when they attacked us in the end. Or after they had died."

He stopped then because there was nothing else to say. Veassen was lingering silent in his mind, even as Chriani saw the dark look that had spread now across nearly all the Ilvani listening to him.

It wasn't anger, though. That had been his first expectation, the anger of the Ilvani a thing he'd grown all too familiar with over five months of border skirmishes.

They were afraid, he realized. And that scared him more than he could ever have expected.

Tell them, Chriani. The heir of the exile's blade. It is time.

Chriani felt the words resonate in his mind, Veassen's voice shifting his own thoughts away. He pushed back against it, fought to find the will to simply dismiss it all.

In days of war, Veassen said, *one will arise to stand between Ilvanghlira and Ilmari in struggle. One who will forge the final fate of both peoples.*

You know the story, Chriani thought coldly. *Tell it yourself.*

Contáedar spoke up as Veassen went silent in Chriani's mind. Though her back had stayed toward him as she paced to the farthest platform, the warrior turned now with a sneer. "And what makes you special in the Calala's eyes, Ilmari? What draws their interest to a mongrel half-blood?"

"If the hospitality of Sylonna had armed as well as garbed me, calling me that would be the last thing you'd ever say." Quick words, spoken in the moment. Chriani was too scattered to truly feel anger, but the instinct to anger had a life of its own, it seemed.

With a fluid motion, Contáedar whipped one of her backswords from its scabbard, tossing it in a smooth arc across two terraces and the fountain between them. Chriani didn't move as it stuck blade first into the wooden floor, one pace away from where he stood.

He stepped up to wrench the sword out, hold it fast in both hands. He felt himself assessing the blade's weight and balance, feeling his senses shift forward as he slid away from Dargana. Contáedar was moving for him, drawing her bloodblade and her other sword with mirrored motions across her stomach and back.

"This action is forbidden," Laedda called. And with a speed that spoke to the rigid code of discipline among the Ilvani and managed to surprise Chriani all at once, Contáedar slid to a stop. She sheathed her weapons with a dark look, her breath coming sharp, mouth set in a narrow line.

She looked to Chriani as if waiting for the other sword to be returned. He carefully slipped it to his own belt, mindful of the edge that would have cut through its double-thick leather as if slicing paper. He was certain that if he had to draw the weapon, he would leave the belt and his leggings on the floor at his feet.

Contáedar slowly turned away. As she advanced to the edge of the central tier, her hand stayed at the hilt of her bloodblade.

"The Calala seek the heir of the exile's blade," Chriani called to her back. His voice carried across the chamber, the anger still in it. He felt the same subtle shift in the attitude of the Ilvani as he'd felt at the first council. "They believe that your legends speak of the narneth móir of the exile warlord Caradar. It was claimed by Chanist when he struck Caradar down in the dying days of the Incursions. I claimed it when it was stolen from Chanist. The cult wants it. Now they hunt me for it."

Where his hand rested on the hilt of Contáedar's sword, Chriani felt it shaking. He squeezed his fingers to stillness, cautious of the bare blade pressing against his leg. An undercurrent of dark tension was twisting through the Ilvani where they paced around him. The mention of Chanist, of Caradar, of the Incursions.

"That's why I'm here," Chriani said. There at last, a sliver of truth. But having said it, he realized he had no idea what came next.

Contáedar laughed to set his mind at dark ease. "This fool was seized from his Ilmari captors in fetters. Arrested and bound by his own people. Rescued from them by Ilvanghlira riders, who took him stripped of weapons and armor." Her back was still to Chriani as she spoke, her words for the assembled Ilvani. Dismissing him even as she spoke of him. "How does the heir of the exile's blade allow it to be taken into laóith hands?"

"The Ilmari didn't take the blade because it was already hidden by my hand," Chriani said. "As it had to be for one who serves in the Prince's Guard of Brandishear. One who sits at the side of the prince high." The words rang hollow even as he said them, but they were the best point of defiance he could think of. "I knew to protect the blade. I knew to keep it safe."

Contáedar spit in response, still not looking back.

"The cult of the confessor is old even by the ages of the Ilvani." Veassen spoke to break the tense silence. The seer's voice carried the thinness of age across the chamber, even as Chriani felt it strong in his mind. "Two paths along which its power flows. Ilvani who take the rites of confession fall under its sway and control. They can be committed to any cause of their masters."

Across all three tiers, the Ilvani began to shift again, moving more quickly than before. No speech passed between them, though. All of them listening, but seemingly afraid to meet the seer's gaze.

"The coins are of Talaeria, the lost province. The lands that are now Crithnalerean, where the power of the lóechari rose and was abandoned millennia past for fear of the destruction it might reap. Two coins are placed in the hands to pay the price of service, one in the mouth to pay the price of confession that is the vow of service. Then the ritual of confession sees the coins bound into the body by arcane force. Magic fueled by the power of the memory that is the price of admission to the cult."

"These things are told," Laedda said. Chriani heard the words pass through a third of the assembled Ilvani, rising as a whispered reflection while the master continued. "The act of confession during the rite burns away what has been confessed. The acceptance of the lóechari's power is a corruption of oath to clan and Valnirata, even as the act of acceptance burns clan and oath away."

Chriani could hear the unease in Laedda's voice. Could see it reflected in the faces around him.

"The rites grow more powerful with each new lóechari claimed," Veassen said. "The bond of the coins burns bright. It compels action, coopts the mind and spirit. And if that action fails, if the agent who commits life and strength to the rites of confession fails in the missions assigned by the cult, the coins exact the price for failure. A death of mind and spirit even if the body has already fallen. The faithful twisted and left broken from within. Two coins in the hands, one in the mouth. As this envoy has seen and described."

Whispers again from the other Ilvani. More of them this time. *These things are told…*

As the seer's words filled his ears and mind, Chriani felt the fear grow stronger. No sign that Veassen was anything but calm as he spoke, but his thoughts carried a revulsion sharp enough to turn Chriani's stomach. He felt words that weren't words. Not interfering with what the seer was saying, but working on a deeper level. Some kind of meditation. A whisper of thought expressed as the faintest hiss of voice, subconscious.

It was the sensation of making the moonsign, he realized. The desperate hope that came from the familiarity of a gesture, from the connection of body and spirit and faith. Except this was a symbol not of the body but of the mind, the Ilvani with their own wards against the darkest magic.

He felt something shift into place. He tried to focus his thoughts, distanced himself from Veassen, though he felt the Ilvalantar still come easily to his mind.

"The act of confession during the rite burns away what has been confessed." Chriani repeated Laedda's words, heard them echo in his own mind and Veassen's at once. The seer was listening to him now. That was something new.

He remembered the Ilvani at the camp, their eyes clear as they fought, as they surrendered. The eyes clear in those who had died at once. Then the terrible transformation, the power tearing through them with no warning.

"If the rites take the confession from mind and memory, then can the confession itself be forced and then forgotten?"

All the Ilvani were whispering now, Contáedar and her four followers the only ones who stayed silent. *These things are told.* Chriani heard Dargana's voice join in from behind him. No fear in her, though. Just a razor-sharp hatred for what she had come to understand even as he did. He fought the urge to make the moonsign himself.

"The rites grow more powerful with each cultist claimed." As he said the words, Chriani felt the thoughts shifting in from somewhere unseen. Felt the pieces fall into place, even as he realized the puzzle was one whose full scope he hadn't seen before. "And with that rise of power, what if the confession burns deeper? What if knowledge of the cult itself is taken by the rite, leaving those afflicted with no sense of what they've done. No knowledge of who they serve until their orders are triggered. I've seen it."

The faint hiss of whispering faded, silence hanging for a time. Chriani wasn't surprised when Contáedar was the one to break it for a second time.

"This is laóith trickery." The war master's voice was ice. "We patrol the Crithnalerean frontier as we always have. Where is this cult? Where are these golden warriors of legend, building an army for Calala?"

"Hiding," Chriani said. More pieces falling into place. "Because they know that to reveal themselves would bring the Laneldenari down on them. They're setting things in motion, testing their power first against the Ilmar."

Contáedar sneered. "So if the cult fights against the Ilmari, both sides do our work for us. Let them kill each other…"

"And what's your plan for after, then?" Chriani saw the war master's expression darken, noted how his interrupting her was raising her ire. Good. "War against both sides of the forest? Or are you waiting for Calalerean to use its cult magic against Brandishear, then planning on striking after both are weakened?"

"No." A firm voice rose from the third tier before Contáedar's anger could force a response. Chriani looked away from the war master's cold gaze to see Farenna there. The Ilvani captain had his hand at the hilt of his backsword. "No," he said again. "I speak for myself only, but I speak with the voices of veteran warriors. The Valnirata do not need war, friend Chriani. We do not seek it. Our truth is more complicated than that."

"Captain." Contáedar took three steps toward Farenna, the backsword in her hand edging up. A hiss of alarm spread around the two of them as the Ilvani closest to them both edged away. "You usurp the authority of your war master at this council."

"I show all deference to your rank and will in the field, war master. But I am at this council as captain of Sylonna, and am your equal here."

"I will not…"

"The captain of Sylonna will speak." Laedda's voice cut across Contáedar's with the force of a blow. Chriani saw the war master shudder with the effort of silence. She lowered her blade, but slowly.

Farenna nodded to Laedda. He began to pace, turning to face the others by turns. Even so, it was Chriani his gaze returned to, time and again.

"I have fought for Valnirata and Laneldenar for long years. I have trained three generations of carontir since the wars before. I killed Ilmari soldiers in those wars. I have killed Ilmari rangers in the time of so-called peace, for crossing too far into Laneldenar. For pursuing us where only Ilvani may tread. I have killed exile bandits pressing in from Crithnalerean. I do these things for duty and order. But also because the love of combat flows in me, and has since I came of age in battle against the Ilvalachna in the wars before."

Chriani saw Dargana tense from the corner of his eye at Farenna's mention of hunting the exiles, but his own attention was taken by the rider's mention of *the wars before*. From Barien and the ranger loremasters alike, he knew that this was how the Ilvani referred to the Incursions. No formal name given to them, because doing so would force the Valnirata to admit a resolution to that dark conflict. To remember that they had lost.

"In battle," Farenna said, "all Ilvani crave the strength that comes with victory. We crave that sense of majesty for our people. In war, we find the strength of life, but our lives are more than war. And we have grown too used to the strength of war giving meaning to our lives. What we need is the wisdom after long centuries to see this."

The incursions were the wars before, the loremasters had said, because that phrase brought with it a sense that war was a continuous thing. In the wars before, the Ilvani had pushed out from the Greatwood seeking blood and triumph, then fallen back under the threat of a unified Ilmar standing against them. A threat wrought by Chanist, the young prince whose rise none of the Ilvani could have foreseen. And just as there were wars before, there would be wars still to come, inevitably.

Chriani wouldn't have judged Farenna old enough to have fought against Chanist. Most Ilmari veterans of those campaigns were long retired to quiet duty, the fireside, or the grave. The Ilvani aged more slowly than the Ilmari, he knew. A hundred years and more was a good life for them. Something easy to forget when the similarities between the two peoples were so sharp.

"Ilmari and Ilvanghlira were a single people once."

Veassen's voice rose to embrace the brief silence that hung as Farenna's words faded. Chriani felt a chill trace along his spine, the words echoing his mother's from so long ago. He couldn't remember thinking them, wasn't sure when the seer would have pulled them from his mind. But then he watched as a half-dozen of the scattered Ilvani whispered the same words in echo to Veassen's voice. Some kind of reluctant benediction. A thing the Ilvani knew, that some of them believed, he realized.

He had never suspected it, would never have dreamed it. His mother repeating words that his father must have told her.

Contáedar wasn't one of those whispering Veassen's words. "The captain of Sylonna and the seer of Laneldenar speak treason," the war master shouted. "This council's purpose is lost. I call its end."

"Your call is denied," Laedda said evenly.

"I speak no treason, war master." Farenna stepped up to within two paces of Contáedar, his voice grim. "I speak of the future. And your fear of that future is your affair, not mine." He turned away, leaving the war master ignored behind him. Chriani half-expected her to draw against the captain, but she simply stalked away.

"If a dark power does rise in Nyndenu," Farenna called out to the assembled Ilvani, "then entering Crithnalerean in force alerts the lóechari and the Calala to our purpose and our fear. But our patrols are known along the frontier, and push often across the forest wall when the Crithnalerean threaten. I have ridden to the Ghostwood more than once since Calalerean's movement north, though the forest and its spirits sing their same silence as ever to my ears."

"Then how is the cult to be found?" An Ilvani in blue robes spoke up, circling close to Farenna.

"With the assistance of this envoy and the fate that weighs on him."

Chriani felt a faint chill at the captain's words. A surge of whispering rose around him, the Ilvani watching intently. The flash of fear was bright in their eyes again, their minds open to him somehow through Veassen's thoughts. He could feel the ward against dark magic. The words that weren't words.

"Friend Chriani," Farenna said with a deep nod. "You spoke of the Calala hunting you. Show this council their weapons."

Chriani stood in silence a moment. Then he slipped two fingers within his belt and found the larger pocket there. Carefully, he pulled the two talismans from it, their bloodstone shards still dark.

He heard the whispers around him shift and echo. *Gavalirnon...* Farenna stepped forward, his hand extended. Waiting.

Chriani passed the captain the newer talisman, claimed along the Hunthad. Farenna examined it carefully, stepping away from Chriani as blue-white light flowed within his hand. As he whispered an incantation, that light flared to a brilliant pulse of ice-white. Farenna turned slowly, eyes half-closed. Listening for something, Chriani thought, but the silence that had descended upon the council chamber was absolute.

Farenna opened his eyes, holding the talisman straight out before him. He stood that way for a long while, staring at the stone on its thin steel chain before he spoke.

"I focus this magic and feel for its source, and it calls me north to Nyndenu."

A new chorus of whispers broke across the council chamber. Even Contáedar's entourage had joined in now, the war master the only Ilvani who was silent.

"I can trace the lines of dweomer in this hunter's heart, back to the source it reports to. I turn the power of the lóechari against them. Where they dwell in the Ghostwood, the hunter's heart will lead us, and the riders of Laneldenari will find and destroy them."

The council chamber was a storm of voices suddenly. As Veassen listened, Chriani felt them filter through his mind without really trying. Support for Farenna's plan, and arguments against. Alongside the call for action against the Ghostwood, cries for movement against Calalerean itself. Calls for restraint and second thought before action was taken.

Chriani heard it. Understood it. From a starting point of disbelief — in him, in the story he had to tell — the Ilvani had swung around full in the name of the fear of whatever power had been found in Crithnalerean. In the name of a legend Chriani heard circling around him now, caught from the cacophony of voices like a child snatching fireflies from the night air.

"The half-blood..." they were saying. *"Heir of the exile's blade..."*

They believed him because of whatever connection they imagined he had to prophecy and power. The connection the Calala Ilvani believed in, and in whose name they had hunted him. And it didn't matter that none of it was true.

All that mattered was that in that moment, in the fanciful terms of Veassen's children's tale, Chriani understood with sudden clarity that he had been granted a single desperate chance to undo the damage that fate and his own failures had done to him.

"No," he shouted.

The voices faded to abrupt silence. Farenna's expression showed the surprise present on all the Ilvani except Contáedar, whose eyes showed only contempt.

He wasn't sure where the notion had come from. It was sharp in his mind like it had always been with him, but it carried no sense of Veassen's voice.

"You need alliance with the Ilmari to do this," Chriani said. He ignored the war master's gaze to focus on Laedda and Farenna, and the Ilvani standing close by them. Trying again for Barien's voice. The even tone, the sense of careful thought behind every word. "You need to bring the four principalities into alliance with the Ilvani of Laneldenar against the cult, as I came here to do."

"The Valnirata take no orders from laóith." Contáedar's voice rang out ice cold as she paced forward. Her four followers were with her but had pushed away. Just out of sword range, Chriani noted.

"This is no order," he said carefully. "This is an offer of assistance. Of the truce the Ilvani want and need. The reason I came here from Brandishear. If you move against the lóechari in force, if you push a Laneldenari army into Crithnalerean and the Ghostwood, signal fires will light the length of the Aerach frontier. The assault from the east will come before the next dawn. The invasion of western Crithnalerean from Brandishear comes before dusk that same day. They won't wait for the Calala Ilvani to push north to meet your assault. Because they won't know that the Ilvani are fighting the Ilvani, and they won't care."

"You are disgraced," Contáedar sneered. "By the testimony of this captain, you have no authority…"

"I make my own way among the Ilmari, and it's no concern of yours. I have the confidence of the Prince High Chanist who sent me here. The first strike needs to come from the Ilmar. Brandishear and Aerach have their forces already set across Crithnalerean and the Clearwater Way. The north of the Ghostwood is their range, as the south is yours. You set a pact between Ilvani and Ilmari. Destroy the cult together to end the threat against both realms. Prove that Ilmari and Ilvani can have common cause and purpose."

The words rang in his own ears as if someone else was speaking them. Barien's voice, carrying the warrior's conviction even in the Ilvani's complex tongue.

It was a good story, as stories went. And it didn't matter to Chriani that it was the greatest lie he had ever told.

"I will see it done," Farenna said. "Chriani rides with me."

The energy in the chamber shifted. Chriani had to fight to slow his breathing.

Contáedar stepped toward him but it was Farenna she shouted to, anger twisting her voice to a steel-sharp edge. "The lóechari seek the half-blood, and you would deliver him to them!"

"You have claimed the Ilmari's story as fabrication, war master." Farenna's tone was deferential, his grey-black eyes steel hard. "Have your thoughts changed?"

"No Ilmari rides with the carontir!" Contáedar snarled in response. "No Ilmari army breaches Valnirata on this half-blood traitor's word. Captain of Sylonna or no, you presume too much."

"As do you, war master, if you believe that your will supersedes the will of this council."

Contáedar's eyes burned like bright coals. She shifted away with a grace that suggested she might have forgotten Farenna was there. No one was watching her, though. All eyes were on the captain.

To Laedda, Farenna turned and saluted, right hand up to touch the war-mark at his shoulder. "I am captain of Sylonna. Chriani is the guest of Sylonna. It is my right, and my choice, for Chriani to ride with my carontir. I mean to discover the location of the lóechari in Nyndenu. This information will be shared with the Ilmari through this envoy, whose fate ties him to Laneldenar and all Valnirata. This fate we shape together to build the foundation of the lóechari's fall, if the council wills it so."

There it was, Chriani thought. This was his way home.

"The vote," Laedda called out. No more preamble than that. No more discussion.

One by one, starting with those closest to the speaker and shifting outward, the Ilvani raised their hands. Some made the full salute, hand up and held at the war-mark. Some pressed a cursory touch to the shoulder, their expressions unreadable.

Only Contáedar and two of the Ilvani with her kept their hands at their sides, looking at Chriani as they did. The other two of her followers had broken with her in the end.

"It is decided," Laedda said. And with nothing else spoken, the Ilvani began to move for the first tier and the open stair beyond.

Contáedar was among the first to go, stalking a curving path away from Chriani. She avoided the stairs, leaped down to the lower tiers, her footsteps sounding out in a way Chriani expected was meant to show her anger. He still had her sword at his belt.

Farenna stepped up beside Chriani, nodded deeply. The newer talisman was still in his hand, still pulsing within its cocoon of blue-white light. "We ride at dawn."

Chriani nodded in return, glanced around to see Dargana watching him. The look in her eyes was something he couldn't read. "Dargana rides with us," he said. "If she wants. With your permission."

"It shall be." Farenna and Dargana exchanged the salute. Then the captain joined the others walking for the edge of the platform, disappearing beyond shadowed walls and across the stairs.

In the end, Chriani and Dargana were left alone in the council chamber. The sentries at the entrance stood impassive, not seeming to care whether they stayed.

Veassen had vanished. Once more, Chriani hadn't seen him go.

"You did well," Dargana said at last. She was eyeing the sword at his waist, Chriani not sure whether she was talking about it or more general events.

"It wasn't me," he said quietly. "Veassen was in my head."

"I gathered that when you stopped needing me to translate. It wasn't all him, though. You did well."

"If you say so."

Dargana gave him the thin smile. Then she paced across the tier, down the stairs, and away.

Chriani walked to the second tier and toward the fountain as Dargana's footsteps faded. He let its blue light wash across him as he paced around the platform, watching to make sure there was no movement at the sentry station before he opened his mind to the steel ring at his finger.

I am here, Chriani. Veassen's voice rang clear in his thoughts.

Are you ready to tell me what in fate's name is going on? Chriani thought.

I can tell you that you have done a thing today few could do. I will help you in any way I can...

You told me to say it. The heir of the exile's blade. Chriani had to focus to interrupt the speaker's voice in his head, feeling it falter. *At the council yesterday, then today. Why?*

Because that is why they listened to you, Chriani. That is why they believe.

That and that alone? It's madness.

It is faith, Veassen said. *There are subtle differences.*

If he could have laughed within his mind, Chriani would have done so. *They think the heir is me. You think that.*

I believe that the lóechari believe you are the heir, Chriani. And that I saw you here to speak the legend yourself.

I said it because you told me to, Chriani said darkly.

I bade you say it because I saw you say it, Chriani. I saw it before it happened.

Chriani bit down on the frustration he wanted to voice. He was fairly certain the seer heard it anyway. *Then what happens next? If you see it all before it happens?*

Fate and the future are not a fixed tableau. Events move and shape themselves according to our will, but there are fixed points toward which we move. The fate of Ilvani and Ilmari is mutable. It shifts and changes according to the hearts and passions of those within the Greatwood and without. I have lived with those passions for long years, Chriani. And at the end of my life, I understand the price that both Ilmari and Ilvani have paid for them.

Why didn't the council just ask me if I was the heir so I could tell them 'no'? Put an end to it?

They would hardly trust one who made open claim to such a destiny. Fate must be lived and proved, Chriani. Not merely spoken.

Again, Chriani felt a gentle mocking in the seer's tone that reminded him of Barien.

I sense all possible futures, Veassen said. *I see the fixed points that might lead to those futures. You are one such point, Chriani. You have touched something beyond your own life, whether you willed it or…*

Chriani pulled the steel ring from his finger. As he did, he realized the leather-strung talisman taken in Rheran was still in his hand, squeezed tight to leave an impression of its dark bloodstone shard in his palm. He slipped both it and the ring to the gold-lined pockets of his belt as he turned away.

— CHAPTER 12 —
THE GHOSTWOOD

CHRIANI DIDN'T SLEEP any more through the end of that night than he did through its start, though he felt himself slip in and out of the same state of fitful dozing. Dargana hadn't returned to the shared platform by the time Chriani made his way back, the sentries at the council platform the only Ilvani he saw along the way.

When he awoke to the faint glimmerings of first light through the leaves above, Dargana was with him. She was sitting cross-legged, the slowness of her breathing telling Chriani she was resting. He worked the knots from his muscles as he stretched across the platform floor, his body finally feeling rested even as his mind was racing, his heart beating fast with a sense of agitation he didn't understand.

Then he remembered that he'd been dreaming of Kathlan before he woke. He felt something twist in his chest, forced his mind to push the memory down. But in the shadow of its disappearance, a kind of clarity came to his thought. A focus and purpose that resonated in his mind.

In the heat of the moment on the floor of the council chamber, it had been Kathlan who forced his hand. He had understood it then, but hadn't let the thought loose in his mind. Aware that Veassen was listening. All his talk of common threat, all his repeating of what the seer told him to say. It was what it was, but none of it mattered anymore.

He would go back to the Ilmar. Back to Kathlan. That was his mission, his goal. The only thing that mattered.

He could find the cult. Find the common threat that might undo even the smallest amount of the generations-long animosity between Ilmari and Ilvani. Find a foe that both could hate, that both could fear. Chriani could do this. He would bring the information back to Chanist, would convince him of the urgency of the cult's threat.

He would win a place for himself again in Brandishear when it was done. He had to go back.

Dargana stirred as he stood, Chriani not sure whether he had disturbed the exile or whether she had simply been waiting for him. She blinked awake, quickly took in the shadowed platform around her.

"It's almost time," she said. "You'll want to use the baths again before we go. The waters will strengthen you. Help you compensate if you don't sleep again for a while."

Chriani said nothing as another memory unfolded. Something lurking beneath the memory of dreaming Kathlan, he realized.

He had been dreaming of the cult as well.

He had dreamed the rites. Some vague version of the lore Veassen had fed to his mind, coins in each palm, one in his mouth. He could taste the metallic tang of bright gold in memory, could feel it burning his hands as magic coursed through him.

The act of confession during the rite burns away what has been confessed...

In the dream, Chriani had felt his memories torn from him. He felt the coins flaring molten-hot, searing his flesh as they became part of him. And as they did, he had made the confession he made to Kathlan that night. Felt it burned from his mind and forgotten — a chance to truly forget, to wipe away everything that had happened with Lauresa from his mind. Undo all the pain he'd ever caused, feeling it scoured away as if it had never been.

"Are you all right?"

Dargana's voice brought him back from the shadow. Chriani was staring down to his hands, the black ring and the steel ring clutched tight there. One in each palm, as the coins of the dream had been. He couldn't remember having retrieved them from his belt. He nodded to the exile as he turned for the ladder, slipping both rings back to their hidden pockets as he went.

Dargana appeared at the baths as Chriani was finishing, slipping behind the screens as he dried himself. He had soaked quickly in the steaming water, but even that was enough time for someone to once more steal onto the platform to leave new clothing behind for him and Dargana both. Armor this time. Supple grey leather overlaid with a sash of steel links, both cut away to leave the war-mark at his shoulder exposed.

"When this is done," Dargana called out, unseen in the tub beside him, "you should come with me." She spoke the common Imperial tongue once more.

Chriani didn't understand the statement at first. "To where?"

"Crithnalerean. Ride with me. You're an exile twice over now. You'll be a good fit."

Chriani felt a chill pass through him as he slipped the armor on over tunic and leggings. He didn't answer directly. "Considering that none of us actually knows what we're doing beyond Farenna saying he can follow the talisman's magic back to the cult, it's hard to talk about it being done. Never mind what happens after."

A rush of water came from behind him as Dargana slipped from her bath. Chriani heard her footsteps, glanced back to see her wiping water from herself as she inspected the armor laid out for her. He caught sight of the exile's war-mark for the first time since she'd covered it in Rheran, saw its more complex reflection of his own mark. The same core of tight lines was set at the center of both, the sigil of Halobrelia. But then both expanded out to their own pattern. Different stories told. Different names to be read there.

"And I'll be going back to Brandishear," Chriani said quietly. He heard the words hang, not sure why he'd felt it necessary to say them.

Dargana glanced over as she pulled on smallclothes, slipped her tunic and leggings on. "Indeed? I don't know your soldiers' code in Brandishear, but I'd be surprised if desertion and accusations of treason didn't carry some kind of penalty."

"I'll be going back."

"You were last seen escaping an Ilmari camp beneath a hail of Ilvani arrow fire."

"Anyone with eyes and half a mind will understand the Ilvani weren't shooting to kill that night."

"I've ridden the Clearwater Way my whole life. Half a mind is as good as most of your captains get."

Chriani's armor was an unexpectedly good fit, the leather moving with him as if he'd worn it all his life. An empty scabbard stood against the rack where the armor had hung, Chriani hitching it to his belt. The backsword he'd taken from Contáedar slid into it easily.

"What do you believe?" he said. "From what was said yesterday."

"Why are you asking?"

"Because you don't seem the sort for superstition, yet you came for me. You've stood by me."

"Maybe it was fate."

Chriani glanced over to see Dargana tightening the buckles of her leather. A thin smile underlay the exile's words as she checked the fit of her scabbards, making an adjustment where her bloodblade hung at her hip.

"I want my homeland back, half-blood," she said. "I believe in the need to kill Calala by the score for what they've done to Crithnalerean. I believe Veassen when he talked of seeing you as the key to defeating the cult. But why that might be, and what you and your prince and the Laneldenari do with the rest of the Ilmar after that, is no concern of mine. Just as it's no concern of yours anymore. You should ride with me."

Dargana headed for the ladder, Chriani lingering behind her. But as she slipped down it, she slowed. "However this ends, you need to watch me, Chriani. You need to make sure I'm not lóechari."

Chriani's mind was silent suddenly, all his other thoughts gone. The wind through the trees overhead was a voiceless whisper. The exile's smile had faded.

"What are you…?"

"I was a month in Calalerean." Dargana's voice was even, Chriani feeling her choose her words carefully. "Getting close to the cult so I could watch them, then waiting for them to move against you. Seeing the blind agents since then, with their memories of the rites taken from them, if you're right about that… The Calala might have turned me, and I've got no way to know…"

"That's enough on that." Chriani heard a fear thread through the words as he said them. From the ladder below him, Dargana's dark gaze was locked to his.

"I'm not asking you to kill me here and now. I'm just saying watch me. Stay close. If you see it happen, you'll know what to do."

The degree of calm in the exile's voice was as unnerving to Chriani as the task she was setting for him.

"It won't come to that."

Dargana shrugged. "You'll know what to do," she said again as she descended the ladder once more.

Chriani said nothing as he followed.

He didn't know the route they were taking, but Dargana made no sign of uncertainty. Countless Ilvani were out along the ladders and bridges and platforms of Sylonna, walking or lingering in the rising light. Watching Chriani as he passed.

The lights of the forest-home were bright in the trees above them, spreading to a shimmering haze as the wind set boughs and branches, bridges and platforms to a gentle swaying. The two of them reached the ground in a broad paddock. Stables of green cloth stretched over ridged wooden frames surrounded them, pushing back into the shadows beneath the trees. The morning was mist and grey light, a wind blowing through the branches high overhead and the ground crawling with a fast-moving fog.

Chriani saw seven horses waiting, five Ilvani preparing to ride. Farenna was there, as was Taelendar, he noted darkly. He recognized the other three from the troop that had ridden to the Hunthad, but Farenna was the only one to acknowledge him as he approached.

All the riders were dressed as he and Dargana were, in leather and chain. They wore green-grey cloaks over it, like the ones slung across the backs of the two horses not yet bearing riders. Dargana approached a lithe black mare, the other horse a grey gelding that watched Chriani, assessing him with a too-intelligent eye.

Farenna called to him, speaking the Ilvalantar once more. "The grey is yours, friend Chriani."

The horses of the Ilvani took no other riders, Chriani knew. He stood there in a moment's uncertainty, then reached out tentatively to stroke the neck of the grey. He felt it shift into him in greeting.

Next to the horse, he found a bow and two well-stocked quivers, a wide belt pack filled with the paper-wrapped bread and flasks of mead. He strapped both quivers across his back, hefted the bow carefully. It was a light recurve horsebow, its feel familiar enough. But even through a first quick sense of its balance and pull, Chriani understood that it was the best weapon he had ever held.

The Ilmar had modeled their own bows on those captured from the Ilvani for generations, but whatever knowledge the weapon masters of the Ilmar had stolen from the folk of the Greatwood, there were subtleties they'd missed. Or was it Ilvani magic imbued into the bow's tightly wrapped wood and horn? Chriani felt a wave of unease, then felt an even stronger sense of irritation at himself. He couldn't make the moonsign, but he touched his fingers lightly to his heart as he drew the bowstring back to his chest.

Farenna swung on and astride his white stallion, pacing to the front of the squad. "We ride," he said.

As always, the steeds of the Valnirata bore no saddle. Chriani was acutely conscious of how his experience at bareback riding amounted entirely to a half-dozen short sessions training for retreat tactics, plus the frenzied flight that had taken him to Sylonna. From his first meeting with Dargana, he remembered that her Ilvani exile band had ridden with saddles, but she showed no hesitation or uncertainty as she jumped up to her mare's back now.

Chriani managed to pull himself onto the grey without alarming it, which he took as an achievement. Farenna set out at a walking pace, the others falling into line behind. Chriani took the second spot from last, Dargana behind him. He was glad of that, assuming that if he fell off on the journey, she'd be the least likely to succumb to the temptation to run him down.

As they picked up speed, the grey's pace stayed smooth beneath him, the horse responding to rein and knee with equal ease. By the time they crossed the broad stone road that marked the boundary of Sylonna, Chriani felt an unexpected familiarity. Steadier on the horse's back than he would have expected as the troop surged out along a twisting trail at a run.

He looked back once to Sylonna as they passed beneath the first of the sentry platforms, but the hidden city had already vanished into the wall of green behind them.

If the ride from the Hunthad had seemed chaotic to Chriani's mind, the path they cut now through the twilight forest was a maddening pattern of switchbacks and sudden turns. A maze unfolding around them as they rode. Farenna led them at speed along the deep wood's twisting network of intersecting trails, his hand up to flash signals behind him. Warning of quick changes in direction, their course shifting onto side trails. Chriani couldn't remember any signals on their ride from the Hunthad to Sylonna, which made him understand that every Ilvani in Farenna's troop had known that route by heart. This course was new to them, though.

Farenna slowed often, the rest of his riders spilling out of formation behind him. When he did, Chriani could see a pulse of pale blue light at his hands as the captain held the bloodstone talisman high, its steel chain wrapped around his fingers. With no one but Dargana behind him to see, Chriani made the moonsign more than once. This was only the light of Farenna's magic, though, the dark chip of stone still showing no pulse of blood-red the one time Chriani circled close enough to see.

It was strange to his eyes to see a mage armored in mail, but the Ilvani sorcerers were also warriors by nature, proficient with weapons and armor in a manner the Ilmari war-mages almost never rose to. Or perhaps the Ilmari mages simply embraced any excuse to stay out of combat. Farenna's chain-clad arm was set outstretched and sweeping before him each time they stopped, his eyes closed as if he was sensing the direction of the unseen connection between the relic and those who created it. Then he would spur ahead without a word, the others following down side trails or pushing through undergrowth and pale bracken to reorient their course.

Over a long first day of riding, that course led them steadily north, Chriani judged, watching daylight shift through the trees as the day wound on. The unseen sun was bright above them, the light filtering down from the canopy as wind-shifted waves of green. Without that light, Chriani was certain that his sense of direction and distance would have been long gone.

They made short stops at regular intervals as they had before, Chriani feeling less fatigue overall as his body grew accustomed to the rhythm of the grey beneath him. His balance had continued to improve, so that he had less need to lock his legs as tight to the horse's flanks as he had behind Farenna.

While they rested, the Ilvani focused on their horses more than they did themselves. Chriani did his best to rub down and clean the grey without the felt and tools his ranger's saddlebags had always held, following Dargana's lead when he needed to. The animosity he had felt from the Ilvani on the ride from the Hunthad had mostly been replaced by a lesser indifference on this ride. Taelendar remained the exception, her expression ice cold each time Chriani's gaze accidentally crossed hers. The other Ilvani had yet to speak to him, though. Chriani kept his distance, did his best to give them no excuse.

They took their long rest after dark that night, Chriani more than ready to sleep by the time they stopped. He sought out Farenna first, though, not used to the silence of the ride that had left too many questions churning in his mind.

The captain sat alone as he ate, but he nodded to welcome Chriani where he crouched beside him.

"How do you ride, friend Chriani?"

"Haven't fallen off yet. I'll take that for now."

Farenna smiled as he offered Chriani a portion of his bread, but Chriani shook his head. Not hungry for some reason. Too much on his mind.

"How much farther?"

"We break the wall of Muiraiden at daylight," Farenna said. "Were we to cross the sand hills at speed, we would be within and nearly across Nyndenu before the sun falls. But our goal is closer than that, I think."

Chriani didn't know whether it was some lingering sense of having had Veassen in his mind, or just his unexpected immersion into this new world over the previous two days, but his understanding of the Ilvalantar was sharper somehow. "You can tell where the cult is? Your magic?"

Farenna nodded. "The lóechari's power as I sense it is not far into the forest. A reason, perhaps, that our patrols have seen no sign of them. They would understand that moving within sight of the wall of Muiraiden would give them away."

"What about griffons? Can they see us from the air?"

"The gavaleria reach into Crithnalerean only under extreme need. The griffons sense the old magic there. On the ground, the Calala have pushed north in secrecy, to hide their numbers and purpose from Ilmari patrols. That stealth works to our advantage, for now."

They broke out from the Greatwood as the sun was rising molten-bright to the east, as Farenna had said. On any map Chriani had ever seen, the Ghostwood was an island of the Greatwood, splintered off from Muiraiden by the open space of the unmarked border between Crithnalerean and Laneldenar. He had seen that border from the north and at a distance, marking it as an expanse of sand hills that cut between the great stands of trees. Seen from the south, though, that narrow sea of sand was marked with an archipelago of dark groves that spread out between the two forest walls, like the Ghostwood had been torn away from the Greatwood and left a trail of fragments behind.

The ruined groves where Dargana had taken him and Lauresa were the forest's northern flank, close to the Clearwater Way and edged off by the scorpion wastes that spread into the Sandhorn. Chriani and the Brandishear rangers had passed within far sight of that flank as they rode the Clearwater Way two weeks before, but Chriani had kept the shadow of what happened there far down in his mind.

All the land from the Sandhorn to the Greatwood in the south had been the territory of the Crithnalerean exiles. Dargana's people. But Dargana had called the Crithnalerean broken now. They saw the signs of that as they rode north, making their way carefully across the unseen frontier. They slipped from grove to grove when they could, watching for a long while against the threat of patrols, then sprinting across open scrub and sand into the next pocket of green. In each sheltered copse, they saw abandoned settlements — well-built shelters and corrals blended seamlessly into the trees, almost invisible until they'd been stumbled into.

Chriani saw broken arrows scattered, signs of horses having stampeded. No bodies, though. No evidence left to warn Ilmari patrols of whatever clash of Ilvani had happened here.

The sun was at its height as Farenna called an unscheduled long stop within a broad grove of limni, the Ilvani watering their horses at a small stream that twisted through the trees and north toward where the wall of the Ghostwood loomed. That was the direction the captain faced as he knelt with the talisman in his hand, shrouded at the edge of the grove. The pulse of blue-white light that surrounded the relic was brighter now.

"Stay sharp." Dargana's voice came from behind Chriani, her black mare sidling toward him. "If there's trouble, this is where it starts."

"I've fought the Ilvani before." Even at a whisper, Chriani's response caught the attention of Taelendar, who gave him and the exile a dark look.

"You've fought the Ilvani on your ground," Dargana said. "Along the frontier. You've never seen Ilvani fight Ilvani in their own lands. Just watch yourself."

Chriani simply nodded as he stepped his horse forward. Dargana spurred up to stay alongside him.

"Watch out for the unexpected," she added, but in Ilmari. Her voice was the faintest hiss in Chriani's ear, not wanting the others to hear her.

His response was lost to a change in the echo of the grove behind them. The wind was faint within the trees, but it shifted suddenly. The sound deadening, then rising again. Drawing closer. Dargana and Taelendar both heard it as he did, twisting their horses around, shifting back into shadow as they drew weapons. Their movement was enough to alert Farenna and the others, blades drawn and gleaming in the half-light. No one spoke.

The war-band appeared through the trees as a straight-line attack, racing toward them in unnatural silence. Not just the voiceless assault that was the Ilvani trademark, but a deadening of all sound that could only come from spellcraft, and which had let the Ilvani draw close enough to mount their ambush. They were a force of six in matching grey leather, some kind of uniform Chriani had never seen before. Most had blades in each hand, their horses running free, silent hooves tearing the ground.

Even as they closed, Chriani saw the flash of gold in all the grey-armored Ilvani's eyes.

It happened almost too fast to follow. Farenna's riders spread to both sides as they shot forward, Chriani following Dargana by instinct. Trying to choose a target as the Ilvani squad split to surge past on both sides. Hoofbeats rose from out of the silence as they did, Chriani sensing how that silence was centered on the lead rider. That leader was the first to fall, Farenna racing past him with sword and long-knife raised, flashing in silence and a spray of blood. Then the ambush leader had fallen and his spell was broken, and the drumming of hooves filled the grove as the Ilvani tore each other apart.

Chriani had fought against the Valnirata a half-dozen times. Those dark days along the Clearwater Way. Minor skirmishes on the frontier, including the assault that had followed him to Rheran without his realizing it. He had grown up on tales of the deadly battle prowess of the Valnirata. Had seen it directed against him and the rangers who rode at his side. But before seeing that combat skill unleashed against itself, taking both sides of the battle, Chriani realized he had never seen and could never have imagined the full extent of its deadly perfection.

As they had when pursuing the rangers from the Greatwood that day, the Ilvani rode at full speed — but toward and through the enemy ranks, not away. No one fleeing, no one seeking distance or trying for range. Horses crashed past each other through the trees, twisting in and cornering back in impossibly tight turns, no one slowing. Blade on blade rang out again and again, coursing like a whirlwind of blood and steel.

Chriani wasn't fast enough to be part of it. His horse was surging, trying to run, but he was balking at the reins, the trees of the grove too close. He desperately wanted to take up his bow, but there was too much cover. Too much movement for him to focus, though that didn't stop the Ilvani from firing point-blank. Arrows hissed into the center of the fray from riders on the outside, were slashed from midair with sword and knife by riders at the center.

The attacks of the archers were joined by the bright light of spell-fire, flashing to all sides now. That light was the warning that let Chriani spin to see an Ilvani warrior crash into view ahead, racing straight for him.

He kept the reins lashed tight in his left hand, felt the backsword's unfamiliar balance as he arced it into motion. He caught the downward slash of the figure's sword on his own blade, ducked below the follow-up attack of the long-knife that arced above his head. Then the Ilvani's golden eyes went wide as Chriani twisted around, following through the arc of his swing to hack through muscle and bone at the shoulder. The warrior lurched as he was torn from his horse's back, tumbling to the ground.

Chriani thought of Kathlan. Thought of the wonder she might feel to see this fight play out, the perfection of movement in horses and riders. A stray thought, tugging at him. Making him falter as another Ilvani surged past him, slashing out. The grey moved to evade, faster than Chriani could ever have commanded it. He rolled with the horse but got his blade up too late, the Ilvani tagging his shoulder with her long-knife as she flashed past.

The grey had twisted around and was racing after the Ilvani by the time Chriani realized she was breaking from the grove. Fleeing north. He dropped the reins and pulled his bow, the sword tossed to the ground behind him. Instinctive action, not thinking. Passing out of the trees and into bright sunlight, a hundred strides of open ground spread out ahead of him, the Ilvani warrior already halfway to the green shadow that marked the wall of the Ghostwood. She was riding a twisted course around low stands of scrub, keeping anyone behind her from a straight-line shot.

Chriani made no attempt to guide the horse, letting it pick its own course as he twisted to adjust his position. He let two arrows fly, saw one of them hit, catching the Ilvani in the shoulder. She lurched but held on, disappearing into the trees.

Hoofbeats rose from behind him, Chriani realizing that they'd been following him the whole time. Though he felt like his horse was running at full speed, Dargana and Taelendar were beside him, then past him, racing into the trees where the cult warrior had disappeared.

A dozen paces into shadow, Chriani saw them pull up quickly. He nearly lost his balance as the grey slewed to a stop.

In a stone-strewn clearing, the Ilvani warrior and her horse were both dead, a long swath of torn moss and scattered rock marking where they'd fallen. To judge by the way Dargana and Taelendar were circling, watching the trees warily, neither of them had been the ones who finished the warrior.

Chriani moved in closer, paced the grey around the dead Ilvani. She'd been caught under the horse as they'd both dropped, its weight holding her fast now as the last of a deep-rooted convulsion took her. He saw the flash of gold at her mouth. A coin gleaming through a trickle of blood.

The horse falling made no sense to Chriani, and he wondered if the throes of the Ilvani's unnatural death had spooked the animal, sent it tumbling to break its neck. Ilmari horses often shied from spellcraft, but surely the horses of the Ilvani would be inured to magic. Unless the power of the coins carried a darkness that even the Ilvani steeds would fear.

He wondered further at what had dropped the warrior in the first place. His arrow shouldn't have been enough to kill her, but she might have been wounded already. Or perhaps her fleeing the battle had triggered the death that her confession to the cult had promised her.

From the corner of his eye, Chriani saw the pulse of blood-red light at the fallen warrior's wrist.

He was off his horse without thinking, Dargana hissing a warning that he ignored. The hunter's heart that the lóechari wore was a match to the ones they had tracked him with before. A jagged chunk of bloodstone set in gold, strung on silver cord this time. But this one was pulsing as brightly as the first talisman had when Chriani found it. The Ilvani dead in the black grove, his body broken before the forest shrine.

He remembered the oily touch as that first talisman had reacted to him, stumbled back from this one like he was afraid he might brush against it accidentally. As he did, he pulled the talisman he carried from his belt, checked for the golden disk meant to ward him from the Ilvani's detection. Panic rose in him at the thought that he had lost it.

The badge of Chanist's mages was still set in its place, though. The talisman he had carried from Rheran was dark, not so much as a glimmer of light seen within the stone held in his shaking hand.

Hoofbeats behind him heralded the arrival of Farenna and two of his riders. Chriani understood that meant one missing, saw the grim look on the captain's face.

"Eladen has fallen," Farenna whispered, "as have the lóechari. We hid his body and theirs, let the light take them…"

He stopped short to see the talisman's pulsing light, hissed a warning to the others. They dropped to the ground as one, taking cover behind their horses with bows drawn. Dargana kept axe and dagger in hand, shifting back into the shadows. Her gaze was tight to Chriani's, some kind of warning there, but he looked away. Farenna knelt beside the body, whispered an incantation as he plucked the glowing talisman from the dead figure's wrist.

"It's not me that led them to us," Chriani said. He showed the lifeless stone in his hand as Farenna stood, saw the talisman the captain carried at his own wrist just as dark. "They were tracking someone else…"

The faint creak of a bow drawn behind him was the barest sliver of sound. Obeying an instinct he couldn't name, Chriani threw himself to the ground, pushing Farenna down. He heard three arrows pass over-head, heard the crack of skull on stone as the captain hit the ground hard beneath him. Farenna convulsed as his body went limp, Chriani rolling away.

He looked up to see Taelendar toss her bow aside, drawing her sword. A light of molten gold was burning in her eyes.

If the rites take the confession from mind and memory, then can the confession itself be forced and then forgotten?

As Chriani rose, Dargana shouted a warning and fell back. Not fast enough. Taelendar twisted, shifting to cut through the rider next to her. The arrow that rider had nocked shot wild into the trees as his bow dropped, arms flailing as Taelendar severed his spine. He had ridden beside her since Sylonna, Chriani remembered. The two of them had rested at each other's side on the long ride from the Hunthad. His mind was fractured images, memories playing out like slow-flowing water.

Our patrols are known along the frontier, and push often across the forest wall, Farenna had said.

The other rider saw Taelendar's attack, saw her spin toward her with blade held high. No time to process the scene before her, the first rider still falling, but she understood the gleam of gold in Taelendar's eyes. The rider shouted out in anguish as she shot Taelendar twice at point-blank range, Chriani feeling something break in her voice. The sense of betrayal there. The Ilvani normally fought in silence, showed no sign of pain.

The rider's arrows took Taelendar in the side but didn't slow her. She died as she was drawing her sword, Taelendar's blade punching through leather and bone at her chest, out through her back again.

The moment it took Taelendar to kick the body away, pull her sword free, was enough for Chriani to grab his bow and loose an ar-row. He wasn't fast enough to drop her, though, his shot arcing across to score a glancing cut to her shoulder as she shifted. Dargana ap-peared at Taelendar's back, slashing in with dagger and axe, but Taelendar rolled beneath the attack, drove the exile back with a slash-ing strike across her mailed shoulder. Then the Ilvani warrior was run-ning for Chriani.

His next shot took her in the stomach even as he backed away, barely dodging a backhand blow that would have taken his arm off if it had hit. In the Ilvani's expression, Chriani saw the single-minded focus of the cultists they had faced in the forest, on the rooftop in Rheran. No sign or sense of the animosity she had shown him before, replaced now with a deeper malice. A thing beyond anger, beyond any hatred of the heart or mind. As Taelendar swung in against him, forcing him back again, her golden eyes were the blank gaze of a scrubsnake, of the fell wolves of the southern mountains. The rare creatures that kill not for want or need, but because killing is all they know.

He stumbled, dropping to his side and forced to roll back, his bow useless beneath him. Taelendar swung high. Then she died before her blade could fall, Dargana's axe spinning in to strike the back of her head with a sickening crunch.

The warrior collapsed to the ground, her sword falling beside her. The grove was quiet again. The wind was rising, the horses moving to their fallen riders. Farenna groaned as he fought his way back to consciousness, shakily stood.

"By grace and fate, no..." Blood was running freely from the captain's temple where it struck rock when Chriani pushed him down.

The horses were nuzzling the bodies, their expressions showing something uncomfortably close to grief. That same grief was seething in Farenna as he dropped to his knees at Taelendar's side. He cried out as her dead body began to writhe, twisting as on a puppeteer's strings. Watching her convulse as the dark magic that had infected the warrior tore her apart.

With a snort, her horse stepped back, turned and ran from the grove, heading south. The two others followed quickly behind. They would race back to Sylonna, Chriani knew. A warning of what had happened.

He found the new talisman where Farenna had fallen, scooped it up. Its bloodstone was dark. As the captain moved to the other bodies, Dargana carefully retrieved her axe where Taelendar lay. Chriani could see the tension twisting through the exile, her dark gaze locked to the dead warrior's sightless eyes.

"Did she ride alone on patrol here?" As Chriani called to Farenna, his voice seemed unnaturally loud in the stillness. He picked up his bow, retrieved his arrows where they'd spilled. He nocked as he paced around the clearing, looking for something but not knowing what. "They found her. Turned her with the rites, then burned the memory of that from her mind. Like the ones Dargana and I saw. Something triggering her…"

"Be silent, Ilmari."

The edge of anger in Farenna's voice caught Chriani by surprise. It was something he hadn't heard in the captain before, not even in the heated debate of the council of masters. He recognized that anger all the same, though. Had seen it in Barien years before.

In the spring that he had taken the tyro's writ, Chriani had ridden with Barien to Elalantar, part of a twenty-strong troop escorting the Princess High Gwannyn and her children to her mother's funeral rites at Ysorka. They'd met fell wolves along the road, down from Eberedar Pass and prowling the farmlands late in the season. Barien and two others of the guard had nearly been killed in the effort that slew three of the great beasts and drove the rest away.

Chriani had seen healing magic up close for the first time that day, huddled back and under guard with the other children. He had seen also the fury in Barien — not at the attack, but at the injury that had been done to the guards who followed him into the fray. He was bleeding badly himself, one arm bitten almost to the bone, but the warrior made sure the others were healed first. Made sure the princess high was safe before he sat for the healers.

Chriani had never seen anyone die under Barien's command. He saw Farenna now, though, the captain's eyes closed as he knelt by each of his fallen warriors in turn. Whispering words lost to the shifting of leaves in the wind.

It didn't seem like a reaction an Ilvani would make. Chriani felt the realization settle uncomfortably in his mind, hating himself for it even as the thought formed. The coolness of the Ilvani in combat, their stoic silence as they fought, their lack of emotion when captured. That was the Ilvani character he saw, the bearing he knew. It was too easy to assume that what was seen was all there was.

For all he should have known better, he played the same games that all Ilmari played. Looking for the differences that might mark them as separate from the Ilvani. Keeping those differences close to heart and never looking for the rest.

Ilmari and Ilvani were one folk once. Veassen's words, and his mother's.

From the corner of his eye, the corner of his mind that worked against all his anger and uncertainty, Chriani saw blood. It was pooling beneath the dead horse of the Ilvani warrior he and the others had pursued. He knelt to see the jagged wound that had slain the animal, understood now why it had dropped. He understood as well that it was falling beneath the horse that had killed its rider, the magic of the coins claiming her only after.

He focused, tried to push past the sound of Farenna's voice. He let his senses push out, caught the scent of bowel rising against the stronger sense of blood, iron-sharp and all around him. Something not right with the wound. Made by a short blade, not by one of the Ilvani long-knives. A jagged edge to it where it had caught the unfortunate horse low in the belly, slashed through its organs even as it pulled up toward the ribs.

A whisper of movement sounded in the trees beside him. Chriani turned, had an arrow set to his bow without thinking. Dargana was directly in front of him as he pulled back hard, drawing on her. Then she twisted away even as the arrow hissed toward her, dropped to the ground as Chriani knew she would. Understanding that he was aiming at whoever was shifting carefully through the shadows behind her.

The arrow struck something, unseen. Chriani heard a voice cry out but Dargana was already moving, pushing in to where a figure was stumbling back, trying to get clear of the underbrush.

Chriani had another arrow nocked, Farenna on his feet and beside him. Along a broad side path, Dargana was locked tight to a figure in grey. Steel flashed, Chriani trying to take aim, but the fight was moving too quickly. Then Dargana slipped around and behind, managed to get her assailant in a chokehold.

A jagged knife came up in the figure's hand, the horse's blood still streaking it. Chriani put an arrow into that arm to match the one already in the figure's leg, the knife tumbling as another cry was swallowed by the trees. Dargana twisted the wounded warrior over and face down, breaking off both arrows in the process. She grabbed the hood and the hair beneath it to pull back, set her bloodblade to an exposed throat.

Chriani knew who it was before he saw her, recognizing the knife where it had fallen. He had pulled that same blade from his own shoulder less than a week before.

"Let her up," he said.

"I don't think I heard that right," Dargana hissed. Her blade marked a razor-thin line of blood where it was pressed to the Uissa assassin's throat.

"What is this?" Farenna whispered. He sheathed his sword and drew his bow, circling to scan the trees for movement.

"She's an Ilmari assassin working with the Laneldenari," Chriani said to the Ilvani captain. "She was a prisoner in the camp the night you came for me. Dargana, let her up. She's got two arrows in her. She won't be moving fast or far."

The exile's expression showed how much she trusted Chriani's judgement in the matter, but she did as he asked. The assassin set her teeth against the pain as her arms were pulled behind her, Dargana whipping a leather cord from a jacket pocket to bind them. Then she stood, stepping back quickly as if she still expected a counterattack. The assassin simply rose to a kneeling position, though, arms pinned behind her and trembling with the effort. Where the stumps of arrows punched through her tunic and leggings, the grey was marred by a spreading stain.

"Check the perimeter," Chriani said to the exile. "Make sure no one else heard the fighting. But I'm guessing she came alone."

As Dargana slipped away into the trees, the assassin's face was an emotionless mask, her pale eyes watching him. Chriani saw sweat beading on her brow, though, knew she was heading for blood-shock despite her look of defiance. It was the same look he'd seen when she was first captured, and as she was slung to Venry's horse during the Ilvani attack at the camp. She wasn't smiling this time, though.

Farenna was still pacing, circling through the trees like a wounded wolf. The cut at his head was still bleeding, along with a deep gash to his shoulder Chriani hadn't seen before.

"You're hurt," he said. "I can bind…"

"I need no help from you, Ilmari. I need answers." The anger was still heavy in the captain's voice, but directed now at the prisoner. Farenna spoke the Ilvalantar still, but the assassin's expression told Chriani she understood. "The lóechari know our movements, turn our strongest warriors. You said this one works with them."

"She was with a group of Calala, but their cult ties were hidden until they changed. They didn't know what they were. Blind agents. Like Taelendar." Chriani heard Farenna hiss in anger, realized it was the wrong thing to say. He remembered the assassin watching the death throes of the cultist in the Ilvani camp. The look of fascination she'd worn. "I don't know how much she knows."

"Then she's of no use to me."

The long-knife flashed from Farenna's belt to his hand faster than Chriani could follow. He was barely fast enough himself to get between Farenna and the prisoner, seeing a darkness flash in the captain's eyes that told him he was on dangerous ground.

It was a thing no Ilvani would have done, he knew. The quick obedience, the rigid discipline. Farenna pressed forward as if expecting him to step aside, stopped short when Chriani drew his sword instead. Standing frozen, eye to eye.

The assassin said nothing. She made no move, the arrows in her trembling with each breath.

"She helped us in the ambush," Chriani said carefully. "When the last lóechari bolted, the assassin's the one who dropped her horse. She kept the cult from finding out we're coming."

"The lóechari will come soon enough. Their magic shows us to all of them through these ones' eyes."

"They'd already seen us, through Taelendar." Chriani showed Farenna the now-lifeless talisman before he slipped it to his belt. "They were tracking our approach through her. Watching since we left Sylonna, probably. They'll be coming, yes. But they're blind for now."

The captain glanced to the dark stone still at his own wrist, but the anger didn't soften. "You said this one works with the Calala. How do we know she wasn't scouting for them? Fighting among them from the start, then throwing her lot in when it became clear her allies had lost the fight?"

"No one else in sight," Dargana said to interrupt them. She had circled back from the other side, Chriani not even hearing her as she slipped through the trees and back onto the path. "But the noise we've been making, anybody could know we're here."

"If there were more Ilvani, they would have joined the attack," Chriani said.

"They will quick enough, Ilmari." Farenna stepped back finally, his dark eyes cold.

Chriani turned to look down at the assassin again. He let his memory run, showing her as he'd seen her a week before. Seeing subtle changes in her. A gauntness to her look. Her bare feet were dark with dust and muck, even as dried blood showed at her blunted toenails.

"She's been running," he said thoughtfully. "For days. She must have broken free from the Ilmari." He spoke to the assassin, challenging her. "You've been following us."

Farenna laughed, his expression showing a clear contempt. "No Ilmari walks the paths of Laneldenar unseen."

Chriani didn't respond as he crouched before the assassin. He thought about the black ring now hidden in his belt, taken from an

Uissa assassin who had passed unseen under eyes just as alert as any Ilvani patrol. He lifted her face so as to meet her pale gaze.

"You've been following us," he said again. "Why?"

At the corners of the assassin's mouth, set against the pain where the arrow wounds bled slowly, Chriani saw the flicker of the smile again.

"These assassins take up arms with the Calala," Farenna said. "Seeking revenge against the Ilmari by fomenting war."

"No." Chriani felt the details shifting in his mind. More to it than that. "If they wanted revenge against the Duke Andreg in Aerach, there's a hundred easier ways to get it." An unexpected anger twisted through him at the mention of Andreg's name. Thinking suddenly on the duke and his guard, smashing Uissa in response to what had happened along the Clearwater Way during the deep winter of eighteen months past. This duke he'd never met, who he hated on principle for what he was, had made retribution for what the order had done. A thing Chriani would never do.

"The order's just as like to want revenge against the Calala Ilvani," Dargana said thoughtfully, "for killing a score of their warriors who thought they'd carry out the princess's assassination in Ilvani livery."

As he had when the assassin was captured, Chriani thought of that night along the Clearwater Way, and the Ilvani attack that had saved him and Lauresa from the Uissa warriors sent there to kill her. "Which means you don't care about revenge," he said to the assassin, thoughtful. "But you care about power. Don't you?"

The pale smile flickered just briefly.

"What was it Venry said?" Chriani tried to remember the Aerachi lieutenant's words. "Andreg smashed the order at midsummer. The assassins of Uissa, scattered across the frontier and straight into Crithnalerean. Into the Ghostwood. And you found something there. Old Ilvani magic you knew the Calala craved and would pay for."

It was no more than a guess, but Chriani saw the assassin smile again.

"You're smarter than your betters give you credit for, lord."

When the assassin spoke, her voice rang as clear as her eyes. A tremor threaded through that voice as well, speaking to the pain she was in.

"Who are you?"

"Tician."

The smiled flickered at the assassin's mouth again in response to Chriani's surprise. Showing how he hadn't really expected an answer.

He had come up against the Uissa agent sent to kill Lauresa more than once. Had killed him in the end, but never heard him speak. Never knew his name.

"Why are you here?"

"I was following you," the assassin said. "On contract from the Calala Ilvani. When their tracking magic failed, Uissa was called. I was in Rheran when the attack came. The Calala sought me out the next day."

"You were in Rheran why?"

"Business. Nothing to do with you or anyone you know, lord."

"You'll tell me anyway."

"I won't," Tician said. "I'm pledged to duty and a code, the same as all of you."

Dargana laughed, but it was Farenna who spoke. "Then why are you so free with your name and your mission, assassin?" He circled around her, his long-knife down but still in hand.

"Because my contract with Calalerean is done, and I'll tell you anything you ask about them. That ended when I saw the coins transform the Ilvani on the Hunthad. The blind agents, as Chriani called them. I don't take well to secrets held against me by my employers." Her eyes shifted from Farenna to Chriani. "And because I know I'm done without your aid, and I'm not ready to die yet."

Chriani laughed this time. "Saving your life would be poor trade for you trying to kill me."

"Your life or death was none of my concern. I don't know what the Ilvani wanted with you, and I don't care. I was just hired to track you where they couldn't. I watched you leave Rheran, then followed you along the Clearwater Way. The Ilvani were waiting across the frontier, south of Werrancross, from where we followed."

"They told you nothing?"

"They told me you carry something they want. I already knew what it was, though, from when you and the exile had your heart-to-heart off the Wayroad. I was there, listening."

Chriani felt the quick touch of memory, his horse spooked that day as he and Dargana talked. He saw Tician's eyes flash to Dargana's, saw her smile in response to the exile's dark look.

"If I'd been paid to kill you," the assassin said, "I could have done it then, Chriani. Or at the Leisanmira campfire. You would have made an easy target."

"You should have tried it. At least one Leisanmira there would have made short work of you."

Tician smiled again, then grimaced as if the effort had cost her.

"You said you would help us," Farenna said. His tone had changed.

Chriani glanced over to the captain, saw a sense of calm restored in him. Tician seemed to see it too, nodding cautiously.

"I help myself, Ilvani. But I can tell you what I know of the plans of the Calala if it's worth something to you."

"That worth will be determined in Sylonna. You will ride back with us…"

"No," the assassin said. "We go forward. We find the temple and the black tree. You want my help, that's my price. I won't go back to Uissa empty-handed."

Chriani saw Farenna's expression tighten, angry again where the assassin had interrupted him. "What do you know of where the lóechari hide?" the captain said at last.

"I know what I overheard moving south along the Hunthad with the Calala. They spoke of their orders coming from somewhere called Markura. A holy site, they named it, but none of them had been there. Or at least none of them remembered it. I know you seek the source of the power that Calala holds in Crithnalerean. I know how you plan to destroy it."

"Four who followed me are dead," Farenna said coldly. "This mission is done. We return to Sylonna."

Chriani saw a sense of resignation in Tician's eyes. Then he saw her moving, but even seeing it wasn't enough to let him react in time.

A sense of slowness overwhelmed his senses, like he might be submerged to the neck in ice-cold water while watching the assassin tumble along its surface. From where she was hunched down on her knees, Tician lurched to her feet and spun in a single, smooth motion, lashing out with her injured leg in a kick that took her fully off the ground. Chriani was only starting to move, but it was enough that the blow caught him in the shoulder rather than the head, where she'd been aiming.

The assassin pulled her legs up while still in the air, pushing her bound arms down behind her. Her hands wrapped around beneath her feet and were in front of her suddenly, even as those feet hit the ground and she was running hard for the trees.

Chriani was up and after her. He heard Farenna hiss behind him in a way that told him he was blocking the Ilvani's shot, the assassin choosing her course carefully. She was fast but still injured, her gait stiff where her wounded leg slowed her. Chriani caught her in three steps but she spun around again, struck him in the temple with her bound hands.

The double-fist strike sent a wave of shadow through his mind, sent him stumbling. Chriani saw the fear in the assassin's eyes as she twisted away again, sprinting once more for the trees.

She stumbled as Farenna's thrown long-knife took her between the shoulders. A moment of stillness seemed to catch her, her body teetering as she tried reflexively to grasp the knife, but her bound hands couldn't reach it. Chriani managed to catch up to her as she pitched sideways to the ground.

He pulled the knife, cast it away. Blood was at the assassin's mouth and at the new wound. A slow flow, but the pale blue eyes stared sightlessly past him. He heard her choke out a last breath as Farenna stepped up beside him.

"You trust too easily, friend Chriani." The Ilvani warrior snatched up his knife, his voice cold again.

Chriani said nothing as his fingers pressed to the assassin's neck. Trying to feel for her blood, but it was already still. She must have been more badly injured than he'd thought. Pushed herself too far into bloodshock with the acrobatic display that had nearly taken his head off.

Farenna reached down, grasped the body by the hair and hefted it. "We waste our time here," he whispered. His face was a mask as he set his long-knife to the assassin's throat.

"Leave her!"

Chriani heard the words as if it might have been someone else shouting them. He wasn't aware that he'd moved until he was driving into Farenna's throat with his elbow, sending the Ilvani stumbling back. All the captain's rage was redirected toward him as he righted himself, but Chriani's own heart was filled with an anger that burned equally hot.

"You dare...!" the Ilvani shouted.

"I'll dare as far as you, Farenna, but I'm done with this. Ilvani and Ilmari alike, screaming vengeance. Carving oaths into the dead. Enough of it."

Farenna's grey-black eyes were cold, his knuckles white on the knife. Chriani hadn't drawn a weapon, knew that if he did he was dead. From the corner of his eye, he saw Dargana with hands at her axe and dagger, though. Waiting. He hadn't expected the rage that had risen so quickly in him, though he recognized it all the same.

The assassin had been worth something to him alive. Another bargaining chip he might have used to buy his way back into Brandishear. An Uissa agent with intelligence of the Valnirata. He could have delivered her to Chanist's war-mages, or even to Vishod's, after the Laneldenari were done with her.

She'd been afraid. He'd seen it in her eyes. It made a difference to him. He couldn't say why.

Farenna said nothing, even as the anger in him ebbed again. He sheathed his knife. "Our mission is done, Ilmari," the captain said.

Chriani shook his head in response, but it was Dargana he spoke to. "What do you know about a temple? Markura, she called it?"

"A lot of names come out of the Ghostwood. A lot of places lost within it. I don't know this one."

"We're going to find it," Chriani said.

"We return to Sylonna." Farenna's tone had lost its edge, but Chriani was reminded all the same that the captain wasn't used to being challenged.

"You can ride for Sylonna. Tell Laedda and the rest that you let Dargana and I finish this alone."

"When I accepted you among my riders, Ilmari, it came with obligation and trust in equal measure."

"Just like you took obligation from Laedda and the rest of them when you swore to see this mission through."

"The lóechari track us…"

"They were tracking Taelendar, meaning they know she's dead. They're as likely to think she took us down first as anything else. By the time they figure out…"

"The troop is broken, Ilmari. I will not discuss…"

"Your troop is standing in front of you, waiting for the order to push on, lord." The title didn't make any sense among the Ilvani, but Chriani said it by instinct. Packed it with all the usual sense of challenge that the word had carried when addressed to any of the officers whose orders he'd defied.

"Our mission was to seek intelligence of the lóechari, and what we have learned is dire enough," Farenna said.

"Even more reason, then, that you need Aerach and Brandishear. Even more reason to try to learn how the cult puts its power into play. Find a way to undo that power."

Farenna stood in silence a long while. Chriani saw his gaze flit back to the dark amulet at his wrist.

"I will complete the rites for the fallen," he said at last. "Prepare to ride."

While Farenna occupied himself at the bodies of Taelendar and the other dead Ilvani, Chriani searched the assassin's body, already growing cold. He expected to find magic. Some kind of talisman, or a ring like his own to explain her ability to follow them unseen. However, he found nothing on her except her scabbard and a belt pouch filled with Ilvani bread and mead. Stolen from the same provisioned glades they had rested in along the trail from Sylonna, he guessed. He checked every seam of her tunic and leggings, searched the pouch and her belt for secret pockets. He emptied the mead flasks and broke the bread open, but she carried nothing else.

When he returned to his horse, he remembered that his backsword had been cast aside while he rode. Contáedar's sword. He took Taelendar's blade to replace it, wiped the blood from it on her cloak before he slipped it to his scabbard.

Chriani and Dargana were both ready by the time Farenna swung up onto his horse. He whispered an incantation to set the dead talisman at his wrist pulsing with blue-white light once more, studying it carefully. Then he spurred forward to shoot along a shadowed trail hung with moss, Chriani and Dargana following close behind.

— CHAPTER 13 —

MARKURA

THE LÓECHARI RAN in near silence, the grey of their leather all but swallowed by the shadows beneath the trees. They matched their pace to the hiss of the wind as if by instinct, shifting with the movement of the forest canopy overhead as it shed sunlight to spread in ripples and waves across the ground. All five were on foot with bows drawn, moving a half-dozen paces apart and facing away from each other. Scouting the full circle of the forest around them, no way for anything to move unseen within their field of view.

Then one of them died, almost as silently as he moved. Chriani appeared behind him out of empty air in the same instant his arm came around the Ilvani's neck. His other hand plunged a long-knife straight in through leather and bone to the archer's heart.

The power of the black ring at his finger had let Chriani follow the cult patrol unseen, but he felt that magic disrupted as he struck. The forest around him shimmered back into place, like the shadow the ring's power set across his eyes was burning away.

A hiss sounded from the closest Ilvani as Chriani was spotted, as he'd known he would be. He shifted back to let the body crumple before him, threw himself behind a screen of young limni as a hail of arrows slid past to one side. Then he shifted back again, dodging more arrows as he made sure the Ilvani could see him.

The four of them came together in a line as they closed, driving Chriani back into an open clearing. No cover for him as another hail of arrows arced toward him. Then those arrows passed through the space where he'd been standing as he vanished again.

At the same moment, Farenna and Dargana shot from the screen of the trees where they'd been waiting, dropping the two scouts at the outside where Chriani had led them into perfect position. He appeared again at the far side of the squad an instant later, taking what he assumed was the captain in the lower back, punching a long-knife in beneath a chain shirt whose lacquered links gleamed black. With a second knife, he came in across the Ilvani's throat, ending it as quickly as he could.

Four down in less time than it would take to describe it. The last Ilvani panicked, dropping her bow and bolting into the trees. Farenna's bow sang out faster. It was over.

Chriani stood for a while over the body at his feet. It had been Farenna's plans and orders to do it this way. Let Chriani get close, then use him as a lure to draw the others into ambush. Kill them quickly. No other options.

It wasn't something Chriani was used to. Killing up close, no chance for quarter. Not for the first time, he thought of how fighting with a bow, fighting from horseback across the shadowed spaces of forest paths, felt so much cleaner than this. Less chance to think about the dead as they fell beside and behind you, unseen. No reason to ever look into the eyes of the ones you'd killed.

The gold light that was in all the cultist's eyes still burned brightly in the leader's gaze, staring sightlessly upward. His mouth was twisted in a grimace of anger, defiant even in death. Then that grimace was changed to a silent scream of pain as all five bodies began to convulse.

Chriani had to look away, waiting for the dark magic to pass. Not wanting to see the coins appear again.

"Their uniforms," Farenna whispered when it was done. "Before the blood sets. Unless you and your ring wish to go alone, Ilmari."

The attack had been Farenna's plan, built around the magic held in the black ring. Chriani had all but forgotten that the captain knew about that magic, from the time he'd tested it on their ride to Sylonna. The need to move unseen was paramount. The lóechari patrols had the advantage of numbers and position. An intimate knowledge of the territory. The mind magic of the coins meant that Chriani and the others had to move quietly. If they were spotted, they would have to strike just as fast.

They had left the horses a half-league behind them, at the point where the trails narrowed to barely visible footpaths. Shortening the reins across their necks to keep them from catching on anything. It hadn't seemed right to Chriani to simply let them run free, but Farenna was insistent. "They will wait for us," the captain said.

They stripped the Ilvani cultists of their leather and weapons quickly, trading off pieces between themselves to find the best fit. Farenna's mood was dark again, a weight pressing down on the captain as he claimed the chain shirt of the leader, directing Dargana and Chriani to take specific badges and gear from the other fallen scouts. The details of rank and insignia among the Ilvani had a subtlety to them that Chriani had no hope of understanding, leaving him to trust Farenna's directions.

The plan to steal uniforms for the final approach to whatever lay at the end of their trail had been the captain's as well, but he had rejected Chriani's suggestion that they take the armor of the scouts they had skirmished with earlier. Chriani understood his reasons now, seeing subtle differences in the leather of the riders and the armor of the foot scouts on closer patrol.

Farenna spent a good amount of time adjusting Chriani's armor, even ordering him to remove it once so he could don a tunic beneath it. The captain cut away part of this to reveal the Halobrelia sigil at the heart of Chriani's war-mark, then set his armor and some sort of sash of rank to carefully conceal the rest of it. The four names scribed in his own hand, which would give away the irregular nature of the mark the first time it was seen.

"You will need to stay behind us," Farenna said to Chriani when they were done. The hunter's heart he wore was still dark, but the light of the captain's spell-magic was pulsing brighter as he held the talisman high, felt for whatever message it had been giving him as he read its unseen connection to the place where its power originated.

The captain and Dargana wore the cult armor and regalia as effectively as the lóechari themselves, but the faintness of the Ilvani features Chriani had inherited from his father would give him away far too quickly. Up to the point where his own stupidity had revealed the war-mark to the Aerachi and his life had broken apart, Chriani had lived that life by trusting in the minimum amount of subterfuge it took to hide who he was from the Ilmari around him. The Ilvani wouldn't be so easy to fool, though.

"Chriani's ears won't be as big a problem as all our eyes," Dargana said evenly. "Any of the cult get close enough, they'll see we're not them."

Chriani shrugged. "They might take us for their blind agents. Or we just keep our distance."

"Easy to say when we have no sense of who we might meet or what it is we search for," Farenna said coldly.

It took Chriani a moment to realize that the captain was looking to him for response, but he had none. He had no plan. Not really. Just a picture of how he wanted this to end, and an instinct for action that would carry him toward that end if he let it. An instinct he had learned to trust. The problem was, his instinct carried him and him alone. He had no way to explain it, no way to ask anyone else to trust it.

It had happened that way with Kathlan, he realized. Not seeing it in that full light until this moment, the truth hidden away within its place of shadow where all of Chriani's fears would hide. This was the same instinct that had sent him out of the stables in Rheran before dawn to follow Lauresa, because Barien with his last breath had ordered Chriani to protect the princess. This was the instinct that carried him along the Clearwater Way, that had brought him home to Kathlan.

This was the instinct that had forced his tongue to silence over the truth of what had happened along that road. The instinct that had driven the slow wedge between Kathlan and him. The instinct he had turned away from when he told her the truth.

"We find the temple," Chriani said at last. "We uncover what it is. We need to see the magic. This isn't our fight to win, but the Ilvani sorcerers, the Ilmar's war-mages, need to know what's here. That's the only way we'll beat them. Break the magic, then break the cult."

"And if we can't?" Dargana said.

"Then we find out where the cult is vulnerable. Take that back and regroup. Try again."

"And what of the lóechari's interest in you?" Farenna asked quietly.

"The cult wants Caradar's dagger," Chriani said. "It's got nothing to do with me." He almost believed it.

During the ride from Sylonna, Chriani had already been trying to think through the Captain's question, to sift the pieces of the puzzle in his mind. The cult seeking him, and why. All of Veassen's talk, and Chriani's absolute certainty that whoever or whatever the blind seer's legends sought, it wasn't him.

The lóechari attack had left him reeling, though, his thoughts scattered. Taelendar's death had shaken him. The transformation she had undergone. No warning. No chance to save her.

He didn't think on what Dargana had asked him. Wouldn't meet her gaze now.

The quiet anger Chriani had seen in the Ilvani warrior was one he recognized. Her challenge to him on the ride from the Hunthad to Sylonna. Acting without thinking. Chriani understood it because he had lived with it his whole life. Likewise, he understood how Farenna had been able to tame that rage. The command and control he had demonstrated, shaping and honing the anger in Taelendar like the edge of a blade.

Barien had tried to shape the anger in Chriani the same way. He had almost succeeded. Chriani had been the one to stop him.

The day his grandfather died, his mother already dead a year before, Chriani had expected to follow them both in short order. And though Barien's intervention had staved off that fate, Chriani had been pushing toward his own end every long day since. The thought came to him now with a clarity that angered him. A thing he should have understood a long time before but hadn't. The piece of the puzzle he couldn't see.

The pack wolf's instincts sent it to the edge of the herd, set it to pick off the weakest prey. Part of the delicate dance of survival, balancing risk and safety. It was the ultimate reason why those creatures thrived. By comparison, the instincts of the fell wolf were what kept those great monsters in check. Their need to not just hunt to survive, but to destroy for the sake of destruction. To fight simply for the sake of fighting.

Lauresa had said it to him. *You judge by the instinct of emotions that have their own will, and you never understand that will until too late. You never learn to think except by your rage.*

Kathlan had said it. Barien. It hadn't mattered in the end.

They were running now, flat out along the trails that cut through the Ghostwood's twisted stands of limni, draping moss and black mold to the ground. Chriani could be quiet when he needed to. He had always trusted to the senses his father's blood had given him, to his ability to see the shadows, hear the faintest movement. He had always made good use of the instincts for speed and silence that his mother had instilled in him. But as the three of them drew closer to the unseen temple, he realized that he was a pretender to the senses and the stillness, the speed and grace of the Ilvani. Nothing more.

He stayed behind Farenna and Dargana, and was grateful that neither of them looked back to see him struggling to keep their pace. He could move at speed easily enough, and he could move in near-silence when he wanted to. But Chriani had only rarely pushed himself to do both at once, and he felt his footsteps thudding out around him now as if he might be driving cows before him as he ran.

Because they were armed and armored as a lóechari patrol, they did their best to maintain the pace of the squad they had ambushed. The fear in Chriani was of what would happen if they came across another patrol, no way to guess what routes they ran or what call signs they might be using. He had kept the black ring on, a plan in place that if they were stopped, he was to fall back unseen, then come around from the other side. Farenna and Dargana would buy him time enough to strike, or so they hoped. In the end, though, they detected no signs of the cult except tracks along the paths, no signs of any other Ilvani ahead or behind.

They saw the shadow then.

The day was still bright above the forest canopy, but the wood had been steadily thickening as they advanced, the gloom darkening to the point where even Chriani's eyes were having trouble picking out detail in the far distance. So it was that a deeper darkness caught at his sight even before Farenna and Dargana had seen it, Chriani hissing as he halted.

The three of them melted back into the trees, watching. Waiting. The forest was silent, no sign or sense of any movement around them.

"What is it?" Dargana hissed, but Chriani simply shook his head. He remembered the lights of Sylonna as they had approached the hidden city. A shimmering brightness like white fire through the trees. This was the opposite of that. An undulating shadow that billowed like cloud but never spread, visible only by the fringe of faint illumination that vanished at its edges. Sunlight through the forest canopy, swallowed by a roiling darkness.

"Chriani…"

Dargana's whisper carried an edge of urgency, Chriani turning with bow drawn. But through the underbrush where the exile was pointing, he saw no threat. Just a grove of dead limni, stunted and gnarled, and set around a five-sided stone dais crusted with black slime and moss.

They approached the shrine carefully, the moss-thick ground muffling their footfalls. Chriani could feel the uneven spread of stone beneath them, guessing at the extents of the unseen courtyard that wrapped around this shrine like the one he'd seen along the Greatwood's western edge.

He saw crows again, drifting through the trees as the three of them approached. There was no sight or scent of death this time to draw them forth, so that Chriani understood it hadn't been the dead Ilvani that had drawn them the first time. Just the shrine itself. Some unseen power there as there was power here, wrapped in shadow against the shimmer of the westering sun. Even in that shadow, the shrine was identical to the images of Chriani's memory, and set with the same intricate inscriptions. The ground showed no sign of other footprints. No sign that anyone else had stood there in long years.

"Can you read the glyphs?" Chriani asked Farenna.

The Ilvani captain nodded as he traced his fingers along the lettering etched sharp into weathered stone. They came away black with mold. "The language is old, but close to the tongues of Muiraìden. The engravings speak of the fallen *Myllasir* and the power they still hold from beyond time. Power they will share with those who seek it here. Power that waits to return and rule once more."

The name wasn't one Chriani had ever heard before, but the echoes of the tale were familiar enough. The Ilmar swore to fate, but it had been long generations since most folk believed that fate could be bent by prayer. The Ilmari had gods once, but had long since outgrown them — or at least that's how Barien had described it.

Under the long years of Empire, there'd been no formal purge of the old ways. You could still see the temples in Rheran and other cities, though they had turned to healing halls and libraries long ago. Testament to a slow decline and a turning away from the faiths of old. A new focus on magic and truth that gave folk something else to believe in.

"Ilmari and Ilvani alike have their old gods," Chriani said, thoughtful. *Ilmari and Ilvani were one folk once.*

"No gods hold sway in Muiraìden, Ilmari." Farenna rounded on Chriani as he spoke, a sudden edge of anger twisting his words. "Gods, kings, or emperors, no one rules the Valnirata."

From above, the crows shrieked as they took to the air, the fast beating of wings sounding out. Chriani saw the captain's hand stray to his blade. He took a step back by instinct, but Dargana was there to move between them.

"Enough of the history lesson," she said curtly. But she was watching Farenna as Chriani was, the captain distracted. Glancing back to the dark sigils tracing their way across cold stone.

"Forgive my outburst," he said to Chriani. "The Ilvani say that the oldest legends incite the oldest passions. This is a shrine to lost leaders. The Myllasir, who are legends among the Ilvani, and who superstition claims will return once more when their people are in darkest need."

From when Dargana had brought him to the northern flank of the Ghostwood, Chriani remembered asking what the Valnirata Ilvani could possibly have to fear in the empty lands of Crithnalerean. He hadn't understood her answer. *The past, half-blood.*

"We need to get closer," Farenna said. "We climb."

Like his ability to move unheard and unseen, Chriani's skill at climbing was better than most. But it, too, was put to shame by the grace with which Farenna and Dargana fairly slithered upward along the gnarled trunk of the great limni the captain chose as their access point to the forest above.

Shifting from hold to hold, branch to branch, Chriani managed to keep the pace set by the two Ilvani, but he needed both hands to do so. The bow across his back hindered his movement, the scabbards for his sword and the long-knives he had claimed from a fallen scout hammering at his legs as he went. Dargana and Farenna climbed one-handed, each with a long-knife drawn and ready as they hauled themselves up.

The height of the forest was a network of natural bridges twisting forward into the gloom. They advanced carefully, moving across shifting planes of branches and rope-thick vines high above the ground. Farenna led them, picking out a single path between multiple courses that reflected the network of paths along the ground below, but rising and falling even as they moved forward. Chriani saw the Ilvani captain slow to assess different routes more than once, but he made no sign of testing the strength of the branches and vines they clambered along. Just trusting to some innate sense of the strength of the forest that Chriani was forced to share.

As the shadow they had seen ahead of them loomed larger, Chriani could make out details set within it. The shapes of broad platforms were lines of smoother darkness cutting across the gnarled lines of trees thrust up from the ground below, the shadow seeming to wash across them. But as the three of them drew closer, that shadow resolved itself more clearly as individual strands, all flowing along shifting courses that brought them across and over each other to weave a delicate web of darkness.

Like the forest-home of Sylonna and the ruined terraces of the northern Ghostwood, the site that the assassin had named Markura and called a temple rose as wooden tiers connected by arcing lines of rope bridges and ladders. The site was smaller than the forest-home by far, only a dozen huge limni anchoring its border. As Chriani had seen in the northern Ghostwood, most of its terraces appeared long abandoned, their edges a frozen fall of vines. Even at a distance, Chriani could see where pieces of individual platforms had broken free but were still hanging, anchored at steep angles by moss-crusted ropes.

At the center of the site's erratic rise of bridges and terraces, one great dark tree towered over the rest. Not dead, Chriani saw, its leaves rippling in the wind. It was black, though. Dark as the shadow that pooled around it and flowed on the air.

"What magic is that?" Chriani whispered to Farenna as they stopped to orient themselves along a broad, sheltered branch. "Have you ever seen it before?" He felt his hand at his chest, making the moonsign as if his fingers were under someone else's control.

The captain shook his head, a dark tension in his eyes. "This site is old. Abandoned by the Ilvani long before your Ilmar nations rose. Whatever power it held would have been closed off. Should have been."

Something shifted at the edge of Chriani's gaze. He froze.

Though the three of them were safely ensconced within a screen of leaves, he dropped down, Farenna and Dargana following. Watching where he pointed. There, along the closest of the rope bridges ahead, movement. Three Ilvani stepped out to pace along the bridge's narrow span, its long arc resonating with their steps.

"How many are we going to find in there?" Chriani asked.

"No way to tell," Farenna said. "Are you ready?"

The question was for him and Dargana both. Not an order, not this time.

Chriani nodded. "Go."

Stepping into the storm of shadow was like being wrapped by a sudden fall of darkness. Though Chriani knew the sun was still bright to the west, it vanished to sight and mind as they worked their way forward, leaving them in the deep gloom of a moonless night.

Even so, the approach was far easier than he thought it would be. Far easier than it had any right to be. The worst part of their entrance to the temple was the careful climb across a network of open branches that brought them to within jumping distance of a rope bridge along the edge of the site. It was more of a leap than Chriani would normally have risked making, the ground lost to shadow below. He knew he had no choice, though.

Farenna dropped first, leaping into empty air and snagging the edge of the bridge with apparent ease. He hauled himself on and waited while its ropes slowed their swaying, Chriani above him with bow drawn. No sentries appeared, though. No sound was heard.

Dargana made the jump with even less trouble than Farenna. Chriani was breathing deeply as he leaped off the branch and into empty air, arms out as the bridge twisted toward him. He grabbed on well enough but needed Farenna and Dargana to help haul him up.

They made their way quickly to the nearest platform, the darkness spreading more deeply around them. Hanging like an oily sheen on the air, and shrouding a deeper sense of ruin and decay. The wooden slats of the platform were slick with black mold, the scent of it heavy around them. The bridge they had descended had the same appearance as three more leading off the platform — a web of ropes blackened with rot and age, strengthened and supported by newer construction. The platform was anchored by vine-shrouded rope cables that creaked ominously as they moved.

"The black tree..."

Farenna was the one to say it, but all three of them were already looking beyond the platform and to the center of the shroud of darkness that drifted around them. The black tree rose like a skeleton cast of shadow, its branches tearing at air that bled darkness like a gathering storm. Beneath that storm, the platform they stood on was unlit, but they could see lights set along distant bridges and terrace edges at intervals. These were muted, though, each a shimmering glow that faded after a few paces.

"Can you find the way there?" Chriani asked.

"I will do my best, Ilmari. Stay close to me."

"And if we're stopped?" Dargana asked.

"We kill them if we can. We run if we cannot. The horses are due south. They know the way to Sylonna if you make it to them without me."

"No one's leaving anyone behind," Chriani said. "We do this together..."

"Sylonna must be warned." Farenna cut Chriani off in uncharacteristic fashion, an edge of urgency in his voice. A trace of the anger rising there. "Laedda and Contáedar must know what we know. The fate of all depends on this."

Before Chriani could respond, a tremor threaded through Farenna, as if he was trying to hold the anger in check. "I do not order this," the captain said, more focused. "I ask it. In the name of my people, friend Chriani, one of us must return to Sylonna or all we do here is for naught."

Chriani nodded, even as Dargana shrugged. He suspected that the expectation of dying was never a central part of any of the exile's plans.

"Stay close," Farenna said again as they set out.

Whether strictly as a result of Farenna's instincts, or because the cult trusted in the secrecy of the temple site so much that their patrols were lax along its exterior, the three of them made their way across the middle tiers of platforms and terraces unchallenged. They spotted sentries standing at irregular intervals but passed no guards on patrol. Farenna carefully shifted the group's course away along different bridges, up and down ladders to avoid contact. Giving no one any opportunity to see their eyes.

Chriani could see the lóechari's eyes, or so it seemed. Even at a distance, he thought he could make out the pale gleam of gold, but he had no intention of getting close enough to confirm it.

As they drew closer to the black tree, they saw patrols at last. Groups of warriors walking in threes and fours, or lone Ilvani racing along bridges and ladders like messengers. Chriani felt a uniform sense of efficiency in the cultists' movement. A sense of focus he recognized from the golden-eyed Ilvani they had fought in the forest and in Rheran. Something pushing them. Orders followed without question, the Valnirata discipline taken to its worst extreme.

Among all the lóechari, there was a uniform silence. Not a sound could be heard throughout the citadel grove except faint footsteps, rising and falling on the shifting breeze. That breeze washed the scent of rot across them more than once, but when they passed within range of the scattered mage-lights for the first time, Chriani saw that the wind had no effect on the spreading haze of shadow. That darkness flowed and ebbed in no discernable pattern, seemingly of its own accord.

"There."

They had fallen back against the trunk of a limni adjacent to the great black tree at the center of the citadel, Farenna pointing to a narrow bridge arcing high overhead. Chriani had to focus to see it, dark lines almost invisible where they passed over and disappeared within the central tree's black shroud of branches.

It was the lone access point they could see from the terraced platform they sheltered on, its outside edges crumbling in a tangle of supporting rope-cables and vines. There was no sign of anyone traversing the bridge while they watched, but also no sign of any easy access to it. So they climbed again, all of them needing to use their long-knives this time to pull themselves across smooth sections of the limni's trunk where the bark had been torn away.

Though the sound was muted by the wind and the softness of rotting wood, Chriani felt a trace of panic each time one of them hacked into the tree. With no footholds to speak of, each knife had to hold its climber's weight for a tense moment, each of them pulling up carefully to drive the next knife in, then free the first. The vertical stretch was perhaps twice as tall as Chriani was, but by the time they had traversed it and were able to rest within a cluster of broad branches, his arms and shoulders were aching.

While they rested, Farenna flashed a hand in warning. Dargana and Chriani froze, Chriani taking longer than he liked to see the passing patrol that Farenna had sensed. The lóechari paced along the bridge that had been Farenna's destination, but they were gone as quickly as they came. Not even waiting to listen for silence in their wake, Farenna pushed on again, waving for Chriani and Dargana to follow.

Crossing over to the black tree was like falling sideways into dark water. The swirling shadow thickened around them as they slipped across the empty bridge, the air drawing in to a stifling closeness as black leaves surrounded them. The wind-tossed movement of the high branches rang out like the creak of unoiled leather, a wall of faint sound that set an uncomfortable chill up Chriani's spine. The leaves themselves carried the oily sheen of the air, but no one showed any interest in touching them.

Chriani was straining to see through the shadow as he followed Farenna's steady lead, even as he realized the scent of rot was gone. The rope bridge ended on a shrouded half-platform, its far side cracked off and vanished where a tangle of ropes and vines trailed over to the darkness below. The wet footfalls of the platforms they had crossed before faded to soft steps and the creak of wood. The planks of the floor beneath them were seemingly bone dry, cracked with age. The same dead black as the tree's branches and leaves, the shadow seemingly leeching all other color away.

Dropping to hands and knees along the platform's edge, the three of them saw the source of that shadow below.

Chriani felt the blood pounding in his head and chest. His stomach turned as he made the moonsign, kept his hand held tight to his heart when he was done.

The terraced platform below them was no farther away than the jump they had made to reach the first bridge. However, the shadow that pulsed out from beneath and around that platform made the distance seem to shift and shimmer, like trying to gauge the depth of water through its rippled surface.

The wood of the terraces was black like everything around them. Globes of mage-light floated around their perimeter with nothing holding them up, their glimmering light fighting against the shadow. Though the lowest terrace seemed to stand close above the ground, that ground was lost to darkness. They were looking down through a central web of branches that spiraled like funnel lines to a broad pit surrounding the foot of the great black tree. The terraces encircled the bole of that tree as linked rings, set above the pit like balconies extending over a garden below. Except that garden was a sea of oily shadow, out of which the dark storm rose.

Looking up, Chriani saw no other lights within the tree's screen of dark branches, the few platforms he could make out standing half-fallen like the one they were on. Below them, he could see the black tree's roots exposed and twisting down into the pit of shadow, as if its endless darkness was soil and stone.

He didn't know how long they lingered there, just watching. The wind could still be heard, hissing through the black leaves. Over it now, a faint moaning rose and fell. Chriani whispered words that rang out unnaturally loud in his own ear. "What creates something like this? What power?"

Dargana answered, a dark edge in her voice. "Places of this power aren't created, half-blood. They just are. This is what the Ilvani left behind in Nyndenu."

Farenna was staring down, his dark gaze unblinking. Chriani saw the Ilvani captain's anger rising again, heard the rasp of his breathing.

"We must go," Farenna whispered.

"Wait…"

Chriani shifted forward, feeling the broken platform creak beneath him. He'd seen movement on the terraces below, had to focus to pull it from the swirling shadow. Figures were pacing beneath the mage-light, having crossed from a narrow white stair rising in an arc to the tree next to theirs. He counted a dozen all told. Eight sentries set in ranks of two, all wearing the grey leather of the cult. Eight naked figures marched between them, all Ilvani. Not prisoners, though. Their heads were held high, bodies strong. No sign of wound or injury on them.

The figure leading them was in black lacquered mail, the mage-light of the platform edging her with a gleam that showed her form against the darkness. Her white hair was sheared almost to the scalp, the war-mark at her shoulder showing as black and grey. In addition to the mage-light, Chriani saw the pulse of magic at the figure's fingertips, her hands weaving a mandala of golden light that hung in the air as she passed.

"Chriani…" Farenna whispered, but he had already seen it. At the black-armored figure's neck, an amulet hung. Three coins gleamed there with a golden brightness that transcended the mage-light, flaring to push away the darkness. Each was tied through the hole at its center by lengths of golden chain, matching the chain that hung them from the Ilvani's neck.

The figure walked toward a stepped dais that jutted out into the center of the dark maelstrom. At its height, the edge of the dais met a rough pillar of fractured grey stone that thrust up from the darkness below. Its twisted lines seemed to catch at that darkness, gleaming like the storm of shadow was sunlight. Faint ripples suggested movement within its gnarled surface, reflecting the limbs of the black tree spreading out high above.

The naked Ilvani bowed their heads before the figure in black, whose golden light spun around her now to wrap each supplicant in a glowing nimbus. With one hand to the amulet at her neck, she thrust her other hand against the chest of each figure in turn, the golden light flaring each time with a brightness that made Chriani shield his eyes.

When he looked back, the eight figures were dropping one by one to their knees. Each had arms spread wide, head back and mouth open. In each hand, on each tongue, a light of molten gold was burning bright.

"We've seen enough, half-blood," Dargana hissed, but Chriani simply stared, rapt. He wanted to stand but couldn't. Telling himself this was for Chanist's mages, for Laedda's sorcerers. This was their mystery, not his.

The spellcaster in black screamed in what he recognized as an Ilvani tongue, though he understood only a single dark phrase. *Lóech arnala irch niir.* One by one, the naked figures closed their hands, snapped shut their mouths as a convulsion of pain twisted through them, dropping them to the terrace floor.

Chriani felt their screaming more than heard it. An animal sound, no voice to it except a pain that focused in and centered on his own heart, pounding furiously. He could feel the magic. Could sense the power from below forcing its way into him, scouring him from within. The fear coursing through him now like something alive as he scribed the moonsign against his heart again and again.

The screaming stopped. One by one, the figures rose, shaking. Their hands and mouths were empty.

He felt Farenna stand behind him. "Go," Chriani whispered to the captain. "Go now."

"Half-blood!"

Dargana shouted her warning as Chriani was pushing back to rise to his feet. He dropped again and shifted left by instinct, rolling for the open space behind him. He didn't see what had alarmed her, listening for arrows from above, spell-fire from the platform below.

He felt Farenna's backsword miss his neck by a finger's breadth. Saw the blue glow within the steel flare as if hungering for his blood. The captain let the missed blow arc around, swinging down without breaking stride as he surged forward. Chriani was still down, rolling to dodge as he tried to find room to rise, the blade hammering down once, twice, three times.

As Farenna tried to kill him, Chriani saw the golden light blazing in the blood fury of his wide-open eyes.

A spray of red-black lanced out from the captain's shoulder as Dargana tagged him, distracting him for the moment Chriani needed to roll up to his feet. He drew both long-knives, lashed out at Farenna as Dargana shifted into flanking position, but the Ilvani captain was moving at a speed that defied nature. He drew his own long knife, fending off Chriani along one side as his backsword struck off Dargana's attacks, the blade flaring blue-white each time axe and bloodblade hammered uselessly against its dweomered steel.

"You should not have come…" the captain hissed, directing his attention to Chriani as Dargana shifted left to reposition herself. "You are doomed here, Ilmari." He spun to switch blades, driving into Chriani with his sword now, pushing him back along the platform with the force of each blow.

Chriani remembered when Taelendar and the others had fallen. He remembered Farenna on his knees beside her, mourning with an anguish that had torn at him even to watch it. There had been no falseness in the captain's pain for the loss of his warriors. No artifice in the anger that demanded vengeance, but the cult magic had been in him even then. Too deep to touch, too deep to see.

"They're coming," Dargana called. Chriani risked a glance downward, saw that their fight had been observed. The sentries on the terraces above the well of shadow were running.

"They come for you!" Farenna screamed. "You will be sacrificed like all nonbelievers!"

Chriani pressed in hard, managed to catch the captain's shoulder with one of his knives but felt it glance off the shirt of black chain. Farenna's voice carried a pain he didn't recognize. The antithesis of the deadly silence that all Ilvani carried into combat. As if something was breaking in him, he gave voice to each new strike, shouted out in rage when Dargana's bloodblade caught him below his mail, tearing a bloody swath through leather and flesh.

Chriani irnash! Lóech arnala irch niir!

From the forest, Chriani remembered the Ilvani breaking the silence of that first deadly chase. Driven to call his name.

Movement sounded out around them, the ropes that anchored the platform shivering.

"Half-blood, go!" Dargana was shifting, trying to catch Farenna again on his wounded side, but the captain spun to hold her off. "Use your ring. I'll hold them here."

Chriani felt the black ring at his finger, all but forgotten there. He focused its power with a thought, watched the shadow that cloaked them all shimmer beneath an additional layer of darkness as he vanished from sight. He didn't run, though. Just dropped around and under a desperate sword strike as Farenna lashed out, swinging wide in a way that told Chriani the captain could still hear him. The momentary distraction was all he needed, though.

He drove into Farenna with both knives, feeling their steel punch through leather and bone. The Ilvani captain screamed as Chriani shifted back into view, the captain's blazing eyes finding his. Dargana was behind him, hacking in at Farenna's neck, but he got his shoulder up to take the brunt of her axe blow. Chriani was in too close, momentarily slowed as he tore his knives out to prepare for Farenna's counterstrike.

The Ilvani captain turned instead, driving forward with all the strength left in him. The backsword lanced out, an extension of his arm. Its blue light burned brightly as it took Dargana through the stomach.

It happened slowly, as it always did.

Chriani saw the look of shock and pain on the exile's face as she was lurched off her feet, lifted from the ground by the force of Farenna's thrust as it pushed out through her back. Then he pulled free, the sword slipping from her on a trail of blood as she collapsed to the ground.

Chriani couldn't move as Farenna wheeled on him, sensing himself open. Knowing there was nothing he could do in that moment to stop the strike that would kill him. But Farenna only screamed again, his golden eyes burning with a molten light.

"Do you understand now Ilmari? Do you feel now what it means to lose what you were? To watch them die?"

Chriani screamed. No words. He was moving again, flailing away at Farenna with a frenzied series of knife strikes. He couldn't think, didn't care that his voice would be bringing the sentries down on them even faster. He shifted as he attacked, lashing out at Farenna's wounded right side, but the captain's blade danced with the same lethal precision in his left hand.

"You should have been killed at the first sight of the temple! You will be fed to the shadow well and your spirit consumed, half-blood. My orders…"

Farenna faltered. Chriani saw it, drove in to sink one knife into his side. The captain screamed in response, hammered out with an elbow that drove Chriani back, tearing the knife from his hand.

"My orders…" Farenna stumbled back. He was shaking suddenly, Chriani pushing in again, but the backsword came up to block him. No counterstrike, though.

Chriani stumbled back, knowing he had time to use the ring.

He didn't. He felt the understanding shift into place in his mind.

In the forest, he had pulled Farenna down at the sight of Taelendar turning. He had heard the captain's head hit the ground, had seen the blood at his temple as he rose, shaking.

He should have been triggered then. Farenna and Taelendar alike, overwhelmed by the unseen power that coursed through them when the cult's tracking magic was exposed. The moment when they realized what they were, when they embraced the dark instruction the lóechari had placed within them.

In the second council. *I have ridden to the Ghostwood more than once,* Farenna said. The cult had gotten to him and then burned the memory of their corruption away, but the captain had held their power off. Had fought back against that dark magic with a strength of will that Chriani could barely comprehend.

"Farenna…" He fought to focus his thoughts, his voice. "This isn't you. You have to fight it. You have to remember…"

Footsteps rang out loud from below them, sentries racing along adjacent platforms. Preparing to climb.

Farenna drove in with two sweeping blows, Chriani backpedaling away from both of them. The captain was slowing, Chriani's other knife still buried to the hilt in his stomach. A swath of blood was trailing behind him across the wood of the platform floor as he pressed in.

"Veassen is a fool hiding behind greater fools… the heir of the exile's blade, an Ilmari stripling…"

"Farenna, fight this. Remember who you are."

"The blade belongs to Caradar... The exile king will carry it once more..."

"They did this to you," Chriani shouted. "They captured you on patrol. They brought you here. When you led us in, you were leading us back, but you kept us away from their patrols because you knew where to look for them..."

"You will be sacrificed to shadow!" Farenna screamed. "Like all nonbelievers. We follow the Myllasir to the destiny of the Ilvanghlira."

The Ilvani captain was injured. Dying, Chriani knew. But still fast enough. He feinted left, Chriani not seeing it until he was already driving in. The backsword came up and across, its razor edge catching Chriani's leg and cutting almost to the bone. The blade's steel flashed blue, the pain lancing white-hot from his leg to his back.

Chriani felt himself fall.

Dargana was still breathing. He noticed it in the slowness of the moment as he hit the platform hard, felt his own breath leave him.

Farenna stood over him. Teeth set against the pain, the captain drew Chriani's long-knife from his stomach. A gout of blood followed as he dropped it to the floor.

"Fight it, Farenna..." Another layer of shadow was shifting across Chriani's vision. He tried to focus, tried to will the power of the black ring to life, but the pain at his leg made even that much thought impossible. He tried to press down to stop the flow of blood, but his hands were numb.

"This is the destiny of the Ilvanghlira..." Farenna whispered the words uncertainly, as if trying to make sense of them. "The beginnings of forgotten fate..."

"The fate of the Ilvani is to live, Farenna. You said it yourself." Chriani fought desperately to clear his mind, to seek out the memory of the council floor. "The war that starts with this cult ends everything, but that isn't what the Ilvani want. It isn't what you need."

Farenna blinked. For just an instant, through the haze of pain that rose in time with his pounding heart, Chriani thought he saw the golden light in the captain's eyes flicker like a dying fire.

In war, we find the strength of life, but our lives are more than war, Farenna had said. *What we need is the wisdom after long centuries to see this."*

"The war the cult starts will never end. The Ilmar first. Then Calalerean against Laneldenar. Then the rest of Muiraìden. Then where does it stop?"

The platform shuddered as three sentries pulled themselves up along the trailing ropes at its shattered edge. Chriani heard still more movement around him, a steady pulse of sound that he realized was countless rope bridges vibrating under the weight of running footsteps.

The three Ilvani pressed in with long-knives drawn, the golden light blazing in their eyes. Their faces were the grim masks of rage and defiance Chriani had seen before, matching Farenna's expression as he stepped toward them, limping.

Then the captain's blade came up. A blur of red and blue-white. The three Ilvani died, no chance to show the surprise they must have felt as Farenna cut them down.

The captain screamed. The sword shook in his hand as he collapsed to the platform floor, convulsing. The light of gold was back in his eyes, and Chriani's realization came in a moment of horror. He was too distracted, too unfocused to think of it. He had succeeded in turning Farenna, in digging deep to find the spirit and strength in the warrior that could counter the magic that had corrupted him. And in so doing, Chriani had killed the captain with the surety of a knife in the heart.

Farenna had failed in his mission and the dark pledge he had forgotten. It was over.

The magic of the coins was surging in the captain, choking off the pulse of life in him. But with a shout whose strength Chriani could feel, Farenna pushed himself up, staggered to his feet. He locked his arms against the spasms that were forcing them to the side, sword shaking in his hands as if his grip on it would keep the coins from appearing in his palms.

Three more Ilvani appeared, Chriani not seeing where they'd come from. They pushed in toward him as if they were afraid he might run.

"Friend Chriani..." Farenna whispered. His dark eyes were wet, blood at his lips. "Do not fail..."

He ran for the three Ilvani, surging past Chriani to angle himself toward the platform's edge. They stared for an instant too long, as if they instinctively sensed the magic that bound Farenna to them, unable to comprehend the reality of him turning against them.

He was injured, close to dying, but the captain moved with all the grace that had led Chriani and Dargana through the forest and into the trees. He let his arms go wide, the sword gripped tight in his left hand, as he struck with all the power that had dropped three cultists in a heartbeat. He took knives in the shoulder and stomach as he drove forward. It didn't slow him.

The sentries made a hiss of alarm as they stumbled back beneath the force and fury of Farenna's attack. Then they were gone.

Chriani was at the edge of the platform, couldn't remember moving. He reached out as if he was trying to grab for Farenna, hoping that the captain had managed to hang on somehow. Hoping he'd see him clinging to the edge with a grim smile, waiting for Chriani's hand.

Instead, he saw all the Ilvani hit the well of shadow below. Their bodies dissolved within a pulse of black flame, Farenna claimed last. He saw the blue light of the captain's sword flare and die, then saw its steel shatter as it was consumed. A pulse of thunder shook the platform like it might be a sailboat in a storm wind, a wave of sound and force and shadow that rose and swirled around Chriani and wouldn't stop.

Dargana was breathing.

Chriani was on his feet, couldn't remember standing.

It was pitch black around him, his sight extending barely two paces to all sides. The storm of shadow was a shrieking gale as he dropped to Dargana's side, saw her eyes open. The wound at her stomach was barely bleeding, but the tremor of blood-shock was pushing through her, a red-black stain at her lips.

"Go..." she whispered.

Chriani lifted her carefully. He slung her across his shoulder, wrapped his arm around her tight. He had no awareness of how much she weighed, his body moving of its own accord, fed by a strength he couldn't name.

If he'd had healing, he could have saved her. The taste of a simple draught at her lips and he would watch the blood slow where it spilled from her, watch her wounds knit closed. But that magic was a world away now.

He used the only magic he did have, forcing his will into the black ring. Feeling the shadow cloak him, watching it cloak Dargana where he held her tight.

This wasn't about saving her. It was about keeping her safe, keeping her from the cult and its madness until the end.

He could feel the movement of the platform as he hit a rotting ladder, sensing it lurch beneath his weight and Dargana's but hold fast. He could feel the sentries around him but couldn't see them. Knew that meant they couldn't see him.

He didn't look back as he climbed.

— CHAPTER 14 —

THE ROAD BEHIND

CHRIANI HAD NO MEMORY of the route he took. Couldn't see how far up he'd come when he fell to his knees finally on the wet planks of a narrow platform edged by a low wall, hemmed in by close-growing branches and a screen of leaves.

He was thinking of Barien, confusion twisting through his mind as he wondered why he was carrying the hulking sergeant on his back. He wondered why his body felt so light. He thought of the road to Elalantar, Barien bleeding out, fighting the blood-shock as he waited for his guards to be healed. Then Chriani was there on that road and it was Barien dying, bleeding out on grey grass that was the stone floor of the archives quarter in the Bastion, where the sergeant had fallen.

He felt the pain of that night, slipping out from the shadow where it hid. Felt the anguish of knowing Barien was dying, and that there was nothing he could do to stop it.

He fought through the shadow in his mind. He reminded himself where he was, told himself that this was the blood-shock coming for him. He was on the rotting platform again. Dargana was at his shoulder as he forced himself forward, the pain in his leg flaring to a white light behind his eyes, threatening to send him down. He fought it, pushed into the shelter of the wall and the screen of leaves before he carefully, gently, let Dargana down to the ground.

The shadow cloaked them still. The trunk of the tree around which the platform wrapped couldn't have been more than four paces away, but Chriani saw nothing but darkness in all directions. Dargana looked up at him, her eyes clearer than they had been. He was trying to speak, trying to find the words to tell her he was sorry, but he heard her voice instead.

"Chriani... where is the blade of Caradar?"

He shook his head. "Don't speak," he managed to say. The taste of metal was in his mouth, the scent of rot filling him. "You're safe."

She laughed then. No sense of pain in her, which Chriani knew as a sign that she was close to the end. "I'm already gone and you know it," she said. "And I need to know this. Please."

He would tell her the truth. He knew it even before he spoke, felt the decision set itself in his mind with a strange clarity. A test of sorts, he thought. Seeing if the truth was even something he was capable of anymore.

"I gave the blade to Lauresa. She knows to keep it hidden, to let Andreg guard it without realizing it. It's safe with her."

He expected the exile to be angry. He expected to see her contempt one last time, her mouth set in the familiar sneer. Dargana's face was a mask, though, the dark eyes showing only curiosity.

"The blade that killed her grandfather. That nearly killed her. That's a strange gift to give, half-blood. Why?"

It was a question Chriani had asked himself, almost from the moment he handed the bloodblade to Lauresa in a shadowed glade of the Ghostwood eighteen months before. He had pushed it aside then. Too many other things to think about. Had pushed it aside each time the thought came back to him, each time word of the new duchess came from Teillai to Rheran across the Clearwater.

There were birth celebrations in Aerach, almost a year ago now. He had felt the question come back to him then, but he understood the answer only now. Holding Dargana's freezing hand in the dark, waiting for the end.

"Because Ilmari and Ilvani were one folk once. And they need to be again. The hate has to stop. Some good has to come of all the blood of the past. Or the Ilmar has no future."

"And you think she's the one to do it? Living ensconced as some duke's pet in Aerach?"

"She's strong enough," Chriani said, and he felt a sense of other lives splitting off from his own. Splitting off from those long days of the deep winter eighteen months before. Another life Lauresa might have lived if she'd been left to choose the terms of her life. "If she's not able to do it herself, she'll show others the way."

The hand that was squeezing Dargana's was warm. Chriani looked down to see her bloodblade clutched in his shaking fingers. He hadn't seen her press it to him, hadn't thought she could still move.

"Carry it from here," she whispered. "Don't let the lóechari claim it."

"I'm sorry..." Chriani said at last, but Dargana hissed him to silence.

"Keep both blades safe. Find your path, half-blood. And know that Veassen was right."

A chill twisted through Chriani. But whether in response to Dargana's words or the faint trace of footfalls rising through the shroud of leaves around them, he didn't know.

"Veassen's a fool," he said. "And this was a fool's errand. We shouldn't have…"

"The heir of the exile's blade," Dargana whispered. "You have fate behind you, Chriani, whether you like it or not. You'll know what it means…"

She was silent after that.

Chriani crouched beside her for a long while. Silence hung around him again, but he could see the great trunk of the limni at the platform's inside edge now. The shadow was lifting.

Dargana was ice cold to his touch suddenly. Something had changed. Chriani tried to focus, wondering whether he'd blacked out. Still no sound of sentries, but the hissing alarm-call of the Ilvani was rising in the distance, faint on the wind.

As he reached down to close Dargana's eyes, he saw the platform clearly around her. White wood mottled black and grey, shot through with mold. And no sign of blood anywhere except where faint traces had come off her armor and the soaked tunic beneath it.

She hadn't bled here. Not a drop of her life spilled out, because she hadn't died here. Which meant she'd been dead already. Had probably slipped away even as Chriani climbed.

That made no sense, though. He felt for the shadow deep in his mind. He pushed the thought away.

With Dargana's bloodblade, he cut strips from her tunic, used them to bind his leg where Farenna had cut him. The razor sharpness of the Ilvani backsword had probably saved his life so far, the cut perfectly straight and all but sealed. Nothing torn, none of the fast blood hit that would have pumped his life away.

You have fate behind you, whether you like it or not, Dargana had said. She'd been lying before, in the council chamber. It was more than revenge she was out for. She'd believed in something. She'd believed in some at least of Veassen's children's tales.

She'd believed in Chriani and was dead for it now.

You'll know what it means.

But he didn't know. Couldn't think on it. It was too late.

He stood up carefully, felt the pain at his leg surge against the shadow in his mind, skipping through thoughts as if he might be flipping pages in an atlas. What they'd seen coming in, the route to the temple that had left so many dead behind him. Horse patrols on the perimeter, sentries in the trees. Cult agents among the Ilvani of Laneldenar, their minds in shadow, their movements tracked. No way to risk action from the Greatwood as long as the magic of the cult was maintained.

He had done what he set out to do. What they had all set out to do.

Farenna had accepted Chriani among his riders. Obligation and trust.

He was the last one left. He needed to get back with what he knew. To Sylonna, to Aerach, it didn't matter. His horse would know the way back to the hidden city. A faster ride, no chance of getting lost. But if he rode for Aerach, made it to the frontier fast enough, it might stop the Ilvani from following. He could return to Kathlan, take the rites with her. He would ride into Teillai a hero.

Chriani heard a laughter that he realized was his own voice. He forced himself to silence, shook his head to clear a wave of darkness settling there. His focus was drifting, his thoughts slipping away from him.

He needed to run. That was all.

He slipped Dargana's bloodblade to his belt, clenched his fist to feel the warm touch of the black ring there. A rope bridge was visible at the far end of the platform, the storm of shadow all but faded back to its original web of dark lines. Chriani was already running as he vanished from sight.

The shadow that surrounded him as a sign of the ring's power forced him to move slowly, needing to focus on the path ahead and the sounds of movement around him. The sentries and warriors of the cult were racing across the dark network of bridges and platforms that surrounded the black tree, spreading out from that center even as Chriani tried to find his way down to the ground.

The dead shrine they had passed through was his goal, but the path was elusive. He needed that landmark to find the horses again, he knew. Too much of a chance to get himself lost in the forest if he set out at random. He needed to retrace the route Farenna had followed to bring them in, but he felt himself trapped in a maze of three dimensions. Picking out course after course, only to have each one vanish into dead ends, fallen platforms, and sentries standing watch at key bridge points.

He learned quickly to check for signs of traffic, avoiding bridges and ladders that showed no use. He had missed those signs the first time and nearly been lost, moving onto a bridge whose ropes had rotted through and torn away to nothing beneath his first step. He had caught the platform's edge, just barely. Had seen sentries below him, pointing up to mark his position where they heard him hit, then racing back into the shadows.

Those sentries were in constant motion around him now, a presence felt in the distance even as their exact positions went unseen. Chriani's senses couldn't follow them, couldn't track through the chill that twisted through him, turned all his thoughts to points of brightness and shadow in his mind. It was the blood-shock, still trying to settle in on him but fought with all the strength he had left.

Though the power of the ring protected him from the sight of the lóechari, he caught them reacting to his passage more than once. He was moving as quietly as he could, shrouded by equally faint footfalls and hissing shouts to all sides. It wasn't enough, though. They could hear him, could sense him somehow. He thought of the keenness of his own senses, the gift of his father's blood. But it was nothing compared to the hunters' sight and hearing of the Ilvani as they closed in around him.

His leg had been agony at the start, but he had forced himself beyond the pain. Pushed past it to find a steady, shuffling pace. His foot and lower leg had long since gone numb, though, the pain replaced by a dull ache that rose higher with each step. He was slowing as a result, fearful of a stumble sending his leg out beneath him. The power of the ring, the shroud of shadow it spread over the darker storm from the well, made it that much harder to judge distance as he moved.

If he fell, if he twisted or broke his ankle with a misstep, it was over.

He was descending along a platform's anchor rope, forced over the edge when three sentries had appeared along the bridge he'd been hoping to take. He hung by his arms and legs, shifting carefully. Timing his movement with theirs so the tremor in the rope wouldn't be seen. He heard them pass by, was nearly down to an empty platform below when he felt the numbness of his leg flare to an unfamiliar warmth.

Where both legs wrapped around it, the fraying rope had torn at Chriani's makeshift bandage. The wound was bleeding again, and badly. He saw it dripping freely, watched as a spill of blood shimmered to become visible as it left his body. Coalescing out of thin air to a red rain as it fell.

He dropped to the platform quicker than he'd wanted to, putting the weight of the landing onto his good leg. Even through shadow, he saw the red-black gleam trailing behind him, saw it flowing down to trace his footsteps as he moved.

Onto the next ladder, climbing to reach a terrace that he thought might lead him to the ground, Chriani heard a hissing from behind him. He glanced back to see an Ilvani scout low to the platform he had just fled. She was running a hand along the planks, was sniffing the blood she'd found there.

"Laóith!" Against the silence in which the Ilvani were hunting, her voice rang out like an alarm bell. Hissing rose in the darkness all around, calls of response. Chriani hauled himself off the ladder, hit the terrace running. He felt movement behind him but didn't look back.

He didn't know how much time he had, but he knew this was the end.

He pushed himself along a short bridge, dropped at the end of it to lower himself to another platform below. He could see the ground, the dark spread of rotting leaves. Footsteps above him, hissing voices from below. If he took the time to stop and rebind the wound, they would likely find him. And even if they didn't, he wasn't sure whether he'd be able to move again if he stopped, the numbness in his leg turned to a grating sensation now with each step.

They would find him. He felt his scattered thoughts spinning past him, but they all circled around that point of final understanding. No chance to doubt or deny it. They could capture him. Would torture him, most likely. The Ilvani sorcerers would have truth magic. They would have the magic of the black arrow, consuming his will. And then what?

He knew things, he realized. An idle thought, drifting in from the darkness where all Chriani's past days were hidden away. He was of rank and commission now, had ridden with the rangers. He knew the movements of troops along the Brandishear frontier. Knew the defenses of Konaugo Post and other camps. He'd finally been trusted with that knowledge, had proved to Barien, to Kathlan, to himself that he had what it took to be part of the prince's guard. He had been granted a position of power at long last, and now all Chriani could think about was whether he'd give all that away.

If he were dead, would that protect him? He didn't know, wanted to know. He felt the thought sharp in his mind, digging in like the spike of pain at his shoulders as he hauled himself up a ladder, not knowing where he was going anymore. He was climbing with his arms alone, using his good leg to support himself but unable to bend the other enough to reach the rungs.

The Ilvani hated the healing magic of the Ilmari, feared the raising of the dead. An abomination of the spirit, they called it. Chriani knew this, had learned it. But would they use such magic on their enemies? Bring the dead back to speak again, or to endure more of the torture that had killed them in the first place?

Kathlan would have known. Her love of lore. She would be able to tell him. Chriani wondered where she was.

He knew about Lauresa. A sudden thought, stark in his mind, pushing all else away. He knew where the blade of Caradar was hidden, knew who held it. If the Ilvani caught him, they would know.

He landed hard on an empty platform, slipped on a patch of black mold and had to stop to right himself. A silence hung around him as he looked down to see the black tree looming close. He could see the platform, could see the white stair below him. He was running the wrong way.

The platform shook beneath his feet, Chriani turning to see an Ilvani sentry crouched where he had dropped from above. A hiss of warning sounded out, the sentry's teeth set in a feral display, golden eyes blazing as he launched himself toward Chriani at a run.

He shifted in time, but just barely. The Ilvani was attacking by instinct, by whatever sense told him where the invisible Chriani had been standing an instant before. Dargana's bloodblade was in his hand, but Chriani couldn't remember drawing it. He drove in hard, one chance to strike unseen. He stabbed up below the ribs but the Ilvani rolled with it, took the blade across his stomach. A flash of blood and steel against his leather. Barely a wound.

Chriani was visible. He felt the shadow fall, saw the Ilvani's golden eyes focus on him as his leg gave way. He pitched over onto his good knee, felt a flare of pain that held him immobile. The Ilvani loomed over him, ready to strike.

He wanted to throw Dargana's blade, wanted to send it into the shadows, see it fall to the forest floor. *Don't let the lóechari claim it,* she had said, but he didn't have the strength to lift it.

He waited for the Ilvani to end it. Felt a shifting uncertainty in the corner of his mind that was still watching, conscious of his vision narrowing, turning to shadow at the edges. But the sentry turned away suddenly, spinning as if hearing something behind him.

Chriani watched the sentry stand there for what seemed a long while. Then the long-knife dropped from his hand as he crumpled slowly to the platform floor.

A bloody gash crossed the warrior's abdomen where his armor had been laid open. Not the scratch Chriani had made, but a rough wound, up and under the ribs. A small dagger, a jagged blade.

He saw the Uissa assassin standing over the fallen Ilvani, the knife still in her hand. Bright red streaked her arm to the elbow, contrasting the darker stain of blood dried on her tunic and leggings, though the arrows Chriani had left in her were gone. She was watching him, thoughtful.

"Each time we meet, warrior, you look surprised."

Chriani was prone on the ground, couldn't remember falling. The assassin had moved, was on top of him now. Her fingers were at his lips and chest, warm.

"Wait," she whispered. Tician, she had called herself. He remembered that.

He felt his mind clear. He felt the pain at his leg flare for an instant to white-hot fire, then fade just as quickly to the dull ache that healing magic left behind.

"Now move."

The assassin hauled him to his feet with a strength that belied her size, her slender frame. A surge of strength pushed through Chriani as he rose. He had Dargana's bloodblade still in hand, clenched it tightly as he followed Tician to the edge of the platform. His pace was unsteady, his leg still aching even after the healing magic she'd given him. Not a draught, but something else. Spellcraft, Chriani thought. The wound had closed, though. His step was erratic, but he could feel it at least.

Footsteps were pressing in around them as she went over and down, latching onto one of the rope cables connecting the platform to a larger terrace below. A roof of branches covered them as they passed through it, Chriani tensing as he fell into green shadow, no way to see the terrace as he dropped.

He hit hard and stumbled forward, the healing magic leaving a sense of fragility behind that hadn't yet passed. Tician was waiting for him, her knife in hand as she reached out to grab him. He responded by instinct, twisted around to block her, the bloodblade at her throat.

The assassin smiled. Her own knife was at his leg, Chriani realized. She ignored the bloodblade as she cut through the ruined cloth he had used to bind the cut, grabbing it up and throwing it over the edge of the terrace to a dark platform below.

"Something for them to find," she said. "So they're not looking too closely here."

Movement sounded out above and around them. Bridges stretched off to right and left, but the platform's edge where Tician stepped up to it was open to the air. No way up or down that Chriani could see.

The assassin stood there for a long moment, not moving. One hand held up before her as if in warning.

The platform shivered faintly beneath Chriani's feet. Movement on one of the bridges, someone approaching. But as he shifted close to Tician, all the questions he meant to speak died on his lips as a pulse of silver light opened up before her. She spread her arms wide, the light expanding in response. Shimmering as a circle beyond the platform's edge.

The assassin leaned back to grab Chriani's hand. She pulled him forward, leaping into empty air. Chriani fought the urge to break away, forced himself to follow. He made the moonsign as he went.

His feet struck something solid, his legs buckling where they'd been pulled up in the reflex of a jump. The silver light was a globe around them, wrapping them like a shimmering wall. Tician twisted around, drew her hands together as the portal faded.

Chriani looked down to see darkness below them. He had to fight back the instinctual panic that told him they were floating in empty air. "What is this?" he whispered.

"Sanctuary," the assassin said. "Escape."

Chriani made the moonsign in response. "You were dead," he said. There were more pressing questions, he knew, but this one was at the fore of his mind.

"Not as much as you might think. And thank you for intervening when the Ilvani captain tried to make it certain. Stilling the blood was difficult enough in the moment. I'm not sure I could have started it again in time to kill him."

Chriani felt the steel-sharp calm Tician exhibited now. He remembered the helplessness she had shown when Dargana captured her near the edge of the Ghostwood. A trace of fear in her then that Chriani understood had never been real.

"I'm sorry for what happened to him," the assassin said. No real emotion in her voice, though. "And for the exile. I lost you when you vanished with the body. I'm sorry it took so long to find you."

"And how much is you being sorry for anything worth?"

The assassin said nothing as Chriani's gaze caught movement beyond her shoulder. Lóechari sentries were hitting the platform at a run. Two ran to the edge, dropping alongside it in a way that made him sure they were set to leap out into the air after them. But then both fell back after scanning the shadows below and around them, their gazes slipping past Chriani and the assassin where they floated two paces away.

"They don't see us because we're here now," the assassin said. "No longer there. This space is set aside from the world for a time. They can't reach us."

"You're a spellcaster," Chriani said. "Faking your death in the forest, passing into Sylonna and pursuing us unseen. Healing me."

Tician smiled like his assessment pleased her somehow, but she shook her head. "Spellcraft takes a dedication I don't have time for. My magic is a deeper part of me."

She carried no ring. He saw that much. No chain or amulet at her wrist or neck. He had searched her body in the forest, found nothing on her. He didn't understand, but he had no time to wonder at it. "They can read your magic, though. Spell or no spell."

"Indeed. They know you're passing unseen with magic. They'll be looking for you that way. So we need to keep moving."

Chriani saw the platform receding even as the sentries left it, disappearing along both bridges, lost to the shadows. He made the moon-sign again, ignored how the assassin's smile broke briefly to a smirk. Her hands were close together, thumbs and forefingers touching as she let them trace across the interior of the silver sphere. Its course changed as she did so, as if under her direction. Chriani felt no sense of motion, though. Just a feeling like the silver space around them held stock-still while the dark shapes of trees and platforms swept slowly past.

"You saved my life," Chriani said. "Why?"

"You saved mine, more than once. I owed you that much." Tician's pale blue eyes held a playful light that made the straight-line scars beneath them seem even more sinister.

"You're a mercenary. An assassin. You don't act for what you owe, you act for what you can earn." Chriani saw the assassin smile. "Why?"

"Fate and magic are intertwined," she said in response. "The power of magic can warp reality. Bend time and understanding. That's why Ilmari fear it so much during their short lives. Why the Ilvani live longer than us."

As the silver sphere rose, it shifted through a screen of branches. Chriani lurched back instinctively as they appeared to push in through the shimmering wall, but they turned translucent as they did, passing through him where he stood. A sensation like vertigo shunted through him, his feet slipping to send him a step down toward Tician. He pushed himself back quickly, tried to focus as the ghostly branches passed behind them.

"Answer the question. Why did you save me?" Chriani felt a faint trace of anger twist through him. The last and unlooked for sign that he was returning to normal.

"I am, warrior. I'm interested in your fate, and the lines that magic weaves within it..."

"No," Chriani said coldly. "I'm done with pretending to go along with any talk of fate."

"Strange words to come from the heir of the exile's blade." The assassin smiled again.

Chriani slipped farther down toward her, forced himself back once more. He was conscious of the fact that he would slide inexorably toward Tician if he didn't hold on, but his legs were cramping from the awkwardness of keeping himself pushed back and up along the silver sphere's sloping floor. The assassin's bare feet seemed to offer a better grip along that surface of light, her hands still locked together as she swung them slowly around.

"The heir is a figure of mystery," Tician said. "The legends are fascinating."

"That seems a strange sideline for someone like you."

Tician laughed. "The Order of Uissa is about power, warrior. Knowledge is a key to power, as is the manner in which the past drives the present and the future to come. Like the way the destinies of Ilvani and Ilmari alike are centered in the lines of fate that mark a single warrior's life."

"I held the blade for two weeks," Chriani said darkly. "Chanist held it for years. Tell the Ilvani to go to him for their salvation."

"But it's not about time, warrior. It's about destiny. During the Incursions, Caradar was named as heir by the Ilvani, but the blade was his mother's before him, and her father's before her. Caradar was the one touched by fate, though. Meant to fix the conflict between Ilmari and Ilvani, by drowning the Ilmari in their own blood."

In days of war, one will arise to stand between between Ilvanghlira and Ilmari in struggle. One who will forge the final fate of both peoples.

Tician smiled as if she could sense Chriani's thought. "All the best prophecies leave themselves open to interpretation."

"A good enough reason to ignore them."

"A good reason to try to figure out which interpretation holds true. The Calala named you the heir, Chriani. I don't doubt that you surviving two attempts on your life and singlehandedly taking out a war-band in Rheran have made them believe it even more now than they did at the start. I suspect that's why they set a shadow on you in Aerach rather than arranging another assault when I led them to you. Why they sent their blind agents, as you called them."

Chriani felt a chill slip through his mind. A brief surge of anger that turned to something sharper, tracing along his spine. "I don't even hold the blade."

"The Laneldenari knew that, but it made no difference to what they saw in you. The Calala knew that Chanist held the blade after Caradar fell, but never said a word to connect the prince to the prophecy. Hidden or in hand, the Valnirata believe the blade's fate ties to you, now."

Chriani told himself that the anger was just from fear, told himself it meant nothing. The pieces of the puzzle were shifting, but he forced them aside in his mind.

"If you know so much, tell me why the Ilvani seek the blade."

"I know the history, not the will of the cult. Veassen spoke truth as well when he said the Laneldenari don't know. Just that the cultists seek the power of the past, and they believe the blade to be the key that unlocks that."

Within the silver sphere, they were passing now alongside platforms and terraces lit by mage-light. Chriani could see cots and bedrolls set out as makeshift barracks, but these were deserted. All the cultists on the move, searching for him.

"The cult found that power here," Chriani said, staring to the darkness. "You sold it to them." It was only a guess, left over from when Tician had been bound before them in the forest. He saw the truth of it in her eyes now as he had then.

"Uissa discovered the temple when we fell back to the Ghostwood," she said. "Nowhere else to go, thanks to the duke of Teillai. We stumbled across the site but found no sign that even the Crithnalerean had walked here in a century. They were as afraid of the power here as the Ilvani that fled from it a hundred generations before."

"And that didn't give you pause?"

"We're mercenaries, warrior." Tician smiled. "We act for what we can earn. We found the temple, but there was no power here. Only ruins, and the coins of the confessor, hidden away. The amulet the dark sorcerer wears. You saw it."

"And you gave it to them."

"We sold the coins to the Calala, because we had no means to assess what they might do. But we knew the Ilvani did. We kept our contacts with the Calala to stay close to them. We waited. We watched."

"And you've seen. You were with us with Taelendar turned. You saw what happened to Farenna. You were watching when Dargana died."

The assassin said nothing in response.

Below them now were terraces flooded by water, pouring out from shattered fountains. Their wood and stone had broken away, but the magic at their heart still produced its endless bright flow. None of it had been restored, none of it so much as touched from what Chriani could see. It was as if the Ilvani's reverence for the power of the past had forced them to a fearful worship of that past. Insinuating themselves into what was here, for fear of what might happen if they disturbed it.

"You won't have the blade," he said quietly. "If that's your goal in saving me."

"A novel plan, except I'm certain you'd kill yourself before you led me to it. I promise I'm not tempted by the price on your head, Chriani."

"Then what?"

"The coins of the amulet channel the power of this place," Tician said. "They're bound to the shadow well and the sorcerer. Viranar, they call her. White hair, black robes. You saw her. We didn't know the power the coins held. But then the Calala Ilvani made a full-scale invasion of Crithnalerean while we watched. We saw the golden-eyed ones set out on their hunt. We discovered what they were hunting for. And we don't like the idea of them getting it any more than you do."

"So what are you planning?"

"Not what I'm planning, warrior, but what we're planning. This is for both of us."

Chriani heard the tone of careful diplomacy in the assassin's voice. The bravado had vanished beneath it for a moment, the bright blue eyes expectant.

"We're going to steal the coins of the confessor," Tician said evenly. "We're seizing the amulet. You want to break the cult's power. I'm here to help you do it. I've saved your life to take you back with me to

Uissa. Give you a place and purpose, because you know in your heart, Chriani, that you have nowhere else to go."

Something had changed. He felt it.

Outside the silver sphere, Chriani saw the rough platform camps of the Ilvani surrounded by the furnishings and features that had once filled those platforms, scattered like shadows now. Stone benches were shattered and slumped across rubble-strewn floors. The remains of lac-quered screens stood even where their paper had rotted away, long ropes of mold hanging now from black frames.

"I walk my own path," he said at last.

"The paths you once walked are closed, warrior. You're an exile from two lands. Always caught between two worlds, and now cut off from both. And when the road behind is closed, you can look only ahead. There's another future in front of you, starting here tonight. The coins represent the future of the balance of power in the Ilmar..."

"And Uissa wants to control that."

Tician smiled. "We will control it, one way or another. But you're connected to the power here. I was listening when you spoke in the council at Sylonna."

"I said nothing in council. Veassen was in my mind. The blind seer." Chriani shook his head, dismissive. "And even if I believed a word of what Veassen had said, why in fate's name would you think I'd follow you?"

"Because I believe it," Tician said, and Chriani saw the light of truth flash in the bright blue eyes. "I believe in all the fates that wend through us. I've seen those fates laid down, seen them shattered and rebuilt. Your princes seek to chart the fate of peoples and nations with the movement of armies and merchant fleets. They set a future of chaos into motion, hoping it resolves to a world somehow richer and less terrible than they began with. Uissa seeks order. We chart change by manipulating one line of fate at a time. Save a thousand lives on a battlefield by engineering a single death whose effects can ripple through a thousand-thousand lives..."

The assassin's words cut off to rough silence even before Chriani shot the bloodblade to her throat, as if she'd realized just a moment too late what she was saying. How he would hear it.

He locked himself tight to the sphere, but his boots were slipping, edging the blade along the assassin's neck. She made no move to defend herself, her hands still locked together, set against the silver light.

"You need to stop talking now," Chriani said. The blue eyes

blinked once to mark a minimal nod of Tician's head. Chriani let the blade drop. His hand was shaking. "Uissa's contract to kill the Princess Lauresa would have plunged all the Ilmar into war. You don't talk of saving lives."

Tician nodded again. She let her gaze slip back to the view outside the sphere. Her hands shifted to set the spaceless sanctuary rising once more, drifting through mage-light and green shadow. "The coins could change all that," she said carefully. "You know their power. The means of sharing intelligence across whole armies. Soldiers bound by the magic of the past."

"The coins channel the shadow. They'll have no power away from here."

"The coins can channel any power you wish to send through them," Tician said. "We didn't understand that when we found them, but we know it now, as we know their full potential. The Ilvani kept the coins here because of the natural power bound here. They knew what this place once was."

"Laneldenar and the Ilmar will raze the temple. If you were at the council, you know our goal."

"But the coins will endure, and in the hands of the Ilmar or Laneldenar, their power leads to the same end, warrior. And you know what that end will be."

The skein of shadow shimmered below them. Chriani looked down, saw a figure moving along a wide expanse of white, glimmering in the mage-light. He slipped the bloodblade back to his belt.

"Take us down," he said.

Tician glanced down to follow his gaze, squinting. Her eyes would see only shadow, Chriani knew, but she shook her head just the same.

"The magic of the well of shadow is too powerful. It bends the fabric of the world, just as this sanctuary does. It'll destroy dweomer as easily as it destroyed your friend and the sentries he took with him. We'll have to get closer on foot. If you're with me, Chriani."

Below them, the shadow rippled again. It was the dark sorcerer, Chriani saw. Her hands were in motion around her, tracing out the lines of golden light that hung in the air for a long moment, then faded away.

An understanding settled in Chriani's mind.

"If I join…" He felt the words catch in his throat, couldn't speak them. "If I help you. How does this end?"

The assassin smiled. Her hands shifted as the silver sphere rose. "With the coins in the hands of the only force in the Ilmar who can keep their power in check. Uissa doesn't seek to rule, warrior. We simply want to be, and to carry on our craft and trade."

"Murder."

"Order," the assassin said. "Intelligence. Knowledge that the rest of the Ilmar has long forgotten."

Chriani said nothing. He focused his thoughts, shook his head to clear it.

"Think on it, warrior. Memory is the true threat of the coins. The confession drains away the past. A hole carved out in the mind, and the power of the cult threaded through that hole to hang all their supplicants like the coins on their chain." A sense of earnestness was in Tician's voice. A sense of careful persuasion. "Armies of Ilvani with any memory of morality stripped from them. Armies of Ilmari who've forgotten how to fear death. Soldiers who remember every skirmish ever fought, who can recognize and name every enemy that any ally on their side has ever seen. Knowing every battle plan as soon as it's uncovered."

"The blind agents," Chriani said. As much as he wanted not to, he saw it exactly as the assassin meant him to. "Spies and assassins bound by the coins. Undetectable until the magic triggers in them."

"And the Ilmari will have a distinct advantage in that regard," Tician said. "If you were thinking that your princes claiming the coins from the Ilvani would make a difference. The Valnirata have a short supply of Ilmari they could bind to their service. But the Ilmari have you, warrior, and plenty of others like you. Loyal Ilvani and half-bloods. You'll be the first ones forced to your knees to take the rites. The memory of your lives lost so they can send you to the Greatwood, then wait as you fall into a life you never had. And they'll know everything you see while they wait for whatever trigger turns your eyes to gold and forces you to kill everyone around you in their name."

"The coins are Ilvani magic. The Ilmari won't be able to…"

"The war-mages of your princes won't let anything stand in the way of their understanding the coins' magic. They'll invade Crithnalerean for a start. They'll tear the Ghostwood apart in search of its secrets."

All his life, Chriani had looked out to see a future in front of him that it seemed he would never touch. Then death and fate had pushed him forward to seize that future, unexpectedly. Had torn it from him just as fast. And in thinking on it, he understood that the assassin was right.

He was gone from his own past, as if that past might have been a story told about someone else. No place for him among the Ilvani. No way back to the Ilmari. Everything lost and nowhere to look now but forward. Chart a new course. Draw his fate out from the tangle of torn threads that had been his life. And out of all that, what would he find? What would be left to him when everything else was gone?

Kathlan.

The thought came to him unbidden. The question and the answer, the same. Kathlan was what was left to him, because Kathlan had been all there ever was.

He wished he'd known it sooner.

Kathlan was all that was left to him, but all he could do now was make sure she was safe. Make sure that the worst of all the Ilmar's futures never came to pass.

The silver sphere drifted through a dense screen of branches again, Chriani feeling the same sense of unease as they turned to shadows and passed through him. He shuddered with the sensation, felt himself slip down, half-stumbling as he tried to hold on. He was next to Tician, his healed leg touching hers. Blood came away from his leather, darkening the stains on her leggings as he tried to shift away.

Her fingers were long and smooth, Chriani not noticing them before. Not so much as a tremor in them, though she'd had her hands held out before her all this time. He remembered the Ilvani sentry dying so quickly that he hadn't had time to realize it. He knew how fast those hands could move.

He would have to be faster.

"The mercenary who came for the princess," Chriani said quietly. "The events in Rheran, and along the Clearwater Way. What was his name?" It was something he had wanted to know for so long now, but had never thought to have a chance to ask.

Tician hesitated. "Valoch."

"Did you know him?"

"Yes."

Chriani was silent a moment, his eyes on Tician's. Closer to her now.

"I'm sorry," he said.

"You have nothing to be sorry for. Fate works its way through all of us. We don't wait for it to find us, for it waits for us in the end."

When Chriani had gone after Lauresa, there had been no hesitation in him. No sense of waiting for fate to find him. He had chosen his path with a clarity he had never known before, had put his life on the line and nearly paid with it. Telling himself along the full length of that winter road from Rheran and back again that Lauresa was worth that price.

He hadn't been wrong about that. Not exactly. But he remembered something now, felt the emotion as raw as it had been in those first days of his return to the Bastion. He remembered understanding that if he had died on that path, he would have lost something whose worth he'd never truly known. The value of his own life. Something that had come to him only after the darkness of those days had overwhelmed him. Left him broken and made whole once more.

Kathlan. He felt her in his mind now. Felt her touch, tasted her scent as if she might be standing behind him.

Lauresa was a past that had been taken from him. A thing that might have been but wasn't. Chriani had waited for that fate to find him, had chosen to close his eyes rather than watch it pass him by. On the winter road from Rheran, he had reached back for that lost thread, tried to touch it one last time, because it had been the easiest thing in the world. But in his heart, he had always known he was looking backward. Had always known he'd need to look forward, to turn for home before that journey was done, because Lauresa was a past already lost.

Kathlan was a future he had never expected to see. That was something else.

He looked down to see movement below and around them, sentries passing each other along what appeared to be one of the lower platform tiers. The black tree was somewhere behind them. There was no sound except Tician's breathing, close to his ear.

She couldn't see the movement below them. Just shadow to her Ilmari eyes.

As fast as Chriani moved, she almost stopped him. Would have stopped him if she hadn't had her hands locked together, but he understood how that gave him the advantage he needed.

She had forced her hands together when she sealed the silver sphere against the space outside. She had kept them together all the time since, as she controlled the sphere's movement. Chriani brought his arms up between her arms now, driving them hard to the side to knock her hands apart and free.

He felt the lurch as the sphere tumbled. Silver light rippled before him as the portal cracked open. Then he pitched himself forward to fall through it and into open air beyond.

— CHAPTER 15 —

THE BLACK WELL

CHRIANI HALF-EXPECTED the assassin to follow him. He expected to feel a knife in his back or hear her scream some oath of vengeance, but there was only silence in his wake as he fell. He hit the platform hard, rolled with it as best he could. He felt the air knocked from his lungs regardless, felt a sharp point of pain at his ankle as it twisted beneath him.

He slid to a stop along wet wood, the scent of mold sharp in his senses. He slipped the black ring off his finger, fumbled within his belt and hid it there beside the plain steel band. At the same time, he pulled the hunter's heart from its pocket and plucked the golden badge from its space. He felt the warmth of the disk as he threw it off the platform, watched it disappear into shadow below. The talisman flared bright for a moment in his hand before he hurled it away. The hiss of alarm sounded out around him as he rose to his knees.

"Let me confess!"

Footsteps pressed in, six Ilvani there. He heard more moving behind them, heard the creak of the adjacent bridges as they closed. A blaze of gold filled the shadows around him, the lóechari's eyes flashing bright.

"I was a soldier for the Ilmari!" Chriani shouted it in Ilvalantar, kept his empty hands out to his side. "I rode with the Crithnalerean and the Laneldenari." The closest cultist lashed out at him, forcing him to roll back to evade his knife. "I came to the temple to join you. I know intelligence of Brandishear and Aerach, of the Laneldenari and the Order of Uissa. I'll tell you everything."

"Hold!"

A voice from the edge of the platform rang out with a tone of absolute authority. A tall Ilvani warrior stepped forward, his appearance and armor uniformly pale, the color of spoiled milk. All but the golden eyes, blazing unnaturally bright.

He stepped in close, set the backsword in his hand to Chriani's throat. Chriani met his gaze, wouldn't look away.

"I'll tell you everything," he said again. "Let me confess."

The warrior stepped back to lash out with his foot, catching Chriani in the stomach. He took the full force of the blow, felt ribs crack as it laid him out. Then hands were on him, lifting him roughly to his feet.

He looked up but saw no sign of the silver sphere, as he knew he wouldn't. He thought he could feel Tician's presence, though. Could feel her cold gaze on him as the lóechari dragged him off into the darkness.

He was beaten as they half-pulled, half-carried him down through a labyrinth of terraces and bridges. Chriani fought to stay on his feet as he ran. They had lashed his wrists tightly together with silk ropes, one of the Ilvani pulling on the trailing lead as if it was a leash. Someone had seized Dargana's bloodblade from his belt, the pale Ilvani holding it now where he sprinted at the head of the company.

Through the haze of pain that filled his head, flaring each time he felt a fist across his shoulders, the flat of a blade against the back of his legs, Chriani saw the pale Ilvani studying the bloodblade. Reading the marks that etched its steel. More than once, he turned back to Chriani to assess the war-mark at his shoulder, a dark look in his golden eyes.

Chriani remembered how Dargana had reacted when she first saw a narneth móir in his hands. *Tell me where and how you obtained it that I might slay every laóith and half-blood hand to have touched it since, and I may let you die quickly.* He tried to meet the Ilvani's gaze, defiant. Conscious of wanting to push the anger as much as he could. Conscious of the fact that pushing it too far might get him killed.

They hadn't found the rings in their hidden pockets within his belt. They had searched him too quickly, had used spellcraft to seek for magic on him, but they had missed the gold foil and what was hidden within it. It was the first of the many turns of fortune Chriani would need if he was to survive long enough to do what he needed to do.

He felt the black well before he saw it. The same stomach-turning sensation he'd felt when they watched the rite. It was the premonition of decay, like the instant of knowing that wine had soured even before its taste had settled on the tongue. Except it wasn't an instant, but an ongoing churning revulsion that rooted in his stomach and spread through every limb.

He nearly retched as the Ilvani dragged him over the white stair to the black terraces beyond. The storm of shadow could be felt here as well as seen, pouring across him like a scalding rain. It was in his eyes, in his lungs as he fought to breathe. He had to focus to see through it, catching sight of Ilvani standing in short rows between the floating globes of mage-light. More lóechari were shifting in from behind them.

Sentries called in from across Markura, seemingly. Coming to witness Chriani's capture and whatever would follow it.

He was dragged to a halt, the pale Ilvani turning back to stop beside him. A kick to the back of Chriani's leg sent him to his knees. He took it in silence, looked up to the Ilvani's molten gaze.

"Let me…"

A steel-hard blow took him across the back of the head. Chriani felt himself slip down into shadow, felt the warmth of the platform beneath him. He thought he remembered trying to call out again, and another storm of pain descending.

No words, half-blood. Words only get in the way.

The voice in his mind spoke one of the old Ilvani tongues. But as with Veassen, the words were clear to him, their understanding defined by the mental link across which they moved. Chriani blinked his eyes open but still saw only shadow. He had to force himself upright for the haze to lift.

The sorcerer in black was pacing around him, all the Ilvani sentries except the pale captain having shifted back. They all stared in silence, Chriani feeling the weight of their gaze like an itch that rose even above the pain of the blows he had endured.

He tasted blood at his lips, did his best to not make any sign that he was trying to speak again. He focused.

Let me confess…

The sorcerer's thoughts cut through his, punching into his mind like an attack. *I already know your plea, half-blood. I heard it on the terrace above, as I saw you struck down when you spoke it. I am master of this place, and keeper of the coins of the confessor.*

Viranar, he thought. Focusing on the name Tician had given him while he pushed all thought of the assassin from his mind. He could only hope she hadn't been lying.

The dark sorcerer nodded. *You know far too many things that an Ilmari should not. Are you a mystery meant to be solved? A puzzle to be broken apart in the hope of understanding how it fits together?*

I'm an heir of the Valnirata from my father, and wanted for treason in Aerach and Brandishear alike. Chriani let the truth of his words resonate in his mind, drawing on all the power and pain of what had happened. He let the memory of Kathlan push through him, let the sorrow of her in his heart frame each word. *I lost everything once dear to me. I joined the Laneldenari, but they're dead. But through them, I know what this place is, and now I've seen its power. I want to be one of you. Please.*

Chriani felt a ripple of reaction shift through the sentries around him. He understood that whatever link of memory the lóechari shared through their rites, his thoughts in the mind of the sorcerer Viranar were filtering through to everyone. He fought to feed them his anger, had to dig deep beneath the fear to find it.

Viranar whispered an incantation, her voice at Chriani's ear strangely hollow compared to her thoughts in his mind. A tingling rose at the back of his neck, the pulse of dweomer twisting through him. Truth magic, he guessed.

The sorcerer's thoughts shifted at a level below words. Waiting for him. Curious.

I know things, Chriani said. *I was a ranger of Brandishear. I had contact with guards under the duke in Teillai, and I know the useless games that the princes play for power, Chanist and Vishod. I was in a war-council in Sylonna. I know Laedda and Contáedar, and what they know of the lóechari, and what they don't yet know. I'll tell it all to you.*

Viranar didn't move, but Chriani felt a command slip out from her to the pale Ilvani at his side. A name hung unspoken there. *Raecla.* He felt a nod from the captain to two sentries on either side of him.

Chriani was pulled to his feet, a wave of nausea flowing through him to follow the pain at his neck and back. His hands were still tied, aching where the circulation had been cut off. He fought to move his stiff fingers as the dark sorcerer paced away, feeling himself pushed roughly forward to follow her.

Her destination was the pillar of grey stone. She stepped onto the dais where the eight Ilvani had taken the rite, Chriani three steps behind her. He heard footsteps following that he was sure marked the pale captain, Raecla. He didn't turn back to confirm it. He stumbled as he reached the pillar, saw its fractured lines gleaming with an oily light. He saw the movement shifting within it. Realized up close that it wasn't a reflection as he'd first thought.

Looking beyond the platform's edge, it was as though he could see down beneath the surface of the world itself. The well of shadow was a surging whirlpool of dark magic, crusted to solid form like the skim of ice that would form over even fast-flowing water if the cold was sharp enough. As from the platform above, he saw the great roots of the black tree twist and plunge downward into darkness. But seen up close, he could make out the white rot that shot through those roots, and which sent pale veins coursing up the tree's black bark and twisted branches.

So tell me. Viranar's voice shivered with a seductive quality that made

Chriani tremble. Not with any desire of the body, but of the mind. He felt her pressing against his thoughts to dull their frantic thrashing, like another's hand soothing the sting of a burn with a cool salve.

Promise me first. Let me take the confession. Let me forget.

He let the pain of his mind take him again. He remembered Kathlan's face in the tent when he'd told her the truth, remembered the pain of her voice driving into him like a dull blade. The memory of her face as she'd turned away from him, the ache at his chest as he'd ridden away into the Greatwood. Away from everything his life had been.

No Ilmari has ever taken the rites of confession.

I'm Halobrelia. In his mind, Chriani was defiant. *I belong here. I'm meant to be here.*

The dark touch of the well's magic flared as if in response to Chriani's thoughts, almost overwhelming him as Viranar paced before the pillar. In the new wave of nausea that coursed through him, he could feel all the Ilvani draw strength from the magic as it flared. The power coursed through Viranar even more strongly, Chriani seeing the fire at her hands, the light of her golden eyes pulsing beneath her skin now. At her neck, the three coins were blazing bright.

With his hands bound, Chriani couldn't raise them to make the moonsign, but his frantic fingers clawed the crescent shape across his stomach as he fought to stay standing. He let the fear flow through him, not caring that Viranar would feel it. His mind was memories of Barien suddenly, and how the warrior had always been dismissive of the Ilmari suspicion of spellcraft. He let himself remember learning with shock that Barien had channeled magic himself as Irdaign did, as one of the spell-singers of the Leisanmira.

He told himself that if it had been Barien standing here instead of him, he would have been doing the same thing Chriani was doing. Making the same choice. The pain that came with those thoughts was raw still, the loss of the warrior's presence like a butcher's blade had cut part of Chriani's life away. A wound that wouldn't heal, wouldn't ever close.

"My name is Chriani. I'm the heir of the exile's blade."

He needed to say it out loud to focus the words. He expected to be struck down, but there was only silence in response. The touch of Viranar's mind to his quickened somehow. An intensity to her thought. A sudden storm of fear and hope, but wary.

A command slipped out to Raecla behind him. As the pale captain stepped forward, his golden gaze burned into Chriani, malice and bloodlust shining even brighter in his eyes. But from his belt, the Ilvani pulled a familiar talisman. Chriani saw the furious surprise in the pale face as the talisman's bloodstone chip flared to a blood-red glow like the Darkmoon in a clear winter sky.

Chriani noted the frantic pulse of that glow. Felt it echoed in the hammering of his heart.

The shadow that wrapped the platform shifted. A shudder passed through the storm of darkness that swirled and rose around them, like the web of thought and mind that connected him to the lóechari was connected in turn to the shadow well itself. That shadow's breath of decay wrapped tighter around him, the mage-light of the platform shimmering, but Chriani kept his gaze fixed tight to Viranar.

They knew him now. Every single one of the lóechari felt and re-membered the fatal pursuit in the forest, the failed attack in Rheran. The deadly storm of magic that had consumed them on the Hunthad. All of them had been there, all of them had fought and died and knew Chriani's name through the power of the coins.

We sought to claim you, and you came to us. The sorcerer's voice shifted within the framework of her spell, its magic still reading him. *You are a mystery within a mystery, half-blood.*

I came here because you can't claim me. You tried and failed. I join you willing-ly, or not at all. But I need to understand my part in this.

He let all the raw emotion of his heart and mind free, anchored by the understanding that everything he had been was gone. He was noth-ing to the Ilvani, nothing to the Ilmari. He felt that knowledge push past the shadow where the secrets were held, leaving no room for those secrets to seek the light.

I don't know what I am, he said. He felt Viranar recognize and accept his fear. *I never knew what I was meant to be. But the Laneldenari told me. The heir of the exile's blade. The one who'll break the stalemate between Ilmari and Ilvani and change the balance of power in the Ilmar.*

Chriani waited, his heart still racing. The blood-red pulse of light shone out in the pale Ilvani's hand.

I brought you the exile's blade. Chriani tried to force the thought to-ward Raecla. *But that's not enough.*

He felt the pale captain's uncertainty. Felt the anger that masked it as he drew the bloodblade Chriani had carried. He felt Raecla's reaction through the link that made his dark thoughts part of Chriani now, fo-cusing on all the names and history he read in the symbols on the blade. Then those thoughts become Viranar's as the captain reverently stepped toward her, bowing as he handed the dagger to her.

It was Dargana's bloodblade, but it was a match for the blade of Caradar. The engraving on it the same, to Chriani's eyes at least. Dargana had been able to read the dagger he'd taken from Rheran. Had known it was Caradar's from its engraving. She was Crithnala, though, and of Caradar's own house. He had to hope the Calala wouldn't be able to read Dargana's dagger with the same skill.

He had to hope both of the Ilvani were seeing what they needed to see. What they so desperately wanted to see, even as Chriani had no sense of where that hunger came from.

It would keep him alive, though. Long enough to end it.

He felt the pieces falling into place around him. Almost ready.

The sorcerer's hunger for the weapon was a fire in his mind. For an instant, he was seeing through her eyes across the link they shared, the blade limned in the golden light that flowed from her hands.

The coins and the blade. The blade and me. Chriani forced the words out through a tightly woven defiance, summoning up every bit he could still touch of the anger at the center of his life. *You need to let me be part of this. You need to let me forget.*

You would embrace this willingly. As Viranar's voice filled his mind, Chriani understood that it wasn't a question. She was reading the blade in some way, but his thoughts were leading her. Pulling her in the direction he needed her to go.

"I'll do it willingly so long as you give me what I need. Just let me take the rites. Let me touch the power of the coins. Let me forget."

He spoke the words aloud to distract the sorcerer, feeling her thoughts divided in her mind as she stepped close to him. Her hands were raised before her, the bloodblade clutched tight in one, the amulet in the other. The three coins on their golden chain were burning so brightly that Chriani had to squint to look at them.

"What would you give up in taking confession, heir of the exile's blade?" As Viranar spoke for the first time, her voice carried an edge of excitement. A hunger and expectation that Chriani could feel. A sense of having already claimed the thing she wanted more than anything else. But at the same time, he understood how that want wasn't coming from her at all.

The golden light was in his mind. A separate consciousness. A tangled skein of dark thought that set his blood boiling.

"I want to forget the pain I've caused," he whispered. His mind was battered by the shadow around him, but he fought back against it using the memories. Barien's body in his arms, the slow spread of blood across a pale stone floor. Lauresa weeping in a winter grove, the sun bright, the warmth of her magic wrapping them against the freezing air. Kathlan sleeping while he watched her, the day bright and blue-white at the window of the loft.

"Let me forget the people I've hurt. Let me forget what I've lost." Chriani felt the shadow like uncounted insects crawling across him, tasting his skin with sharp tongues.

Viranar laughed as she stepped up to touch his face. The hand that held the amulet traced its way along his cheek. "No true Ilvanghlira would ever ask such a thing."

"You're right," Chriani said.

A burning cold struck him as he grabbed the amulet with his bound hands. The shadow around him flared with a molten light, the world turned to gold suddenly. He pulled down with all his strength, feeling the soft gold of the chain snap around Viranar's neck as the coins came away in his grasp.

Then he disappeared.

This was a good way to die.

When he was younger, in the days before he had taken the winter path to Aerach and back to Rheran, Chriani had thought often about the matter of his own death. He was a soldier, had been made a tyro of the prince's guard at ten summers, even if he'd spent most of the years since then ensuring that he would never make rank or take the field. He was a warrior, whether a soldier or not. Skilled enough with bow and blade that he made a routine habit of showing up guards with far more experience. He'd won his share of fights as a result, had lost a few besides.

He had ridden the roads of Brandishear at Barien's side. He remembered the feeling as he watched fell wolves appear on a sunset road in Elalantar, Barien riding them down without hesitation, his seconds close behind. He remembered being herded back to the train with the royal heirs, flanked by four more guards. Just another one of the children to be protected. Lauresa was there. Barien was her warden, was there first and foremost as her escort, but Chriani hadn't known the princess then.

The guards had been focused on getting Princess Gwannyn and the royal heirs ready to ride, so that when Chriani stole a knife, the young squire whose belt it was claimed from never felt a thing. He slipped it to his own belt, let his jacket cover it. He was ten years old and a new-made tyro, and he decided in that moment that if the wolves got past

Barien, if they advanced against the princess high and the royal heirs, he would fall defending them.

It would have been a stupid way to die. He realized that only years later, thinking on how his efforts to play the hero would have distracted the guards who were there to do the job for real. But the thought had stayed with him through each barracks fight, through each patrol at Barien's side. Always thinking on how it might end for him, and what good or ill might come from that, and what would be said when his life was done.

It was a stray thought, fixing in his mind now as he watched the world fade around him, saw the startled look in Viranar's golden eyes. He'd been moving his stiffened fingers, no one seeing them slip within his belt as he had tried to make the moonsign, the magic of the well overwhelming him. No one seeing him slip the black ring to his finger, conceal it with the shaking of his hands.

He had thought about his own death when he upheld Barien's last orders to defend Lauresa, following her on that winter path to help her do what she needed to do to protect her homeland. To protect all the Ilmar. But then when he came back to Kathlan, he had stopped thinking it. Had stopped wondering about what battle or accident would eventually take him. Even riding the frontier for five months, Chriani had been keenly aware of the risks, had measured the threat of the Ilvani. But he'd never let him himself imagine what it might lead to in the end.

He hadn't realized that had changed in him, not until the endless moment of thinking it right now. He hadn't let himself understand why.

He had come back to Kathlan. He had made his choice for her then, as he made it for her now.

It was over for him. This was a good way to die.

Viranar was trying to snatch the amulet back even before Chriani vanished, but he was faster. Every muscle in him, every facet of his senses had been focused on the golden coins as the sorcerer moved closer to him, step by slow step. He had done his best to focus her thoughts on the coins to ensure they'd be in hand, offering himself to her so that she would take him as bait. The only thing he had left to give, the only ruse still open to him.

Chriani had marked the distance to the platform's edge as six paces, knowing it would be the longest run of his life. He heard Viranar scream, felt her voice tearing at him like a bright blade. The sentries were moving for him, faltering as he vanished. He ducked down to roll between the closest two, then was up and running.

Break the magic, he had said to Farenna. *Then break the cult.* He couldn't finish it anymore, but he could start it. Shatter the dark power that was channeled here for the others who would follow him. They would pick up the fight.

The well of shadow would destroy whatever touched it, Tician had said. Chriani had watched it consume Farenna. Had seen it destroy him, body and armor alike. Had seen it consume the magic of the captain's sword.

He had no way back to the Ilvani. And even if he could make it back, what would he tell them? Farenna was gone. Corrupted. Captain of Sylonna and one of their best warriors, Chriani had no doubt. And if he could be broken, there was no telling who else among the rangers patrolling the Ghostwood might have already been captured by the cult and had the memory stolen from them. How many might have taken the rites of confession without knowing it. No way to tell how many others would turn on the Laneldenari in the heat of battle, setting Ilvani against Ilvani in a storm of red steel and golden eyes.

He had no way back to the Ilmari. Not anymore. He could break for Aerach, find his horse and hope it would let him cross the Hunthad into Ilmari territory. It might not, though. The Ilvani horses were trained to return home if their riders were lost, and Chriani knew he was the grey's temporary master at best. Even if he made it out, he'd have to find the Aerachi. Would have to hope they didn't execute him on the spot, hope they believed his story.

Even if they did, it would be war again, Chriani knew. An Aerachi force marching on the Ghostwood, Brandishear holding back the Calala Ilvani as they surged north into Crithnalerean to defend the secrets of this place. It would be a brutal assault. Probably futile. The only chance for the Ilmari would be to try to catch the lóechari by surprise, try to cripple the power here before breaking it.

Or Chriani could do that for them. Even with no way out when it was done.

Someone else would pick up the fight. That was the thought that drove him the six steps marking out the rest of his life. The Duke Andreg in Teillai. The prince's guard in Brandishear. Kathlan, leading a squad of her own before long.

Chriani would give them all that chance if he could.

He heard spells being cast, felt a tingling at the back of his neck as he ran. Detection magic, he guessed, trying to pinpoint his location. Some charm to undo the invisibility that cloaked him, perhaps. He had a moment to worry about whether they might unleash spell-fire at him, taking out him and the closest lóechari at once. A necessary sacrifice.

From the corner of his eye, he saw sentries shifting to block access to the bridge, guessing he was trying to flee that way. Not suspecting that he had chosen a different way out.

He was two steps from the edge, looking down to the darkness below him. He put Kathlan's name in his mind and held it there. No time to speak it.

He was one step from the edge when a pulse of crippling pain drove him to his knees.

He was ready for that last step. Ready to slip over into the shadow, taking the coins with him. But in the light of molten gold that filled all his senses, Chriani understood that the coins of the confessor had other ideas.

This close to the well, its shadow was like black oil filling his lungs. Chriani had felt it getting stronger with each step he took toward it, fighting to push through it, but the full extent of its force hadn't become clear until it pounded down on him like a crumbling wall. He was drowning now. Freezing, burning, a cold scouring him from the inside even as fire spread from the coins white-hot in his hands.

He wasn't dying. He knew that somehow, instinctively. He felt the magic of the shadow well licking at his life, tasting it hungrily but waiting to consume it. But the pain that coursed through him with each pulse of darkness made him wish with real honesty and for the very first time that he were dead.

Chriani's body twisted in a convulsion of pain that locked his muscles tight, no way to let go of the amulet even if he'd wanted to. The black ring at his finger went cold as its power waned, the closest sentries turning toward him as he became visible again. Bows were raised against him. A dozen archers drew a bead on him as a convulsion knocked him backward, sending him even farther away from the edge. Raecla was moving toward him with backsword drawn, but Viranar's voice was in all their ears and all their minds at once.

"All hold! The infidel is mine!"

She was next to him suddenly. Chriani didn't see her move, but whether because he'd blacked out or the sorcerer had used magic to cross the space between them, he didn't know. She grabbed at the coins clutched tight in his still-bound hands, used them to lift Chriani as if he weighed nothing. She had Dargana's bloodblade in her other hand, knuckles white where she gripped it.

It wasn't the blade she thought it was, Chriani reading the sorcerer's knowledge of his deceit in her frenzied eyes. He could see himself through those eyes suddenly, flashes of the pain that lined his face, his twisted body. The link that connected Viranar to all the other Ilvani was in him now as the power of the shadow well coursed through him. He felt her rage, felt the hunger for his death that drove her. Whatever power Chriani's lies had seemingly promised her was already forgotten.

As she raised the blade, readying a killing stroke, another convulsion took him. But Chriani was ready for it this time. He let it drive him forward, angled himself with the last of his strength to smash his head into Viranar's. He heard her nose break beneath the force of the magic coursing through him.

The sorcerer screamed as she staggered back, dragging Chriani with her. Her knife hand spasmed, swinging wide as she tried to keep her balance. Her grip on the amulet was still iron-tight, even as Chriani's hands began to slip. A haze of her blood clouded his eyes, but he saw her gain control of her other hand, striking with the bloodblade for his throat. He was screaming as he forced one hand open, managed to lock it around hers to send the dagger wide.

A bright pain across his cheek and ear told Chriani he'd been struck, but he managed to hold on. One hand was at the amulet, the other at the bloodblade as Viranar's fingers cracked beneath the convulsive strength of his grip. But with his wrists still bound, his body bent, he couldn't find any leverage to force the blade back toward her.

His hand slipped, just a little. A bright flash of pain seared him as the dagger scored his palm, set a new line of blood there.

Then a bright blue light was in his mind, turning the haze of molten gold across his eyes to the gentle color of a winter sky.

Something had changed.

Chriani felt the link to Viranar and the other Ilvani fade away like quickly shuttered windows. One by one, they closed to darkness where a golden light had shone a moment before. In its place, he felt the white light resolve to the sharp lines of a war-mark he recognized. The sigil of Halobrelia that marked his shoulder, that had marked Dargana's shoulder. The lines acid-etched across her dagger, his blood spreading out along those lines now to mark the name of his father's kin as a red-black stain.

You have fate behind you, whether you like it or not.

Dargana's voice was around him, as if the exile might have been standing at his side. He felt her strength fill his mind, felt his tight-locked muscles surge with an energy he didn't understand. He twisted his hands around to tighten his grip on the dagger, locking himself to the amulet where Viranar was desperately trying to tear it from him. The coins still burned brightly, but their heat was gone.

You'll know what it means.

His wrists were bleeding beneath the ropes but he ignored the pain. He heard a scream that he realized was his own voice as he held Viranar fast.

He felt Dargana in his mind. He felt her strength and resolve, her bitter anger driving the pounding of his heart. He felt her memories as the flickering light of a shadow play, flashing across his sight. Voice and image, impression and sensation, all of it moving faster than his thought and sense could process. Chriani understood it all the same.

The power of the coins was in his mind like a living thing. He felt that mind opened up and laid bare, his memories set down like charcoal lines on blank parchment. Single images frozen fast, words and voices plucked out of mind and time. A connection between magic and memory. His eyes burned with a white light that he could see through Viranar's frenzied gaze.

Chriani felt the blood and passion of the fallen Dargana erupt from the blade the exile had carried her whole life. He felt the lives of all the exile tribes reflected in her — and through her blade, all those lives burned now in him.

He understood a lifetime spent seeking a path between the extremes that defined the exiles, as clear as if he had lived that life himself from the day he was born. Trying to cleave between the two bright points of hatred that defined the Crithnala. Hatred of the Ilvani who had driven them north into exile, out of the Greatwood that had been home to their people for all time. Hatred of the Ilmari who haunted Crithnalerean along its borders and across the Clearwater Way, and who hunted the exiles even in the only lands they could call their own.

A hundred generations of hatred became a seething passion in his pounding heart. He felt an ageless indifference, saw with his own eyes the act of turning away from the Greatwood. Felt the need to push even farther north to avoid the Ghostwood and its dark pasts, the Clearwater Way and the battles that would always be found there.

He knew Dargana's father in the blink of an eye. Felt her child's reverence at the tall figure who had carried her before him on horseback, dark hair flowing behind him in the wind. He knew her mother an instant after that, seeing her laid to rest on a brush bier, draped in white cloth that hid the marks of the Ilmari arrows that had slain her. He knew her brothers. One who rode the Sandhorn in scorpion mail. One who had left Crithnalerean for the forests of Elalantar long years before, disappearing into what passed for life among those Ilvani who called the Ilmari nations home. Chriani knew the Ilvani who had followed Dargana as leader, who had ridden skirmishes against Ilmari patrols for long years. He knew their names, watched them live. He felt her love some of them for a time, felt them drift away or die, one by one.

He remembered his own father. The images of his childhood were refocused and reframed by the magic that scoured his thought and mind, all his memories twisting through Dargana's like the magic that filled Chriani might be trying to weave a single life between them. But where the slow-frozen panes of loss and ache intersected, a dissonant clash of color and form erupted, driving into Chriani's heart like a fist. He felt the loss of Dargana's father, understood how it had driven her. Forced her to find her own strength, forced her to fight.

He felt the loss of his own father. Understood how it had crippled him instead. Threatened to break him.

All his weakness, all his anger. All the lessons of his life that he had forgotten or would never learn. The empty space inside him that his father had left, that his mother had tried to fill before fate took her from him, too soon. Barien and Kathlan. Everything they had tried to show him, with Chriani thwarting them every step of the way. That legacy of failure he would carry with him to the last moments of his life.

Those last moments were almost on him. Chriani blinked.

He was caught in the timelessness of memory, sensing and seeing the scene move around him. A slowness of body, a quickness of thought and mind. It let him judge the movement of Viranar as she pushed back against him, let him use that movement against her as he thrust straight down with both hands, twisted the bloodblade around.

The loops of chain that bound the coins of the confessor were twisted around their conjoined hands as Chriani punched the dagger up beneath the sorcerer's ribs and into her heart.

It didn't kill her. He had no idea how. He felt the scream her life made as her skin pulsed gold and a strength twisted through her, forcing him back. She lashed out with her hands, tried to gouge his eyes out. Tore at his throat with her teeth, the blood of her broken nose making a red-black mask of her face.

Chriani fought back with a strength only partly his own. He felt Dargana's hand at the bloodblade as he tore it free and struck again, feeling its balance and weight with a lifelong familiarity that countered the hindrance of his bound hands. He punched the blade into Viranar's chest, turning it to lock within a cradle of splintered ribs. Then with both hands, he used that bloody steel lever to turn the sorcerer, smashing into her face with his head again to drive her back toward the edge of the platform. One step away.

He recognized the sensation of arrows slamming into him, but he couldn't feel their bite. He was dying, didn't care anymore. He would finish it, for Kathlan and the others. For Dargana. It was done.

He tore the dagger from Viranar as he punched into her with his foot, driving her back. The blade slipped from his blood-soaked hand to hit the platform somewhere behind him. He let go of the coins as he staggered backward, the sorcerer's hands tearing at them, trying to reach them as both she and the amulet fell back screaming into shadow.

The swirling darkness erupted to a storm of dead black like it had when Chriani watched Farenna fall, and the sentries the captain had taken with him. He saw Viranar's body consumed by shadow, flesh and bone drawn away to black tendrils and unspooled like tangled yarn. The coins flared with the molten light of a winter sunset, then shattered with a crack like thunder. Then they were gone.

Chriani was on the ground, couldn't remember falling. He could barely see as the darkness descended on him, swallowing him whole. But as the coins were consumed, he felt the last tentative touch of the link of mind and memory fall away. The eyes of the Ilvani closest to him flickered gold to green, and grey and brown, black and silver. He heard shouts of alarm, footsteps racing away from him. Then there was just the sound of the black storm.

He tried to stand but couldn't. He tried to drag himself forward, but there was no purchase to be found on the blood-slick platform. A wave of pain crashed down over him, the taste of metal fading from his mouth. A half-dozen arrows were perforating his legs, jutting out of his back and shoulders.

Fire was bright in the distance, flaring even through the darkness. The hiss of arrows rose, hoofbeats pounding hard, growing louder. He didn't understand it.

He heard the call of Ilvani voices shouting out in alarm. The Valni-rata fought in silence, though. Something had changed.

"Laóith!" they screamed.

His hands were free. Chriani felt the raw flesh at his wrists marked by cleaner cuts where he must have used the bloodblade to slice through the silk ropes. He couldn't remember it. The blade was in his hand, though, and he was using it like a climbing axe as he drove it into the platform, pulled himself slowly forward like he was scaling some sheer wall.

He couldn't remember where he was going, couldn't understand why the pain had stopped. The bloodblade was warm in his hand, Dargana's strength still clutching it. Holding it fast even as his own strength failed.

"Chriani!"

He thought he heard Kathlan calling to him, but she was a world away. He had done it for her, though. The Ilmari could catch the cultists by surprise now, their power crippled. The Laneldenari were safe from the treason that had infected them without their seeing it.

Things would be better now, he hoped. It was done.

"Chriani! Fate and faith, no!"

The glow of mage-light was bright around him. He tasted a bitterness at his lips, then felt himself lifted off the ground by a storm of pain that took his sight away.

He was gagging, more liquid forced to his lips, but he couldn't drink it fast enough. He felt hands on him, heard other voices calling from far off.

"...dead three times over..."

There was a darkness, then a light.

"...fate and fucking moonsign, what's keeping him..."

Someone was calling his name, telling him to hold on. He thought it was Dargana at first, her voice in his mind again. *Find your path, half-blood.* But then he recognized Kathlan, speaking softly.

"It's all right... It's all right..."

Someone was holding him, and he wished suddenly and with all his life and heart that it could have been her. Not just a dream. One last moment in Kathlan's arms would have made it better, he thought, before the darkness took him away.

— CHAPTER 16 —

ONLY MEMORY

HE WAS BACK IN RHERAN, but it was a memory, not a dream. A subtle difference within the cascade of images, of scent and sound that washed through him in the dark. Chriani didn't understand how he knew. He just accepted it. Welcomed it in what he knew must be the last moments of his life. The past running before him at the end, like the old warriors all said.

He and Kathlan had come together at the harvest fest, High Autumn of three years before. He remembered it with a strange clarity, all his present darkness seeming to sharpen the sight of the past. A night of wine and song around the market court fires, Kathlan taking up a duet with Barien — an ethereal lyric of fathers and daughters, love and time that had driven into Chriani's heart like a blunted stake as he watched her.

Late that night came a moment he had long known was coming. From the time Barien had taken him in at eight years, he had told Chriani — had warned him repeatedly — of the danger of showing the warmark at his shoulder to anyone in the Bastion, anyone in the prince's guard. Though she worked within the walls of the keep and alongside tyros and squires alike, Kathlan wasn't of the Bastion or the guard. But this did little to temper the fear that churned in him as he felt that moment drawing closer. Both of them overwhelmed by the celebration of a summer gone, and by spiced wine and firelight, and by an intensity of feeling that left Chriani light-headed as Kathlan led him to her loft above the stables beneath a moonless sky, stars blazing bright and warm.

Chriani had fumbled his way through the overtures. Had attempted to keep his shirt on at first, but Kathlan was having none of that. He had known the day would come at some point, but he hadn't expected it quite so soon. Had no idea how to stop it, how to stop her. No idea what would happen as she pulled his tunic off his shoulder and saw the mark there.

She hesitated, to be sure. But in the end, all she said was, "Tell me." So Chriani did. He told her all of it, the words rushing from him in a flood that spoke to how long he'd been holding them inside. The things he'd only ever told Barien before. The reasons why he'd kept them secret for so long.

When he was done, Kathlan told him her story. Where she'd come from, how she'd gotten to Rheran, her parents dead. "I'll keep your secret," she said in the end. "Don't worry about what's done."

The rest of that night was a blur to him now, with the months that had followed it almost as much so. He had turned away from Kathlan for a time. He had gone to Aerach and returned, and had forgotten in the year and a half since then how many things had changed with that return.

He had forgotten what it felt like to accept the solitude. To expect that he would always be alone. Had forgotten how long it took him to break past that. He should have known it sooner, he thought within the dream. Waiting for the darkness to close around him for good.

He should have told Kathlan what she was to him when he had the chance. He should have told her what she'd done.

Chriani awoke to daylight and the feel of healing magic coursing through him, clearing his thoughts, washing away the pain. A half-dozen points of a bright aching were fading in him now, where arrows had pierced him. At least two of those carried the sharp sense of having hit bone, but even that pain was only memory now.

His arms and legs felt like glass chimes, so fragile that they might shatter if he moved too quickly. His skin was clammy, warm against the chill in the air. It was the brief weakness that came with the magic of healing, but Chriani had never felt it so intensely before. He thought on what that might mean about how close to death he had been. Then he pushed that thought away, down into the shadow where it would hide for a time.

Kathlan was holding him. He couldn't see her, but he knew her presence all the same, feeling her arms around him where he lay slumped on his side.

He was conscious of the sounds of distant shouting, horses on the run. Scattered bowshot over the faint hiss of wind through the trees. Something dark was falling all around him, carrying the scent of charred paper. His vision flickered as he tried to focus, thought for a moment that he might still be dreaming.

He felt Kathlan's breath at his neck. Knew it was real.

"Kath…"

"You need to not move for now," she said quietly. "You've taken enough magic to bring a full squad back from just this side of dead. The healer's not sure how you held on so long."

"I did it for you..."

It was all he could say, the thought etched in his mind as if he was finishing a conversation he'd started with himself a long time ago. He felt the words burning bright, shining like steel scraping at the darkness. He could see torches along the platform, the floating motes of mage-light gone. The black well's haze of shadow was before him, but it had changed somehow. Swirling more slowly, drifting down instead of venting upward. Above him was the faint glimmer of a sunset sky.

The well was silent, he realized. The falling darkness was the slow storm of leaves shedding from the great black tree, swirling down around them like a gentle rain.

Slowly, Chriani raised himself up to sitting, Kathlan's arms disengaging from him. He didn't turn back, couldn't look at her yet. More slowly, he stood. He felt a wave of dizziness wash through him, quickly pass.

He turned to survey the terraces around him, seeing them littered with arrows but only three Ilvani dead. A half-dozen guards in the livery of Aerach were spread around him and Kathlan, walking a slow patrol along the edges of the platform. They were alert, cautious as if they expected a horde of Valnirata to suddenly swing down from the adjacent trees. Beyond and below them, where the well of shadow had been, Chriani could look down to see nothing but ash now. The roots of the great tree were cracked and splintered where they thrust up above that grey-black field. Between two of those roots, the twisted pillar of stone had collapsed to a lighter grey stain.

He moved carefully, took three cautious steps toward the bodies. All warriors in the grey armor of the cult, felled by Aerachi arrows. Some part of his mind that cared about such things noted that the pale captain Raecla wasn't among them. Chriani set the thought aside. It didn't matter anymore. It was over.

Tician wasn't there. That thought stayed with him a little longer, though Chriani expected that the assassin must have bolted the moment the Aerachi arrived in full force. But as his gaze swept the platform, he saw the blood trail he'd left from the edge nearest the black tree, where he had tried to step over and into oblivion. Tried and failed. He marked the smoothly arcing lines that said he'd been dragged a half-dozen steps from that edge, then marked the rougher movement where he had clawed his way forward with the bloodblade in hand.

The ropes that had bound him were cast aside at the point where he'd started moving on his own. He didn't remember cutting them. Could only recall the wounds at his wrists that a knife hacking through the ropes had made.

He saw the rough edges of those ropes where they'd been severed. Not by the razor-smooth edge of the bloodblade, which he had dropped as Viranar died, then claimed again somehow. It was a smaller knife that had sliced through them. A jagged blade, someone freeing him before the Aerachi arrived. Tician had dragged him from the edge, had cut his bonds. She found Dargana's dagger, set it back in his hand.

The assassin had saved him. Again. Chriani set the thought aside, let it slip into the shadow. It was over.

"Sergeant Kathlan. It's all but done in the woods." The voice carried a strength that echoed heavy footfalls along the platform, a tall figure wearing the insignia of an Aerachi captain approaching at a brisk walk.

"And here, lord," Kathlan called in response. She shifted in toward Chriani, who understood that by doing so, she was blocking the incoming officer's view of him for just a moment. He felt her push something into his hand. The black ring, which she must have taken off him.

"That's Captain Shara," she said as Chriani slipped the ring to his belt. "He commands this troop, made me an acting sergeant. You're going to come with us. Do you understand?"

Chriani nodded, turning toward the captain, but Kathlan stopped him with a hand. He saw the cinched rope restraints she held.

"I need to arrest you," she said quietly.

From the corner of his eye, Chriani sensed a pattern to the movement of the guards around him that he hadn't noted before. He understood that he was at the center of the patrol they walked. It was him they were watching, their eyes straying to the Ilvani leather he wore, the war-mark that armor revealed at his shoulder.

"I understand," he said. Pieces falling into place. Whatever chance had brought Kathlan to his side in time to save him, this was an enemy extraction, not a rescue mission. The charges against him as a result of the war-mark at his shoulder being revealed, the fear of whatever plots of the Ilvani he was part of, were both strong enough that a full troop had been sent into the Ghostwood to find him. Repayment for his betrayal.

"I understand," he said again, but for the benefit of the Aerachi captain this time as he stopped close. Shara was an older veteran, wind-burned and close-shaved, thickly muscled in the manner of one who'd been a warrior all his life. Chriani was surprised, though, to see an even temper in his gaze. None of the bluster in Venry, or the raw hatred he remembered from Jeradien's eyes, and which he saw echoed in three of the guards around him now.

Dargana's bloodblade was on the platform two strides from where he had woken. Kathlan stooped to pick it up, wiping it clean with a cloth from her belt pouch before she handed it to Shara. He showed no fear as he took it, held it up to examine it. Chriani saw only admiration in the captain's gaze for the quality and construction of the blade.

As Kathlan stepped close, she pushed Chriani's wrists together, preparing to bind him. They would leave his hands in front of him at least, for riding. Chriani raised his hand to stop her, felt the quick tension in her.

"Captain Shara. Before I'm arrested, I have a favor to ask."

The captain's eyes flicked over to Chriani from the bloodblade, angled so that the light danced across its glyph-etched steel. "You're in a poor position for favors, son."

"How many did you lose in the assault, lord?"

Shara's eyes narrowed. Chriani had no reason to hope for a conversation with the captain, but something in the Aerachi's manner made him speak. Reminding him of Barien.

"Eight wounded, none dead," Shara said, "by the grace of fate and steel. Lucky for you and your cause, I'd say."

"It wasn't luck, lord. When you approached the temple, you would have seen the patrol trails, but I'm guessing you met no sentries." Shara made no response, but Chriani saw acknowledgement flicker in the captain's eyes. "You have war-mages with you. I saw fire in the trees, then heard arrows to follow. You saw the Ilvani scatter, then. They were fleeing even as you attacked."

"The Ilvani excel at skirmish tactics, son, but they know better than to stand against Aerachi rangers on a mission. They broke when they read the odds…"

"They broke because I slew the mage who led them and shut down the magic of this place. I'd wager that your mages are on the ground right now, reading the dweomer around the black tree. Feeling it fade. Ask them. And know that if I hadn't done what I did, this assault would have ended differently."

Shara was silent a moment. His eyes drifted from Chriani to Kathlan and back again. Carefully, the captain set the bloodblade into his belt. As he did, Chriani realized that he had never wondered before at whether the narneth móir held any of the magic said to be second nature to the Valnirata Ilvani. The crafting and history of the blades had always made their legend powerful enough in his own mind, even before he'd seen one for the first time. But he was thinking now of the real power Dargana's blade had fed to him in that desperate moment at the platform's edge. The memories of the exile leader, and the strength of her that had saved his life.

"Lieutenant Venry has accused you of treason, son." Captain Shara said it evenly. Almost apologetically. "He has the duke's ear in this. Fighting against the Ilvani doesn't absolve you of working for them in the first place."

"I have one favor to ask of you, lord," Chriani said again. "When that's done, Venry and your duke can accuse me of whatever they like."

They left him unbound so he could climb, but Chriani had four guards within striking distance the whole time as he led an Aerachi squad to the sheltered platform where Dargana's body lay. The exile showed no sign of having been disturbed, her eyes still closed as if she might have been sleeping. The blood on her had dried to black against the grey of her lóechari armor. The guards stepped in front of Chriani to let him know he wasn't to approach, but he could see the platform clearly around her.

It was approaching dusk, the unnatural night imposed by the shadow long gone. In that light, and the glimmer of the torches the Aerachi guards needed to fill the shadows, Chriani could see clearly what he thought he'd seen when he left Dargana there. No blood pooling beneath her. No trail of red-black across the platform to mark where she'd been bleeding out as he carried her.

He couldn't think on it right now. It was over.

Kathlan stepped past him, Chriani seeing the sadness in her as she helped search Dargana's body, no weapons on her.

Under Chriani's quiet direction, Kathlan tore off the insignias and sash of the cult, left the exile armored in plain leather. Then she directed the guards who wrapped Dargana in an Aerachi cloak and bound it tight with rope. Using those ropes, they lowered her carefully to the ground, Chriani and his guards following.

Kathlan tied his hands when they reached the forest floor. Another guard searched him, checking his belt quickly for hidden weapons but not finding the other treasures it concealed.

Shara ordered two guards to carry Dargana's body, neither of them looking much like they cared for that duty. Then Chriani fell into line with the others as they marched south through the trees.

As they walked, Kathlan stayed by his side. The uneasy lightness of the healing magic was finally beginning to clear, his senses sharpening. He saw three Ilvani bodies scattered along the trails they passed, all of them with arrows in the back to indicate they'd been fleeing. He let his gaze slip across all the Aerachi guards, but saw no one he recognized from Venry's squad.

"Who are they?" he asked Kathlan quietly. "How did you get here?" Even as he said it, he understood how it should have been the first question he asked. His mind was still clouded, all the uncertainty that had dogged him since the Ilvani attack in the Greatwood swirling now like black sand. Kathlan was the only thing clear to him, like somehow her being there had become the only aspect of his life that was important. The how of it happening was just some minor detail.

"They're a troop of ranger scouts from Teillai. They know this frontier. They've been in the Ghostwood, most of them. Hand picked for skill and loyalty."

"Hand picked by who?"

"Lauresa and Irdaign."

Chriani felt the names in his mind like a faint breath of summer air. The warmth that threaded through him made him realize how quickly the day was cooling as the sky darkened overhead.

"We rode with Venry's rangers back to Teillai after the attack," Kathlan said. She spoke quietly, though Chriani's guards were staying closer to Captain Shara ahead of them, unlikely to overhear. "The Ilvani didn't come after us, but you know that. I kept the Brandishear squad together but there was nothing we could do but follow the Aerachi. We went straight to Castle Osthegn so Venry could report to his duke. I sent the squad back to Rheran to report after Irdaign found me there."

The forest around them showed movement in all directions, the Aerachi rangers converging on some rendezvous point that Shara led them toward.

"Found you? How?" Chriani felt the words heavy in his mouth. Knowing he needed to say something, but fairly certain he already knew the answer.

"Same way she found you, I reckon. Said she recognized me from the campsite when you met with her. I asked her how she knew you were coming that night, and she told me. So I asked if she could do it again." Kathlan's hand traced the moonsign, quickly. Chriani caught it from the corner of his eye. "She left a charm on you, she said. She could see you with it. Told us where you were."

Chriani remembered that night at the Leisanmira campsite, and the mark of magic that had seeped through his armor and into his skin when Irdaign sang. He felt the urge to make the moonsign himself. He set it aside. "And then what?"

"Then someone convinced the duke it was important we find you," Kathlan said.

Chriani didn't need to ask who that someone was. *We would have you be safe in all things,* Irdaign had said. Speaking for herself and Lauresa both. He hadn't noticed it then.

Through the trees ahead, a clearing was filled with Aerachi horses coming and going, rangers circling along the Ilvani patrol paths. Archers stood on point, watching cautiously as Captain Shara and the others approached. Chriani felt their eyes on him, didn't care.

He sat beside Dargana's body, two guards watching him while Kathlan and three other sergeants spoke with Shara a short distance away. The troop was a full Aerachi scout force by the look of it, thirty strong or more. Rangers and war-mages, all with field experience that showed in the set of their weapons, the scars of their armor. Kathlan was one of only three females among that number, Chriani noted, and the only one among the sergeants. She stood among their experience as an equal of any of them, though, holding her own as they debriefed.

More than once, Chriani saw the eyes of the sergeants turn in his direction, sensed an undertone of anger in their distant voices that he knew was for him. More than once, he heard Kathlan's voice rise in response.

A field promotion from guard to acting sergeant was a sign of expertise and trust. A promotion from noncommissioned squire to acting sergeant was unheard of. Eighteen months since she had joined the guard, and Chriani had known from the start that Kathlan would wear the sergeant's badge some day. Him being on trial for his life at some point was a thing he probably should have guessed at just as easily.

Even with the sharpness of his ears, he caught only fragments of the conversation between Shara and his sergeants, but it was enough to confirm what he had already guessed. The Ilvani had broken almost immediately, fighting only as long as it took to get them clear of combat, then vanishing into the woods. He heard Shara repeat what Chriani had told the captain, of how the death of Viranar had overwhelmed the

Ilvani, shattering their morale. The overly excited ramblings of the one war-mage among the sergeants gave a hint of the larger story. Magic within the trees, he said, fading now but marking a site of incalculable power. That power broken somehow. Failing the Ilvani that had been bound to it.

None of it was important anymore. Let the rangers craft their tales of the dread Ilvani horde fleeing at the mere sight of Aerachi steel. It was over, Chriani thought. That was all that mattered now.

It would make a good story, as stories went.

The order to ride out came as soon as the officers' council broke. Chriani was given a horse, was surrounded by a full squad with Kathlan at its head. She had Dargana's body behind her, slung over the horse of a wounded Aerachi forced to ride behind another ranger. She was leading the troop on Shara's orders, taking directions from Chriani. He was conscious of the anger that spread through the other rangers as a result. He didn't care.

It had been two favors he asked Shara in the end. For the second, they carried Dargana's body toward the grove where Farenna had set their horses loose, Chriani hoping beyond hope that the three steeds were still there. The Ilvani didn't return their dead to home and family, he knew, but leaving Dargana behind in these dark woods was a thing he wouldn't do.

When he halted, he did his best impression of the whistling call the Ilvani used on their horses, not sure how close he came to the original. The horses heard him, though, appearing through a break in the trees ahead as if they'd been hiding there, just out of sight. They cantered forward toward him, showing no sign of worry or fear at the Aerachi arms and armor arrayed around them.

"Tie the body onto that one," he said, indicating Dargana's horse. As he did, something hit him hard in the back of the head, Chriani twisting around to see the Aerachi guard closest to him with a dagger in hand. He was tanned and scarred in equal measure, fair hair cut long and rough to shade eyes set small in his face as dark points of malice. His weapon was angled so that Chriani understood he'd lashed out to strike with the pommel.

"Another word, you half-blood bastard, and I'll see how you deal with the sharp end."

The surge of anger in Chriani died quickly as Kathlan pushed her horse between him and the wild-eyed guard. "Tie the body on," she said. "And do it right or I'll send you along with her as a peace offering."

The guard scowled as he grabbed the lead of the second horse, two more rangers following him. As they tied the body over the Ilvani horse's back, Kathlan slipped close to the other two mounts, reached out to gently touch them. They accepted her hand easily, rubbed themselves against her in a way that made her own horse shuffle back. Her expression reflected the sheer awe and majesty of the Ilvani steeds, Chriani understanding how much they would mean to her.

He had ridden among the Valnirata. A thing that perhaps no other living Ilmari could say. He didn't know what would happen when the horses made their way back to Sylonna. Dargana would be taken to her rest, given rites. The Ilvani would come to the temple site, he knew. They would find the remains of Farenna's riders who had fallen, but they would never find the captain. Would never find Chriani, never know what had happened to him.

The three guards returned when Dargana's body had been tied carefully to the horse, the ropes padded with cloth against its breast and belly. Chriani spurred forward beside Kathlan, brought himself up close to the white stallion Farenna had ridden. He spoke clearly in Ilvalantar. "Home," he said.

Like they heard and understood him, all three horses twisted away and shot off south into the woods, Dargana's mount in the lead. Their hoofbeats were muffled, falling quickly to silence as they found the trail back to Sylonna and disappeared from sight.

Captain Shara called out from behind them. "We ride out the light and beyond. No rest till we've cleared the Ghostwood." Then with a surge of sound and motion, the Aerachi troop turned for the east, thundering away through the trees.

They rode hard along the course that Shara's rangers had marked out from Teillai. Through the forest, they ran east breaking slowly north, emerging just past the Clearmoon's rise into a wedge of scrubland around which two arms of the Ghostwood spread like horns. They were still well within Ilvani territory but free of the trees and the risk of ambush attack. They set a rough camp late that night, bedrolls only and horses staked. The rangers made no fires but set out full torchlight and patrols on the perimeter. They were on a low rise that gave a wide view of the land around them, but there was no sign of any pursuit or patrol.

They were riding again before dawn, a grey-gold light ahead of them marking their course. The sun was still climbing when the horns of the forest thinned to patchy scrub and open ground ahead, showing that they had left the Ghostwood behind. Their course changed to due northeast then, setting the shortest route for the unseen border ahead. It was three day's ride to Teillai, Chriani heard someone say.

The journey was made with a profound lack of conversation. The Aerachi had seemed unwilling to speak while within the Ghostwood and the Crithnalerean scrubland, as if obeying some rangers' superstition and the fear of unseen Ilvani patrols. Not that any such patrols would have had problems hearing the Aerachi horses from a league away, Chriani had thought more than once. Against the memory of the Ilvani horses running in near silence, the endless din of the troop's passage was like thunder in his ears.

They made a second rough camp that night atop a rise set with fir and grape vines. While the horses grazed in thick stands of wild grass, the guards gathered deadfall for watch fires. The mood was dark among them, conversations undertaken in hushed tones. However, from the glances sent his way at regular intervals while the guards worked and he sat, Chriani was fairly certain what the topic of conversation was. He was too distracted to think on it, though, Kathlan keeping a distance from him that left him mostly alone with his thoughts.

More than once, those thoughts had turned back to Dargana, and a chill uncertainty that was becoming familiar to Chriani as he thought about the events of that dark day. Hearing her speaking, even though all the evidence of the platform told him she was already dead before he set her down there. All the evidence of logic, and his understanding of how badly injured she was before he had first set out with her, climbing with her body over his shoulder.

Her memories were tied to the dagger. Perhaps that was what he was hearing on the platform. The magic of the coins around him, the shadow of the black well flowing through him. That darkness across his eyes, scouring his lungs, filling his mind.

As he sat at one of the watch fires, Chriani thought of Barien. He was eating alone, the four guards charged with watching him all sitting a few paces away. Though his hands were still bound, he was able to deal with bread and jerky, flasks of water and weak ale that were apparently Aerach's standard field rations. He had started with the ale, was feeling light-headed when the thought of Barien came from nowhere, then shifted within the lingering sense of that moment when Dargana's memories had opened up within his mind. He remembered the power of the coins flowing through him, leaving him empty so that he could take the strength her memory offered him. Remembered touching the exile's life as though he had lived it.

He had never really known Dargana. He had felt the rawness of those memories, and the dark emotion that fueled them. There were connections between her and Chriani, but he understood that those connections were things outside the scope of his life. Things he would have liked to know, and that she might have helped him with if the two of them had ever known the chance. Questions about the world his father came from. But those were things Chriani had never thought of as important before his life took its turn along the path that led him to the Clearwater Way. And so he was left with little sense of what he might have truly asked Dargana if he'd had the chance.

Barien had stood at the center of Chriani's life for ten years. Had been the focal point around which that life turned. And with everything that had happened to him, with all the changes that had overtaken him in the past eighteen months, Chriani understood only too well how many questions he would ask Barien now if he could. He understood how much he would give to embrace the warrior's memories, to feel that contact of thought and mind in the same way he had touched Dargana. To feel Barien alive and in his life once more, even as memory. Even for a moment.

He felt the heat of the fire, felt the chill that came in from the edges of the cloak Kathlan had found for him, his bound hands unable to seal it properly. The night was bright and cloudless, the waning Clearmoon still waiting to rise. He had relics of Barien's, he remembered. The wooden dagger. Other things locked tight in the trunk he'd left behind at the Bastion when he took to the field.

Chriani tossed the last of his bread to the fire, catching a dark look from one of his guards in response. And as he stared to the flames, he wondered whether the magic of the coins would have opened up all the memories tied to those pieces of Barien's lost life. Wondered what it would have felt like to touch the warrior's mind that way. Feeling the strength that had driven him, the sense of honor and accomplishment behind the blue eyes and the wide smile. The grim dedication to service that had cost him his life.

He had no idea whether the bloodblade held magic. No idea whether it was that magic alone that had interacted with the dweomer of the coins and the black well. No idea whether the Ilmari had access to magic that might recreate the effect of the coins. Mind magic powerful enough to tear the impressions of a life out of the objects that life had touched would be secret if it existed at all. Milyan or Varyn or another of Chanist's mages would know of it. But even as the thought came to him, Chriani knew that enduring a lengthy questioning under magical compulsion was the only encounter he was likely to have with Chanist's mages again.

"…kill the half-blood bastard now."

He heard the voice rise from where his guards sat, starkly shadowed by the light of the fire. Figures were moving around them, other rangers heading for sentry duty or settling down into bedrolls to catch some sleep before their own turn along the camp's fire-bright perimeter.

The speaker was the guard who had struck him when they retrieved Dargana. Madoc, under Kathlan's command. Chriani had heard his name on the ride but ignored him as best he could, even as he knew that effort wasn't likely to last the length of their journey together.

"Waste of a trial if you ask me," the scarred warrior said, louder now. "We cross the border tomorrow, we can mete out military justice by law. What's the penalty for treason again?"

"Execution," one of the others said with a smile. "They'll hang him in Teillai. Seems too quick a way for a treason-bastard to go, though."

"We can deliver justice to traitors as well as Andreg. A sight more painfully, too."

"You can try," Chriani said quietly.

Madoc shot to his feet without a word, Chriani following. He felt a dangerous anger hanging, spreading out around him. A few eyes were watching, but only his guards were moving.

"Too bad your hands are tied, half-blood." Madoc's tone was mocking as he pushed in, Chriani shifting back to keep himself from being surrounded.

"Best to keep it fair, I thought." With his bound fists, he hurled his borrowed cloak at the two guards trying to circle around behind him. Beneath it, he was still in his lóechari leathers. He saw the dark rage in Madoc's eyes flare bright in the firelight.

"Stand!"

Kathlan's voice rang out like steel on steel, Chriani seeing her from the corner of his eye as she strode up from the far side of the fire. He sensed the guards behind him go still. He and Madoc both took another step before they stopped, an arm's length away from each other.

"There'll be no rough justice." Kathlan stepped up between Chriani and Madoc, pushing Chriani back with the flat of her hand. He stumbled as he put two more steps between them. "We're bound for Teillai to deliver the prisoner. That's captain's orders, and don't be telling me you didn't hear him as well as I did."

Madoc leered. "Saved by your woman, half-blood. Story of your sotting life, I'm betting."

"I don't think I heard you straight, Madoc."

Though Kathlan had to look up to see the scarred warrior a full head and a half above her, even he heard the steel-sharp edge to her voice. Madoc sneered, though, as he took a step back.

"Begging your pardon."

"That's *Begging your pardon, lord*. Or is there an officer in Aerach stupid enough to have granted you promotion?"

Madoc's hands flexed to fists. "I'll ask after whatever sot stuck your insignia on, then?"

Chriani felt the tension twisting through him, whipcord tight. He started to shift, wanted to get past Kathlan and to the side, get a clear shot at Madoc. There was no way she could have seen him, but her hand flashed up behind her to warn him away just the same.

"That sot would be your captain," she said sweetly. "Shall we take it up with him?"

Madoc spat. "I'll take orders from him if you like. But I don't take a dressing down from any treason-bastard's whore…"

Kathlan punched up with a shot that even Chriani hadn't seen coming. Taking advantage of the size difference between herself and the larger warrior, she put all the strength of body and legs behind the fist she buried in the soft underside of his jaw. It sent his head back with a disturbing crack. He was still reeling from that, stumbling a half step back to regain his balance, when she spun with a roundhouse kick that took him cleanly between the legs.

Madoc cried out with a voice that caught the ear of every other soldier in the camp. He hit the ground hard.

Chriani stood stock-still, watching for the warrior to move, but he stayed where he was. Partly for the pain that hunched him over nearly double, but partly also from the sheer shock of Kathlan's assault.

Standing over Madoc, she flexed her hand. She was breathing slowly. Cautious, Chriani saw, but carried by a control he recognized as the deepest, strongest part of her.

"Just so it's clear," she said. "The second shot was for the insult to me, and I'll be using your leather-cured cock to pick my horse's teeth if I ever hear it again. The first shot was for calling Chriani a traitor." She turned now to the two guards behind Chriani, pitched her voice for anyone else who was listening to hear. "Lieutenant Venry and your duke are wrong in this. But if it takes a trial to prove it to you, then that's what's to happen. By your Duke Andreg's orders. Or do you answer to someone else?"

Chriani felt as though he could touch Kathlan's anger in that moment, knowing it matched the best rage that had ever burned in him. Knowing also that Kathlan would never let it get the best of her. Would never let it control her. She would use it to push herself, just as she'd always done.

He understood in that moment not just that he loved her, but how much. He understood why. Understood how she made him better than he was, better than he could ever be on his own. The anger that had broken him, always, was a strength in her. The stone that shattered his ambition whetted hers.

He didn't know whether that made any difference now. Didn't know whether it was too late.

"Sergeant Kathlan, is there a problem here?"

Shara's voice rang out with a subtle strength that told Chriani he'd heard everything Kathlan said. The captain was pacing toward them from the center of the camp, the horses tethered around a stand of scrub pine there. Madoc shot to his feet, but Chriani noted that he had to strain to stand straight.

"No, lord." Kathlan's tone was even, but Chriani heard the caution in her voice. Not sure if she'd gone too far.

"Did I not see one of your rangers on the ground a moment ago?"

"We've ridden hard today, lord. We could all use rest."

Chriani saw three of the guards behind Shara smirk, though no one dared to laugh.

"Carry on, then."

The captain passed by without another word. Kathlan waited until he'd gone before she spoke. "Madoc, you're with the horses. Stay out of my sight, and unless every Ilvani in Crithnalerean comes out of the Ghostwood tonight, don't let me hear your voice."

Madoc's gaze spoke volumes but he held his tongue. He turned from Kathlan, limping away from the fire and toward the trees. She turned her attention then to the other three who had been sitting with the scarred warrior. Chriani noted that they had all shifted back a few paces.

"Does anyone else have any problems following my orders?"

"No, lord." All three of them, speaking at once.

"Then guard the prisoner. Two on watch, one resting. Set whatever schedule you like. Anything happens to him, you answer to me."

She turned without another word, stalked off toward the next watch fire. Chriani picked up his cloak and wrapped himself with it as the others settled into watch positions. None of them met his gaze.

He could see Kathlan at the edge of the firelight where she set her watch with three other guards. She kept her distance from them, pacing until the deep night, the Clearmoon thin and cold when it finally came. When she and the others were spelled off, she sought out a bedroll, lying down near the fire as the guards banked it high.

Only then did Chriani sleep.

— CHAPTER 17 —

THE FUTURE UNSEEN

THEY LEFT ILVANI TERRITORY at dusk the next day. The land around them had turned from wild grass and scrub pine to overgrown meadow earlier at the sun's height, which yielded at sunset to the first tilled fields dotted with frontier farmsteads, buildings set low and solid behind rough stockade walls.

The long day's ride had been all but silent, Chriani in the van close behind Shara, like the captain meant to undercut any additional discussion of the troop's orders and Chriani's fate. Kathlan was farther behind, so that he saw her only when they stopped to water and graze the horses. In all the time he was alone, he tried to keep her in his mind, tried to focus the emotion that had cut through him the previous night. Understanding that nothing mattered except her. Understanding how much he wished he could have had more time.

They would be in Teillai the following day. The weather was still clear, nothing to slow them. Chriani didn't know what a trial for treason before the duke would look like, but he expected it would be brief.

If he was found guilty, he'd be executed. Kathlan would be there to see it. Irdaign as well. Lauresa.

Over the two days it took them to ride out from the Ghostwood, Chriani had kept escape in his thoughts the whole time. Not focusing on it. Not plotting it specifically, for fear that his anger would push him to try it before it was time. He had been watching the rangers as they rode, though. Had assembled in his mind the makeup of each squad, the tone and tenor of their sergeants. He knew how many outriders Shara liked to deploy, and how often. He noted which of the guards outside Madoc and his entourage were strongest in their intrinsic hatred of him. Which ones were merely indifferent. Which ones seemed most likely to back down from a fight if their lives were on the line.

He recognized the landscape around them, judging that they were within easy ride of the farmstead where he had challenged Venry's rangers for their threats against Dargana. It seemed a long while ago. Though he hadn't seen the river yet, Chriani knew they were close to the Hunthad where it defined the border between Aerach and the Valnirata lands. The farm tracks that crisscrossed the area would hide his own tracks.

If he was taken to Teillai, it was even odds he'd be dead before the next sunset. If he broke from the troop and fate was in his favor, he might make it. He had the black ring to conceal him. He had the Greatwood waiting for him. Perhaps not better odds of surviving than the trial, but they'd be his odds at least. A chance to die on his feet, hands bound or no.

He'd been watching Kathlan, noting when she rested. Not just the previous night, but the nights before and each time the troop had stopped. Because for all the logistical impossibility of escaping the watch of thirty seasoned rangers, there was only one of those rangers Chriani was worried about.

If he tried to escape, if he was pursued and brought down, he wouldn't let Kathlan see him die.

They set a full camp with tents that night but kept well clear of any settlements, Shara not wanting to stop near the frontier farmsteads in case they were pursued. A carontir patrol shadowing them unseen would wait until deep night to attack, at which point having to protect civilians and livestock became a liability. It seemed a fleeting concern, though, with the troop's outrider patrols catching no sight in two days of anything moving out from the Ghostwood behind them.

Chriani had a double tent to himself. They had set him away from the other rangers and the perimeter fires, but with the flap sealed against the wind, he was warmer than he had been sleeping rough the previous two nights. He wasn't sleeping this night, though. He was sitting in the center of the tent, twisting his arms and shoulders carefully, as he had been over the two days of their ride whenever he thought he could get away with it. With his wrists bound, he knew his arms would begin to weaken even after so short a time. He needed to be limber, needed to be ready for whatever might happen.

He was studying the restraints that bound him. A thing he hadn't done while they rode, not wanting to give anyone a chance to see him. The ropes were retied twice each day, their steel cinch checked and locked. Chriani knew he had no hope of opening that lock even with his picks, the keyhole set too far from his fingers. They hadn't changed the rope, though, and Chriani had long since noted the weak spots where the cinch bound it.

He was working those spots carefully now, knowing his time was growing short. But in doing so, he was distracted, so that he heard movement outside the tent only as the flap was drawn. He started back, cursing himself silently for not listening.

Kathlan slipped inside. She quickly sealed the flap behind her.

When he had first entered the tent, Chriani noted two guards sitting close to the fire a dozen paces away. In the quick glimpse through the open flap, he'd seen darkness there now, cloud covering Clearmoon and stars, the guards gone.

Kathlan had a knife in hand, was working at his restraints before Chriani could react. "I took this shift of the watch with Madoc. Show him there's no hard feelings. But he's on a trip to the trees. Licorice root in his wineskin means he'll be there a while, but not all night."

As the ropes parted, Chriani felt his wrists come away raw from each other. With his arms moving freely for the first time in two days, he shifted to embrace Kathlan, but she held him back.

"There's no time," she said. The sense of finality in her voice was something Chriani had never heard before. "I begged Lauresa to talk to her duke for you, but she said that convincing him to send rangers after you was all she could do. She could twist that to make him see how it granted advantage over Vishod and Chanist alike. Him capturing their lost traitor envoy. But for your fate, Andreg won't be taking any counsel but his own."

It was near dark in the tent, Chriani knowing Kathlan couldn't fully see him even as her face in shadow was clear to his eyes. Her hand was trembling at his shoulder, fingers tracing out the war-mark unseen beneath his leather.

"Lauresa and Irdaign promised instead that they'd send word to Prince Chanist," she whispered. "Ask him to entreat Andreg to send you back to Brandishear for trial. Get you out of Aerach."

Chriani felt an unexpected anger rise in him. His fate suddenly in Chanist's hands was a thought that would never have crossed his mind. Something he would never have sought for himself, even to save his own life. "You shouldn't have done that…"

"Chriani, if they get you to Teillai tomorrow, it's your life. There was no other way."

It wasn't true, he knew. He could think of a dozen different ways it might end, though most of them were far from good. But he remembered also his warning to Chanist, and the threat that still hung between them. If the prince high acquiesced, it would be because in doing so, he would see Chriani hand back the only power he had ever held.

"It doesn't matter, though," Kathlan said. "Irdaign said she'd make sure riders from Brandishear would catch us before Teillai to keep it out of Andreg's hands. But they haven't come, so you need to run."

"Kath…"

"Run, Chriani. Use the ring. You need to get away."

"Do not let the fear of what you cannot see control you, Ilmari," came a voice from behind them both. The words were in Ilmari, heavily accented. "For fate leads us to futures seen and unseen, and is yet in both your hands. There is still time."

All the words Chriani could have said in response to Kathlan turned to ash in his mouth. He twisted to get in front of her, felt her press close, the knife in her hand up and beside him. The blood was hammering in his head, the taste of metal in his mouth. He wasn't afraid, though.

"What are you doing here? How did you…?"

Chriani's voice was cut off as Veassen set a faint light to his fingertips, the seer's blind eyes gleaming in the shadows. He was sitting cross-legged a single stride away, the wall of the tent at his back. Chriani felt the air shift as if tugged at by a faint breeze.

"The Aerachi cannot see us," Veassen said. "They will not hear us. My magic protects us, even as it has shown you to me and brought me safely here. But we must be quick."

I have learned and forgotten more spells than are known among all the Ilmari. Chriani remembered the seer saying it, remembered how he had come and gone in two councils without Chriani seeing him. His hand shook from two days of being bound as he made the moonsign.

"Chriani…" Kathlan's voice at his ear was a faint whisper.

"He's named Veassen. He's of the Laneldenari. I know him." It was far too brief an explanation, but it was all Chriani had the strength to say. "What do you want?"

"To ask what you mean to do, Chriani. And to offer you sanctuary if your choice leads you back to the Ilvani."

The absolute silence that followed Veassen's words was stark enough that Chriani could hear a faint hissing from the light that blossomed from the seer's hand.

He thought of Barien, unexpectedly. A timeless moment of memory that carried a conversation with the warrior, and talk of the choices in life that a person could make. Chriani wondered briefly what choice Barien might make if the warrior had been in his position right now, even as he understood the stupidity of the thought. Because Barien would never have allowed himself to be named a traitor in the first place. He would have prevented it, would have fixed it somehow.

That was Chriani's problem. Had always been. Thinking always too late about the things that challenged him in his life. The things he wanted, and how to reach for them. Realizing the answers to the questions only after the questions had come and gone.

"No," he said.

Kathlan's hand was at his shoulder, squeezing hard, but it was Veassen she spoke to. "Can you take him from here? Use your spellcraft?"

The seer nodded even as Chriani shook his head. "No," he said again.

"Don't be a fool for the first time in your life, Chriani." Kathlan twisted herself around to meet his gaze, but he shifted to keep his eyes away from her. "Take the road that's offered you."

He remembered Tician's words within the respite of her sanctuary. *When the road behind is closed, you can look only ahead.* "I know my road," he said. "I go where you go, Kath. I stay at your side until the end."

It was an admission of failure, he knew. Not the strength he had wanted to believe was in him. The strength to break from Kathlan, to make sure she wasn't there to see him die.

If living meant living apart from her, he wasn't strong enough to do it. Not anymore.

"I'm sorry," he said.

"Chriani, please…"

"Did you lie to me?" He pushed his thoughts from Kathlan because he had to, his eyes finding Veassen's. Locking themselves to the seer's blind gaze. The thoughts of Tician unfolding in his mind let slip the things the assassin had said. "If Laneldenar had captured the coins, it would have meant the same end as the Calala Ilvani holding them. Was that your plan when you sent us to find the temple? To claim that power for yourself?"

Veassen smiled. "But you were not sent, Chriani. I saw you make that choice, and in so doing, place the fate of both your peoples above yourself. I saw that you would do what you were meant to do. As you do now."

"Please take him." Kathlan shifted forward toward the seer, hand clutched to her heart and fighting the urge to make the moonsign with a strength Chriani could feel. "If it's in your power, don't let him do this…"

"This is not my fate, child," Veassen said. His white eyes drifted to Kathlan, a sad smile tracing his face. "I hope you understand. Now, do not tarry. My power goes with me, and the dawn is near."

The seer was gone. No sense of him vanishing, no lingering presence of his sorcery. Just again the faint stirring of air, and a silence that seemed to hang for a long while before Kathlan spoke.

"Chriani, please…"

"Get some sleep," he said. "It'll be a hard ride to Teillai. Shara and the rest won't want to be late in."

He was looking to the back of the tent, staring at the spot where Veassen had been, when Kathlan slipped outside and away.

He was sitting there still when Kathlan came through the tent's door flap again at dawn. He hadn't slept.

As she slipped inside, she pulled a short length of rope from inside her tunic. Under the guise of checking Chriani's bonds, she retied him tightly, pocketed the remnants of the rope she had cut the night before. Neither of them spoke.

Chriani stood by as the Aerachi broke camp, the sun bright above the fields to the east but the world around them still in shadow. Darkness hung to the south where the distant Greatwood lay. He noted again the difference to the light in Aerach, remembered sensing it first when he led the Brandishear squad out from the Clearwater Way. He recalled the dawn in Rheran, blazing above the sea like an eruption of bright fire. He remembered sunrise on the frontier, bursting above the dark stain of the forest like molten gold. The dawn of Aerach was muted, though. The land here seemed to embrace the light, releasing it only grudgingly. As if that land longed to cling to the shadow of night for as long as it could.

He heard the order to saddle up, saw his horse being led toward him. He tried to find Kathlan within the chaos of movement as the rangers prepared to ride, but she was nowhere in sight. Madoc was there, though. Chriani noted the ranger's queasy expression, the dark lines beneath his eyes. He couldn't find it in himself to care.

He was on his horse, stepping into place between the four riders assigned to flank him, when he saw movement in the distance.

To the far northwest, a ripple disturbed the shadow that clung to gently rolling fields. Riders on horseback, moving quickly. They were faint still even to his eyes, Chriani knowing that no one else in the troop would see them.

They heard the horn, though. Two short blasts that sounded out faint on a rising wind. Rangers returning.

The sound of hoofbeats quieted as Captain Shara held a hand up at the front of the troop, all eyes turning. The horn sounded out again. Chriani caught Shara's glance back toward him as the captain circled his hand overhead for a change of course. The sergeant at Shara's left sounded a horn twice in response as the troop turned as one to the northwest, cantering off as the sun finally broke away from the ground below.

It was five riders, all in the livery of Brandishear. They were tired, the well-run look of their horses suggesting that they must have set out well before dawn. The Aerachi rangers slowed to a halt, spreading out as the Brandishear squad came within their midst. Chriani didn't know any of them, though he recognized the livery of the Bastion guard.

"Iarva," the sergeant called as she saluted. "Are you Captain Shara out of Teillai?"

"Indeed," Shara said. "What business is this?"

"A message from the Prince High Chanist, for your eyes." From the pouch at her belt, the sergeant retrieved a sealed envelope, passed it to the captain. "We were told you'd be riding from the Ghostwood and were meant to be waiting for you last night, but we were delayed. Ilvani are all across the Clearwater Way. I'm glad we didn't have to ride to Teillai to catch you."

Shara broke the seal on the envelope and unfolded the message within. He read it silently.

"Kathlan. Bragan. To me, please."

A ripple of uncertainty spread through the Aerachi rangers, Chriani feeling it.

He recognized the war-mage he'd seen in the Ghostwood as the other sergeant Shara had called. He hadn't bothered to learn his name before. Kathlan slipped up from the back of the troop, riding wide around Chriani to reach Shara's side. He showed her the letter first, Chriani seeing her read it quickly. She nodded, her face a mask.

To the war-mage, Shara nodded. The mage spoke unheard words, a pulse of pale light surrounding the letter in Shara's hand. Most of the Aerachi rangers made the moonsign. The captain didn't.

"Chriani, approach."

The silence as he spurred forward past his guards hung like a shroud. He stepped his horse up slowly, stopped two paces away. Shara nodded to him before he read the message aloud.

"This letter confirms, by the words of the prince high of Brandi-shear, that Chriani of the prince's guard, regiment of Rheran and the Bastion, is engaged on a mission to infiltrate the Ilvani war-clans." He spoke to let his voice carry, every eye in the troop on him. "For purposes of diplomacy and the safety of the realm has this mission been undertaken, with knowledge limited to Chriani, the prince high of Brandishear, the Captain Ashlund of the Bastion in Rheran, and those three sworn to absolute secrecy in this matter."

As Shara shifted in the saddle, Chriani could see the message. He recognized the writing as Chanist's own hand. He had seen it enough times, on documents and notes and commendations, all piling up on the rough shelves in the quarters Barien and Chriani had shared for ten years.

"As a Half-Ilvani with ties to the Greatwood, but whose loyalty to Brandishear and its crown is above reproach, Chriani has been ordered to take the guise of an Ilvani agent of the Valnirata, and to seek access among them. On orders of his prince high and for the manner in which the truth of this mission might imperil diplomatic efforts between the Ilmar Principalities and elements of the Valnirata, Chriani was not to speak the truth of his mission under any circumstances, even to the point of saving his own life at trial. So do I, the Prince High Chanist, speak it for him."

Something twisted in Chriani's gut. Kathlan still wasn't looking at him, but he saw the trembling in her hands, at her jaw. He understood the weight of the burden suddenly leaving her. The weight she had carried as she came after him, all of it slipping away now.

"Chriani is absolved of all guilt for actions committed in the name of his duty to Brandishear, by request of the Prince High Chanist, and with dispensation from the Prince High Vishod, who speaks for the Duke Andreg under whose service Chriani's duties in Aerach have been done. Chriani is to return to Brandishear at once."

Shara folded the letter thoughtfully. He looked to Chriani like he wasn't sure what to say. In the crowd of rangers around them, Madoc beat him to it.

"This is lies and Brandishear bastardry!" the warrior snarled. "What proof do we have of where these so-called orders come from?"

Shara turned to his ranger with a dark look, but it was the war-mage Bragan who spoke. "I have the proof, master Madoc, and you'll watch your tongue. The message holds the arcane seal of Vishod's court at Aleran, magically marked alongside the arcane seal of

Rheran." The mage's expression suggested how rare such a thing must have been. He spoke an incantation again, Shara holding the letter up this time so that all could see the two arcane sigils that flared across its writing.

Chriani was watching. He thought he saw the quickest flash of a third mark. A flower of five petals, etched in lines of white light. The same sign of protection Irdaign had placed on him.

"Chriani."

He looked over to where Shara had a knife out, nodded to his bonds. He stepped his horse closer to let the captain cut the ropes, shaking his hands out as they were freed.

"Pick your horses and arrange for a change of gear," the captain said as he appraised Chriani's Ilvani leathers. "We've all got riding to do." He nodded then to him and Kathlan in turn, but his gaze lingered longer on her. Chriani saw a sense of respect there that reminded him again of Barien. He tried to think on what Kathlan had done, the lengths she'd gone to, to bring the captain and his troop to Chriani's rescue.

The rest of that troop shifted away now, the rangers waiting in silence as Chriani and Kathlan prepared to take their leave, just like that. She was at Shara's side, talking quietly as Chriani changed into the Aerachi uniform and leather provided for him. He felt eyes on him as he stripped off the Ilvani armor, packed it carefully into the saddlebags he'd been given for his horse. He didn't care.

He pulled off the tunic that Farenna had cut away to reveal the war-mark at his shoulder. He felt that war-mark catch the warmth of the sun for a fleeting moment as he pulled a clean tunic over it. He found the cut ropes that had bound him, carefully unfurled a single cord from one section. He used it to tie his hair back and low, covering his ears. A sense of things going back to the way they were, even as Chriani understood that everything had changed. Futures seen and unseen, Veassen had said.

His secret was known now, and a strength and a sense of freedom like he'd never felt before was surging in him as a result. But he didn't know how long any of it might last. Understanding that he was stepping back into a life whose parameters would change because of what others knew about him. Understanding that he owed a debt to the Prince High Chanist whose terms remained to be resolved. Remembering Kathlan's anger and the shadow drifting deep inside him. All the things he'd been afraid to tell her.

For weapons, Chriani secured a dirk and smallsword donated by Madoc on Shara's orders, along with a spare shortbow from the captain's own saddle. Shara also returned Dargana's bloodblade to him, wrapped tight in oilcloth.

"Thank you for your hospitality," Chriani said to the captain when he was ready to ride. He thought of asking to give his thanks as well to the Duke Andreg, but the words stuck in his throat.

The captain simply nodded as he turned away and spurred off east and north, the troop falling in behind him.

The Brandishear couriers had further business in Aleran, and so rode with Chriani and Kathlan only a short distance before breaking off to the north, leaving them to make their own way back home. The two of them continued along a succession of farm tracks bearing steadily northwest, shadowing the distant border with the exile lands.

Chriani remembered the courier's words about Ilvani on the Clearwater Way, wondering what it might mean. The remnants of the lóechari dispersing, perhaps. Or the scattered Crithnala hearing of the cult's fall and slipping back to the south, pursuing the Calala as they fled. Ashlund would need a full report, he thought, feeling himself falling back into a sense of his own service and duty with a strange familiarity.

He remembered having been banned from the frontier by Captain Rhuddry, wasn't sure how best to deal with that. He started by telling Kathlan, though, confessing the results of his hubris that day.

"It'll work out," was all she said.

They were going back to Brandishear. Chriani told himself he wouldn't think on any of the reasons he had to return to Aerach. Not a secret anymore, or not from Kathlan at least. But just something for another day.

It was a two-day ride to Werrancross, and Chriani filled much of it with talking. He told Kathlan what had happened to him and Dargana, sharing every smallest detail of their flight through the forest with the Ilvani, and of the hidden city and the councils that followed. He told her of Taelendar, and was surprised at the emotion that twisted through him in response to his own words of the warrior's end. He told her of Farenna and of Dargana falling, and of how the Ilvani captain had fought against the curse that consumed him. How he'd saved Chriani's life.

That first day turned to cloud threatening rain, so they sought shelter at a farmhouse in a small steading just past a railed wooden bridge that crossed the Hunthad. With them both in Aerachi uniforms, they were welcomed with open arms by the matron whose farm it was. With her four grown children, she treated them to a meal that might have been the best thing Chriani had ever eaten, even if it hadn't come at the end of a long road.

The farm had two guest rooms used for summer laborers, both of them set up with fresh linen and basins of hot water by the time dinner was done. Chriani would have preferred to share a room with Kathlan, just to hold her after the ordeal that had separated them. But he felt the exhaustion in her that matched his own, and an emotional distance between them that he knew would do better with rest.

He also knew he had one more thing to say to her. Knew that it would be better said by morning than by night.

On the next day's ride, Chriani told Kathlan of the cult. He told her of being captured, feeling himself drawn back to the well of shadow as he spoke, the memory sharp and cold in his mind. He told her of how the cult's magic built on memory, repeating what he'd learned at the council, what Dargana had told them in the Bastion throne room when it all began. He felt the fear in her that was the only natural reaction to such things.

He talked of Dargana's memories laid down alongside his, and the strength in her that had saved him. Then he told Kathlan of what had come before that, not spoken yet. Dargana's last words to him, and how Chriani thought now that she must have been already dead when he heard them. He told her of not knowing what it meant that it had happened that way, and of being afraid. Kathlan made the moonsign as he spoke.

Chriani told her finally of the assassin and how she had saved him. How he was sure she had dragged him back from the black well's edge. The offer she'd made, and the choice he'd made in return.

"I know my path," he said. "I came back for you. I did it for you." Echoing the words he'd whispered in the aftermath of the battle, while Kathlan held him and he clawed his way back from dead.

She squeezed his hand hard as they rode on in silence. Said nothing in return.

That night brought them to the outskirts of Werrancross, and to the same inn the Brandishear squad had occupied on a night of rain nearly two weeks before. To Chriani's mind, it seemed so much longer. They shared a room and a bed, and he felt a hunger in Kathlan throughout the darkness of the night that set a brightness burning in his heart and mind. Watching her as she sat astride him, as she cried out beneath him, her shadowed features shining in his eyes.

They woke early and in silence, setting out as the grey dawn rose. A haze of mist and low cloud hung to blanket the city where it spread to north and east. Chriani and Kathlan made their way toward one of the patrol way stations set up where the north–south trade road forked out to mark the beginning of the Clearwater Way. These were riding posts where merchants and other travelers could wait for the patrols of Aerach and Brandishear, traveling alongside them for safety. Though both he and Kathlan had riding bows, even with a packhorse carrying arrows by the barrel, Chriani wouldn't have dreamed of taking the Clearwater Way alone.

They didn't know how long they'd have to wait, so they sat close along a stretch of meadow grass while the horses cropped. Kathlan's hand was in Chriani's still, the rawness at his wrists where the ropes had bound him already responding to some Aerachi salve she'd given him from her saddlebags. She was still silent, watching the grey sky.

Chriani told her the last thing he had to tell her then. The thing he'd told Dargana. How the blade of Caradar that had seemingly started all this — had brought him to the Ilvani's attention and into their sights — was with Lauresa. How he had given it to her to give to the daughter he would never know. He felt the pain of each word as he spoke it like broken glass on his tongue. Afraid to say it. Knowing how he had to.

"Thank you for telling me," Kathlan said when he was done. Chriani heard the pain twist in her voice as he kissed her, hoping in some way that he might draw that pain away from her. The last thing he had needed to say, done now.

He would have no secrets. Not anymore.

The thud of hoofbeats marked the arrival of an Aerachi patrol at the way station. In addition to Chriani and Kathlan, two merchants with a pair of horses each were waiting for escort, along with what looked like a trio of noble's couriers.

The six rangers nodded to each of them in turn as the others mounted up, Chriani and Kathlan standing, walking to their horses hand in hand. Their fingers parted only as they each climbed up to the saddle.

"I'm sorry, Chriani."

He had paced away toward where one of the merchants was sharing a wineskin with the rangers, all of them laughing. Kathlan on her horse stood behind him, hadn't moved. He reined to a stop, turned back toward her.

"You need to go back," she said. "Ride safe."

The chill of distance was in her voice, and a strength that said these were words she'd been thinking on for a while.

"Kath, what are you doing?"

"Staying, Chriani. You've got your life back. You've got your road to follow. Ride it well."

"No." He kicked his horse forward to step beside her, reached for her hand but she backed away.

"Don't do this," she said. "Don't make it harder."

"It's not…" Chriani felt his mind fumbling for words. "I don't understand." But even as he said it, he realized he did understand. The words came back to him from the tent three nights before, locked in his memory but distant. Not focused on in the moment, for the sake of all the other things he had needed to focus on.

You need to run, Kathlan had said. *You need to get away.* Not *we.* Just him.

"If I had fled that night, you were planning on staying," he said numbly. "Right from the start."

"No, Chriani, I was planning on running, same as you should have. I didn't plan on sticking around for them to understand I helped you, then invite me to share your traitor's fate. But I wasn't going with you. I can't go with you. Not anymore."

Behind him, one of the Aerachi rangers whistled. Chriani turned back, waved to let them know he'd heard. With the courier and the merchants in tow, the squad set off at a trot toward the west.

"I'm no traitor, Kath. You have to believe that. I didn't plan the attack, I didn't call for…"

"Fate and faith, Chriani, you're a fool twice over. I know who you are. I'd trust you with my life, rank and uniform or not."

Chriani felt the words carry through him with a strange echo. He remembered that last night along the Hunthad, and understanding that he trusted Kathlan with his own life. He had vowed to say it to her that night, but the words and everything else had been taken from him.

"Then what…?" It was the only thing he could say now. Too late for all the rest.

He saw it in her eyes before she spoke. Saw the pain there that he knew was greater than any hurt he'd ever known. The truth he'd told her, and all the truths that split off from that.

"At Osthegn, when Irdaign found me. After talking to Lauresa, waiting for the troop to assemble. I saw the girl. Your daughter. Only from a distance, mind. She's beautiful."

In the space deep inside him where the shadow dwelled, Chriani felt something break. He reached for Kathlan again but she stepped her horse back with no more than a flick of her toes.

"Don't," she said. "Just don't. Please."

He wouldn't think on any of the reasons he had to return to Aerach. He wouldn't. Not yet. It was something for the future he had always dreamed of seeing, but that future was in front of him now and turning to darkness before his eyes.

"Tell me what's between you and the princess," Kathlan said. "The duchess. Lauresa. The truth, Chriani."

The words he'd spoken to Kathlan in Venry's camp were in Chriani's mind. The darkness of his confession that night, come back to him as if only a moment had passed. He felt every word that had gone unspoken since then, every lie he'd woven into his life in the years before.

"I told her I would die for her," he said. The truth.

"And?"

"A part of me did. And a part of her died for me. And there's nothing left after that."

Kathlan said nothing for a long while, turning away toward the sea. Its salt scent was fresh on the wind, but the horizon was lost behind a veil of cloud.

"Kath…"

"Do you know what you want, Chriani?"

"No," he said. The truth. "I'm sorry, Kath, but I can't see it yet. But I'm looking, and I'm trying, and I know more than I know any other truth that whatever I want, it has to be with you."

Kathlan nodded as if she understood. Then she turned her horse, began to walk away.

"I'm staying in Aerach," she said as Chriani spurred up beside her. "I'll seek a place in the guard here."

"This isn't the place for you, Kath." Chriani tried to edge around her, reaching for her hand again, but she slipped past him easily. "You know how they think of women in Aerach, and in the guard most of all. You'll work twice as hard to get half as far, even if you manage to find someone willing to take you for what you're worth."

"Good thing I already work twice as hard as anyone else. And I've got Shara, who more than knows what I'm worth. He already offered me a place in his troop, but I told him I wouldn't be comfortable in Teillai. He thinks it'd be because of what happened with you. Not that he's wrong."

"Kath…"

"I'm riding for Aleran. You're riding for Rheran. Shara's given me some names, said he'll send letters to speak for me. Other captains who don't have their heads up their asses. I know my path, Chriani."

A shadow was in his mind, twisting around the words he meant to say. Strangling them down to the darkness where his secrets hid. The other horses were gone, hoofbeats and the jingle of tack already fading behind him.

"Please, Kathlan. I'll do anything you ask of me."

"I'm asking you to go, Chriani. Find your way. Find your place, whatever it's meant to be."

"Kath, I can't lose you…"

"Goodbye, Chriani."

She turned her horse past him with the lightest flick of the reins, then spurred away to the east.

"Kathlan!"

Chriani shouted her name as she picked up speed. He didn't follow, though. Already knowing she was gone.

The fog was lifting, breaking the cloud that shrouded the city and the broad farming steppes beyond. Kathlan was pushing her horse with precision, because she knew that if Chriani tried to follow her, he'd override his own mount before she had any need to slow. No way he'd ever catch her.

She had asked him what he wanted. His life back and in order was the easy answer. And he had that, granted in an unexpected instant by the prince high he had sworn to hate.

There was more to it, though. He felt an understanding settle in on him, his mind trying to make some sense of the pain twisting through him, centered on his heart.

He wanted to know he had made a difference.

The threat of the cult was done. Chriani had accomplished that, had made his decision to stand and fall if he must. He had expected to die, had been thinking of the others who would follow him to finish what he'd started. But in a twist of fate he had never expected, he was following himself now.

He had a report to make to the prince high, he knew. To Ashlund. He would tell them what he could of the Laneldenari, and of what Veassen and the others had said. A chance there for peace, maybe. A chance to build on what had come before.

In war, we find the strength of life, but our lives are more than war. Farenna had said it on the council floor.

War, which is the dream the Ilmari made. Chriani remembered Contáedar's dark hatred, as he remembered Chanist speaking of the Greatwood burned to ash and spread across the Ehadne Sea. But he remembered the weariness in the throne room as well.

I will serve my people at any cost, the prince high had said. That same weariness in Farenna.

Between themselves, he and Lauresa had stopped a war. With Dargana's strength guiding his hand and his heart, he had undone the dark magic that promised a second. But if war came anyway, it would all have been for nothing.

His mind had drifted, he realized. He was alone. Kathlan was gone ahead of him. Behind him, the patrol and its civilian cohort had vanished into the mist.

In the council of masters and in his tent two nights before, Veassen had spoken of fate. *I saw that you would do what you were meant to do.* Chriani held onto that thought now. Felt it shimmer against the shadow within his mind, even as he felt that shadow breaking.

He turned his horse, spurred it to a jog toward the west. The patrol party wouldn't be far ahead of him, but he didn't want to risk surprising them at a gallop. Ilvani were on the Clearwater Way, the Brandishear couriers had said.

He rode toward where the last of the fields of Aerach would fall away to wild rose and scrub grass. He slipped within the mist, felt the sun at his back and shadow before him as he passed along the Clearwater Way and was gone.

FICTION BY
SCOTT FITZGERALD GRAY

SIDNYE (QUEEN OF THE UNIVERSE)

THE EXILE'S BLADE TRILOGY
Clearwater Dawn • Three Coins for Confession
The Timeless King *(Coming 2016)*

WE CAN BE HEROES

A PRAYER FOR DEAD KINGS and Other Tales

BLACKHEATH (with Quinn Hamilton)

THE VOICES OF THE DEAD — Dark Tales & Lost Souls

TALES OF THE ENDLANDS
The Twilight Child • Shadow to Shadow • The Moonsign Scar
Daeralf's Rune • The Game of Heart and Light • The Voice
Black Run • A Space Between • Stories

ONE SIZE FITS ALL (as Gary Scott)

Scott Fitzgerald Gray is a writer, fiction editor, story editor,
RPG editor and designer, and man about town. He shares his
life in the Canadian hinterland with a schoolteacher, two
itinerant daughters, and a large number of animal companions.

More info on Scott and his work (some of it even
occasionally truthful) can be found by reading
between the lines at **insaneangel.com**.

COLOPHON

Thanks and admiration to the following
for taking up arms when the bell sounds.

The Council of Masters
Colleen, Shvaugn, and Caitlin

Seers of the Bastion
Gabriel Duclair, Colleen Craig, Jennifer Landels

War-Mages of the Prince's Guard
François Bertrand, Shvaugn Craig

Engravers of the Myllasir
(studio)Effigy, Pawel Lyczkowski, Tokarev Anton, Margo Black,
Peter Polak, Susanitah

The Odes of the Leisanmira
Alter Bridge, Ramin Djawadi, Tom Holkenborg, Guy Gavriel Kay,
George R.R. Martin, Porcupine Tree, Red, Scott Stapp,
Mary Stewart, Barry Windsor-Smith, Hans Zimmer

THREE COINS FOR CONFESSION

BOOK TWO OF
THE EXILE'S BLADE

Published by Insane Angel Studios
insaneangel.com

Cover, Design, and Typography
by (studio)Effigy

ISBN 978-1-927348-39-0

v1.1
July 2015

We try to make sure that no errors creep into our work, but publishing is a chaotic enterprise at the best of times. If you spot a typo or a formatting glitch in an Insane Angel Studios book, email insaneangel@insaneangel.com with details (including which e-book version you're reading, if applicable). If any errors you spot are ones we haven't yet caught and are in the process of fixing, you'll receive one of our e-books of your choice for free.